One Who Cries had failed the test.

The Warrior pushed away from the railing, charting a path that would intersect with the boy. He held his hands, curled into fists, tightly against his sides as he strode across the crest of the hill and angled toward One Who Cries. This was the moment of maximum danger where recognition could result in the loss of the child. He tried to clear his mind of negative thoughts. His first priority was to regain control of the child.

Later there would be time for analysis. He would have to discover what flaw in the training process had resulted in another failure. At least it was not a total disaster like the last time. Bad enough, but not unalterable.

It was important to keep in mind how much time he had invested in the boy's training. Well worth finding the weakness in the program so that he could modify it for the next time. Not much time remained until the final test. It was painful to think that the boy might be a poor choice.

Like the others, however, One Who Cries was expend-

CRITICAL ACCLAIM FOR MARTHA POWERS AND

BLEEDING HEART

"Keep[s] the reader on edge and offer[s] enough loose ends and possibilities that none of the leading suspects can be eliminated until the very end."

—Booklist

"Maggie is a credible hero . . . and her search for her father-in-law's killer and Tyler McKenzie makes a compelling story."

—Chicago Tribune

"Martha Powers tells a grand story that brings fresh life through her deep characters to the lurking-monster-in-human-clothing thriller."

—Midwest Book Review

"Powers populates the town of Delbrook, Wisconsin, with memorably off-kilter types."

—Publishers Weekly

"Ms. Powers

BLEEDING HEART

MARTHA POWERS

POCKET BOOKS
New York London Toronto Sydney Singapore

This book is a work of fiction. Names, characters, places and incidents are products of the author's imagination or are used fictitiously. Any resemblance to actual events or locales or persons, living or dead, is entirely coincidental.

POCKET BOOKS, a division of Simon & Schuster, Inc.
1230 Avenue of the Americas, New York, NY 10020

Copyright © 2000 by Martha Powers

Originally published in hardcover in 2000 by Simon & Schuster, Inc.

ISBN: 0-7434-2293-7

First Pocket Books printing November 2001

10 9 8 7 6 5 4 3 2 1

POCKET and colophon are registered trademarks of Simon & Schuster, Inc.

For information regarding special discounts for bulk purchases, please contact Simon & Schuster Special Sales at 1-800-456-6798 or business@simonandschuster.com

Front cover illustration by Joseph Cooper

Printed in the U.S.A.

ACKNOWLEDGMENTS

To Lynn Wolfram for being a great friend as well as the good sister who stayed awake during grammar classes. To Captain Arthur Babiak, retired, Bergen County Police Department, New Jersey, who answered endless questions on police procedure and downhill putts. To Gary Kotsiris for sharing his knowledge of falconry and for being patient with my ignorance. To Ruth O'Brien for forcing me to go to the next level despite my penchant for easing through the cracks. To Lauren McKenna and Pocket Books for their support and magnificent covers. To Paul Grange for being a magician with a camera and giving immortality to my favorite dress. To Sue Sussman for enlivening meetings and conferences with her sense of humor and for remembering long-forgotten lines of poetry. Most of all to Bill Powers for the gifts of time and laughter and a sense of what's important in life.

THE SECOND COMING

Turning and turning in the widening gyre
The falcon cannot hear the falconer;
Things fall apart; the centre cannot hold;
Mere anarchy is loosed upon the world,
The blood-dimmed tide is loosed, and everywhere
The ceremony of innocence is drowned;
The best lack all conviction, while the worst
Are full of passionate intensity.

William Butler Yeats

PROLOGUE

TWO-AND-A-HALF-YEAR-OLD Tyler McKenzie opened his mouth in a wide circle and blew against the front of the jewelry counter. A cloud of wet air frosted the glass, then slowly disappeared. Inside, the bright stones shimmered on the blanket of shiny gold. He liked the blue ones best. Like Mommy's eyes.

"Don't do that, sweetheart," Barbara McKenzie said, pulling him back against her side. "A couple more minutes, Tyler. Then we'll go home."

She knew he was tired. They'd been returning presents for more than an hour. He leaned against her leg. He rocked from side to side, then slid down to the floor. The tether attached to his wrist snagged on her belt loop, and he tugged to get it loose.

"Don't pull, honey. You'll tear Mommy's coat."

She unwound the coiled plastic tubing until the strap swung free, one continuous loop from Tyler's wrist to hers. She was glad that she'd remembered to bring it. Between after-Christmas sales and people returning rejected presents, the department store was dreadfully crowded. She always worried about Tyler getting lost.

From his seat on the floor, he stared up at her. His mouth stretched into a lopsided grin, but his brown eyes drooped sleepily. She ruffled the top of his blond head.

"What a love you are, Tiger," Barbara said. "Mommy's hurrying."

Tyler nuzzled her leg, purring like a cat. They'd taken him to the zoo Thanksgiving weekend. They'd made a special trip to see the lion cubs because Tyler loved the Disney movie *The Lion King*. It was the tiger, however, that had drawn his interest. Barbara had to admit it was her choice too. Tyler wasn't afraid of the huge animal. For him it was nothing more than a big cat.

She checked to see that the Velcro strap was secure around his wrist, unable to resist touching the soft skin on his cheek as she straightened up to sign the return slip. Finished, she put her wallet back in her purse, picked up the shopping bag beside Tyler and helped him to his feet.

"Only one more stop," she said as she dusted the seat of his pants with her hand.

Now that Tyler was standing, he was anxious to be on his way. His short legs moved like pistons to get ahead of her as she walked down the aisle toward the escalator.

"Wait for Mommy," she said as he strained against the tether.

She took his hand, making sure the strap that joined them wrist to wrist didn't catch on the treads moving up the escalator. Ken never used the tether when he took Tyler out. He said it reminded him of a leash for a dog. Easy for him to say, she thought. Husbands didn't have a million errands to run while trying to keep track of an active child.

"Jump jump?" Tyler said.

"Almost." She tightened her grip on his pudgy little hand, and as the escalator steps flattened out, she said, "OK, Tiger. Jump."

She raised his arm as he hurled his body forward, then steadied him as he came down in a two-footed landing at the top. He cocked his head, crowing with triumph as he smiled up at her.

"Tyler good," he said.

"Very good. That was an excellent jump," she agreed, giving his hand another squeeze before she released him.

He had just begun talking in two-word phrases. It wasn't always easy to know what he meant, but it was fun hearing the sound of his voice and anticipating what it would be like when he could verbalize more. He'd learned his colors and shapes and even learned the first part of the ABC song.

She let him pull her along as they followed the aisle around to the women's department. She opened her shopping bag and pulled out the knit tunic her brother, Grant, had given her for Christmas and placed it on the counter in front of the salesgirl.

"Last stop," she said, leaning over to kiss Tyler on the top of his head.

Making small smacking sounds, he pushed through a rack of sweaters until he reached the open space in the center. The tether stretched, and Barbara hunkered down to peer under the clothing. Tyler was sitting on the floor, his back against the center pole.

"Tyler hide," he said. He clutched the sleeve of a navy blue sweater, brushing it against his cheek as he tucked the thumb of his other hand into his mouth.

"It's a very good hideout," she said to the heavy-lidded child. "You can take a rest, and I'll be right here."

She straightened up and turned back to the sales-girl, explaining that the tunic was too long and the wrong color. She rummaged through her purse until she found the correct receipt.

The sweaters on the rack shook, and she heard Tyler cooing within his soft nest. At least he was still awake. Her parents and brother had stayed in the house over Christmas, and Tyler had overdosed on excitement and was short of sleep. She knew it was a mistake to let him nod off. He'd be crabby when she woke him.

Leaning tiredly on the counter, Barbara pulled the tether. From under the rack of sweaters, Tyler pulled back. She turned around to face the counter, waiting for the clerk to complete the transaction. The girl pressed keys on the computer, pausing after each action to stare blankly at the monitor. Finally the machine spit out several sheets of paper.

"Here you are, Mrs. McKenzie," the salesclerk said.

She set the receipt down on the counter along with a pen. Barbara signed her name, waiting as the girl stapled the two receipts together. Tucking the charge card back in her wallet, Barbara stuffed everything into her purse.

"Time to go, Tyler. Mommy's all finished."

She pulled the strap, sighing at the lack of response. He must be sound asleep. She'd have to carry him all the way to the car.

"Come on, Tyler. Wake up and we'll go home."

Settling her purse strap on her shoulder, she spread the sweaters apart, following the coiled plastic wire to the center of Tyler's hideout.

The Velcro wrist strap of the child tether was attached to the metal center pole.

Tyler was gone.

CHAPTER
ONE

THE RENAISSANCE FAIRE was in full swing. Coming to Delbrook, Wisconsin, the Friday after Labor Day, it was an event of pure performance art. A whimsical imitation of a medieval market town was erected in a field above Falcon Lake. Costumed players provided a day's worth of events that ranged from plays and musical entertainments to nature exhibits and crafts to a finale of jousting, mock battles and horsemanship.

Traditionally the local schools called a day off on Friday. It gave the teachers a welcome chance to catch their breath after the hectic opening days of the school year. Now that the lake crowd had closed up their summer cottages and returned to the cities where they lived and worked, the residents of Delbrook observed the weekend of the Renaissance Faire as a time for celebration. This year the weather was unusually warm.

Nevertheless, the Warrior was cold.

Beads of sweat stood out on his forehead and slid down the side of his neck to pool at the indentation below his Adam's apple. The late afternoon heat pressed against the top of his head, but a chill, a combination of anticipation and fear, fanned out from the core of his being. His arms and legs tingled and his stomach cramped as he leaned against the railing, staring across the fairgrounds.

To the Warrior, the carnival atmosphere was alien to the serious purpose of the day's visit. The inherent danger of proximity to his home made it a daring choice. He had never worked within his own territory, and had strong misgivings. Even though the risk factor was very high, he had chosen the Faire for the apprentice's first test because it offered the greatest opportunity of success for the boy.

All week the Warrior had been restless. He had spent long nights establishing the guidelines, working out every detail to minimize the danger to both himself and the boy. The first trial in the initiation process was always the most important, setting the tone for eventual success or failure.

Despite the long training period, the boy's youth was a decided disadvantage. The test would prove whether, at four, the boy had mastered the necessary discipline to follow orders without question with all the distractions of a public place.

The Warrior had chosen his vantage point well. From the top of the hill, the outdoor patio of Ye Olde Ale House had a panoramic view of the entire fairground.

Smoke from the cooking pots and the open fires hung in a thick pall above the gaudily painted buildings of the mock town, pressed down by the humidity left behind by the recent thunderstorm. The ground was soaked and dotted with pools of standing water. In a futile effort to lessen the impact of the rain, the organizers had strewn loose straw on the main traffic areas, but despite that the ground had become a quagmire. The wet, mud-streaked crowd added a measure of veracity to the appearance and smell of the make-believe medieval fair.

The Warrior bit his lip. A sense of unease invaded his body. He hadn't counted on the rainstorm that had changed the temperament of the crowd. The sheer boisterousness worried him. In this atmosphere, anything could happen, and in an instant he could lose control of the situation.

Instinct urged him to abort the trial.

His eyes flicked across the crowd milling around the wooden benches next to the jousting field. It was easy to spot the blond boy sitting alone at the far end of the bench closest to the arena. Against the shifting movements of the excited audience, the child's immobility created an oasis of stillness.

One Who Cries was waiting for the signal. It was time for the boy to take the first step on his journey.

The Warrior could remember when he began his own training.

He had been older than One Who Cries. Twelve and lost in a world of pain and despair. He had found the answers to his search for freedom in reading about the culture of the American Indian. The tough disciplining of young boys captured his imagination, especially the tests that led to becoming a warrior. He'd steeped himself in the rituals and the customs, picking and choosing the elements he liked best and the ones he thought would enhance his own spirit.

The warrior symbolized power. And counting coup brought ultimate power.

A coup was a war honor that emphasized bravery, cunning and stealth over actual killing. It was the greatest achievement to touch an enemy with a coup stick in the heat of battle and leave him alive to wallow in shame and self-reproach. The triumphant warrior captured the enemy's spirit, which was worse than death to a man of the People.

Like a young American Indian boy, he began to train so that he would be worthy to take on the mantle of the warrior. In this he had no mentor to guide him. He would be his own teacher.

He had invented the first test when he was twelve.

During a week of planning he had fine-tuned the rules. He would select an enemy in a public place. For the coup to count, he had to touch the very center of the target's back. It must be a one-fingered touch, solid enough to elicit some reaction from the victim.

Level one had been easy to master.

Suddenly the Warrior straightened, hands tightening on the railing as he noticed the activity in the arena. Several horses had entered the jousting field.

The crowd applauded and shouted as the colorfully draped mounts with costumed knights on their backs pranced nervously around the ring. A loudspeaker bellowed over the noise of the audience, but the words were unintelligible at this distance.

Soon. It would be soon.

Eyes intent on the back of the blond head, the Warrior waited. He stood tall so that the boy would be able to see him clearly when he turned to catch the signal. The noise and commotion faded into the background as the Warrior concentrated on the child. He narrowed his focus, as if by sheer willpower he could guarantee success.

Still seated on the bench while all around him people shouted and gestured at the activity, One Who Cries looked too frail for the test ahead.

Despite appearances, the boy was in peak physical condition. He had been prepared for this moment through a strict regimen of healthy food, exercise and a highly structured schedule of activities.

The Warrior had made today's test extremely simple. It was the first time the boy had been released from confinement in a year and a half. Primarily the test was to see if the Warrior could maintain control of the four-year-old with all the distractions of the real world and an opportunity to escape.

What the boy had to do was neither demanding nor dangerous. He needed to wait for the appointed signal that initiated the coup, touch the wooden fence around the jousting field, then look to the Warrior for the signal to retreat and return to the rendezvous point. If he could, it would prove that the boy could be trusted on his own to obey his mentor's instructions.

A trumpet blew. One Who Cries rose to his feet and turned around until he was facing the Warrior. His right hand came up just below his chin and his fingers formed the sign to indicate he was ready. The Warrior raised his own hand and gave the go-ahead.

Heart racing in anticipation, the Warrior watched the boy walk with steady steps to the edge of the jousting arena. He reached out with his left hand and placed his palm flat on the wooden fencing.

Success.

One Who Cries turned around, and even at a distance, the Warrior could see the pride written clearly in the straight carriage of the boy. Now all that remained was the retreat. The Warrior raised his hand, but before he could give the signal for withdrawal, he heard a piercing cry. The boy's body jerked at the sound. His head tilted back, mouth open slightly, eyes trained upward.

A falcon soared high overhead. Even at that height, her silhouette was easily recognizable. With her strong wings, she dug into the air and climbed steeply above the arena. Wings and tail spread wide, she circled in a lazy spiral. A shiver of fear ran through the Warrior's body. This was not a part of the trial.

The falcon was a harbinger. An omen of disaster.

The Warrior started to move forward, watching the boy, who remained transfixed by the bird. The falcon slipped sideways, riding the rising currents of heat, then folded her wings against her body and dived straight down toward the earth, swooping above the crowd before she started to climb again.

One Who Cries opened his mouth in a silent scream.

Covering the top of his head with his arms, the boy raced down the aisle away from the arena. Seeing his distress, people reached out to him, but the boy dodged all attempts to hold him, ducking beneath the outstretched arms until he was beyond the jousting field.

Free of the crowd, One Who Cries slowed. His eyes were open, but he appeared to travel blindly, mind far from the motion of his body. The mud sucked at his feet, holding him to the earth, as he staggered from side to side up the hill. The Warrior could see the heaviness that invaded the small body as exhaustion overcame his initial panic.

The Warrior drew upon his own training to guard his face from showing any interest or emotion, but inside he twisted with frustration.

One Who Cries had failed the test.

The Warrior pushed away from the railing, charting a path that would intersect with the boy. He held his hands, curled into fists, tightly against his sides as he strode across the crest of the hill and angled toward One Who Cries. This was the moment of maximum danger where recognition could result in the loss of the child. He tried to clear his mind of negative thoughts. His first priority was to regain control of the child.

Later there would be time for analysis. He would have to discover what flaw in the training process had resulted in another failure. At least it was not a total disaster like the last time. Bad enough, but not unalterable.

It was important to keep in mind how much time he had invested in the boy's training. Well worth finding the weakness in the program so that he could modify it for the next time. Not much time remained until the final test. It was painful to think that the boy might be a poor choice.

Like the others, however, One Who Cries was expendable.

"Look, Mom. It's Grampa's car," Jake yelled.

The car lights illuminated George Collier as Maggie pulled into her parking space behind the house. As the tall, slim figure rose from the swing on the side porch, she sighed, knowing she didn't look her best. One glance in the rearview mirror confirmed the fact she couldn't look much worse.

"Hi, Grampa," Jake shouted as he got out of the car. "We just got back from my birthday party."

"It was getting late and I was beginning to worry that you'd run into trouble," George said.

"No trouble. I had to drop off the other boys," Maggie said, following more sedately as Jake bounded up the stairs to the porch. "Don't get too close, George. We're both absolutely filthy."

"Good heavens," the older man said as they came into the light. "What happened?"

"We got caught in the rain." Jake held out his dirt-streaked arms for his grandfather's approval.

"Was the party a disaster?" George asked.

"Actually, it was a great success," Maggie said. "Start taking your shoes and socks off, Jake, so you don't drag all that mud into the house."

She brushed at the front of her once white blouse, wondering if the splatters of mud would come out in the wash. A damp strand of reddish brown hair touched the side of her cheek, and she raised her hands to anchor the curly mess behind her ears. Her sneakers made squishing sounds as she crossed the wooden floor.

She frowned at the acrid smell of smoke. She knew George's doctor had told him to give up cigars, but other than to make her father-in-law sneak his guilty pleasures, the injunction seemed to have had little effect. Oh damn! She bit her lip. No point in nagging him. He'd just shrug and ignore her, like Jake did.

"How was the carnival?" George asked.

"Super," Jake said. "Extra super. None of the boys had ever been to the Renaissance Faire. Not even Kenny Rossiter. It was awesome."

"Despite the rain?" George asked.

"Probably because of it," Maggie said. "The whole place was one huge mud hole. If you were eight years old, what could be better. The boys loved it. Believe it or not we cleaned up a bit before we came home. After a day of slogging through the muck and mire, we were a pretty nasty-looking group. And you should see the car. I'll have to have it washed, inside and out."

Jake pulled at the sleeve of George's jacket to get his grandfather's attention.

"These two guys got into a fight and they wrestled in the middle of this mud puddle. They were all covered except for their eyeballs. They looked like white marbles. And when they were all done, another guy squirted them with a hose. Oh, and Grampa, if you gave this guy a dollar, he'd eat a whole handful of mud."

"Good Lord." George turned to Maggie. "How on earth did you survive?"

"Actually, it was a lot of fun," she said. "Once I realized the boys were having a great time and there was no hope of staying clean, I just sort of relaxed. It was like being a kid again. And the big finale at the jousting arena was well worth the aggravations."

Since Jake was too excited to be very helpful, she knelt down on the porch and grabbed one foot as he braced himself with a dirty hand on her shoulder. She removed his shoes and peeled off his socks as he regaled his grandfather with the events of the day.

Male bonding, she thought wistfully as they chattered away, oblivious to her presence. That was the one thing she could never give her son. After all these many days since Mark's death and all she'd done to help him, she couldn't hold back a twinge of jealousy that George could give Jake more than she could.

"Grampa, they had these horses and these knights with poles and they'd run at each other. And smash! They'd knock each other off the horses and then finish the fight with swords. I don't think anyone got killed." There was a trace of disappointment in his voice.

"Well I should hope not." George shook his head. "I'm sorry I missed it. It must have been a real spectacle."

"Just wait'll you see. Mom bought me one of those cardboard cameras, and I took tons of pictures. I even got one of Kenny throwing up."

"A bit too much pizza and cotton candy," Maggie explained, standing up. "He was back in action almost immediately."

"Sounds like quite a day," George said, smiling down at the excited child. "I can't wait to see the pictures."

"We took them to Kruckmeyer's Pharmacy to be developed. I'll have them back tomorrow, so you can see them before we go to dinner."

In the dim porch light, Maggie noted the bright color rising high on George's cheek and guessed the reason he had been waiting for them.

"Well, you see, son," George said. "I know we talked about going to dinner and a movie tomorrow, but I've run into a problem."

Jake's eyes narrowed slightly as he stared up at his grandfather.

"I got a call this afternoon and I have to go to the

country club tomorrow. There's going to be a poker game." His eyes shifted between Jake and Maggie. "We won't be able to go to a movie, but there's no reason we can't have dinner together. I thought you and your mom could have dinner at the country club and then we'd take in a movie on another night."

"That's OK, Grampa," Jake said. "Mom already planned a special dinner for tomorrow. We can go to a movie next weekend, if you want."

His voice was flat, and Maggie felt a lump in her throat at his lie. She dug the house keys out of her pocket.

"It's still pretty warm out," she said, opening the screen and unlocking the door to the second floor apartment, "but I don't want you catching cold. Give Grampa a careful hug, then run along upstairs and take a shower."

She ignored the relief on George's face as Jake hugged him then raced up the carpeted stairs. Maggie sighed as the screen door slammed.

"Is he never still?" George asked.

"Not often. Even in his sleep, he tosses and turns as if he's fighting dragons or herding cattle in some imaginary world."

"I don't recall his father being quite so physical," George said. "Mark read a lot, and at Jake's age he was content to play with his collection of action figures."

Maggie chuckled. "Jake is his own action figure."

"The boy seems to be more cheerful. Not so sad and moody as when you first moved here."

"He's better. He's made some friends in this past year, and that's helped. But if you look beneath the surface, the anger's there. Deep down, he still blames me for his father's death."

"I thought he was over that nonsense," George said. "He must know it wasn't your fault. It was a car accident, for God's sake."

Maggie shrugged. "I know that, but Jake sees it differently."

"Do you have any regrets about moving here?"

"Not when I see how well he's adjusted. Right after Mark died I thought it would be better to stay in our house in Chicago." Maggie shrugged. "I suppose part of it was an attempt to keep as much the same as I could for Jake's sake. The other part was inertia."

"I can understand that," George said. "Mark's death was a shock to us all."

He took a deep breath and blew it out as if to cut off any more discussion. Maggie knew that George had never really come to terms with his son's death. He rarely spoke about that first year, but Maggie knew from others in Delbrook that her father-in-law had lived as a recluse, only coming out when he could find a card game or when he'd run out of alcohol.

It had been a letter from Nell Gleason, her mother's friend, mentioning George's situation that convinced Maggie to move to Delbrook.

"Don't worry, George. I'm very glad we came. With you here, Jake has a real sense of family. He misses his father a lot and loves spending time with you."

"I like it too," George said. He reached out and squeezed Maggie's shoulder. He ducked his head, his words mumbled as he continued. "I know these last two years have been hard, but you've done a damn fine job with the lad."

Maggie was surprised and touched by her father-in-law's momentary softness. Normally he was not a demonstrative man. Mark had referred to his father as The Tall Silence, and the nickname fit. George was the first to admit he wasn't into that "New Age touchy-feely crap," but in the last two years Maggie had grown to love her father-in-law dearly.

"Thank you, George." She leaned forward to kiss his cheek.

"I'm sorry it didn't work out for the movie tomorrow," he mumbled. "They're counting on me to be at the poker game, and I'd hate to disappoint them."

Better to disillusion one small boy, she thought. Aloud she said, "There will be other times for a movie."

"I hate letting Jake down," George said, echoing her own thoughts.

It was difficult to be angry with George. He was far too aware of his own weaknesses. She knew he had done his best since Mark's death to be a strong male influence for his grandson. For that she would forgive a great deal.

"Why don't you come over Sunday for dinner? Jake's dying to tell you all about the birthday party."

"I'd like that," George said. "In fact, tomorrow I go right past Kruckmeyer's Pharmacy on the way to the country club. If they're ready, I'll pick up the photographs from the Renaissance Faire."

"That would save me a trip. I played hooky today, but tomorrow I'm working all day. Come about five on Sunday."

It was clear that George was pleased with the olive branch.

"Jake's a good kid, Maggie. Every day he looks more and more like his father. He'll be a real heartbreaker when he grows up. Just like his dad."

A heartbreaker just like his dad. His words kept repeating in her ears as she watched her father-in-law walk down the stairs to his car.

"A heartbreaker? Not if I can help it," Maggie muttered aloud, sitting down on the porch swing.

George's weakness was cards; Mark's had been women.

Mark with the bedroom eyes, who had attempted to sleep with every woman he met. Mark, who had ignored his marriage vows the moment the ink was dry on the wedding license. Mark, whose car had swerved off the road, killing himself along with the twenty-five-year-old woman carrying his child.

Oh yes. Mark had been a real heartbreaker.

He had broken her heart long ago. And for different reasons his death had broken the hearts of his father and his son. There were times when she wondered if any of them would ever heal.

He had been gone for two years, and yet Maggie had not been able to move beyond her anger. To George and Jake, Mark had been a wonderful son and father. Dead, he had become Saint Mark. They both assumed that she was as devastated as they were.

"Mom?"

Maggie jumped at the voice behind her. "Sorry, Jake, I was daydreaming."

"I knew you didn't hear me when I came down." He plopped down on the wooden seat beside her, leaning his head against her shoulder. "Grampa gone?"

"Yes." She put her arm around his bathrobed figure and leaned close to smell the shampoo in his hair.

"No movie. That really bites," Jake said. "Big time."

Although Maggie might have worded it more strongly, she forced out a motherly response. "Life is like that sometimes. You could see that Grampa was sorry."

"He's always sorry."

Maggie heard the hurt in his voice. "And what's this about the special dinner I had planned?"

He grimaced. "I guess I sort of lied, Mom."

"Lies stink. They always end up hurting people. Even when you're trying not to." She smiled to take the sting out of her words. "Do you know what I've been thinking about for tomorrow night's dinner?" He shook his head. "A big pepperoni pizza."

Jake's expression lightened. "DeNato's makes really great pizza."

"Excellent plan. And on the way back we'll stop at Hoffman's Video and pick up *Godzilla*. You haven't seen that in at least a week or two."

"It's my favorite."

"Don't I know it."

She pulled him to his feet. He put his arms around her waist, and when he spoke, his voice was muffled against her rib cage.

"Thanks, Mom."

It was times like this that were the toughest for Maggie. Jake was only eight, but his father's death had made him more aware of her feelings than he normally would be. He knew she was trying to make it up to him because George had bailed out of the movie. Jake's forced sensitivity to her emotions was one more thing she blamed on Mark. Tears pricked her eyelids as Jake pulled away.

"And thanks for the party. It was the best."

She grasped the chains to haul herself out of the swing. She was stiff. Jake's clean smell made her far too aware of her own odor. Definitely time for a shower.

"Race you," she said.

She released the swing chain and ran across to the open doorway. He was right behind her as she swung open the screen door. He slammed the inside door, and then, crowing with delight, he shot past her and scrambled up the narrow flight of stairs.

"What if Hoffman's doesn't have the Godzilla tape?" he called back over his shoulder.

"Then we'll rent a wonderful old musical with lots of singing, not to mention tap dancing."

"Yuck," he groaned.

With what little breath she had left, Maggie sighed. It was good to hear him laugh. For a long time after Mark's death, Jake would barely speak to her. She had thought he was asleep the night that Mark had asked her for a divorce. But Jake had been awake. He'd heard them arguing and heard his father slam out of the house in anger. The next day Mark had been killed.

Jake had blamed Maggie. If she hadn't fought with Mark, he reasoned, there wouldn't have been a car accident. Therefore it was Maggie's fault that his father was dead.

Although she had told George that Jake would eventually understand, the truth was she wondered if he ever would.

CHAPTER
TWO

THE WARRIOR OPENED the door of the locked room and stepped inside. He pressed the switch on the wall, and the string of lights, suspended close to the ceiling, illuminated the windowless room.

In the low light, he didn't see the child immediately. He wondered if he'd regressed and was sleeping in the corner under the wooden shelf as he did whenever he made a mistake. No. A lump under the blanket at the foot of the bed indicated his location. Shoes silent on the packed mud floor, the Warrior approached.

Curled in a fetal position, the boy's rounded back was pressed into the corner. His head burrowed into the pillow, arms hugging the softness against his stomach and chest. Tufts of blond hair stuck to the skin on his sweaty forehead. His eyes were closed, eyelids trembling in the depths of sleep.

The Warrior reached out his hand to stroke the cowlick rising at the front of the boy's hair. From the moment he had seen those splayed blond strands, resembling a crown of feathers, he knew the child was the chosen one. The others had been forerunners. This child was the successor.

He debated waking the child just so he could see the startled look of fear in the clear blue eyes. It happened every time the Warrior came to the boy's room. After that first awareness, the child would squeeze his lids shut, and when he opened them again, his face would be blank of all expression, his senses alert to the Warrior's every command.

One Who Cries shuddered, reacting to the dreams that populated his sleep. He rolled over onto his back, one arm flung out and hanging over the edge of the bed. The blanket bunched around his hips, revealing his naked chest and stomach.

The Warrior leaned over, staring down at the tattoo above the nipple on the left side of the boy's chest. It was small, only an inch and a half in height and width, but each color was clearly delineated.

The black line around the red heart was etched with the same meticulous care as the golden feathers on the arrow that pierced it and the teardrops of blood that rained down from the wound.

Bleeding heart.

When he had seen it in a book of graphic arts, he had taken it as his personal icon. It held no religious connotation for him. The heart shot through with an arrow symbolized his belief that a warrior could conquer any obstacle, even death. A true warrior was invincible.

The apprentice's tattoo was a duplicate of his master's.

The Warrior rubbed his fingers over the original tattoo that lay beneath the cotton shirt on his own breast. The heartbeat transferred to the tips of his fingers, moving up his arm until it reached his shoulder then spread out, running along his nerve endings to the outer reaches of his body.

The child stirred as if he felt the connection between the two of them. His eyelids fluttered, partially open, showing a thin line of white. A soft cry came from deep in his throat, but he did not wake.

The Warrior remembered how concerned he'd been when he'd made the stencil. Unlike the others he had tattooed, the boy was too young to understand the necessity to remain still, so it could not be used as a test of bravery or endurance. He worried too that One Who Cries might be traumatized by the sight of his own blood welling up around each needle prick.

Because of the placement over the breastbone and the additional pain, the Warrior had decided to take the safe route and tranquilize the boy. He'd used restraints so that even if the child roused during the procedure, his movements wouldn't affect the precision of the outlining. It wasn't so important when he did the shading. Then a slight movement wouldn't mean an unsightly mistake. He wasn't a "scratcher"; he took pride in his professional skill.

It had taken two weeks for the tattoo to heal. The scab had formed and fallen off and all had gone well until the skin dried and shed. Although the bleeding heart was perfect, the skin around the drawing had been warm to the touch and the boy had run a slight fever for two days. The Warrior kept him sedated, and on the third day the fever broke. One Who Cries woke with clear eyes and no temperature.

The tattoo was the best he'd ever done. Just the

sight of it gave the Warrior a new determination to help
the boy succeed.

The door closed with a click. Tyler McKenzie didn't
move. He waited, listening to the silence. One time he
had opened his eyes too soon. The man was still there.

A, B, C, D, E, F, G. He didn't know the rest of the
alphabet song. He sang the letters in his head. One time.
Two times. Three times. Sometimes he forgot the letters. He tried not to cry when that happened.

He opened his eyes slowly, searching for the single
bulb shining over the door. He let go of his breath, his
body shaking with the explosion of air. Every time the
man left, Tyler was afraid he would turn the light out. It
wasn't very bright. He couldn't see the corners of the
room.

The dark was scary.

He caught his breath at the rustle from across the
room. He couldn't see the mouse cage on the table. It
was in the shadows. With one chubby finger he tapped
three times on the wooden shelf bed with his fingernail.
The sound was soft but clear in the silent room.

Scrabbling. Mouse noise.

Tyler pushed the blanket away and dropped his feet
to the floor. One foot at a time. Silent on the mud floor.
His chest touched the edge of the table, and he reached
out to pull the mouse cage closer.

He had given a name to each of the white mice. Tiny
was the smallest. Pinky's nose was always shiny. Toes had
a black foot. Ears had black spots on his ears. Shorty had
only half a tail. Fatso tried to eat all the food.

He peered close, searching for Mouse Ears.

The mice tumbled over each other in the cedar shavings. His heart raced when he spotted the mouse with the spotted ears. He counted the rest. Five left. Fatso was missing.

Tyler bad. Tyler sorry.

A tear inched out of the corner of his eye, and he looked over his shoulder at the door. The man didn't like it when he cried. Or talked. When he was bad the man would bring the bird.

Tyler squeezed his eyes shut to block out the picture of the bird with spread wings and hooked beak. His cheeks were sticky. He touched them, rubbing at the dried tears. He was proud that he had only cried a little when the man held up the mouse and fed it to the bird.

Not Mouse Ears.

He put his finger out and slid it between the cold metal wires. Mouse Ears bit the end of it. He let the mouse bite him one more time, then pulled his hand back. He returned to the bed, climbed up and wedged his body into the corner where the shelf attached to the wall. He wrapped the blankets around his shoulders and hugged the pillow to his face. Tucking it in the crook of his neck, he settled himself, his fist against his lips and his thumb in his mouth.

The sucking sound lulled him to sleep.

Maggie set the stack of books on the shelf behind the sales counter and brushed Styrofoam particles off the front of her skirt. She rolled her shoulders to loosen the tight muscles after a full day in the bookstore. Saturdays were always busy, and today had been no exception. A quick glance at the clock on top of the register told her Jake was due any minute and it was almost time to close.

After adding the packing slips from the boxes to the stack of them on the old-fashioned metal spindle, she looked around the bookstore to see what she had left to do before closing. Scanning the store invariably brought a smile to her face.

She had worked as a book editor in Chicago when she was married to Mark and had always fantasized about owning her own bookstore. Designing the layout and envisioning the furnishings and decorations had occupied many a coffee break and sleepless night. The reality of her dreams was even better than she'd expected.

The entry door was a sparkling pane of beveled glass, framed in solid oak with an ornately embossed brass faceplate and a matching oval doorknob. The first floor of the house had been gutted. Now instead of walls, wide archways led from room to room, an open and airy space. Only the bathroom and the laundry room remained closed off.

Light streamed into the bookstore from the wide bay window and glass door in front and the double-hung windows on either side of the house. The contractor had told her it would be less efficient for the air-conditioning in the summer, but the sunshine-filled store was reward enough for the higher electric bill.

The contractors had suggested removing the gently curved staircase to allow for additional space within the store. With its old polished oak banister and the intricately carved newel post, Maggie wouldn't even consider it. Instead she had a door installed at the top of the stairs for security.

After straightening up the paperwork on the counter, she walked across to the café that had once been the kitchen. With thoughts of the amount of food she had consumed yesterday at the Renaissance Faire, she avoided the plate of homemade cookies that was always available for customers and staff.

"More coffee?" she asked the man seated in the cushioned wicker chair at the glass-topped table.

Brent Prentice, one of the homeowners on the south side of Falcon Lake, was a frequent visitor to the bookstore. At fifty, he was a distinguished man with dark eyes and thick black hair with patches of white at the temples and around the nape of his neck. Her father-in-law's best friend, Brent was a charmer with his gentle, almost old-fashioned manners.

"I'd love some, Maggie."

He started to get up, but she touched his shoulder to keep him in place. It amused her how he had succumbed to the comforts of the bookstore. When the renovations had been completed, Brent had been disapproving of the café atmosphere. He had warned her that books would be ruined with the addition of coffee, hot chocolate and pastries. She was convinced it was her homemade scones and raspberry preserves that had sold him on the idea.

"I see you found the new book on Florence," she said, leaning over to pour the coffee.

"My dear, it's a definite find. And very apropos. Connie and I are leaving next month for four weeks in Italy."

He picked up a paper napkin and wiped up a spot of coffee that had splashed on the table, then folded the stained napkin into a neat square and placed it beside his cup. Maggie smiled as she replaced the coffeepot.

"I'm already jealous. In four weeks you'll be able to see quite a bit."

"That's what Connie says. She's been after me for the last several years to take some time off. I would have preferred to go on a safari or trek somewhere exotic, but she only wanted Europe." He ran a well-manicured hand across the glossy page. "I suppose if I can see buildings like these, I shall be content."

"I agree. These are quite fantastic," Maggie said, leaning over to look down at the book on the table. "I was quite taken by the photography."

Brent riffled through the pages and showed her several pictures explaining the architectural importance of some of the ornamentations.

When he finished, Maggie said, "The store is closing in about ten minutes, but there's no need to rush. I have a few things to do before I lock up."

"That's quite all right," he said, closing the book. "Connie and I are going to the poker game at the country club, and I have to make some calls before we go. I'll be right along."

She knew he was waiting for her to leave so he could return the book he was reading for a fresh copy. She tried not to be annoyed, since both Brent and his wife never left the store without buying several books. Back at the front desk, she found Connie Prentice waiting for her.

"Would you be a dear, Maggie, and hang this in the window?" Connie asked, holding up a poster announcing a luncheon for the Ladies Golf League at the country club.

Although she could feel herself bristle at the patronizing tone, Maggie smiled across the counter at the woman.

In contrast to Maggie's plaid skirt, white blouse and loafers, Connie wore a lemony silk dress, matching yellow slingback pumps and was carrying a yellow-and-white clutch purse. At thirty-six, Connie was only four years older, yet she invariably made Maggie feel like an awkward schoolgirl.

"I'd be happy to," Maggie said, taking the cardboard and picking up a tape dispenser. She turned to the bay window that looked out over the park and the lake and tapped the glass panel that was about shoulder height. "How about here?"

Connie raised her hands to flip the ends of her blond hair away from the sides of her face. Her wide gold bracelet caught the late afternoon sun coming in the window, flashing brightly.

"Maybe a couple inches higher," she said. "Ah. That should be all right."

"It's a good spot. People coming along the sidewalk always peek in the window to see if the store is open."

Maggie taped it to the glass, then turned back to see Brent holding several books and standing diffidently behind his wife. Sensing a presence behind her, Connie turned, glowering at him.

"We're running late." She pushed a stack of books toward Maggie. "Pay for these, Brent, while I run to the drugstore for some aspirin. I'll meet you at the car. See you soon, Maggie."

Connie waved her hand, and with a sharp click of heels across the wooden floor, she breezed out the front door, leaving behind a tense silence and the heavy scent of her perfume.

Ignoring the woman's rudeness, Maggie rang up the charges and handed Brent the bag of books. She walked with him to the door, opening it and stepping outside.

"I need a bit of this fresh air," she said, walking down the stairs toward the park.

"It may be September, but it still feels like summer," Brent said.

Maggie lifted her head and breathed in the slightly moist air coming off Falcon Lake. The early evening was beautiful. The twilight painted the lakefront with warm reds and oranges, which added to the nostalgic appearance of the old houses that lined the park. Most of the houses in the five-block section had been converted into small stores and upscale boutiques. The street was closed off between the park and the stores. Parking was available in public lots and in the business section of town that ran on the street behind.

With the end of tourist season, a sense of peace and tranquility had settled over Delbrook. Instead of a crowd of boisterous teenagers, only some year-round residents were strolling along the shoreline of Falcon Lake or sitting on the benches around the fountain in the center of Wolfram Park.

The park had been named for one of the early traders who settled in Delbrook. Although the historical society had discovered later that Wolfram had been jailed for horse stealing, all attempts to change the name had run into stiff opposition from the locals.

Just as they reached the sidewalk she heard Jake's footsteps as he trudged around the side of the porch.

"I'm right here, Jake," she called.

Her heart sank as she saw the slumped posture and sulky expression on his face. She smiled halfheartedly at Brent and braced herself for her son's outburst.

"I hate Wisconsin," Jake said, coming to a halt directly in front of Maggie. "I wish we'd never come to live here."

His mouth was pulled into a thin line as he sloughed off his ever present backpack and dropped it on the ground beside her.

"Aren't you forgetting your manners?" she said quietly, placing a steadying hand on his shoulder and turning him to face Brent.

"Sorry, Mom," he said, the tips of his ears reddening in embarrassment. "Hi, Mr. Prentice. I didn't really mean what I said about Wisconsin."

Brent smiled indulgently at the boy. "Sometimes I wish I'd never moved here too. Looks like you've had a bad day."

"Sort of, sir," Jake said.

"What's the tragedy?" Maggie asked, smoothing his black curly hair with her hand. "When you left for Kenny's this afternoon you were looking forward to a wild romp in the woods. Didn't you have fun?"

"Kenny's dad yelled at us because we were making too much noise." Looking down at his shoes, he hesitated, then raised his head and peeked up at the adults through his dark eyelashes. "And we sort of tramped on some flowers he'd just planted."

"Ah," Maggie said.

"You have to remember," Brent said, "that Mr. Rossiter's business is landscaping, and the flowers and bushes he plants are sort of like advertisements for his business."

Jake gave a grudging nod, but his expression didn't lighten. "We told him we did it on accident, but he still made us help him do some digging." After a momentary pause, he asked, "Can I go to the playground?"

Maggie winced at the whiny tone but nodded. "Just for a few minutes while I talk to Mr. Prentice."

As if released from some invisible tow rope, Jake bounded across the grass to the small playground beside the lake. He veered toward the ladder of the slide, then circled it and instead ran up the sloping metal, reaching out to grasp the sides in order to pull himself up the last few feet. At the top he turned and sat down, pushing off from the platform, sliding smoothly to the ground. Jumping to his feet, he twirled around and started back up the slide.

"I see the painters finally completed their work," Brent said.

"They finished this morning." Maggie crossed her arms, standing beside Brent as he looked back at the house. "A few touch-ups to do, but by and large it's finished."

She stared at the house, trying to be objective. It was a small, two-story house with a wide porch across the front and around the left side. A miniature "Painted Lady." She had chosen Wedgwood blue paint for the clapboards and a rusty red trim on the slats of the porch railing, the stairs and the shutters of the house. Blue, yellow and white were the accent colors.

The bookstore took up the entire first floor, and the second floor was the apartment where she and Jake lived. On either side of the front stairs were stone planters filled with multicolored impatiens and snapdragons.

"So the bookstore has a name," Brent said, pointing to the freshly hung sign over the front door.

"Since this is the last house on the street, I decided to call it The Book End. Better than 'Bookstore,' but not altogether imaginative."

"I like it," he said. "Who made the sign?"

"Tully Jackson."

"Tully?" His tone was arch.

"I know everyone in town thinks the man is crazy."

"That's because he is," Brent said, clearly shocked. "He's not that old but he sits in a webbed lounge chair beside that old junker car at the boat landing all day. The man lives out of his car and talks to himself, for cripes' sake."

Maggie chuckled. "Don't be so stuffy, Brent. I've talked to him and I've seen the inside of the car. It's full of old clothes and odds and ends, but I really don't think he lives in it."

"How'd you find out he could carve and paint signs? He usually rants when anyone gets too close." Brent brushed the front of his suit coat as if he had come in contact with the man.

"Actually, Jake made the first approach. When we first moved here we took a picnic lunch to the park beside the boat ramp. You know Jake. He wandered over and started talking. I was a little concerned since Tully looks so peculiar."

Brent raised both eyebrows and stared down his nose at Maggie. "Peculiar nothing. He's nuts! The man wears a plastic raincoat and a white satin top hat. He looks like the Wild Man of Borneo with that long hair and beard. You've got to worry about some kind of bug infestation. Really, Maggie, you and Jake ought to steer clear of the man. He could be psychotic."

"There doesn't seem to be anything wrong with him. He's a bit shy when you first talk to him, but he warms up after a while. Jake has sort of adopted the man. We see him once a week when we go down to the lake to feed the geese. Jake brings Tully candy bars and comic books."

"Good Lord," Brent said, shaking his head in a shuddering movement. "You shouldn't coddle the man."

At Brent's reaction, she decided not to tell him that she usually brought along homemade soup. Wanting to change the conversation, she called across to Jake who had abandoned the slide for a swing. "Time to go in."

With one last pump of his legs, Jake leaned back, pointing his feet to the sky. When the swing reached the top of the arc, he released his hands from the chains and leaped into space, landing two-footed in a spray of sandy dirt.

"I hate when he does that," she said. "It gives me a queasy feeling in the pit of my stomach."

Brent laughed. "He's all boy, that one. Well, I better get along to the car if I don't want Connie searching for me."

After his exercise in the park, Jake was in a much better humor. Back in the bookstore, he helped her straighten the books on the shelves and fill shopping bags with her regular customers' monthly book orders. When Jake's stomach began to growl, they locked up the store and went out for pizza.

Although in the beginning Jake voiced his disappointment that he wasn't going to a movie with his grandfather, the evening turned out to be fun. To keep Jake from worrying that it wouldn't be available, they'd rented *Godzilla* before going out for pizza. They'd made popcorn and sat on the couch, cheering and booing at the appropriate parts of the movie. After a long week, she was grateful to be in bed by ten-thirty.

The ringing of the telephone jolted Maggie awake. She fumbled for the receiver on the bedside table, automatically searching for the illuminated clock face in the darkened room. Her heart raced.

Two-fifteen in the morning.

She sat upright, pressing the button on the portable phone before it could ring a second time and wake Jake.

"Mrs. Mark Collier please," a young woman said.

"Speaking."

Her fingers, clammy with fear, slipped on the switch of the lamp beside the bed. She threw back the sheet and swung her feet over the side of the bed.

"This is Lechner Hospital calling. I'm sorry to tell you, but George Collier has been injured."

CHAPTER THREE

"I'M SORRY TO TELL YOU, but George Collier has been injured."

Dear God, not again. A chill ran through Maggie's body. Those were almost the same words that she had heard two years ago when Mark had been killed.

"Hello? Are you there, Mrs. Collier?"

Maggie licked her lips before she could speak.

"Yes. Go ahead."

"Mr. Collier has been brought to Lechner Hospital here in Delbrook. The doctor would like you to come."

"Please, can you tell me how badly George—eh, Mr. Collier is hurt?"

"I'm sorry, ma'am, but I don't have that information. If you come to the hospital, the doctor will be able to answer all your questions."

"Yes. I understand. I'll come right away."

Sitting numbly on the side of the bed, Maggie pressed the disconnect button. It had to be a dream. She squeezed her eyes shut, then popped them open, staring around the bedroom. Nothing had changed. She slapped the receiver against the palm of her hand. She felt the sting. Her shoulders sagged.

She could remember the same feeling when the hospital had called her about Mark's car accident. She had been afraid then to move, afraid that if she broke the circle of numbness, she would be forced to accept the painful facts.

Oh, God, let him be all right. Please, God. Jake and I love him so.

The dial tone droned, grating along her nerve endings. She returned the receiver to the cradle and tried to pull the scattered thoughts in her mind into some semblance of order. She didn't want to wake Jake until she had established his grandfather's condition. He had already been through one trauma when his father had died. She didn't know how he'd react to another.

She opened the bedroom door and slipped across the hall to Jake's room, peering in to see if he was still asleep. In the light from her bedroom she could see his dark curly hair sharply outlined against the white pillowcase. His eyes were shut and his breathing deep and even.

Closing the door, she walked down the hall to the living room. Aside from the stream of light from her bedroom, the apartment was dark. The floor creaked under her bare feet, and she shivered at the sound. She hated this time of the morning before the sun rose. She remembered after Mark died when she couldn't sleep and she had paced the floor, feeling alone and frightened in the big house in Chicago.

In the living room she looked out the side window and felt instant relief as she spotted the lighted pane in Nell Gleason's studio.

Nell was a night owl, especially when she was working on a new painting. Grateful that she wouldn't be waking the older woman, Maggie dialed, rocking back and forth on her heels until Nell answered. Maggie quickly explained the situation and asked if she could come over and stay with Jake. At her friend's immediate acceptance, the knot of tension between her shoulders loosened.

Hanging up, Maggie went into the kitchen, turned on the light in the stairwell and ran down the stairs to unlock the outside door.

Upstairs again, she washed quickly and brushed her hair, fastening it with a wide, tortoise-shell barrette to keep it off her face. The mirror reflected her inner turmoil. Against her reddish brown hair, her skin appeared whiter than usual, and she grabbed a lipstick, adding a bright slash of color to her lips. She exchanged her nightgown for jeans, sneakers and a blue-and-white gingham blouse.

Back in the kitchen, she ran water into the coffeepot, measuring the grounds hurriedly before she turned it on. The normality of the action was somehow comforting. The pungent aroma of fresh brewed coffee began to filter into the air as she heard the downstairs door open and Nell Gleason appeared at the top of the stairwell.

The older woman wore a navy blue sweatshirt and navy pants, both of which were liberally covered with splotches of paint. A line of colored stripes marched up her left sleeve where she had wiped her paintbrush. Maggie could see flecks of paint in her flyaway hair, which was dyed a peculiar color of salmon pink. A streak of magenta ran from the corner of her right eye into the hair at her temple.

"Oh, I'm so sorry about George," the older woman

said, breathing heavily from the climb. She enveloped Maggie in an embrace redolent of turpentine and paint, patting her back as if she were only five and had wakened from a bad dream.

The hug made Maggie feel less isolated. Nell had grown up in Delbrook with Maggie's mother, standing as godmother when Maggie was born. Despite the thirty years difference in their ages, she and Nell were the closest of friends.

"I made some coffee for you, and Jake is still asleep," Maggie said. "Sorry I had to take you away from your painting."

Nell waved her hand. "The piece is almost done, so it's not a problem to leave it. Have you heard anything more?"

"Nothing since that first call."

"An automobile accident?" Nell asked.

"That's what I'm assuming. I hope to God no one else was injured." Maggie's lips quivered as images recalled from Mark's fatal crash flooded her mind.

"Amen to that. Well, there's no point in our imagining the worst. You better get along now and see what the doctor has to say," Nell said. "Are you all right to drive? You look a little white around the gills."

"I'm OK." She scooped up her purse and reached for her keys hanging on the hook beside the door. "The phone call spooked me. Sort of catapulted me back to Mark's death."

"Of course it did. Think positive thoughts and don't worry. You'd better take a jacket. It's chilly out." Nell stood with Maggie at the top of the stairs. "I'll be here with Jake as long as you need me."

"Bless you. I'll call you as soon as I know anything."

Maggie grabbed her windbreaker from the line of clothes hooks in the stairwell and hurried down the steps. Outside she pulled on the jacket as she walked along the side porch to the back stairs where her car was parked.

Let him be all right, she chanted as she drove through the empty streets to the hospital. She prayed Jake wouldn't wake up while she was gone. He would know there was something wrong if she wasn't there. Her mind on automatic pilot, she parked the car and hurried in through the emergency room entrance.

The receptionist asked her to wait while she called for information, then motioned to a security guard who led Maggie through a maze of corridors to a door marked PASTORAL CARE and opened the door.

"Mrs. Collier?" A gray-haired woman rose from her chair, coming forward to take Maggie's hand. "I'm Ann Bhat, the pastoral counselor."

"Please, call me Maggie." Strange how the normal courtesies of life continued, she thought. "I've come about George."

Ann led her to a leather chair in front of the desk and, instead of returning to the far side, sat down in the chair opposite.

"Mr. Collier is your father?"

"No. My father-in-law. George's son, my husband, died two years ago."

Maggie could feel her heart beating in her ears. George must be hurt worse than she had first thought, otherwise she would have been taken to his room. Her body began to tremble, a slight vibration like a running motor.

"How difficult for you." Ann folded her hands in her lap and leaned toward Maggie. "Mr. Collier was brought to the hospital, but the doctors were not able to save him. I'm sorry to tell you, but your father-in-law passed away a short time ago."

"Oh, God, no!" Maggie reached up and covered her ears as if she could block the words. "It can't happen again. He can't be dead."

Dropping her hands in her lap, she closed her eyes, swallowing the lump in her throat. Pictures of George flashed behind her eyelids, a kaleidoscope of memories. George holding Jake at his christening, the older man's face stern as he tried to hold back tears of joy. Jake holding up a string of fish for his grandfather's approval. George holding her as she and Jake stood beside Mark's casket.

She was too stunned to cry. How can I tell Jake about George's death? First his father and now his grandfather. It wasn't fair. How could this happen again?

It was so much like her experiences when Mark died that it was almost past bearing. A nightmarish déjà vu. She could remember bargaining with God, begging Him to keep Mark alive for Jake's sake. She had promised she would give up her editing job and devote her life to making Mark happy.

Her fingernails bit into the palms of her hands as she fought the rising tide of anger that threatened to choke her. God hadn't listened then, and now He'd let it happen again.

"Maggie? Are you all right?"

The grief counselor's voice came from a distance. Maggie opened her eyes, taking in the concern on the woman's face. She was softly pretty and elegant in dress and mannerisms. She looked familiar. Possibly she'd come into the bookstore or Maggie had seen her around town.

"I'm all right," Maggie said, wishing that the numbness she had felt earlier would return to replace the gnawing ache of loss. She tried to pull herself together. "It's a shock, but I suppose not unexpected."

"Not unexpected?" Ann's brows furrowed in confusion.

"I always worried when George was out late with his cronies. I know he drank at the card games, and I never approved of him driving home even if it wasn't very far. Was anyone else involved in the accident?"

The counselor's mouth opened and closed but no sound came out. She shook her head slightly and leaned toward Maggie, once more taking her hand.

"Did someone tell you that it was an auto accident?"

"No. I just assumed it was. If it wasn't a car accident, what happened?"

The phone rang, the sound cutting through the tension in the room. Ann reached across the desk and picked up the receiver.

"Pastoral Care. Ann Bhat speaking." She listened for a moment, nodding her head. "Yes. Mrs. Collier is here now."

At mention of her name, Maggie sat up straighter. What could have happened to George? A heart attack? A stroke? A dozen possibilities whirled around in her head, and she found herself impatient for answers.

"All right. I'll wait until you get here." Ann hung up and turned back to Maggie. "That was Police Chief

Blessington. He's at the front desk and is coming back to talk to you. He'll be able to explain everything."

What does Charley have to explain? Maggie thought, shifting in her seat, unable to sit still. With the police chief involved, it must be more serious than she had anticipated.

"What happened to George? What aren't you telling me?"

Without answering Maggie's questions, Ann rose to her feet and went to the coffeepot on a table in the corner of the room and poured coffee into a dark blue stoneware mug with the hospital logo emblazoned in yellow.

"I think some coffee might help," she said. "Sugar or cream?"

Maggie shook her head. She could see by the closed expression on the older woman's face that she would have to wait for answers. Taking the coffee, she cupped both hands around the mug, drawing comfort from the warmth. She breathed in the aroma slowly to block out the antiseptic hospital smell that she would always associate with death. She looked up at the clock on the wall. Three o'clock. It seemed impossible that so much had changed in just forty-five minutes.

She touched her hand to her forehead. It was hot and sweaty in the still air. She stood up and unzipped her windbreaker. Taking the keys out of the pocket, she shoved them into the pocket of her jeans and pulled off the coat. She bundled it up and set it on her purse.

"Would you like a bag for your things?" Ann said.

The woman seemed grateful that she could be of some help. She bustled over with a bright yellow plastic bag with the logo of the hospital printed on the side. Maggie's hands shook as she took the bag, jammed her windbreaker inside and dropped it beside her chair.

The door into the hall opened, and Charley Blessington filled the doorway.

"Aw, damn it, Maggie. I'm so sorry about George," he said, his voice ricocheting off the walls in the small office.

Charley was a big man, tall with wide shoulders and a solid, muscular body. His thick blond hair stood on end as if he'd been running his fingers through it. Eyebrows, an explosion of blond hair above his silvery blue eyes, dominated his face. At forty-five he had been almost twenty years younger than Maggie's father-in-law, but she knew they had been good friends.

He crossed the room in long strides as Maggie set her mug on the desk and struggled to her feet. He put his arms around her and gave her a quick bracing hug. Then, hands on her shoulders, he pushed her away and looked down, his blond eyebrows bunched over his eyes. I'll get a crick in my neck if I continue to stare up at him, she thought. She smiled at the sheer inanity of the thought.

"That's the girl," he said, squeezing her shoulders. "You got to keep a stiff upper lip when times are tough."

"What happened to George?" she asked.

"Now I know you're anxious to get to the bottom of this, but let me grab some coffee before we get started."

Without waiting for her answer, Charley strode over to the table, reaching out for the mug that Ann Bhat held out to him.

"I'll get some of the paperwork started," Ann said as she headed for the door.

Charley crossed the room and sat down behind the desk. He took several sips of the coffee and then set the mug carefully on the blotter. He leaned forward onto his elbows, staring at her over tented fingers. Despite the smile on his face, Maggie could feel a certain intensity to his look.

"What happened to George?" she asked. "I assumed he'd been in an automobile accident, but when I mentioned it, Ann looked surprised."

"Didn't anyone tell you what happened?"

"No. I just got a call that he was here. I didn't even know he was dead until Ann told me."

"When did you last see George?" he asked.

"Friday night. He came over to find out how Jake's birthday party went. We talked on the porch, but it was late, so he didn't stay long. Then he called today just before he left for the country club."

"Did he seem out of sorts? Tense?"

"What the hell is going on, Charley? George is dead, and no one will tell me anything." Her hands shook with the effort it took to keep her body still. She gripped the arms of her chair and glared across the desk at the police chief.

He held up his hands, palms toward her in a placating gesture. "Be patient a few minutes longer and then I'll explain everything. Did he have anything important to say when you talked to him?"

"He wanted to know what time he should come for dinner."

Maggie came to a halt, shaking her head. She'd talked to him less than twelve hours ago. Last night she'd made a pineapple upside-down cake, and just before she went to bed she'd taken pork chops out of the freezer to make George's favorite recipe.

"I can't believe he's gone," she said. Her eyes stung with unshed tears, and she blinked rapidly to hold them back.

"I feel the same way, Maggie. Doris and I ate at the club last night. I stayed to play poker. We finished up around midnight, and your father-in-law was gloating over the fact that he had won on the last hand. George would have loved going out a winner."

Maggie sniffed and nodded her head.

"Did George call from the country club?" he asked.

"No."

"Did you hear from anyone before the hospital called?"

"I don't like the tone of these questions, Charley," she said, "and I think I'm finished giving answers."

Charley accepted her antagonism with good nature.

"Well now, Maggie, this is going to come as a shock," he said. "Your father-in-law wasn't in an accident. Someone attacked him. We'll have to do an autopsy before we know for certain, but it appears that someone stabbed George."

Maggie pressed against the back of the chair, wanting to put some distance between herself and Charley's words.

"Stabbed? I don't understand," she said. "You mean like in a fight?"

"Well, we don't know if it was a fight. It looks like it might have been some sort of botched robbery."

"A robbery. Oh, dear God. Where was he when this happened?"

"He was still at the country club. On the eighteenth tee."

Charley's reply was so unexpected that Maggie felt totally disoriented. She pressed her fingers against her shaking lips and tried to catch her breath.

"A robbery?" She felt stupid repeating his words. It was like some idiotic comedy sketch. "What happened?"

Charley stared hard at her. She suspected he was waiting to see if she was going to break down. When she managed to pull herself together, he flopped back in the desk chair, his mouth pulled into a grimace of anger.

"At this point we don't know much," he said. "At one-oh-two, we got a nine-one-one call to send an ambulance to the country club. One of the cleaning crew found George. The kid didn't know what had happened, but he saw the blood. He said it looked like George's heart was bleeding. He came racing back to the club for help. The paramedics got there within five minutes, but it was already too late."

"Why was George out on the golf course?"

"It looks like he mighta walked out along the eighteenth fairway to have a cigar." Charley shook his head, rubbing one hand over his hair. "The poker game was over, and I thought he'd gone home like everyone else. When I got back to the club, his car was still in the parking lot."

"You said robbery. Was the car broken into?"

"No. It was locked and undisturbed. We're thinking robbery, because George's wallet is missing and his watch is gone."

"I can't believe it."

"Damn it, I can't either." Charley pushed himself to

his feet, angry color rising to his cheeks. "Delbrook is hardly a high-crime area. Sure, we've had little penny-ante shit. But nothing violent since I've been chief of police."

"Didn't anyone see anything or hear anything?"

"Well, honey, we don't know. The numbnuts who was first on the scene didn't think to hold the guy who found the body." He saw her wince and came around the desk and put his hand on her shoulder. "I'm sorry, Maggie. This is all pretty grim, and for the moment we don't know much. But believe me, we'll find out who did this."

Maggie swallowed hard. "What do I do now?"

"Ann is going to help you take care of things. Because of the nature of George's death, an autopsy is required."

"Oh, God, I forgot about that," she said.

She pressed the palms of her hands together to hold back a shudder of distaste. Death was difficult to handle in any case, but the details surrounding a violent death made everything much worse. She knew. It had been like that when Mark died.

Charley continued. "We won't be able to release the body to the funeral home right away, but I'll make sure everything gets expedited as quickly as possible. Where's Jake?"

"I called Nell Gleason to stay with him."

"Good. I'll take you to Ann, and she'll try to cut through the formalities and get you home before your son is awake. I know this is going to be tough for him, coming so soon after his father's death. You might want to talk to Ann about that."

"I will. And you'll keep me posted?"

"You have my word on that. We'll find out who did this. No matter how long it takes."

Maggie picked up her purse and the yellow hospital bag and followed the police chief through the hospital corridors until they reached the emergency room. To her surprise, she found Brent Prentice waiting for her.

"Nell called to tell us about George. Connie and I didn't want you to be alone," he said by way of explanation. "I should have known Charley'd be here to take care of you."

Maggie was touched that Brent had come. She could see in his eyes his own sadness at the death of his friend, and despite her own sense of loss, she wanted to console him. He opened his arms, and Maggie naturally stepped into the circle, kissing him on the cheek. "I'm glad you came."

He smelled of soap and starch, she thought as she accepted his comforting embrace. It was the perfect combination for him. His fussiness and his old-fashioned mannerisms always reminded Maggie of a time gentler than the fast-paced rudeness of modern life.

"It's unbelievable," Brent said. "Connie and I were with him tonight at the country club along with Charley and the rest of the crew."

Maggie was unable to speak around the lump in her throat. Brent sensed her distress and turned toward Charley. Without removing his arm from around her shoulder, Brent held out his hand to the police chief. Joined in their mutual mourning for a lost friend, the two men shook hands gravely.

"As I was driving over here I was trying to remember when I first met George." Brent shook his head. "Since I grew up in Delbrook, I think I've always known him. Once I came back from college, though, is when we really became friends."

His bottom lip trembled, and he swallowed before he could continue. "He taught me how to fish."

Maggie smiled. "George said you hated it."

Brent sniffed, and his mouth twitched with humor. "I did. Those slimy worms and bleeding fish. Good Lord, how repulsive. He said my face turned green as the grass around the lake. The thing was that he never looked down on me for disliking it. He said a man ought to know how to do things even if he never did them again."

"That sounds like George. He had a succinct way of putting things," Charley said.

"Nell said George had some kind of accident. Automobile?"

Maggie opened her mouth, but before she could respond, Ann Bhat opened a glass door in the hall and smiled at the threesome.

"I told you Charley would bring her here," she said to Brent. "While you gentlemen talk, I need Maggie for a few minutes."

"Go on along," Brent said, giving her shoulder a reassuring pat. "I'll talk to Charley."

Too tired to argue, Maggie followed Ann into the office. The grief counselor helped her through the paperwork, explaining everything as they went along. Thank God Charley had already identified the body. When Mark died, she had been the one to make the identification, and she'd had nightmares for several months afterward.

"I think that's it," Ann said. "Let me give you my business card."

She placed a white card in a slit on the front of the bright yellow folder that contained copies of all the paperwork. Maggie's eyes burned, and she rubbed them. She felt drained. Ann picked up the folder and opened the door into the corridor. The police chief was gone, but Brent waited for her, his mouth set in a grim line.

"Dear Lord, Maggie, what kind of world is this where a man can be killed for his money and a watch?"

"I know. It doesn't make sense. Not here in Delbrook," Maggie said. "Let's get out of here."

"Where are you parked?" Brent asked.

"In the back lot. The emergency spots were all filled."

"I'm in front. Wait for me and I'll follow you home."

"I'm really fine, you know."

He held up one well-manicured hand. "Please. I have orders from Connie and Nell."

Maggie smiled as he strode briskly toward the lobby, then turned back to Ann.

"I don't feel right leaving George here. I haven't even seen him. I haven't said my goodbyes," Maggie said with a catch in her voice.

"There will be time for that later, my dear." Ann patted her arm. "Right now the police work must take precedence. For the moment you can catch your breath, see to your son and think about making arrangements."

"You're right. I can't thank you enough for your help."

"That's what I'm here for. I'll be your liaison for anything that has to do with George. If you have any questions in the next day or two, call me."

"It really hasn't hit me yet. I know in my head that George is gone, but it doesn't have much meaning right now."

"Part of it is the shock of how he died. I know you have many questions, but just take it slowly. Chief Blessington will do his job. Do what you can to keep your strength up. Your toughest job will be to keep a buffer zone between all of this and your son."

Maggie shook the woman's hand as she took the yellow folder and tucked it into the plastic bag along with several brochures that Ann thought might be helpful when talking to Jake. She gave a quick wave of her hand and headed down the corridor, sighing as she saw the ladies' room next to the emergency room door.

The fluorescent ceiling lights added to the ghostly reflection above the sink. She washed her hands, staring at the dark circles under her eyes. Leaning over, she scooped up some cold water and splashed it against her face. It helped a little, she thought as she rubbed some color into her cheeks with a paper towel. She rested the palms of her hands on the edge of the sink and leaned forward, staring at her face in the mirror.

I can't do it again. I can't.

How was she going to tell Jake about his grandfather? Tears rose to her eyes, and she squeezed them shut, fighting for control. She rested her forehead against the cool surface of the mirror and tried to breathe slowly. When her heart beat more evenly, she opened her eyes. For a long moment she stared at her mirror image, searching for strength in the pale-faced woman in the glass.

I have to do it. I have to do it for Jake, she thought.

Leaning over, she picked up the yellow plastic bag and settled the strap of her purse over her shoulder. With one more glance at her reflection, she raised her chin, straightened her back and left the washroom.

The hospital doors slid open automatically. Outside, the crisp breeze felt good after the overheated air in the hospital. Sniffing in the freshness, she walked down the empty sidewalk to the parking lot. She was surprised by the number of cars that remained even at four in the morning.

She wasn't used to being out at this time of the morning. Although the sky was not as dark as when she had first arrived, shadows clung to the edges of buildings and created odd shapes where the streetlights didn't reach. She stopped at the edge of the parking lot, shivering.

She'd been in such a hurry to get to the hospital that she hadn't noticed where she'd parked. The lights in the parking lot threw shadows on the ground, and she could feel her heart beating as she walked down the aisle between the cars. The scrape of gravel made her jerk around, but she could see no movement.

"Nerves," she muttered in disgust. She tried to relax the tension between her shoulder blades with little success. The call from the hospital had frightened her, and now, with George's violent death, the perceived safety of Delbrook was shattered. She thought she'd left the stabbings and robberies behind in Chicago. Alone in the parking lot, she was afraid.

Near the end of the line of cars she spotted her blue Corolla. She increased her speed until she was almost running. Panic had taken over, and she breathed in shallow gasps. Shifting the hospital bag to her left hand, she dug in the pocket of her jeans for the car keys.

She could have cried in relief when she reached the car and hurried into the space beside the door. Keys in her hand, she fumbled for the lock. She couldn't hear anything over the sound of her own breathing and a loud roaring in her ears, but she had an impression of movement behind her. Something hard slammed into her back.

She fell sideways. Her head and shoulder crashed against the car, and she bounced off, sliding toward the ground. She threw out her hands to break her fall. The rough asphalt surface scraped the palms of her hands as she landed in a heap beside the car.

Lights flashed before her eyes, and she blinked to drive away the nausea that engulfed her. A dark figure blocked out the light, and darkness invaded her senses.

CHAPTER FOUR

"MAGGIE? Are you all right?"

She could hear the voice close to her ear calling her name. Lethargy held her in a gentle embrace, and she clung to the floating sensation. Even if she had wanted to answer, her mouth was dry, and when she tried to speak, no sound came out. A sharp pain lanced through her shoulder when she moved, bringing back the terror that had possessed her before she passed out. She squeezed her eyes shut and ignored the voice.

"Maggie." Strong hands shook her. "Maggie."

Despite her fear, she responded to the urgency in the man's voice and opened her eyes. Darkness. She couldn't see anything. Panicked by her blindness, she struggled against the hands on her shoulders.

"It's all right, Maggie. It's Brent."

Recognizing his voice, she sagged in relief. Now that her eyes had become accustomed to the dark, she could see she was lying on the ground between two cars. Brent knelt beside her, the white hair at his temples gleaming in the darkness.

"Can you sit up?"

"I think so. I hit my head."

She raised a hand and touched the bump on her head. No dampness, so at least she wasn't bleeding, but she winced at the tenderness. She took inventory of the rest of her body. Her shoulder and the palms of her hands had taken the brunt of the damage.

"Maybe you should lie there, and I'll go for help."

Frightened to be left alone, Maggie grabbed the sleeve of Brent's jacket to hold him in place.

"I'm all right," she said. "Just help me up."

Brent shifted his hands and lifted her to her feet, holding her until she could get strength back in her legs. The ground shifted, and she closed her eyes, letting her head rest against his chest.

"Maybe we should go back into the hospital so you can see a doctor."

She couldn't see his face, but she could hear the concern in his voice. "No. I'm all right. Just dizzy."

"I should never have let you come out here alone." He patted her back. Awkward thumps that he probably thought were encouraging but only made her head ache. "Just wait until Connie hears about this."

Realizing his concern for her was slightly outweighed by his fear of Connie's recriminations, Maggie felt better, not quite so light-headed. She took a deep gulp of air, and he released her.

"That's it. Big breaths. Then you won't pass out again."

"I didn't faint. Someone hit me."

"What?" Brent grabbed her, and she flinched at the pain as his fingers bit into her left arm. She pulled away, flexing her shoulder.

"Someone hit me," she repeated.

"What are you talking about? I didn't see anyone." His voice was sharp, and he glanced around as if to prove his point. "I drove up and found you lying on the ground."

Brent's car was still running, parked in the center of the aisle with the door open as if he had leaped out when he saw her. She leaned unsteadily on the trunk of the parked car and looked around the parking lot. No sign of anyone and no motion near any of the cars.

"I'm not making this up, Brent. Someone was here."

"Are you sure you aren't a little giddy? When I drove up, the only one I saw was you."

Maggie shook her head, regretting the motion as pain pounded in her temple. "Someone hit me and then stole my purse."

"Stole your purse?"

Her words shocked him. He stared down at her, searching her face before nodding.

"Stay here."

He hurried over to the open door of his silver Lexus, reached under the seat and pulled out a flashlight. He struggled with the switch, smacking the flashlight against the palm of his hand until a weak beam flickered on the ground. He swept it back and forth as he came toward her, then crouched over as he searched between the cars.

"I've found your purse, Maggie. And your car keys." He stood up, brushing at the knees of his pants, then came toward her, the purse held out in front of him like a trophy. "It must have rolled under the car when you passed out."

She gritted her teeth as he handed it to her. "I didn't

pass out. Someone tried to take my purse. Oh rats! Where's the hospital bag?"

"Hospital bag?"

"It's bright yellow plastic. I had it when I left the hospital."

She bent over searching the ground for the bag. Brent halfheartedly flashed the light around, but it was nowhere in sight.

"Are you sure you didn't leave it in the hospital?"

Maggie put a hand up to her throbbing forehead. For a second she wondered if she might have left it in the bathroom. Brent stood patiently beside her, waiting for her to make a decision. It was clear that he didn't believe that she had been attacked, so how would she convince anyone else?

Her head hurt. Her bones ached. She had a few bruises, but she hadn't lost anything of value. There was nothing in the bag but her jacket and the folder that the grief counselor had given her.

"I'll call the hospital later," she said. "All I want to do right now is go home."

"I'll drive you. I don't think you should risk—"

He stopped short as she held up her hand.

"Damn it, Brent! I am not prone to fits of the vapors. I'm perfectly fine to drive. My palms are stinging and my shoulder and head hurt, but I'm fine. Nothing a hot bath won't cure."

Brent rocked back and forth, defensive in the face of her anger. Seeing his distress, Maggie took a deep, steadying breath.

"Please forgive me, Brent. You've been wonderful coming to the hospital, and here I am snarling at you."

"My dear, you've had a dreadful shock. It's no wonder you're upset."

His deep voice soothed Maggie's jagged nerve endings, and she didn't object when he handed her into the car, waiting beside the door until she buckled her seat belt. With almost a courtly bow, he held out her car keys.

"Now don't make a fuss, because I intend to follow you until you're safely home. Then I'm going to stop by the police station. We've never had much crime in Delbrook. Now all of a sudden it's a war zone. Charley Blessington should know about this. After all, if you thought you saw a purse snatcher, it could have been the same man who robbed George."

"If Grampa had gone to the movie with me last night, he wouldn't be dead."

Jake's whispered comment made Maggie wince. She reached out to him, but he backed up against the living room archway, his body rigid. Slow tears slid down his cheeks, and he brushed them away with the back of his hand.

"Grampa promised he would take me. When I say I'm gonna do something, you always make me keep my promise," Jake cried. "Why didn't you make him go to the movie?"

Even though it was an unreasonable question, Maggie couldn't find any defense against his charge. She knew Jake's anger was only a reaction to the news of his grandfather's death. Still, it hurt.

"I know this doesn't make sense," she said, "but it could as easily have happened if he went to the movie with you. It could have happened anywhere."

"Oh, Mom, it's just not fair. I don't want him to be dead."

The words seemed torn out of his shaking body. Maggie crossed the room and put her arms around him. He resisted her touch, his back and arms stiff and unbending. She held him firmly, rocking him as she had done when he was younger. She'd missed cuddling him. These last two years since Mark's death, Jake had kept her at a distance.

Fighting to keep her own tears at bay, Maggie stared dully at the clock on the wall.

Eight o'clock in the morning. Less than four hours of sleep.

When she returned from the hospital, she sat with Nell, talking and making lists of things she would need to do. She was too keyed up to eat, but Nell stayed to give Maggie a chance for a quick nap. It seemed as if she'd only closed her eyes when Nell shook her to tell her that Jake was awake and that she was going home.

The sobs that shook Jake lessened, and his body began to relax. She felt his arms wrap around her waist, and this time he returned her embrace. With that she couldn't hold back her own tears. She wasn't sure whether she was crying for George's loss, Jake's grief or her own feeling of abandonment.

When Mark died, her anguish had been part regret and part guilt. Their marriage had begun with such promise. How could she have let their life together deteriorate until there was nothing left to be salvaged? It was all her fault. She'd failed to keep her marriage alive, and because of that, Mark was gone and Jake was being torn apart by sorrow and pain.

A hiccuping sob brought her back to the present and the devastated child pressed against her. She reached into the pocket of her skirt and pulled out a wad of Kleenex. She smiled as they shared the tissues.

"Come on out to the kitchen, honey. We'll feel better after we've had something to eat."

"I'm not hungry."

"Well, you can sit with me at least. I'm starving."

She pushed him ahead of her across the hall to the kitchen and pulled out a chair at the small table by the window. She ignored him as she brought over silverware and plates. Pouring two glasses of orange juice, she set one down in front of him and carried her own over to the stove.

The phone rang, and the answering machine automatically picked it up. It had been ringing ever since word of George's death got out. Earlier Nell had answered the phone, but when a reporter called, she had turned on the machine.

The room filled with the aroma of scrambled eggs and toast. She set everything on the table, sat down and helped herself to a plateful. Jake drank his juice, and she made no comment when he filled his own plate and started to eat.

"Where's Grampa now?" he said around a mouthful of toast.

Though startled by the abrupt question, she assumed he wanted practical details not a religious discussion.

"He's at the hospital. The doctor will examine him to find out what made him die."

"Will they look for clues?"

"Yes. Then he'll be taken to the funeral home. Just like with Dad."

Jake didn't look at her, continuing to stare at his plate as if choosing a question from a list written on the surface.

"Is he all cut up?"

"Oh, no, honey. This is way different than a car crash. I think Grampa will look like he's sleeping."

"That's what you said about Daddy."

She had been so numbed by Mark's death that she hadn't fully taken into account how frightened Jake would be when he saw his father at the funeral home. The auto accident had been devastating, and although the funeral director had done what he could, the face Jake saw lying in the casket did not exactly look like his father's.

"I'm sorry about that, Jake." Her shoulders sagged at the sudden flash of memory. "Your dad had been hurt really bad. I tell you what. I'll take the first look at Grampa, and if he looks yucky, I'll tell you, and you can decide if you want to look. Deal?"

After a pause, Jake nodded.

Maggie stared at him, debating the next step. He needed to ask questions, and she didn't know what answers were appropriate for his age. She let him finish eating and then she said, "Can I ask you something?"

He raised his head, eyes narrowed and his expression wary. "Sure."

"When your father died you were only six. That's pretty young to deal with death. When someone dies, there are a lot of details to take care of and a lot of questions to be answered. You're eight now and you understand more, so I don't know if you want to know about some of these things or if you just want me to go off and take care of them."

His eyes moved back and forth as if he were reading her face. She remained still, giving him time to think.

"I want to go with you, Mom. I'm not a kid anymore. I guess I need to know about all this stuff."

His response broke her heart. Innocence lost. Welcome to adulthood. She stood up, gathering the dishes and putting them in the sink so that she could keep her face averted. She swallowed back her tears, and when she could speak without her voice giving her away, she continued.

"I'd like you with me, too. I don't think it's going to be awful, Jake. It'll be sad because we'll be missing Grampa, but we can help each other."

The telephone rang. She jumped at the sound but was grateful for the interruption.

"Let's go down to the bookstore and get away from the phone," she said. She reached for her keys on the hook beside the door. "Can you unlock the door?"

"Sure," Jake said.

He grabbed the keys and raced down the hallway. By the time Maggie arrived, he had the door open and had flipped on the lights at the top of the stairs leading down to the bookstore. Jake hopped down the stairs, his shoes clattering on the oak treads. Since it was Sunday and the store wasn't open, she left the door to the apartment open.

Light poured into the first floor from the bay window, and she was glad they'd come downstairs. The bookstore had been her refuge ever since it first began to take shape. She had invested a lot of thought into the layout, and it had taken on her personality. She was more comfortable here among the books than she was in her own living room. The warmth of the room surrounded her, and since George had been so much a part of the renovation, she felt his presence in a comforting way.

She rooted in the cupboards for a bag of French vanilla coffee. It was George's favorite, and she had always loved the smell, just a hint of vanilla, not too overpowering. She stood beside the coffeemaker, breathing deeply as the aroma began to fill the room.

"Look, Mom," Jake said. "Kenny and his dad are here."

He raced across the wooden floor to the front door. Maggie reached up for coffee mugs, listening to Hugh Rossiter's deep voice as he talked to Jake. She should have known he would come. Hugh had been a good friend since she moved to Delbrook. A single parent himself, he understood much of what she had gone through after Mark's death and had offered her friendship and a lot of support with Jake.

She chided herself for a moment of vanity as she pushed her fingers through her unbrushed hair. Too bad she hadn't had time for a quick shower when she got up. It might have made her eyes less red and puffy.

"I hope it's not too early to come over," Hugh said as he came toward her.

"Not at all."

She met him halfway and smiled at Hugh's son, Kenny, as he followed Jake into the café area.

"We've finished breakfast, but there's some doughnuts and coffee cake in the refrigerator," she said.

"I think Kenny's hungry," Jake said, hauling the boy across the room by pulling on the sleeve of his striped shirt.

The two heads were close together, talking in conspiratorial whispers. Kenny was as fair as Jake was dark. He was a fragile-looking child with small bones and a soft whispery voice. Jake and Kenny had become friends in the years when they visited George in Delbrook. The move to Delbrook had solidified the friendship, and now the boys were inseparable.

Although Jake acted as spokesman and had a tendency to be annoyingly bossy, Kenny didn't seem to mind it. He would never be an aggressive child, preferring to have Jake plan and lead the action. Letting the boys fend for themselves, Maggie turned back to Hugh.

"Thanks for coming over."

"Sorry about George," he said.

He put his arms around her. He was six foot tall, so her head rested easily in the center of his chest, and for a moment she relaxed, feeling safe and secure. Catching the nudge between the two boys, she stepped away from Hugh's embrace.

"Can Kenny and I take the doughnuts and some milk into the children's room and watch TV?"

"Yes," she said, grateful to see that the arrival of his friend had done much to lighten the serious expression he'd worn since learning of his grandfather's death.

After the boys were settled and the TV was a low rumble in the background, she poured coffee for Hugh and they sat down at one of the glass-topped tables.

"Brent called to tell me about George," Hugh said. "A robbery! I still can't believe it."

"They're calling it a robbery at this point."

"What else could it be?"

Bewildered at the sharpness of his reply, she shook her head. "I don't know. I only meant that George's watch was an old Timex. Hardly worth enough to interest anyone. And he never carried much cash."

"A robber wouldn't know that." Hugh drank some coffee, his voice sounding hollow behind the mug.

Maggie nodded her head in agreement. She didn't know why the whole idea of a robbery seemed wrong. Maybe because Delbrook was such a quiet town, or maybe because she'd never known anyone who'd been killed during a robbery.

"How are you holding up?" he asked.

"I guess I'm still pretty numb. So many things to consider. Thank the Lord it's Sunday and the store's closed. I don't want to think about this week. There's a big shipment coming in, and I've got to box up the returns and get them out of here. There's so much to think about, and I've got so many questions."

Maggie heard the frantic tone in her voice and closed her mouth on the last words. She felt like a child, wanting to shout, "It's not fair!" When she looked across at Hugh, she could see the compassion in his eyes, and his quiet presence warmed her.

"You want me to take Jake over to my house for the day?" he asked. "Kenny and I are going to take Morgana for a hunt this afternoon. It'd get Jake outside. Fresh air's always healing."

Hugh was the master falconer of the Delbrook Falconry Club. Several times Jake had accompanied Kenny and Hugh on a hunt or a training exercise, and he'd loved the experience. Maggie had seen Morgana, Hugh's hawk, and other birds at local events and had gone with the boys to the falconry exhibit at the Renaissance Faire.

Granted the birds were fascinating and beautiful, but Maggie was still ambivalent whether she wanted Jake to get too involved. He had enough death to deal with, and the wild savagery of the kill frightened her. Naturally the more resistant she was, the more interested Jake was.

"Thanks for the offer, Hugh." She reached across the table and patted his hand. "I know Jake will be sorry to miss a chance to see the bird in action, but I think for right now we need to stick together. I talked to Jake just before you got here, and he wants to go with me when I make the arrangements. He's got a lot of questions, and I'm not up to finding the right answers."

"Kenny and I could go along." He put his other hand on top of hers, dwarfing her hand with his large ones. "You should have someone with you."

Once more Maggie could feel herself succumbing to the pull of Hugh's comfort and offer of protection.

Thanks to the prosperous landscaping business he owned, Hugh was considered, at thirty-eight, the most eligible divorced male in Delbrook and, according to Nell, in most of Wisconsin. An ex-marine, he was ruggedly handsome with the tanned muscular body of an outdoorsman.

They had been dating casually in the last several months. It had begun as outings with the boys, then Hugh had taken her to a couple of movies and a dinner. Maggie enjoyed his company, enjoyed having another adult to talk to, but resisted further involvement.

Although not particularly verbal, Hugh had given the impression recently that he would like her to consider a more serious relationship. He'd been a solid presence in her life since she moved to Delbrook, and she loved his son, Kenny. He would make a good husband and father except for one problem. She wasn't in love with him.

She extricated her hand from his grasp and got up to get more coffee. "Thanks for the offer, Hugh, but I think this is something that Jake and I need to do alone."

"What about dinner? You'll have to eat sometime. Why don't you and Jake come over when you're done?"

"Right now that sounds good, but let me see how the day goes." Wanting to change the subject, she asked, "Were you at the poker game last night?"

"Yes. It wasn't a scheduled game. Connie and Brent were supposed to be out of town. I was going to a seminar on composting over at the college. It was rescheduled."

A diverse group made up the weekly poker games, a blend of different personalities united by their common enjoyment of poker. Not everyone played each time. It depended on who was available and who was eager to play. Several women played, but it was primarily a men's group.

"Charley told me that George was the winner," she said.

"Yes. Going away."

"I'm glad. Was he all right?" She waved her hand back and forth, not sure what she wanted to know. "Was the dinner OK?"

Hugh looked at her as if he didn't understand why she would ask the question. "The dinner was good. He had prime rib. Rare, the way he liked it. We sat at that big round table overlooking the eighteenth green."

Although the details were sparse, just hearing about George's evening eased some of the heaviness in her heart.

"He passed around some pictures of Jake's birthday party over at the Renaissance Faire," Hugh said as if he sensed she wanted to hear more.

"I forgot he was going to pick them up," Maggie said.

"You must have taken the first couple pictures. The others were strange-angled shots, so my guess is that Jake had the camera at that point." He grinned when Maggie nodded. "The best shot of all was the one of Kenny throwing up. Perfectly centered. Unfortunately well-focused. It got a general hoot of approval from the group."

Maggie chuckled. "It sounds like George's evening was just the kind he would have wanted."

"Agreed," Hugh said. "Including the fact he won the biggest jackpot of the night on the last hand with only two pair. A poker player can die happy after that."

Maggie sat at the desk in the bookstore, staring out at the empty park beyond the bay window. The afternoon had turned gray with lowering skies, leaden clouds reflecting in the smooth surface of Falcon Lake. She found it difficult to keep her attention on work as the realization that George was gone sank into her consciousness.

Damn it, George! If you'd done a better job of raising Mark, maybe I wouldn't be sitting alone at this desk
surrounded by bills and order forms and publishers' catalogs. I don't know how to go on. I'm afraid for Jake and
I'm so alone. I hate it! First Mark leaves and now you. I
hate you *both!*

Appalled by her thoughts, she caught back a sob and
squeezed her eyes tight, rocking back and forth in an
agony of anger and fear.

Since she'd moved to Delbrook, George had been a
major part of her life. Someone she could go to for companionship, conversation and a sense of belonging. Already she could feel an empty spot opening in her heart,
a void, part anger for his abandonment and part sorrow
for the future that would never be.

Can Jake handle this latest tragedy?

She could only hope that in the last year he'd seen
the pride and joy in George's eyes and understood the
unconditional love that his grandfather felt for him. She
had left Chicago so that Jake would have the stability
that comes with belonging to a family. Was a year
enough time for Jake to feel secure?

The bookstore was Maggie's sanctuary, but was it for
Jake?

The house had originally belonged to Abigail and
Tina Kitchie, old friends of Maggie's mother. Abby was a
tall, long-faced woman somewhere in her mid-
seventies, while her sister, closer to eighty, was short and
stocky with a bawdy sense of humor and barking laugh.
Twenty years earlier Abby and Tina had renovated the
house into a bookstore and moved into the apartment on
the second floor.

During the time of her mother's final illness, Maggie had seen a great deal of the sisters. The bookstore became an emotional refuge for her and a much needed break from her hours at the hospital. After her mother died, Maggie always stopped by to see Abby and Tina when she, Mark and Jake came to visit George.

It was during one of her visits after Mark's death that Maggie mentioned she was considering moving to Delbrook so that she and Jake could be close to George. Tina had died a year earlier, and Abby mentioned that she wanted to move closer to her daughter in California. Or as Abby put it, she could harass her daughter more easily if she was in the same state. She asked Maggie if she'd be interested in buying the bookstore.

"Mom?"

Jake's call broke into Maggie's thoughts, and she raised her eyes to the gently curving staircase that led from the apartment upstairs to the first floor of the bookstore.

"I'm down here, honey," she replied.

Jake leaned his stomach on the banister and half slid, half hopped down the stairs. Holding on to the rounded newel post, he jumped the last three steps, landing in a heap. The video cassette clutched in his hand flew out and skittered across the wooden floor until it bumped against one of the bookcases in the center of the room.

"Sorry, Mom," he said, scrambling to his feet and racing across to pick up the black vinyl box.

"Did it break?"

"Naw," he said, wiping it off on the seat of his pants. "It's in the case. Can I watch it again?"

"Godzilla?"

"Yes. We don't have to take it back until tomorrow."

Jake really needed some down time, Maggie thought. His face was pale and there was a tightness around his mouth that indicated how strung out he was. If he relaxed with the comfort of his favorite video, he might fall asleep. The days ahead would be difficult enough, and some extra sleep would boost his energy levels to get him through.

"Why don't you watch it down here and keep me company?" she said.

"OK. I can set it up."

He zigzagged back and forth between the bookcases, running his fingertips across the backs of the books as he headed for the archway into the children's room. He opened the doors of a low cabinet which housed a TV-VCR combination. He pried up the top of the vinyl box and inserted the tape. Remote control in his hand, he turned on the TV.

His eyes fastened to the screen, he walked backward, hitting the buttons on the remote to start the tape. Then with a quick glance over his shoulders, he flopped down among the pillows and set the remote control on his chest. As the sound boomed out, Maggie jumped.

"Can you turn it down a little?"

For answer, the volume decreased until it was only a gentle background murmur. She smiled as she watched Jake's instant absorption in the video. Other movies had appealed to him, but nothing came close to his fascination with what she considered, despite its production costs, to be nothing more than a low-budget sci-fi film. Jake's eyes drooped, unfazed by the carnage on the screen, and she had high hopes he'd just drift into a reviving sleep.

Perhaps Jake felt the same sense of safety and security that she had felt the first time she entered the bookstore.

When Abby suggested buying the store, Maggie had jumped at the chance. It was the perfect solution. Maggie would be able to earn a living that would still keep her free to spend time with Jake after school and when he was on vacation. She met with Abby's "man of business," Gerry Goldey, and the financial arrangements were made in record time. They were able to move to Delbrook during the summer, with time enough to get established before Jake had to start school.

For Maggie it was a new beginning. A home and a business untainted by memories of infidelities or unhappiness.

A light tap on the window beside her desk brought Maggie back to the realities of the present with a resounding jolt. Her head jerked around to see Charley Blessington standing outside on the front porch of the bookstore.

She had been so absorbed in her thoughts that she hadn't seen or heard him walking across the porch. His blue-uniformed figure filled the center pane of glass and blocked out the late afternoon sun. When he realized he had her attention, he pointed to the front door.

"I'm sorry, Charley. I didn't see you," she said, unlocking the heavy oak door. "Come on in."

"This is really some place, Maggie," he said, looking around. "I hate to admit I feel rather out of my element. Most I ever have time to read is Wanted posters and financial reports from the mayor telling me about budget cuts."

Maggie had always wondered if the chief of police had really been born in the south or had only assumed the drawling way of speaking to put people at ease. With his folksy chatter it would be easy to underestimate Blessington. George had always maintained that Charley was one of the best card players in the group, able to read the unconscious mannerisms of the others to his own advantage.

He hooked his thumbs into his belt and strolled around, stopping occasionally to look at something that caught his interest. As she might have expected, he was drawn to the true crime and men's adventure section. He peeked into the children's room, smiling as he spotted the sleeping Jake breathing in rhythm with the soft murmur of the TV. He moved quietly after that, making a full circle of the store.

"Poor kid," he said. "He's really had a rough couple years."

He kept his voice low, but even with all the books to absorb the sound, it echoed around the room. Maggie indicated the wing-backed chair she'd pulled up close to the desk. She sat back down in her own chair and waited as he took a seat and shifted his beeper, a cell phone and the revolver on his hip to a more comfortable position.

"How are you and Jake holding up?" he asked.

His expression was earnest, but she had the feeling the question was more a formality than anything else.

"We're doing all right. Shocked, of course."

"Aren't we all?" He raised his leg, resting the ankle on the knee of his other leg, smoothing the uniform material with the palm of his hand. "Dagnabbit, Maggie. We're going to get to the bottom of this. It looks like pretty quickly, too."

"Have you discovered who attacked George?"

"That's why I stopped by, so I could fill you in on what's happened since I talked to you this morning. First off, I want to tell you that someone turned in that hospital bag you lost last night."

"I didn't lose it, Charley." She tried to keep the annoyance out of her voice, but she could feel a flush of heat rise to her cheeks. "I thought Brent explained what happened."

"Well, he did and he didn't." The chief of police appeared ill at ease in the face of her indignation. "Now don't get all riled up. He said you thought someone had attacked you, but in his opinion you'd had some kind of a 'spell,' and when you woke up, the bag was missing."

"Oh for God's sake, Charley!" Maggie snapped. "I'm not some simpering drama queen. I ought to know the difference between a near mugging and a dumb-ass swoon."

"I'm sure you do," he said. "On the other hand, you'd just had a violent shock to your system."

"Bullshit! Someone assaulted me in the parking lot, and it's your job to find out what happened."

Tears of frustration filled her eyes, confirming Charley's opinion of her emotional instability. Biting back any further arguments, she changed the subject.

"How is the investigation going?" she asked.

"We finally interviewed the worker from the country club who discovered George. His name's Dennis Nyland."

"I don't know him," she said.

"You'd recognize him if you saw him. Mid-twenties. Pierced ears and a nose ring. Ponytail and tattoos all over his body." From the tone of his voice, it was hard to tell which Charley disapproved of most.

"Now I know who you mean."

"He cleans the locker rooms at night to pick up some extra cash. Lives at home with his mother and runs a graphic arts business out of the garage."

"Dennis found George?" she asked. "Did he see what happened?"

Charley shrugged, grimacing for an answer. "He says he didn't. His story is that all the guests were gone by twelve-fifteen and he was finishing mopping the floor of the ladies' locker room. It was hot downstairs, and at twelve forty-five, he ducked outside to have a . . . cigarette."

Maggie heard in the careful hesitation that Charley wondered exactly what Dennis had been smoking. She didn't care. All she wanted to know was what had happened to George.

"Nyland didn't want to get caught smoking, so he ducked into the trees and walked along the eighteenth hole toward the tee. He heard a noise up ahead and snuck out toward the fairway until he had a clear view. He saw a man bending over something on the surface of the tee."

Maggie could feel a slight tremor inside her body and wrapped her arms across her stomach.

"Apparently he made some sound, because the man whirled around, and when he saw Nyland, he went streaking off into the trees. Dennis heard the chain-link fence rattle as the guy climbed over into the parking lot of the boat ramp."

"Did he recognize the man?"

"Yes, he did. The moon was as bright as a spotlight. He got a clear view of the attacker." Anger made his voice louder. "The man who stabbed your father-in-law was that homeless nutcase who lives out of his car. Tully Jackson killed George."

CHAPTER
FIVE

"TULLY JACKSON WOULD never hurt Grampa."

At the sound of the high-pitched voice, Maggie and Charley jerked around to see Jake standing rigid in the archway. He had the dazed look in his eyes of one who had just wakened from a sound sleep.

"Now, son," Charley temporized, rising to his feet.

Jake bristled at the placating tone. Maggie beckoned him forward.

He came across the floor slowly, giving a wide berth to the chief of police. He sidled up to Maggie's chair, and she put her arm around his waist, pulling him close to her side.

"Mom, you know Tully wouldn't hurt anyone," Jake said before she could say anything. "He wouldn't."

"I don't know how much you heard, honey, but I think we need to listen to Chief Blessington before we jump to any conclusions. Maybe he can clarify things for both of us."

Charley sat back down on his chair, perching on the edge of the seat, clearly uncomfortable with Jake's presence.

"Did you hear me tell your mom that Dennis Nyland was outside and saw someone up beside your grandfather?"

"Yes, sir. But Tully wouldn't hurt Grampa. Tully's my friend."

"That may well be, Jake. But sometimes things happen that no one intends to happen." He raised his eyes to Maggie as if asking her how to proceed.

"Dennis was positive that it was Tully?" she asked.

"Yes. He said he saw the white satin top hat clear as a beacon, and when the man ran off, that plastic raincoat Tully wears was streaming out behind him like a cape."

"But Dennis didn't see him attacking George?" she asked, wanting to be perfectly certain she understood.

"No," Charley admitted. "He just saw him bending over the body."

Maggie felt Jake's shudder at the chief's words and her arm tightened around him. She wanted to shelter him from hearing any of the details of the attack, but she had learned from Mark's death that it was better to know the real facts than to make up a fantasy to fill the gaps. She could see on Blessington's face his resistance to talking in front of Jake, but she knew it would be easier this way.

"Then what happened?" she prompted.

Charley seemed to realize that she wasn't going to let him off the hook. With a heavy disapproving sigh, he flopped against the back of his chair.

"Nyland ran up to the tee and discovered that it was George."

"Was he dead?" Jake asked.

Maggie flinched at the stark question. She wasn't

surprised, since the thought had been uppermost in her thoughts too.

"Yes, Jake. Your grandfather was already gone. According to the report from the doctor, there was only the one wound in his chest. He was stabbed with a thin-bladed knife. I don't think your grandfather ever really knew what happened. It was very fast."

Jake exhaled a soft breath of air. Obviously he had been worrying, thinking his grandfather had been in pain.

"Then Nyland ran back to the clubhouse and an ambulance was called. The paramedics pronounced him dead at the scene."

Charley waited, as if to give them time to absorb the details before he continued. "I'm sorry I couldn't get this information to you sooner. It took us a while to find Nyland. He was so upset about finding George that when the police released him he went to his girlfriend's house, and they both got drunk. His mother didn't think to tell us about the girlfriend until late this morning. I sent a car over there to bring him in."

"Have you talked to Tully? What does he say about all this?" Maggie asked.

"The bastard's run away." He shot an embarrassed glance at Jake and rubbed a hand over his face. "Sorry, Maggie, it's been a tough day."

Jake's body trembled, but when Maggie looked at him, she could read nothing in the blank expression on his face. She remembered that look from after Mark's death, and she bit her lip in concern. She didn't know if she was doing the right thing by letting him hear all the details. Time would tell.

"We've put out a bulletin on Tully, but so far we haven't found him." Head cocked to the side, Charley eyed Jake. "We've had a car watching for him at the boat ramp, but there's been no sign of him. You wouldn't happen to know where Tully goes when he's not sitting beside his car, do you, son?"

Jake shook his head. "No, sir."

The chief stared at him for a few minutes, as if weighing the truthfulness of the answer. Jake remained perfectly still under the scrutiny, but Maggie could feel the rapid beat of his heart where his body pressed against her side.

"What if he didn't do it?" Jake asked.

Charley was rising from the chair but sat back down at the boy's question. He pursed his lips as if trying to decide what to say.

"If he didn't do it, then we'll get to the bottom of this, son. I know you call Tully your friend, but there's something you should know. I don't want you to think we're picking on him just because he's—eh—different. Police work isn't done that way. It's not like TV, you know."

"Just 'cause he was there," Jake said, "doesn't mean he hurt anyone."

Charley nodded. "You're right about that. When we work on our investigation, we have to take a lot of things into account that might prove whether someone's guilty. So after we heard about Tully, we got a search warrant and went over to the boat ramp and had a look through his car."

Jake's eyes opened wide. "Did you find any clues?"

"Yes, son, we did." The chief leaned forward so that

his face was on the same level as Jake's. He waited until
the boy's eyes lifted to his before he spoke. "I think your
mom told you that some things were taken when your
grampa was killed. On the floor of Tully's car we found
your grandfather's watch."

The Warrior's arms and legs tingled and his stomach
cramped as he leaned against the railing staring down at
the people on the lower level of the mall.

He pressed the knife at his side.

Excitement raced through him as he felt the metal
hidden beneath his clothes. It was too bad that he
couldn't wear it on his belt, visible to everyone's eyes.
The small dagger was beautiful, crafted with aesthetic as
well as practical considerations. He could recall the
shiver of joy as the antique dealer placed it across the
palm of his hand and he stared down at the exquisite
workmanship.

The blade was five inches of thin, pointed steel,
sharpened on both edges. The shiny brass cross guard,
or quillon, extended only an inch beyond the blade. The
hilt was braided silver wire that spiraled to a rounded
knob, on top of which was a raised heart.

A *misericorde*.

To him, it meant "heart of mercy." In medieval
times, a warrior used the knife to kill a friend or an
enemy who was terminally injured but not dead. The
coup de grâce. The symbolism appealed to him.

He'd bought the *misericorde* ten years ago and had
worn it as often as he could without risking disclosure.

The antique dealer had recommended a leather-
smith who fashioned a sheath of deerskin with thin flat

straps for attaching it to his body. Resting along his left side beneath his upper arm, it was invisible. No one knew it was there, but he was conscious of it every time he pressed his arm against it.

Despite his disappointment that he needed to keep the knife hidden, there was something sensual about wearing it against his skin.

He was restless. Badly shaken by the events of the last several days. He needed a chance to rebuild his confidence. Drawing a deep breath, he searched the Sunday shoppers for a worthy opponent for a feathering coup.

He could recall how once he had mastered the touching coup, he had invented the next level of tests. As before, he would choose a target in a public place. This time, instead of merely touching the enemy, he had to place a feather on the enemy's person and walk away without detection.

He had chosen falcon feathers, collected in the woods during the spring and summer molt. In the beginning he used body feathers, but as his skills increased, he began to use the more highly prized flight feathers: primaries, secondaries and tail feathers.

If the occasion was special enough, he tagged with eagle feathers, but that decision had to be considered on a case-by-case basis in order to preserve his limited supply.

He began by slipping the feathers into pockets and bags but eventually gained such dexterity that he was able to insert them beneath layers of clothing, next to the victim's skin. The kick of adrenaline as he watched the unsuspecting "feathered" victim walk away was worth the occasional dark or suspicious look he received when he followed a subject too closely.

His one-day record was an even dozen.

He still found the most pleasure in feathering. Perhaps it was the knowledge that the victims would find the feather when they were alone and know someone had been near enough to touch their private places.

Whenever he felt the restlessness coming over him, he could hold it within controllable limits by searching out risky targets and earning a feathering coup.

He straightened up, hands gripping the railing as he spotted the dark-haired child in the center of the milling crowd below. The boy's head was tilted back, his eyes following the flight of a small bird that had become trapped inside the shopping mall. Silhouetted against the skylight, the sparrow fluttered against the glass, searching for escape.

It was a sign.

He moved to the escalator, eyes intent on the child. A young woman in a clinging jersey dress reached for the boy and led him along one of the corridors of the shopping mall. Impatient for the escalator to descend, he pushed ahead and, when he reached the first level, hurried along the tiled floor in the direction the boy had taken.

Eyes sweeping across the crowd, he spotted them at the entrance to the department store. He quickened his pace, careful not to jostle anyone and draw attention to himself. He wove in and out of the crowd until he spotted the boy and his mother and could slow his pace to follow the twosome.

Suddenly, as if she sensed a threat, the young mother cocked her head and turned to scan the crowded aisles of the department store.

He had seen that look before. A mother protecting her chick. Some psychic signal had warned her of danger, and from now on she would be on the alert. It was basic and it defeated him.

No coup today.

Tyler was hungry.

The man wouldn't come until his tummy made noises. When he was bad he only got one dish of food. It was a big dish, but it was just once. He could tell because of the lights.

When the first dish came, the man left the lights on all around the room. When the second dish came, only the light above the door stayed on.

He slept then.

He didn't like the dark. He was afraid the bird would come back in the dark and bite him.

When all the lights were on and the man was gone, he marched around the room. He liked the sound of stamping feet. He was punished if he talked, so he made noises. He could blow air and make a funny sound when his lips moved. One time a sound came from his mouth. It was so loud and strong it jerked his chest. It came again and again and then it went away.

Across the room he heard the mice rustling. He slid to the ground and ducked under the shelf. He brushed his hand along the back wall until he found the crust of bread left over from the last dish. Crawling out, he clicked his fingers as he carried the prize to the table.

He pulled the mouse cage to the edge. Mouse Ears was still there. Toes was gone. Four. Just four now. There used to be so many. More than he could count.

He broke off a piece of bread and pushed it through the wires. Before his friend could reach it, the other mice gobbled it up. He broke off two small pieces. He picked them up and tapped on the cage with his finger and rubbed the bread against the wire.

Holding the second piece of bread above Mouse Ears, he stuffed the first piece inside the cage. When the three mice ran over to it, he dropped the other piece in front of Mouse Ears.

Tyler good job. He clapped his hands, jerking his head around when he thought he heard a sound outside the door. He pushed more bread into the cage and propped his chin on the table so he could watch the mice eat it.

His tummy growled. He picked up the remainder of the bread and returned to the shelf bed. Snuggling into the corner, he held the bread under his nose. He closed his eyes and smelled it. The mom lady appeared in his head and he smiled.

The moon was high in the sky by the time Maggie drove past the stone lions that guarded the entrance to McGuire's Irish Estates. Despite the grandiose name, the forty houses that made up the tight-knit community were crammed together on a low bluff at the west end of Falcon Lake. She wound through the narrow streets until she came to George's house and pulled into the parking space at the back.

Like all of the houses in the Estates, George's house had begun life as a summer cottage. Some had been renovated so completely that little remained of the original structure, but her father-in-law had kept the framework, adding modern conveniences and insulation to make it a year-round home without losing the simplicity of design.

Turning off the headlights, she sat still, waiting for her eyes to adjust to the dark. As the night settled in around her, her muscles relaxed and the tiredness she had kept at bay seeped into her body in waves of lethargy. God, it was wonderful to just sit quietly. She'd been running all day, doing the best she could to deal with the practical and emotional demands of the day.

Wes Upton, the funeral director, had understood Jake's need to ask questions and had responded matter-of-factly. Later, at St. Bernard's Church, Father Cusick made suggestions for the funeral service that gave both Maggie and Jake a degree of comfort amid their sadness.

Back at the apartment there had been phone calls and visits by friends, and by the end of the day she had been grateful to Hugh for his offer of dinner. Afterward, she called Nell to stay with Jake so she could pick up clothes for George and take them to the funeral home.

She had been getting ready to leave when Jake flew into a temper tantrum. He had handled the grim details of the day with such emotional control that she had been stunned by his agitation.

"Don't go, Mom," he wailed. "Please don't leave me."

She reached out to hug him, but he fought her, his arms pounding against her back and shoulders as she pressed him against her chest. Tears rolled down her cheeks, mingling in the dark curly hair of the distraught child.

Please, God, help me. Don't let me lose him, too.

Eventually Jake quieted, and she helped him get washed and into bed, sitting on the edge and patting his back until he drifted off to sleep. When Nell arrived, he didn't rouse, and despite her own exhaustion and despite the fact it was already ten o'clock, Maggie hurried down the stairs for the drive to George's house.

She turned off the motor, rubbed her tired eyes and stared through the windshield at the house. A light mist hung in the air, painting the clapboards a ghostly white.

The house looked forlorn. Her impression was fueled by the sad knowledge that George would never return to stand on the redwood deck overlooking the lake.

She opened the car door and shut it carefully. In the quiet of the night all sound was magnified. Most of the houses were still summer homes, closed up until next year. Only a few older people, like George, lived in the Estates full-time. These were the hardy golfing and fishing set who rose at the first hint of light and faded with the setting of the sun.

She looked up at the treehouse that hung partially over the parking area. It had been Mark's when he was a boy, and was now a clubhouse for Jake and Kenny.

The single room, balanced between two thick limbs of the maple tree, was accessible by a wooden ladder, nailed to the massive trunk, that led to the trap door in the wooden floor. George had built the original, and Mark had added to it until it was truly palatial. The large room had windows with movable shutters and a tar paper roof that, according to Jake, made the treehouse watertight even during a thunderstorm.

The knotted rope that Jake used for a swing was coiled into a circle and fastened to the trunk of the tree above the platform. She remembered holding her breath as Mark showed Jake how to shinny up the rope. His hands had seemed too small to grasp the thick rope. Both George and Mark had been impatient with her gasps of fear and sent her off to sit on the deck overlooking the lake so that Jake would not be influenced by his mother's qualms.

Maggie blinked rapidly to disperse the tears that filled her eyes. Her emotions were too close to the surface to risk getting caught up in memories. If she got moving, she'd only be here a short time.

Her sneakers crunched on the gravel path that wound down to the back door, sounding overly loud in the oppressive silence. The lilac bushes scraped against the side of the house, a rhythmic complement to the chirp of the crickets. The wind had picked up and clouds drifted across the face of the moon, blotting out the light. She stood still, afraid of tripping on the uneven ground.

As the light returned, she could see the dark shape of the canoe, propped upside down on sawhorses against the back of the house. Originally belonging to Mark, George and Jake were refinishing it.

Maggie set her purse on the top step of the back porch and walked over to the canoe. In the shadow of the house, she could only see the outline, not the natural grain of the wood. She ran her hand along the side, feeling the patches where the wood had been sanded smooth and others where it was still rough to the touch.

Will it ever be finished? Her hand dropped down to the canoe paddle, leaning against the leg of the sawhorse. Fingers tightening on the shaft, she picked it up, setting it on her shoulder and leaning her cheek against the smooth blade of the paddle.

There was no one to take over the project, and Jake was too young to work on it alone. She glared at the canoe. It symbolized all the schemes and activities that would never come to pass now that George was gone.

A burning anger raced through her body, and she raised the paddle from her shoulder, wanting to smash the canoe just as George's murder had shattered their lives.

Another cloud covered the moon, blotting out the light and leaving her in darkness. Deprived of sight, her ears picked up the sound of furtive movements as someone approached the side of the house. She froze at the sound, straining to hear.

The scrape of a shoe on the gravel, the rustle of bushes as someone brushed past and then nothing. Only the silence of an unknown trespasser lurking beside the house.

Oh God, someone was here!

CHAPTER
SIX

SOMEONE WAS TRYING to break into George's house!

Maggie knew that someone had attacked her in the hospital parking lot. Maybe it was him! This time she wouldn't let him get away. Her hands squeezed the wooden canoe paddle as the tide of anger rose to block out any thought except a need to act.

Soundlessly, she slid her feet across the grass, hugging the back of the house until she reached the corner and could see around the side of the house. Between the bushes, she could see the outline of a man silhouetted against the lighter shades of the clapboards. The window in front of him was open, and it looked as if he was preparing to climb inside.

A burglar! How dare he break into George's house!

Infuriated, Maggie sprinted forward, raising the canoe paddle over her head. The man must have heard her charge, because he jerked around to face her before she could bring the paddle down full force. At the last minute he thrust an arm out. The paddle hit his arm, bouncing once before it struck him in the head.

The man dropped to his knees, and Maggie pulled back, raising the paddle for another strike. She was in mid-swing when the man raised his head and shouted.

"Don't hit me. I'm a lawyer."

The sheer absurdity of the words brought Maggie to her senses, and she tried to stop the arc of the canoe paddle. It was too late. The flat blade slammed into his shoulder and knocked him over. In the dim light she stared down at the man lying on his back, his body motionless.

Oh God, don't let me have killed him.

As if in partial answer to her prayer, the clouds parted and moonlight set the scene aglow. The sprawled figure was illuminated, and she could only gasp in surprise.

She had been expecting an ill-kempt second-story man and instead got a yuppie in a dark suit, button-down shirt and a royal blue tie. Even the blood threading down the side of his face didn't change the fact that her attacker looked as if he'd just come from a board meeting not a prison cell. As if to emphasize that fact, a thin leather briefcase lay in the grass at his side.

Maggie threw down the canoe paddle and dropped to the ground beside the man. She put a hand on his chest and sighed in gratitude as she felt the steady beat beneath her palm. She tipped her head back in silent prayer, then as her eyes touched the open window, her heart jolted at the reminder that the unconscious figure had been attempting to climb in the window.

Wanting answers, she poked his shoulder, but he didn't rouse. Safe enough for the moment, she thought. Gingerly she unbuttoned his suit jacket and reached into the pocket inside. She withdrew a thin leather wallet. With shaking hands, she opened it and flipped through the credit cards until she found his driver's license.

Illinois license. What was he doing in Wisconsin? He didn't look like a man on vacation.

Holding the license close to his head, she compared the photo to the man on the ground. In the harsh moonlight, there were pockets of shadow on his face. With his even features, hawklike nose and strong chin he might have been considered a handsome man except for the jagged scar that was now visible, running along the left edge of his jawline from his ear to his chin. The right side of his face, although streaked with blood from a cut on the side of his head, was unmarked.

She took out a business card and tilted it to catch the light so she could read the raised print. His name was Grant Holbrook. He worked for Etzel, Doyle, Glynn & Williams in Chicago, Illinois. In a flash, the words the man had shouted just as she hit him registered in her mind.

"Don't hit me. I'm a lawyer."

In any other situation that statement would have elicited the automatic response of: "All the more reason to hit you." In this case she suspected she'd made a dreadful mistake. No matter what Grant Holbrook is doing outside George's house, if he doesn't die, he'll sue me, she thought in rising hysteria. Better call 911.

She started to rise when she felt the first movement of the man on the ground. Her glance rose to his face, and she caught her breath at the flash of angry brown eyes that glared up at her. Before she could act, his arm shot around her, pinning her to his chest as he brought her face down to within inches of his own.

"Who are you?" Holbrook demanded in a thin whisper that was in sharp contrast to the power in his arm. "Why did you hit me?"

"Oh thank God, you're alive," she said, ignoring his questions. "I thought you were breaking into the house."

"I'm here to see Collier." He shook his head to give emphasis to the denial, then groaned in pain.

At the mention of her father-in-law, Maggie felt even more guilty. "Don't move," she said. "I was just going to call the paramedics."

"No." The word was feeble but definite. "Help me up."

He pushed himself to a sitting position, remaining hunched over his knees while his breathing shuddered in and out of his chest. Guiltily Maggie stared down at the wallet in her hands. She reached out for the briefcase and jammed the wallet and the loose cards into it and tucked it under her arm. Standing up, she leaned over and put an arm under the man's elbow as he struggled to his feet.

"Can you walk?"

"Give me a minute," he said, his voice raspy. "OK."

He towered over her, but in his weakened condition he didn't intimidate her. She led him along the side of the house to the redwood deck that jutted out over the bluff. She took most of his weight as he used the railing to pull himself up the three steps. She eased him down on one of the green plastic chairs and set his briefcase on the picnic table.

"Sit here," she said. "I need my keys."

She ran to the back porch where she'd left her purse, and as she came back toward the deck, she spotted the canoe paddle. She was so appalled by her earlier attack that she picked up the paddle and shoved it under the bushes out of sight.

Back on the deck, she searched for George's spare key that she carried in the zippered pocket of her purse.

The old-fashioned house key turned easily in the lock, and she opened the door into George's living room. She pressed the light switch on the wall, and the center fixture came on. Maggie let out a low cry.

The room was in chaos. The contents of the desk drawers had been dumped in a heap on the floor and all the storage areas had been emptied and lay scattered around the room.

She whirled around, snarling at the injured man in the deck chair. "What were you searching for in the house?"

"I wasn't in the house," he said in an abused voice. "I was looking in the window."

Rising anger gave strength to his voice. It sounded less thready than at first. Maggie bit her lip, wondering if he was telling the truth.

"Why were you looking in the window?"

"Why should I tell you? Who are you?"

In the light from the living room, she could see him raise a shaking hand to his forehead. The feeble gesture filled her with guilt, and she responded automatically.

"Maggie. Maggie Collier," she blurted out.

"George Collier's daughter-in-law?"

"Yes," she said. "Who are you and what are you doing here?"

"My name is . . ." Holbrook reached inside his suit coat, feeling around for his wallet.

"It's in your briefcase on the table," she said in a choked voice. "I already looked through it when you were unconscious."

"Well, damn!" he muttered.

She was embarrassed but still uncertain about who the man was. "Were you climbing in the window or climbing out?"

"Neither, damn it," he snapped. "I need to talk to Collier. I knocked on the back door, but there was no answer. I walked around the side of the house and found the open window. The next thing I knew you were attacking me."

When he finished speaking he sagged in his chair as if the long answer had drained him. What to do? Despite the villainous scar on his jaw, he had made no aggressive moves toward her and seemed genuinely incensed that she had hit him.

"Let's get inside where I can take a look at that cut on your head," she said.

She helped him to his feet, handed him his briefcase and nudged him over to the door. He held on to the door frame as he scanned the disorder in the room. He looked back at her, reacting to the scowling censure in her eyes.

"I did not do this, Ms. Collier!" he snapped. "I may have scared off whoever was in here when I knocked on the back door."

"Maybe," she said, refusing to absolve him until she was convinced of his innocence.

Despite his bedraggled appearance, Grant Holbrook had a presence as he drew himself up to his full height. He wasn't a big man, but somehow the living room seemed smaller than normal. Watching as he scanned the room, Maggie sensed that little escaped the notice of his flashing dark eyes.

She walked ahead of him, turned on the light in the kitchen and found the same disorder. Cupboard doors were open and drawers were pulled out, their contents littering the surface of the kitchen table and the floor. Picking up a pile of papers from the oak table, she dumped it on the countertop beside the sink and pulled out one of the chairs.

"Sit," she said.

Without a word, Holbrook lowered himself to the seat, wincing as he propped the briefcase against the chair leg. In the glare from the overhead light, he looked as if he'd been in a dreadful accident.

Dried blood streaks coated the right side of his face and stained the beige shirt and royal blue tie with dark red ribbons. One of the buttons on his suit coat hung by a thread, drawing her eye as it swung back and forth with every breath he took. There was a streak of mud on the knee of his pants, and the high polish on one of his shoes was dulled by a wide scrape on the toe.

"Dear Lord, you look awful," Maggie said, covering her mouth with a cupped hand.

"I don't feel all that terrific either," he said. "Do you have any liquor?"

Appalled at what she'd done to the man, Maggie reached into the cabinet beside the stove and pulled out a bottle of brandy. She took out a glass, then reconsidered and took out a second one, filling them with ice.

She poured the alcohol into the glasses and carried them over to the table. She stood beside the man, wondering if he should drink with the cut on his head.

"Do you think you have a concussion?" she asked.

"I don't care. Give me the damn glass," he said ungraciously.

She handed it to him and watched as he took a tentative sip.

"What is this?" he said, licking his lips in confusion.

"Ginger brandy. You're in Wisconsin, Holbrook. Only California consumes more brandy than Wisconsin, and it has five times the population."

"Thanks for the news flash," he said.

He took another sip, closed his eyes, breathed deeply and then swallowed. Two more swallows and he set the glass down on the table. She could see his cheeks take on a healthy flush, and a hint of red crept back into his colorless lips.

"Do you need a doctor or should I tell the police to bring an ambulance?"

His eyelids flew open, and he stared up at her. "You can't call the police."

"Why not?"

"They'll take one look and charge me with breaking and entering, and then I'll have to charge you with assault and battery."

"You wouldn't," she said; but one look at the tightness around his mouth and she guessed that he would. She sagged against the counter.

"Where's George Collier?" he asked. "Where's your father-in-law?"

At the mention of George's name, Maggie's hands

began to shake, the ice in her drink clinking against the side of the glass. She sat down in the chair on the other side of the table, took a quick sip and grimaced at the sharp bite of the alcohol. Setting the glass down, she stared across at Holbrook.

This is not the man who robbed and killed George, she thought with a sinking feeling. His question gave some verification to that fact.

"Who are you?" she said.

"I told you before," he said. "Grant Holbrook. I'm thirty-seven, have a law degree from Case Western Reserve University and currently work at a law firm in Chicago. There's a number on my business card that you could call for confirmation from one of the partners. I drove up here to talk to George Collier."

"Where's your car?" Maggie said. "Why didn't you park it out back?"

"I parked it up along the edge of the park." For an instant the corners of his eyes crinkled as if he could read the suspicion in her mind. "I know, it looks bad, but I didn't know exactly which house was your father-in-law's and I wanted to have a chance to look over the place before I announced my arrival."

"Why?"

"I'd never met or talked to Mr. Collier." He shrugged. "I'm the cautious type. No point in rushing in before I'd had an opportunity to check things out."

"You sound like a lawyer," she said.

"I *am* a lawyer, Ms. Collier, and as such I'm trained to be both cynical and skeptical."

"Sorry for the cheap shot. It's been a long day."

She took a sip of her drink, staring at him over the

rim of her glass. With his straight, dark brown hair and tanned features, he had a GQ look, marred only by the scar on his jaw. The ugly raised ridge added a hint of character to an otherwise too-handsome appearance.

"What time did you get here?"

He looked at the clock on the wall. "It's ten-thirty. I got here around ten. It took me a couple minutes to park the car and walk down here. I'd guess you attacked me around ten after ten."

He bit off the words. Maggie got to her feet, uncomfortable with his anger, even if it was justified.

"I want to look at that cut before I decide what to do."

Holbrook shrugged. He took another sip of his drink and watched as she moved around the kitchen. She rooted through the disorder until she found several terry cloth towels, a basin for water and a small first-aid kit. Steam rose from the water as she set the basin on the table. She dropped one of the towels in the water.

"You should take off your jacket and tie," she said.

He reached up and loosened the knot at his neck, pulling the tie out of his collar.

"Oh shit! That's my Hermés tie," he said, staring in disbelief at the bloodstained silk. "Damn thing cost a fortune."

"Maybe I can get the blood out."

He snatched it out of her reach, folded it carefully and slid it into the pocket of his suit coat. "You've already done enough."

Ignoring his comment, she stepped behind his chair and helped him remove his coat. She could see his mouth tighten as he saw the dangling button. His hand shot out and he grasped the button, snapping the thread, and slapped it into her outstretched hand.

She jumped at the abrupt movement, frightened by what he might do next. Her hand shook as she shoved the button into the pocket with his tie and hung the coat on the back of his chair. She moved back to the basin of water and wrung out the wet cloth. When she turned back to face him, the sight of the blood on his shirt banished her fear.

No wonder he was so bad-tempered. He'd lost a great deal of blood. Gently, she pressed the wet cloth to the side of his face. She could feel his jaw clench as she wiped the blood away from his cheek.

The cut was just inside the hair line above his right temple. He sucked air into his lungs and pulled away as she touched the tender area.

"Hold still," she said.

"Watch what you're doing. It hurts."

"Don't be such a baby, Holbrook."

She refused to let him know how the sight of the gash on his head made her almost physically sick. If she'd hit him a little lower on the temple, the injury might have been far more serious.

"What did you hit me with?" he asked.

"A canoe paddle."

"It felt more like a sledgehammer."

He relaxed under the soothing strokes of the wet cloth. When his face was free of the dried blood, he looked considerably more civilized. Despite the scar, he was a handsome man, and she could see why he'd be so full of himself. He would have a devastating effect on susceptible young women. Luckily she was neither an ingenue nor a young innocent.

"It doesn't look as if you need stitches," she said. "It's stopped bleeding."

She picked up the wet cloths and the basin of bloody water and took them over to the sink. She washed everything and wrung out the towels, hanging them over the arm of the faucet to dry. Finished, she returned to the table and sat down.

"At the risk of sounding redundant, Ms. Collier, where is your father-in-law?" He cleared his throat and leaned toward her. "I have to talk to him. It's very important."

Searching for words, she shook her head, but before she could say anything he hurried on.

"I've come a long way in order to speak to him."

"Please, Mr. Holbrook," Maggie said. "I'm not trying to prevent you from talking to him. I'm trying to tell you that it's just not possible. George Collier is dead."

"He can't be!"

Holbrook slammed his fist on the table with such force that Maggie jumped, pressing against the back of her chair. The color leached out of his face as the action jarred his already injured body. The muscles in his face and neck rippled as he fought to control his fury. He stared at her, sucking in his breath as he read the truth in her expression. He had half risen out of his chair and just as suddenly collapsed back onto the seat.

"Another wild-goose chase." He muttered the words, more to himself than to her.

For some reason the news of George's death was a devastating blow. Defeat was written in the sag of his body, the emotions so genuine that Maggie felt sorry for him. Curious to find out the connection between this stranger and her father-in-law, she sat quietly.

"I'm sorry for your loss," he said in a voice devoid of inflection. "I hope he wasn't sick long."

The words were a conditioned response to her grief. He didn't look at her, staring down at the surface of the table instead.

"He wasn't sick," she said. "He was killed in a robbery."

It took a moment for the words to penetrate. He raised his head, eyebrows furrowed on his forehead. He was like an animal on a scent, nostrils flared and every sense alert.

"When did this happen, Ms. Collier?"

"I'm not sure it's any of your business, Mr. Holbrook."

At her words, his expression became even more intense.

"I'm not asking out of idle curiosity. I assure you it's very important."

"Did you know my father-in-law?"

He shook his head. "I was given George's name by a friend of his in Chicago. Hamilton Rice."

The mention of George's friend caught Maggie by surprise. She wasn't prepared for the emotion that swamped her as she thought of their long-term friendship.

"Oh rats," she said. "I'll have to call Ham and tell him what's happened."

Knowing how close the two men had been, she could almost picture Ham's reaction. Her mouth trembled, and she pressed her fingers against her lips until she was more in control. She cleared her throat before she could speak.

"Ham and George have known each other for years," she explained.

"I gathered from what Hamilton said that they were fishing buddies."

"Yes. Ham used to live here in Delbrook, but he moved to Chicago years ago."

Maggie wasn't sure why the mention of a mutual friend should go such a long way toward giving credibility to the stranger, but it did. Although she didn't trust him completely, she felt less on guard than she had been.

"I know you don't know me and have little or no reason to trust me," he said. "I drove all the way here from Chicago to talk to your father-in-law on a very serious matter. I didn't know he was dead. It would be very helpful if you could tell me what happened to him."

She took a sip of her drink, letting the liquor roll over her tongue before she swallowed it. She could feel it spreading through her body and took another long swallow. Back against the chair, she rested the cool glass against her cheek and raised her eyes.

"I don't know a lot about what happened to George," she began.

It was strange retelling how she'd been called to the hospital and learned of George's death. She had repeated the story so often during the day that the sentences had taken on a certain structure and rhythm that imparted an element of news reporting to the process. There was safety in the rote recital. She could keep her emotions in check and free her mind to concentrate on other things.

His eyes never left her face, and for a moment she felt self-conscious. His entire attention was concentrated on her as if he was analyzing her words, her voice and her expressions to gain a complete picture of the events.

He probably is, she thought. After all he is a lawyer, used to observing and judging. She wondered what kind of law he practiced and if he was any good at it.

"You said George won the poker game last night?" he asked when she finished. "Was the betting particularly heavy so that someone at the country club might have been tempted to rob him?"

Maggie shook her head. "No. The winning was all on paper. At the end of the evening, the chips are counted and added to the running tally that's kept at the club. At the end of the year the players settle up. Money isn't the reason for the poker games. It's the joy of the competition."

"Did George normally carry a lot of cash?"

Maggie smiled. "No. He was extremely frugal."

"Do the police have any idea who did it?"

"According to Charley—that's Chief of Police Blessington—the person they think attacked George is Tully Jackson. A very peculiar man who sort of lives at the boat ramp parking lot that abuts the golf course. He was seen bending over George, and then took off when a worker from the country club spotted him."

"You sound as if you don't think he did it."

"I honestly don't know." She shook her head at the continued confusion in her mind. "Tully is one of those people that just doesn't fit into society. I think he might be homeless, but I don't even know that for sure."

"Is he crazy? Psychotic?"

"This sounds stupid, but I don't know. Lost. Troubled. Shy. All of those are just words that apply to him but don't describe him adequately. I lived in Chicago and I've seen people like Tully pushing grocery carts containing all of their possessions. Long scraggly hair. Unkempt beard. Talking to themselves. Panhandling."

"I know the kind you mean. A lot of them are war veterans who just can't deal with society. Many of them are suffering from post-traumatic stress syndrome. Does he look like a vet?"

She snorted. "What does a vet look like? Tully is somewhere in his forties. I don't think he's mentally handicapped, but he has a very childlike quality about him. I realized early on that he was more comfortable talking to my son, Jake, than he was to me."

"Have the police taken him into custody or charged him?"

"They would if they could find him."

"He's run off? Sounds like a pretty strong admission of guilt."

Maggie shook her head. "If Tully didn't do it, my guess is he's hiding out somewhere."

"You don't think he's left the area?"

"I don't think he'd leave without his car. It's filled with his belongings. I saw Tully a couple of weeks ago. He has an old lounge chair that he sits in. I gave him a new beach towel because the one on his chair was looking pretty threadbare."

Maggie could remember the shy smile he'd given her when Jake presented the towel along with two Snickers bars.

"He held it up to admire the huge sunflowers on the towel. He said he was afraid it might rain later in the afternoon, so he'd save it for the next day. 'In the meantime,' he said, 'I'll keep it with my treasures.' He folded it up carefully and placed it on top of a pile of things in the backseat of the car."

"Where's the car now?"

"I think the police have it." When his expression intensified, she grimaced. "I forgot to mention that they found George's watch in Tully's car."

He blinked once. "And that doesn't convince you that he killed your father-in-law?"

She shrugged. "They didn't find George's wallet."

"Do you think Tully might have been the one who searched the house?" Holbrook asked.

"Tully strikes me as a person who has an old-fashioned idea about territory and privacy," she said. "I don't think he'd come into George's house uninvited."

She noticed that as her story unfolded and he began to ask questions, his energy level increased until he appeared strong and well focused. She wondered if his earlier frailties were an act to garner sympathy. If so, she'd just run out of patience.

"All right, Mr. Holbrook," she said. "Let's hear *your* story."

Mired in her own suspicions, she spoke more harshly than she intended. Other than a raised eyebrow, the man showed little reaction. He was silent for a moment, rubbing one shoulder and rolling it forward as if it was stiff. It was probably bruised from the second time she'd hit him, and she felt a twinge of guilt when he caught her eye and then leaned forward onto his elbows.

When he spoke, his voice was soft, but each word was enunciated clearly.

"Two Christmases ago, Tyler McKenzie, a two-and-a-half-year-old boy, was kidnapped from a shopping mall in Cleveland, Ohio."

Maggie shuddered at the bald statement. If he'd hoped to capture her attention, he'd calculated right.

"Dear God in heaven," she said. "Have they found him? Is he safe?"

"No, they haven't found him. And I try not to think about whether he's safe or not. He disappeared as completely as if he'd been beamed up by aliens."

"I remember once when my son, Jake, wandered away while I was trying on some shoes. I couldn't have taken my eyes off him for more than a minute." Her voice thickened as she remembered the fear when she'd looked up and found him missing. "I doubt if I've ever been more frightened in my life. I pity this boy's parents. I can't imagine how one survives the loss of a child."

"The parents are coping as best they can. In the beginning I think they existed in a kind of limbo." Holbrook's tone was thoughtful. "Listening every day for a phone call. Watching the door and the street for a glimpse of a small blond boy running toward them."

He coughed to cover the emotion that had crept into his voice.

"Were there any witnesses? Suspects?"

"No witnesses ever turned up, and the police have exhausted every lead without coming up with any suspects. They couldn't find a trace of Tyler. As a final desperate measure, the parents announced a reward for information leading to the safe return of the boy. Flyers were made up and distributed throughout the Midwest. It's been posted on the Internet. Message boards, an e-mail campaign, that sort of thing. Since the amount of the reward was sizable, the police were flooded with calls."

"How much was it?"

"One hundred thousand dollars. The money has been deposited with my law firm in Chicago, and people who don't want to go to the police can contact us directly."

He turned around to reach the jacket on his chair and pulled out a square of paper. He unfolded it, pressing it out flat before he handed it across to her.

At the top of the page in bold type were the words: "Have you seen Tyler?" Beneath the headline was a color picture of a little boy wearing a Christmas sweater. His blond hair stuck out beneath a stocking cap, and a stuffed tiger was cradled in his arms.

Maggie stared down at the flyer and the sweet innocent face of the missing child. Instantly her mind conjured up pictures of Jake at two, and she could feel the muscles across her stomach contract at the possibility that something could happen to her son.

She looked carefully at the picture, but there was nothing familiar about the boy. She wanted to recognize him, but to the best of her knowledge she'd never seen the child before.

Her throat tightened and she had difficulty swallowing back the bitter taste of fear as she read the paragraph about the child's disappearance. Below that there was another line of bold type specifying the reward. At the bottom of the page, also in bold type, was an e-mail

address: FindTyler@aol.com. Beneath that, the telephone number of the police and another number to
contact the law firm handling the reward were listed.

Her hands shook as she handed back the paper.
"This is truly a horrific situation, and I pray to God you
find the boy. But what does any of this have to do with
George?" she asked.

Holbrook didn't answer immediately. He folded the
paper carefully and put it back inside his jacket. When
he faced her, his eyes were hard, the scar standing out
along his clenched jaw.

"After Tyler had been missing a full year, the case
was pretty much closed. The investigation was no longer
active, although interest was generated occasionally by a
phone call or some other possible lead."

"And the parents?" Maggie asked.

"Although they never stopped wishing and hoping,
they became resolved to the fact that they would never
see Tyler again. Some of the people involved in the investigation believe that Tyler is dead." He paused, swallowing several times before he continued. "Maybe it's
easier thinking that he's dead than that he's being hurt or
abused. In any case, that's where the case stood until
today."

"Tyler was found?"

"No. Nothing that spectacular," he said. "This
morning I talked to Hamilton Rice, a friend of your
father-in-law. Mr. Rice wanted to know if there was still
a reward for the missing boy. I said only if the child was
recovered alive. He said good because George Collier
knew where to find Tyler."

CHAPTER
SEVEN

"YOU'RE CRAZY," Maggie said, slapping her brandy glass down so hard on the table she was surprised when it didn't break. "How would George know where to find Tyler?"

Her fingers tightened around the glass, and she had to restrain herself from throwing it at him.

"That's what I came up here to find out," he said.

"And that's why you were skulking around George's house? You thought he might be holding this child for the purpose of collecting the reward."

Her comment was not a statement; it was an accusation. Grant held up his hands, palms toward her in a defensive position. He couldn't hold back a wince as he moved his shoulder, but she ignored any attempt to elicit sympathy.

"I'm not saying your father-in-law was in any way involved," he said. "I may have taken time to look around the property, but I approached with no prejudice. I knocked on the back door."

"I should have hit you harder," she said, her eyes flashing with her anger. "George Collier was an honest, caring person. The idea that he would be involved in a kidnapping is not only insulting, it's downright libelous."

"I'm not accusing your father-in-law of anything, Ms. Collier. All I'm telling you is what George's friend told me."

Maggie's mouth pulled tight. "When did you talk to Hamilton Rice?" she asked.

"This morning. Around ten o'clock."

"Look, Holbrook, the whole story about the little boy is appalling, but I think there's a huge mix-up here. At the time you talked to Ham, George was already dead."

Too restless to remain seated, Grant pushed his chair back and stood up. He held on to the back of his chair as he waited for the light-headedness to pass.

"Do your ministrations run to a couple of aspirins?" he asked.

Her eyes narrowed at his sarcasm, but the reminder of his injuries left her off balance. He'd have to remember that. He needed all the leverage he could get. He had to have her help. Everything depended on it. With a sigh she stood up and reached into the cabinet above the sink and handed him a bottle of painkillers.

"Should you take them when you're drinking?" she asked.

"Probably not," he said.

He pried open the top of the bottle, poured two tablets into his hand and swallowed them down with the last of his drink. He added more brandy to his glass. When he held the bottle up, she shook her head.

"I want to repeat that I'm not accusing George Collier of anything," he said, "but the mere fact that your father-in-law has been murdered at this particular time seems highly suspect. Will you let me explain why I came to talk to George?"

"All right, Holbrook," she said. "Make your case."

She sat back down, staring up at him, her chin raised in returning antagonism. She appeared tough, but the dark circles under her eyes indicated that the circumstances of George's death had taken a physical as well as an emotional toll on her resources.

Taking a long pull of his drink, he studied her. Despite the fact that her reddish brown hair was disheveled and she wasn't wearing any makeup, she had a soft Irish beauty with her pale skin and crystalline blue eyes. She was a little younger than he—at a guess, early thirties— with a petite but nicely rounded figure.

Working as a criminal defense lawyer in Chicago had jaded Grant. He trusted few people in his life, and yet even after their inauspicious meeting, he liked what he saw in George Collier's daughter-in-law. She wasn't easily intimidated. She'd shown courage in attacking him. Ms. Collier would make a formidable ally. Although she didn't know it, he needed her more than she needed him. God willing, they might be able to help each other.

"Your father-in-law's friend Hamilton Rice called last night, but I was out and didn't get the message until this morning. He told me that George had telephoned him yesterday, Saturday evening, from the Falcon Lake Country Club."

"That's where the game was."

Her surprise at his mention of the name of the

country club helped get him on a credible footing. Grant rested his hip against the kitchen counter. The booze and the aspirin were helping to ease some of the aches in his body. Now all he had to do was stay sober long enough to convince Ms. Collier to help him.

"George asked Hamilton if he remembered the little boy who was kidnapped in Cleveland. Apparently they had been stuck in the Cleveland airport for about five hours right after Christmas. Not last Christmas but the year before."

"Every year George and Ham go to Florida for a week of fishing." She spoke slowly, as if she were reaching back for the memories in order to confirm or deny his words. "Two Christmases ago they flew to Cleveland to pick up John Pfeifer and Ralph Glaser for the flight to Miami. A blizzard hit the Midwest, and the four of them were snowed in at the Cleveland airport for five or six hours."

"I know it's a long time ago, but do you remember what day it was?"

"Yes. The reason I remember is that they were worried that they wouldn't make it to Miami for New Year's Eve. They had planned to celebrate in style and had wanted to get down a day earlier. They were stuck in Cleveland on December thirtieth."

"Tyler disappeared on December twenty-eighth. The reward was announced on the thirtieth. If they were in Cleveland, anywhere near a television or a radio, they would have seen the news stories."

Maggie took a sip of her drink, then pushed the glass away as if it were distasteful.

"Look, the phone call may be true, but the rest of it

has to be some sort of fantasy on Ham's part. Something that George said might have gotten scrambled."

"From what Hamilton said, your father-in-law sounded pretty excited. Hamilton couldn't hear him very well because there was background noise, but George indicated that he'd just come across some information that might help locate Tyler."

"Look, Holbrook, George and I were very close. I talked to him just before he left for the country club, and there was nothing in his attitude or behavior that indicated he possessed information of this magnitude." She shook her head to add weight to her words. "Believe me, I would have known."

"What if he discovered the information once he was at the country club? Wouldn't it be possible that he'd call Hamilton right away?"

"I suppose he might have."

Her tone was grudging. She shrugged. Wincing, she reached up, massaging her shoulder with her fingers.

"I've been obsessed with my own injuries, but I suppose I should have asked if you'd been hurt in our 'introduction' outside," he said.

"Thanks for caring. In this case you're off the hook," she said. "Someone tried to steal my purse, and I think I've pulled a muscle in my shoulder."

"Someone tried to rob you?" he asked. "When?"

"Last night. Well, actually it was early this morning when I was coming out of the hospital."

"After you were called about George?"

She nodded.

"What happened?"

"I don't really know. Someone shoved me and

grabbed for my purse as I fell. I hit my head and wrenched my shoulder on the way down. Luckily a friend of mine came along and scared off whoever did it."

"And your purse was gone?"

"No. I had a pretty good grip on it. Whoever it was ended up with a plastic hospital bag full of paperwork and my old windbreaker."

Grant forced his body to remain still while his mind whirled with conjecture.

"What did the police say?" Grant asked.

"Not much. They're pretty busy with the investigation into George's death."

"Couldn't this have some bearing on the case?"

"No one believed that I'd been attacked." A flush of indignation rose to her cheeks. "The general opinion was that I'd had some sort of panic attack, passed out and made up the story out of embarrassment."

"Did you?"

She shot him a dark look.

"No. I was uneasy from the moment I stepped outside the hospital. You know how you have the feeling someone is around and watching you. An itch in the center of your back. I never saw anyone. Just had a feeling of movement, a hard shove on my back and then I was falling."

"So only the hospital bag was missing?"

"Yes," she admitted. "Someone found it in the parking lot during the day and took it into the hospital. The assumption is that when I fell, the wind inflated the bag and sent it sailing out of reach."

"I'd like you to think about something, Ms. Collier," he said. "Doesn't it seem strange that in less than twenty-four hours Delbrook, Wisconsin, has become a dangerous place to live? One stabbing and two robberies?" He waved his hand toward the mess in the kitchen. "And by the looks of it, you can count this as number three."

Maggie ducked her head, but not before he spotted the flash of fear in her eyes. He could tell that her father-in-law's violent death had shaken her badly. If her reactions were like most people's in a case of random violence, she would be ignoring the inconsistencies and trying to convince herself that George had been killed by a passing stranger who had committed the crime and fled. With a young child, the thought that a killer was still in the area would be frightening to contemplate.

"What you're suggesting is that whoever killed George also tried to take my purse and then came over here to burglarize the house?"

Her brows were bunched up as she waited for him to deny it.

"That would be my guess. I suppose you could make a case for someone knowing that George was dead and using the opportunity to rob the house, but somehow I don't think that's what happened. It looks to me like someone was searching for something."

"Why? Why is this happening?"

Grant came back over to the table and sat down across from her.

"Let's say that George is at dinner and discovers some information about Tyler. He's not sure about it and he calls Hamilton to check if the boy is still missing. Does that seem reasonable so far?"

Eyes steady on his face, Maggie nodded.

"In the meantime, someone realizes that George has this information and confronts him. There's a fight, and George is stabbed."

"Do you mean Tully?"

"Let's call him X. This is all hypothetical anyway, so just go with me for a moment."

He was comfortable going over the elements of a case, weaving the various strands of the puzzle in hopes that they'd form some kind of pattern. All he could do was try to connect what they knew with what might reasonably be assumed to have happened.

"For the sake of an argument we'll say that X didn't mean to kill George. When it happens, he panics. He tries to make it look like a robbery. You said yourself that George's wallet and his watch were stolen."

"If he tried to make it look like a robbery, why would he attack me and then come here?"

"Say there's a piece of evidence that George has that the murderer wants. Maybe he doesn't find it when he searches the body. So X goes to the hospital and waits around until he sees you coming out with a hospital bag. He could have assumed that you had George's personal effects and decided to make a grab for it."

"But there was nothing in the bag," she said.

"He wouldn't know that."

"And when he didn't find what he wanted in the bag, he came here to look?"

Holbrook nodded.

"What's he looking for?" she asked.

"I wish I could tell you." He didn't intend for his tone to come out so strident, but he was frustrated that he didn't know.

"Didn't Ham give you any kind of a clue?" she asked. "What exactly did he tell you?"

Grant rubbed his hands over his face, the beard stubble rasping against his palms. God, he ached. The pounding in his head had lessened, but it was hard to concentrate. He wished he knew how far he could trust her and how much information he could safely give her without putting her in danger.

His first consideration had to be Tyler's safety. According to Hamilton, George must have discovered something relatively solid or he never would have made the call. And the fact that George might have been killed because of that knowledge made it all the more important that Grant keep his own counsel.

"What did Ham say?"

Her repeated question brought him back to the present.

"Nothing really. He told me that it was George's story to tell. He was only making the initial contact. I didn't press him because I assumed I'd be able to get the information directly from your father-in-law. I called George, but there was no answer. I tried off and on today, but by five, when I still hadn't reached him, I decided to drive up here."

He took a quick glance at the clock above the stove. Eleven-thirty.

"It's not too late to call, if that's what you're thinking. But I'm the one who has to make the call," Maggie said. "Ham needs to hear what happened from me. Besides, he'll be more likely to tell me exactly what George said."

Grant reached down for the leather briefcase beside his chair. His mouth tightened at the sight of his wallet, license and business card lying loose inside. He looked across at her, and she raised her chin in defiance.

He took the business card and set it on the table as close to her as he could reach. She turned her face away as if she hadn't seen the gesture. Flipping open the wallet he replaced the license, then reached inside the flap for the piece of paper where he'd written Hamilton Rice's phone number. He pulled out his cell phone, dialed the number and handed the phone to her.

As she began to speak haltingly about George's death, Grant stood up and walked into the living room to give her some privacy. Although moving made his teeth ache, he knew he needed to keep his muscles from stiffening.

Avoiding the cluttered areas where the burglar had dumped things, Grant wandered around the first floor, trying to draw a sense of George from his environment. The main room led out to the deck and off a short hall to two small bedrooms and a bath. The first bedroom was George's. It was spartan and neat except where the intruder had dragged things out of the closets and drawers. The walls were covered by family pictures, and Grant leaned close to examine them.

After he'd gotten the call from Hamilton Rice, he did as much as he could to check into the background of George Collier and his family. Before he arrived in Delbrook, he already knew about Maggie, Jake and the death of George's only child, Mark.

Pictures of George and his grandson generally included a string of fish. Jake looked very much like his father, a handsome dark-haired man who dominated the photos, white teeth flashing in a tanned face.

Maggie photographed well, her Irish coloring enhanced by the outdoor settings. Feisty as she was, Grant was beginning to think of her as Maggie. She was less formal than he was, and neither the title of Mrs. nor Ms. fit her. Looking at the pictures, he was intrigued by the look of vulnerability in her eyes.

"Keep your head in the game," he said aloud.

The second bedroom was set up partially as an office. As he took in the outdoor prints and the meticulously cared-for fishing equipment, he became more and more convinced that George was not involved in the kidnapping but had stumbled onto something that resulted in his death.

Thoughtfully he walked back to the kitchen, stopping in the doorway. Maggie sat at the table, the cell phone still in her hand. Hearing him enter, she stood up, and he could see the sheen of tears that filmed her eyes.

In death it was always the little things that caught at the heart, he thought. He could bet that she was thinking of her father-in-law's long friendship with Hamilton Rice and that she was hurting with the knowledge.

She closed her eyes and took a long, sniffling breath. When she opened them again, she had regained some control.

"Ham is driving up tomorrow afternoon. I told him that there would be a wake for George in the evening and a memorial service on Tuesday." She held out Grant's cell phone. "Thank you. Ham said he thought someone should stay in the house until he gets here. I said I would ask if you would do that."

Stunned by the vote of confidence, Grant said, "Hamilton must have done a whale of a sell job."

"Apparently you have mutual friends," she said.

He caught a hint of a smile in her eyes, and gave a nod of his head in acknowledgment. Her partial acceptance of him released some of the tension that had knotted his stomach. It was provisional, so he'd still have to tread carefully. He'd do whatever it took to get the information he needed.

"What did George tell him?" he asked, putting the phone in his briefcase.

"Ham said George called from the country club around eight-thirty Saturday night." Her eyes opened wide, and she shook her head. "I can't believe that's only yesterday. I feel as if this all happened days ago."

"It's a lot to absorb. Any death is traumatic, but violent death takes a stronger psychological toll, Maggie," he said.

It was the first time he'd used her first name. Aside from one startled glance from beneath her lashes, she made no comment.

"At any rate," she continued, "dinner was over and they were taking a break before the card game. Ham said George wouldn't say much. He was talking from a pay phone just outside the bar. The upshot of the conversation was that he asked Ham to find out if Tyler was still missing."

"Did he mention Tyler by name?"

"No. He referred to him as the child kidnapped in Cleveland. Ham knew immediately who George meant.

I don't know if Ham told you that he went to the Internet, checked various sites until he found one of those flyers you showed me. That's how he got your name and your phone number. George told Ham not to contact the police directly."

"Did George say that he'd seen the kidnapped boy?" Grant asked.

"No. He said he'd seen a picture of him. At least he thought it was the missing child, but he wasn't sure."

"A picture? You mean a photograph? How would he get a photo of Tyler?"

Grant heard her sharp inhalation of breath. It didn't seem possible that she could get any whiter, but her skin took on a translucent appearance as if she'd received a massive shock.

"The pictures," she said.

A jolt of excitement zinged along Grant's nerve endings. "What pictures?"

"My son, Jake, just turned eight. I bought him a camera for his birthday party on Friday, and he took pictures all day long. A friend of mine, Hugh Rossiter, was at the country club the night George was killed. He was telling me about the evening, and he said that George passed the pictures around the table during dinner."

Grant prowled around the edges of the kitchen, too restless to remain still. "Do you remember what was in any of the pictures?"

"No. I haven't seen them. George said he'd pick them up and bring them over today when he came for dinner."

Her chin quivered, and he knew she was thinking that there would be no more family dinners with her father-in-law. Just as he thought she might burst into tears, her eyes opened wide and she stared across at him.

"Do you think it's possible that George saw Tyler in one of the pictures?"

Since that was exactly what Grant thought, he tried to keep his expression from giving his own thoughts away. In the twenty months since Tyler had disappeared, there had been so many false leads that he knew better than to jump to conclusions. Even so, his heartbeat accelerated and his depression lifted a fraction.

"It's possible. Or at least someone who looked like Tyler," he cautioned. "It was just one roll of film?"

"Yes. I got him one of those cardboard cameras that you use once and then throw away. I can't even recall how many exposures there were."

"Did your son use all of the film?"

"Yes. I took a few pictures when the boys first arrived. Jake had invited four of his friends from school."

"Were you here at George's house?"

"No. At my house. If you came via the expressway, you drove through the center of town. My house is at the end of the historic area, facing the lake and Wolfram Park. The boys all met in the park, and then I drove them to the Renaissance Faire."

"The Renaissance Faire? The festival across the lake at Camp Delbrook?" Grant asked.

He tried to keep any show of excitement out of his voice. He'd come across Camp Delbrook in another context, and it might prove to be the connection that he was looking for.

"Yes," she said. "Delbrook Community College owns the land and supplies counselors and other volunteers to run a camp for inner-city kids from Milwaukee during the summer. The camp closes on Labor Day, and the Faire opens the following Friday."

"So the majority of pictures were shot by your son at this Renaissance thing?"

"Yes. I may have snapped a couple pictures while the boys were eating, but for the most part, Jake took the rest."

"Do you know where the pictures are now, Maggie?"

"No. I didn't know George had them until Hugh told me, and with everything that's happened, I haven't really given them a thought."

Grant stopped pacing and leaned against the countertop, facing her. He ran a hand over the back of his head and massaged the tension at the base of his neck. The pounding had lessened to a low-grade headache that should be gone by morning.

"If George had the pictures at the club," he said, "they should have been on his body. Unless whoever killed him took them."

Maggie shuddered. "If that's true, then why would the murderer search the house or steal the hospital bag?"

"I don't know."

"How old was Tyler when he disappeared?"

"Two and a half."

"So he'd be four now," Maggie said. "When he disappeared he was just a baby, chubby face, stocky body. By now he would have turned into a boy, lengthened out, his face leaner with more individual traits apparent. He would have changed so much that I can't believe George would have been able to recognize him."

"I thought of that the moment you told me about the photos. I know it sounds crazy, but all I can think of is all the people who have recognized other children from the fuzzy photos on the side of milk cartons. It gives me hope."

She bit her lip, her expression hesitant. "Look, Holbrook, instead of talking to me about all this, you should be talking to Charley Blessington, the chief of police."

"You're the only one I can talk to at this point." When she opened her mouth to object, he raised a hand, palm toward her. "Hear me out. If by the wildest chance any of my premise is true, there's a good chance that Tyler is in the vicinity. What do you think would happen to the boy if whoever was holding him got wind of the fact that I was here searching for him?"

Maggie's hands flew up to cover her mouth. Her haunted expression indicated her understanding of the situation.

"If your father-in-law was killed because he discovered something about Tyler, then anyone who was at the country club has to be considered a suspect. And you said yourself that Chief Blessington was at the dinner and stayed for the poker game."

"But Charley was George's friend. Everyone at the game knew him and liked him. These are all good people."

He couldn't hold back a sharp bark of laughter. He almost resented her naïveté.

"I was born a cynic, Maggie, and dealing with the law over these years has given me a jaundiced view of mankind. For what it's worth, good people can do bad things. They're not perfect. They have all the faults and frailties that are a part of our humanity."

"So what you're telling me," she said, her voice soft and expressionless, "is that I can't trust anyone?"

"That's exactly what I'm saying," he said, and she winced at the acid in his tone.

"How do I know I can trust you?" she asked.

"Believe me, Maggie, despite what happened earlier between us, you have absolutely no reason to distrust me. In fact, I'm the one person you can have complete confidence in, because I have the most at stake."

"For a moment I forgot you were a lawyer, Holbrook." There was a definite bite to her voice. She needed to strike out at him. "I should have remembered you have a major stake in the hundred-thousand-dollar reward. So you're just in it for the money?"

"No, not the money," he said. "I put up fifty thousand dollars of the reward myself. All I want to do is to locate the boy. Tyler McKenzie is my nephew."

CHAPTER
EIGHT

"ALMOST BACK TO NORMAL, George," Maggie said, wiping a dusting cloth across the surface of the desk. "Just your bedroom to finish."

Maggie was grateful that there was no one in the house to hear her running dialogue with her father-in-law. She'd spent the morning removing the evidence of the break-in, and to keep the pain of her loss from over-whelming her, she'd talked to George as if he were watching her every move. She hoped he was. Touching his things had made him seem very close.

With a final brush of her hand across the back of George's desk chair, she hurried across the living room, opened the door onto the deck and stepped outside.

The day was cool with a hint of the crisp fall days ahead. Leaves were beginning to fall, covering the ground with a carpet of mottled colors. Reds, oranges and luminous yellows overlaid the grass. The soft throb of a motor on the far side of the lake floated up to her. The beauty of the moment juxtaposed with George's murder made a shocking contrast.

Murder. Robbery. Kidnapping.

The words seemed alien to the shimmering water

and the brilliant fall coloring. How could evil exist in such a setting? Only two days since George had been killed, and still there were so many questions.

When she arrived at the house after dropping Jake off at school, Grant Holbrook had been gone. On the kitchen table was a note saying the police had OK'd the cleanup of the house and that he had gone to town to run some errands and pick up food for lunch. She had to admit she was nervous about seeing him again, because she had begun to question the agreement they had made the night before.

"Have I made a pact with the devil?" she wondered aloud.

Even though Ham Rice had told her that she could trust Grant, she had wanted to go to the police and tell Charley Blessington the whole story about Tyler and the photographs. Only when Grant indicated that George's involvement might be questioned did she agree to keep everything from Charley.

She'd told Grant that she wouldn't speak to the police until she was convinced that George wouldn't be accused of anything, but she didn't tell him the real reason for her acquiescence.

She couldn't let Jake question his grandfather's character.

After two years Jake finally had begun to recover from his father's death. She had talked about Mark's virtues and his faults so that Jake would not grow up believing his father was perfect. She had never lied to him, but since she was the only one who knew that Mark had been unfaithful, she had felt no need to explain that part of Mark's character.

The sudden death of his grandfather threatened Jake's psychological well-being. She could see it in his volatile emotional outbursts. He was dealing with anger, abandonment and sorrow. Once again she felt the need to protect Jake from anything that would taint his memories of George. What would happen to Jake's equilibrium if his grandfather was suspected of being involved in a kidnapping?

Anyone knowing George would realize the whole idea was ludicrous, but she wasn't willing to take a chance that, in the frenzy to find answers, George's call about the kidnapping could be misconstrued.

"Back to work," she said aloud as she pushed herself to her feet. "Just time before lunch to finish your bedroom, George."

Putting fresh linens on the bed, Maggie fluffed up the pillows, smoothing a hand over the appliquéd black-and-white loon in the center of the quilted comforter. Turning her head, she checked to make sure that everything was in order.

She stood at the door of the closet and brushed her fingers across the soft leather elbow patch on the sleeve of George's black-and-white tweed sport jacket. She'd given it to him for Christmas soon after she'd married Mark, and it had always been his favorite. She raised the cuff, touched it to her cheek, then dropped it back into place.

She pressed her hands against the small of her back, stretching backward to ease her tight muscles. The physical labor had been a godsend to keep her from thinking about the confusion in her own mind, but now that she'd completed her chores, her mind was flooded with the pain of reality.

She stood still, her eyes closed against the threat of tears. She was alone again. She didn't know if she had the strength to start over and shore up the protective barricades she'd built after Mark's death.

"Maggie?" Connie Prentice's voice sounded from the back door.

"Come on in," she called, jolted back to the present.

"There you are, my dear. I saw your car parked out back," Connie said. "Brent and I just had to stop in to see how you were doing."

She crossed the living room, her high heels clicking against the floorboards, and put her arms around Maggie, kissing the air in the general vicinity of her right ear.

Flowery perfume swirled around Maggie, and she stepped away from the cloying scent. Connie's eyes dropped, a quick scan from Maggie's hastily bound-up ponytail to the soles of her ancient loafers. She didn't exactly sneer, but it was close to being offensive.

"Thanks for stopping by," Maggie said, holding on to her temper. "Where's Brent?"

As if on cue, the back door opened. "Maggie? Connie?"

"In the living room," Connie called out.

Heavy footsteps crossed the kitchen floor, and Brent Prentice appeared in the doorway. His expression was grave as he crossed over to kiss Maggie's cheek. The lines in his face seemed to be more deeply etched than when she'd seen him at the hospital.

"How are you holding up?" he asked.

"Pretty good. Jake and I are both tired but doing OK."

"I can't believe he's gone. George was always such a vital man. A real presence." Brent's eyes teared up. He sniffed several times, then reached in his pocket and pulled out a freshly ironed handkerchief. Turning away, he blew his nose, walking over to stare out at the lake.

"Mr. Sentimental," Connie said, flipping her hair away from her face. Her tone was caustic, and she smiled to take the sting out of it. She sat down on the couch, settling her skirt becomingly before she patted the cushion beside her. "Now, Maggie, come and sit down and tell us what you know."

Wavering between amusement and annoyance at Connie's usurping the role of hostess, Maggie remained where she was on the far side of the glass-topped coffee table.

"Would you like some coffee or tea?" Maggie asked.

Although Connie opened her mouth to speak, Brent's reply came first.

"No thanks, Maggie. We just finished lunch at the country club," he said. With one final blow of his nose, he tucked the handkerchief back in his pocket.

"Everyone was talking about George. I still can't believe it happened after the poker game," Connie said. "Both Brent and I were there of course. George was still at the club when we left."

"The word is that Tully Jackson's involved." Brent's mouth was pursed with distaste.

"I wouldn't be at all surprised. That man always gave me the creeps." Connie shuddered. Her painted nails clicked nervously on her wide gold bracelet, her personal trademark. "He never said anything to me, but he was always staring. All that hair and those probing eyes. I always thought he was dangerous."

"You never know with those types. Probably mental," Brent concluded. He brushed some invisible specks of dust off the sleeve of his navy pinstripe suit. "I understand that there'll be a wake tonight for George."

"Yes," Maggie said. "Charley Blessington called this morning to say George had been taken over to Upton's Funeral Home."

"Is there anything we can do?" Connie asked.

Her eyes flicked around the room as if to suggest a major cleanup was needed. Maggie was grateful that she hadn't stopped by several hours earlier to see the aftermath of the break-in.

"I appreciate your asking, but everything is pretty much taken care of."

She glanced at the clock on the wall and realized that Grant would be back soon. Hoping to get Brent and Connie out of the house before she was required to make any introductions, Maggie stood up.

"If you think of anything, you just have to call," Brent said.

He reached out to help Connie to her feet. For a moment she hesitated as if she wanted to stay, but then shrugged, batting his hand away as she rose to her feet. He took Maggie's hand and slipped her arm into the crook of his. He patted her hand as they walked out to the kitchen.

"I'd be happy to stay and give you a hand," Connie said. "I hate to think of you dealing with this all alone."

"How sweet you are to offer," Maggie said, opening

the back door, "but I'm just taking everything one day at a time."

With another flowery embrace from Connie and Brent's formal kiss on the cheek, the couple left. Maggie closed the door, leaning against it as she watched them walk along the path to their car. Just as she took a deep sigh of relief, she saw Grant turn into the street and pull into the parking spot next to Brent's car.

Maggie's stomach gave a free-fall lurch. She had agreed that Grant could pose as Mark's cousin, but she wasn't comfortable with the deception. Since it was Grant's idea, she would leave the introductions to him. Turning on her heel, she walked out on the deck to straighten the patio furniture. Only when she heard the back door open again did she return to the kitchen.

Grant was standing beside the sink, a bemused expression on his face, a grocery bag cradled in his arm. His suit and shirt, covered in a plastic bag from Sylvester's Dry Cleaning, hung from the back of a kitchen chair, and a bag from Copeland Haberdashery was on the seat.

"I don't know who that woman was, but she asked enough questions to give my law partners a run for their money in the investigation of witnesses," he said by way of greeting.

"Connie's a real estate agent," Maggie said, "who, along with her husband, was one of the poker players the night George died."

"I liked him, but she gave me a hellava grilling. I thought at one point she was going to ask for my fingerprints and a copy of my stock portfolio."

"Did she believe your story?" she said, feeling the buildup of tension across her shoulders and her neck.

"I think I passed. She and Brent looked surprised when I said I was Mark's cousin, but neither of them really questioned it. I explained that you'd asked me to stay here so the house wouldn't be empty."

"What if they check up on you?"

"Then they'll find I'm exactly who I said I was. A lawyer from Chicago who's come for George's funeral."

He set the bag of groceries on the counter, then turned to give her his full attention. He could see she was shaken by his first encounter with someone from Delbrook.

"Look, Maggie," he said. "I know you're afraid that I'll be denounced as some sort of impostor. Keep in mind that even if that happens, it won't impact on you. Your story is that I introduced myself as Mark's cousin and you had no reason to disbelieve me. Since you didn't know I even existed, you can claim total ignorance if someone questions you."

"I know. It's just that I hate lying." She bit her lip as if her honesty were some kind of character flaw.

"You don't have to lie. I'm the one that has to, and believe me, I'm very good at it. Some people say that's how I make my living."

He could see that she wanted to make a sarcastic retort, but her eyes flicked to the cut on the side of his face and she swallowed the comment. She might not like subterfuge, but she had strong reasons for going along with it.

"The key to lying is to stick as close to the truth as possible. I had a long talk with Hamilton Rice this morning. I told him everything I told you, just like we agreed. He's willing to claim that he knew me through George and had called to tell me about his death." He grimaced, pulling at the lobe of his ear. "Actually, he said he would once he'd laid his baby blues on me and checked my bona fides."

"Ham's the cautious type," Maggie said.

"Will he be able to hold up his end?"

"Among his many jobs, Ham was a private detective for years. He earned most of his money as a skip chaser."

"I think I'm going to like this guy." He smiled with genuine amusement at this latest news. "Hamilton says it's safest to say I was related to George's late wife, Edna. She wasn't from Delbrook. Someplace in Minnesota. I've decided that if anyone asks, I'll say my mother and Mark's mother were cousins. If pressed for details, I'll describe my favorite aunt, Hadie Yates. I won't have to make up any strange stories. She was a real corker."

He could see her eyes soften under his light banter. How nice it must be to never have a need to lie, Grant thought. To live life openly and honestly without hiding your feelings or playing mind games. For a moment he resented her uncomplicated life.

"I'm sorry," she said as if she could read his mind. "I understand why this is necessary. I'm just having a hard time with it. I'll get better."

"You don't have to get better. The important thing to remember is that as far as you know, George was killed in a robbery. Pretend I really am a relative, come to give you moral support."

"All right. I can do that."

"Good girl," he said, hoping he didn't sound condescending. "Let me put this stuff away, and then I'll fix us some lunch."

While he took his suit and the bag of clothes into the other room, Maggie put the groceries on the counter and set the table. When he returned, he began to arrange the ham and cheese on a platter, moving around the kitchen as if he was long familiar with it.

Despite the fact she didn't trust him and wasn't sure she liked him, she was surprised at how comfortable she was in his company.

He was wearing new blue jeans, a tweedy brown knit shirt and a pair of Docksides. Except for a slight stiffness when he moved, he was none the worse for his contact with the canoe paddle.

"What did the police say about the break-in?" she asked.

"No fingerprints," Grant said in disgust. "I suppose anyone who watches TV nowadays knows how to avoid them. The police officer dusted around the window and a few other places, but it was apparent right away that Officer Chung was getting nothing but smudges."

"Did you tell her that it looked more like a search than a robbery?"

"She thought someone was looking for cash. She filled out the paperwork and said that because of George's death, she'd give the report directly to Charley Blessington. Said to tell you she was sorry about George and she'd talk to you at the October meeting of something."

"Sophia and I belong to the same church guild. She's doing a program on her trip to Seattle where she helped the police set up a soup kitchen like one our guild established in Milwaukee."

He got out a jar of mayonnaise, uncapped it and set it on the table.

"Did you take your son to school this morning?"

"Yes. I decided to close the bookstore until after the funeral, which freed me up to talk to Jake's principal this morning. She said the structure of the school day would give him a feeling of security and he'd have less time to think about his loss. The teachers were prepared to discuss George's murder in class today, and Jake will have a chance to talk about his grandfather's death with his peers."

"Sounds like a good school."

"They've been very supportive. Both now and when we first moved up here."

"Your boy's had a tough couple of years," he said.

He didn't ask her how she was coping with this second tragedy. The sadness in her eyes and the droop of her body when she didn't know he was looking gave ample evidence of her grief.

"On the way over here I stopped at Kruckmeyer's to ask about the photographs," Maggie said.

She got out plates and napkins and poured a glass of milk, then, without asking, opened a cold bottle of beer and placed it on the counter beside him.

"The pharmacy doesn't keep any copies of the pictures."

"That doesn't come as a great surprise." Grant took a quick swallow of beer. "The camera?"

"That's destroyed, and everything goes into the incinerator." Maggie sighed as she pulled out a chair and sat down. "Unless George left them someplace in the country club, someone has already taken them. If that's true, what are they searching for?"

"I wish I could tell you," Grant said.

He placed the platter of ham and cheese on the table and opened the plastic wrapping on a loaf of rye bread. While she made a sandwich, he brought over a bag of potato chips and a jar of pickles.

"Is this enough food?"

"Perfect," she said, taking a bite of her sandwich.

"Why don't you give me a little background on that couple I just met while we eat," he said as he dropped down on the chair across from her.

She raised the red-and-white checkered napkin, and for a moment her chin quivered as if she'd suddenly been reminded of George. She wiped her mouth slowly, and when she dropped the napkin, he could see she was back in control.

"Connie Prentice is the granddaughter of the town founder, Delbrook Falcone," she said.

"Falcon Lake was named after him?"

"No. The similarity is just a coincidence. Delbrook was a major contributor to the Audubon Society. He named the lake for the birds in the area and the town for himself."

"It's got to be a great ego trip to have a town named after you," Grant said.

"My mother used to tell me stories about old Delbrook," Maggie said. "He'd been a big hunter in his youth. Always in the woods with a gun, until one day he got a little careless and winged one of his neighbors. Gave up hunting for conservation and wrote treatises on the habitats of local birds. A bit odd, but otherwise a pretty interesting old coot."

"How about Brent? He looks a lot older than Connie. Love match or the making of a dynasty?"

"I'd say the latter. Connie's thirty-six, and Brent just had his fiftieth birthday in June. According to local gossip, Connie's father, Edmund Falcone, was Brent's godfather and paid for his education. He's an architect. Edmund hired him to draw up plans to renovate the original Falcone house on the south side of the lake. An old rambling place, added onto over the years."

"Is it still there?"

"No. It burned to the ground. It happened about a year after Connie and Brent were married."

"Is Edmund still alive?"

Maggie shook her head. "There's some kind of mystery surrounding his death and the fire. He'd had a stroke and was confined to bed. I don't know if he died in the fire or shortly after."

She watched as Grant carefully spread mayonnaise on his bread, working it precisely to the edges before layering on the slices of ham. She had to laugh when he measured the dimensions of the bread and cut a single piece of Swiss cheese to fit exactly. He spoke without looking up.

"Go ahead and snicker," he said. "I can't help it that I'm set in my ways. I like things very precise. It comes from being a bachelor for thirty-seven years."

"Anti woman or just anti marriage?"

"A little of both." He cut the sandwich into two equal rectangles, wiped the knife and set it beside his plate. He took a good bite out of one of the halves and chewed reflectively before he spoke again. "I came pretty close a couple years ago. Her name was Veronica. She was the daughter of one of the partners in the law firm where I worked at the time."

"Sounds like an upwardly mobile move."

"I thought so too." He saluted her with the beer bottle. "It was a pretty heady situation. I got so caught up in the social whirl that I lost my focus for a while. Veronica wanted me to run for political office. As she and her father always said, Chicago needs good Republican candidates."

"Can a Republican win an election in Chicago?" she asked in amusement.

"Not that I'm aware of." He finished off his sandwich and applied himself to the potato chips. "There's something very seductive about being wooed by some of the biggest moneymen in Chicago. Celebrity is very sexy. People ask your opinion and may even listen to your answers. You're invited to all the 'in' black-tie affairs, and everyone tells you that you're just what the party has been waiting for."

At some point he'd forgotten that he was talking to her. It was as if he were giving a monologue on the drawbacks to stardom. She was surprised by the note of bitterness in his voice and wondered what had caused it.

"Did Veronica break it off or did you?"

"Mutual consent. I had an accident, and it was as if this"—he tapped the scar on the side of his jaw—"were the outward sign of a character flaw. It marred the perfect profile of the man she'd hoped to mold into a handsome, debonair political animal."

"She can't have been that shallow," Maggie said.

He stared across the table, his face turned up to the light so that she could see the scar. She wondered if he was expecting her to recoil in horror. When it was new, it might have been ugly. Red and swollen, the edges jagged. Once healed it was noticeable but hardly disfiguring.

"Maybe not. Veronica always sat or walked on my right side. If she couldn't see the scar, she could forget that it was there. She wanted me to have plastic surgery, but I'd grown used to it." He ran his thumb along the ridge. "Each day the scar became less obvious, but in Veronica's mind it grew bigger and uglier until she could no longer stand to look at me."

"Was it a car accident?"

She could see the muscles beneath the scar ripple at her question. She should have remembered she was a stranger not a friend.

"I apologize for asking such a personal question," she said.

"Since I've dropped into your life without asking permission, I'd say you have a right to satisfy your curiosity as to the kind of person I am."

He finished off his beer, setting the bottle precisely in the center of the table. His head was bent, so Maggie couldn't see the expression on his face, only hear the condemnation in his voice.

"The early part of last year, I spent a great deal of time trying to drink Chicago dry. Although I only have a hazy memory of this edifying period of my life, my friends are happy to point out that it was not a pretty sight." He reached for the beer bottle, switching it from hand to hand as he spoke. "I wasn't a happy drunk. I was a mean, pissed-off bastard, looking for a fight. Naturally I discovered several bar patrons happy to oblige."

"You got the scar in a bar fight?"

He raised his head, his mouth twisting into a cynical smile.

"For a moment you sounded just like Veronica. Technically it wasn't a bar fight. Two guys jumped me as I was leaving the Silver Stallion, a bar in a particularly seedy section of Chicago. They robbed me, stripped me naked and were considering cutting my throat when the cops arrived. Saved by Chicago's finest."

Maggie caught the bitterness in his voice and wondered what had brought on the binge drinking. Then she knew.

"This was after Tyler disappeared."

Wanting to spare him, she made it a statement, not a question. He blew out a sigh of relief that he hadn't had to spell it out for her. His body sagged against the back of the chair. Maggie remained still, letting him set the pace.

"Two Christmases ago I went to visit my sister, Barbara, in Cleveland. I'd been much too busy with my campaigning that year to do much traveling even though she'd asked me to come several times. My nephew, Tyler, was growing so fast, and she didn't want me to miss seeing him."

He didn't look at her. His eyes were focused on the empty beer bottle as he rolled it back and forth between the palms of his hands. The words came out slowly, as if it were the first time he'd spoken them aloud. Maybe it was, Maggie thought.

"Veronica was incensed with my decision. Christmas was a prime time for fund-raising parties, and she was furious when I told her I was going. My decision was made primarily to prove to Veronica that she couldn't dictate to me. When I got to Barbara's I was bored."

"Too much domesticity for you?" Maggie asked.

"I was plunged into toddler hell," he said, the corner of his mouth curling in self-mockery. "I'd never been around children for any length of time. Tyler was cute but much too young to hold my interest for more than a few minutes. He had a dog, and the two of them climbed all over me whenever I sat down. The dog was a mutt with bulging eyes in a gooney-looking face. His name was Barney. Did you ever hear that old song 'Barney Google with the goo goo googly eyes'?"

Maggie chuckled. "Small world. George used to sing it to Jake when he was little. Jake loved it."

"So did Tyler," Grant said. "For a year after he disappeared, I used to wake up in a cold sweat with that song playing over and over in my head."

The muscles in his jaw bunched, and Maggie heard the pain behind his words.

"Barbara's husband, Ken, is an oncologist with the Cleveland Clinic. I like and respect the man, and he was kind enough not to kick me in the ass for my behavior. We managed to survive Christmas. Forty-eight hours after I arrived, I announced I had to return to Chicago for some important meetings."

He set the beer bottle down, steadying it with his fingers, then rose to his feet. He began to pace, moving restlessly back and forth between the refrigerator and the sink.

"Veronica was delighted, seeing my early return as a

capitulation to her demands. Barbara was less thrilled. She and Ken had just discovered that she was pregnant with their second child. She had been having bouts of morning sickness and was hoping that I'd help her with Tyler because Ken had an emergency call to the hospital. I was firm in explaining that I couldn't stay. I was too busy. I had important people to meet."

Maggie could feel the buildup to his story in the way he bit off each word, speaking in short angry sentences.

"Barbara had asked me if I could watch Tyler while she ran errands, but I'd managed to get an early flight out. She drove me to the airport, and since she had no one to baby-sit with Tyler, she took him with her to the mall. She was making Christmas returns." He took a deep breath, swallowing once before he continued speaking. "She was returning the present I'd given her when Tyler was kidnapped."

CHAPTER NINE

PLUSH MAROON VELVET DRAPERIES and silky sheers hung at the windows, breaking up the long wall of gold embossed wallpaper that lined one side of the room. The furniture, wood surfaces rubbed to a burnished sheen, represented no specific period. The chairs and couches were upholstered in rich tapestried material illustrated with quaint medieval hunting scenes. Underfoot the thick patterned carpet leached sound from the room and suggested a place for quiet contemplation.

The Warrior stood inside the doorway, letting his senses absorb the emanations of death that permeated every corner of the funeral home.

He had decided to come at the last minute. If he didn't make an appearance, it would be noted and an explanation would be required. Now that he was here he realized that it was going to take all his control to act appropriately and not draw attention to himself.

His mind conjured up a medicinal odor, but any hint of antiseptic would have been overridden by the cloying scent of flowers that were scattered around the room in vases and baskets and wire stands flanking the mahogany casket.

Flowers. Flowers in myriad shapes and colors. Live flowers, not silk. Dying from the moment they were cut.

Maggie stood beside Jake at the front of the room. He approved of her mourning clothes, a light blue silk dress with a pleated skirt and white collar and cuffs. The simple lines gave height to her petite figure, and the soft color enhanced her lightly tanned skin with a touch of golden highlights.

Jake looked very grown up in his navy suit and white shirt. He rocked from foot to foot as if he hadn't fully broken in the new shoes he wore. Aside from that, he didn't fidget but remained attentively next to his mother. Occasionally he leaned his dark curly head against her arm or touched her with his hand as if to reassure himself that she was still there.

The Warrior made suitable gestures of sympathy. Maggie's responses were warm, her voice tinged with the pain of loss. Despite an outward appearance of fragility, she was a strong woman. He could see in her steady gaze the ribbon of courage that started in the core of her body and infiltrated her entire being. Her crystalline blue eyes startled him. They contained the concentration and focus of a warrior.

The observation startled him, and he moved away to speak to the boy.   Jake, like many only children, was comfortable with adults, talking with ease and a degree of interest that was unusual for a boy of eight.

Maggie had done an excellent job in training Jake.

Much to think about, the Warrior thought, as he stepped away so others could offer their condolences.

Between the family group and the casket was a brass metal easel that held a rectangular posterboard covered with pictures. He drew closer, his eyes skimming across the photographs, seeing George's face in most of the pictures. He wished he could remain in front of the collage, but he knew he would have to approach the coffin.

Viewing the body. The concept was alien to his beliefs.

The body was only a shell that housed the spirit. The wake was an anachronism, an ancient tradition that glorified the corporal aspect of life over the spiritual.

He stood about a foot away from the ornate kneeler placed at the front of the casket. The maroon velvet coverings on the hand rest and knee pad were clean and free of stains, but the nap was slightly worn from use. He preferred to stand.

He would miss George.

Who could have guessed that such diverse events would come together, converging on that night, as if it were fated? Nothing had prepared the Warrior for it. No tingle of apprehension had shivered up his spine Saturday night when the poker game was over and George said he wanted to talk.

They walked along the fairway, and George told him about being in Cleveland and seeing the media frenzy about a missing child. Then in a voice filled with exhilaration, George had told him he'd recognized the kidnapped boy in the pictures taken by his grandson at the Renaissance Faire.

In a movie, the Warrior would have rejected the coincidence, and even now he had difficulty believing that something so random could nullify the meticulous planning he'd done to ensure safety from discovery.

George had no concept of the Warrior's involvement. He was too full of excitement that he'd recognized the child and was eager to present the evidence. The Warrior could still recall how his heart had hammered in his chest when the stack of photographs from the Renaissance Faire was passed to him and his fingers touched the slick surface of the first picture.

The poorly focused faces of three grinning boys filled the majority of the frame of the photo. George's teeth flashed in a wolfish smile as he tapped the picture, pointing to a small blond child in the background. Seated on the wooden bench beside the jousting arena was One Who Cries.

The Warrior's fingers stiffened, and he almost dropped the pack of photos. Until George pointed it out, the Warrior hadn't even noticed the child on the bench. One Who Cries was easily recognizable.

Impatiently George showed him the next picture. Again, the half-turned face of One Who Cries could be seen in the background.

What an improbable twist of fate. Sweat beaded on his forehead and his skin was moist as he handed the photos back to George. The Warrior knew without question that he would have to destroy the evidence.

It would be simple enough. George had slipped the bunch of pictures inside the carrying folder. The negatives would be in the short half-pocket of the folder.

They had walked along companionably, George excited and talkative as he smoked a cigar and discussed the significance of the pictures. He spoke with the ease of friendship, and by the time they reached the eighteenth-tee box, the sense of betrayal was so strong that the Warrior was primed for an explosion. The sight of the folder of incriminating pictures triggered the attack.

George stood motionless, holding the photographs, his eyes wide in question as the Warrior opened his shirt and pulled out the knife. The Warrior thrust it home with his right hand, the palm of his left braced on the raised heart at the top of the dagger.

Misericorde. Heart of Mercy.

George never saw the knife. The tattoo of the bleeding heart on his friend's chest held him transfixed.

"Tattoo."

He uttered the single word before he pitched forward onto the surface of the tee.

The Warrior stared down at the body. Moonlight reflected off the blade of the knife, a flicker of gold combining with the dark red of blood.

The folder of pictures lay on the grass under George's hand. He knelt down beside the body and pulled the folder out, encountering no resistance from the limp fingers. The reality of what he'd done began to seep into his consciousness, and he glanced at George's face, wanting to deny the truth of his actions.

A shout made him glance up, and he saw the ghostly figure of Tully Jackson appear out of the darkness.

He didn't turn around. He knew his presence had been discovered, and every instinct told him that he had only moments to escape before he was recognized. Moving quickly, he reached inside George's jacket for his wallet, then tore the watch off his wrist. He ran to the back of the tee, ducked between two weeping cherry trees and skirted along the edge of the next fairway until he reached the heavier brush along the fence separating the golf course from the parking lot at the boat landing.

Jamming the pictures and the wallet in his pocket, he slipped the knife back into the sheath at his side and rebuttoned his shirt. He reached the chain-link fence, racing along beside it until he spotted a low-hanging tree limb. Sprinting toward it, he reached up and grabbed the limb, using his momentum to lift him as he vaulted over the fence and landed in a heap on the other side.

Tully's car was only five feet away. He crept past it and spotted the partially open window. Careful not to touch the car, he rubbed the fingerprints off George's watch and stuffed it through the opening.

He didn't waste any more time. Keeping to the shadows, he ran along the fence to the far end of the parking lot where he had left his car after the poker game, tucked tightly against a thicket where it was almost invisible. Keys in hand, he climbed into the car, started it and drove quickly out of the parking lot.

Reliving the night of George's death, the Warrior's breathing grew ragged. He could close his eyes and feel the rapid beat of his pulse, a remembered combination of exhilaration in the act of killing and fear of discovery and punishment.

It had always been that way. An intermingling of pleasure and pain. Counting coup. He had always thought of killings as death coups. Just another variation on the tests.

A cough reminded him that he was not alone in the funeral home. He needed to stay in the moment.

He took a step forward and placed his hand on George's shoulder. The suit material was smooth against his fingers. He would have liked to touch his friend's chest, to see if the wound would emit any vibrations, but knew that action would spell disaster.

"Goodbye, George," he said and silently turned away.

The food was getting cold. Tyler hadn't touched it since the man left it. It was the second dish. He should eat and go to sleep. His tummy hurt. His nose was stuffy and his eyes itched. That always happened when he cried. Even so he didn't make any sound.

He heard the scrabble of the mice and pulled a corner of the blanket over his head. He lay on his side on the bed shelf, his ears covered, and stared at the food.

It was the brown meat. He liked it because it was easy to chew. The white meat was always cut in little squares, but it wasn't juicy. The tiny green trees were good, but he was glad the dish had lots of the orange sticks. They made a snapping sound when he chewed them.

Was Mouse Ears gone?

A tear slid from the corner of his eye and landed on the back of his hand. He had dropped the feather. He didn't want to squish it tight, so when he tried to put it where the man told him, it fell on the ground. When they got back to the room, the man took another mouse. Tyler kept his head up like he was told, but he made his eyes see funny so he wouldn't be able to tell which mouse was gone.

Scritch. Scritch.

Even with the blanket over his ears he heard the sound. He hammered his heels against the shelf bed.

The dish bounced. His stomach would keep hurting until he counted the mice. He pushed the blanket away.

He reached out and grasped the top of the mouse cage. Resting his chin on the table, he closed his eyes and pulled the cage closer until the cold wires touched his forehead. Slowly he opened his eyes.

Shorty. Tiny. And the last mouse was under the shavings. Tyler poked a finger inside the cage. Nose twitching, Mouse Ears peeked up at him.

Tyler smiled.

"That's quite an outfit Mrs. Gleason is wearing," Grant said, his eyes intent on Nell as she stood talking to Walter Kondrat, another one of the poker players, on the far side of the bookstore. "I suppose it's suitable for a memorial dinner in Wisconsin."

"Your trouble, Holbrook, is that you've been hanging out too long with the trendy set. You're an arrogant snob." Maggie's voice was sharp, offended by his caustic remark.

Unlike Nell's usual attire of sweat suits, liberally dabbed with paint, or something from her vast collection of denim, she was wearing a black cotton ensemble consisting of a batwinged blouse with lace inserts, a midcalf, tiered lace skirt and black open-toed wedgies, bound to her feet by black hemplike ropes that snaked around her legs in a spiral. A small black bow was tucked into the salmon-tinted curls just above her ear.

Despite the gravity of the occasion, Maggie had to chuckle, tipping her head slightly to get the full effect. "The outfit suits Nell," she said. "She's an artist."

"Landscapes or poodles?" Grant asked.

"Lawyers are always quick to judge. You should keep a more open mind, Holbrook," Maggie said. "Nell is a splash painter."

"A what?"

"You know. Like Jackson Pollock."

"You're kidding."

He stared across the room, and she could see he was having trouble coming to grips with this revised vision of the woman he had taken to be an eccentric.

"I've only been in her studio a few times," Maggie said. "It's an experience. The floors are covered with several layers of old sailcloth she uses as tarpaulins. After she's prepped a canvas, she lays it in the center of the floor. She works on large surfaces. Usually six feet by eight feet. Then when she's all ready, she puts on some classic CDs. Her favorite is Pink Floyd's *The Wall*."

"Now I know you're kidding."

"The different paints are mixed in old coffee cans until they're just the right consistency. Then, with the music blaring, she moves around the canvas, hurling paint with long-handled brushes until she's satisfied."

Grant's eyes had a glazed look as she finished. "Is it a hobby or does she sell them?"

"She sold the last one for twenty thousand to a woman in Beaver Dam who wanted what she called a 'sofa-sized' painting to draw together all the colors in her living room."

"Good God Almighty!"

Grant stared at Maggie as if trying to decide if she was making the whole story up. When he saw she was serious, he bowed his head, placing a hand over his heart.

"My apologies to Mrs. Gleason and the entire state

of Wisconsin for my earlier cutting remarks," he said. "If Hamilton hadn't warned me to stay away from her, I'd go over and apologize."

"Ham's right," Maggie said, placing her hand on his arm. "Nell's as sharp as they come. She'd be the first one to suspect you aren't who you say you are."

"I'll remember that," he said. As he saw Doris Blessington heading in their direction, he wandered away.

Maggie followed him with her eyes. She'd been very aware of him over the last two days. He'd handled himself well at the wake yesterday, the memorial Mass this afternoon, and now the dinner at the bookstore. He'd kept a low profile, not intruding on the other mourners but speaking to them easily when they approached him.

She had worried initially that his intensity and the fact he was a stranger to the people in Delbrook would make him the focus of undue attention, but he blended in so easily that his presence barely raised a ripple of conjecture.

"I think George would be pleased," Doris Blessington said as she kissed Maggie's cheek and looked around the room. "The memorial Mass was very touching, and I'm sure he would have been delighted with the dinner here at the bookstore."

"I thought Jake would feel more comfortable here," Maggie said. "I can't take credit for the other arrangements. George had already done that."

"You don't say."

Doris leaned closer to Maggie, eyes glinting at the possibility of some tidbit of gossip. Her behavior didn't ruffle Maggie. The police chief's wife was known for her personality rather than her intelligence. An adorable child, a beautiful teenager and a handsome married woman, she had been flattered, pampered and protected all her life.

Since Doris was never required to be anything but decorative or entertaining, she found her calling in providing the latest in local news and rumor, reporting it without passing judgment or reveling in the transgressions of others. She didn't hesitate to disclose her own family's affairs, so people seldom took offense. On the other hand, they rarely shared secrets with her.

"After Mark died, George made all the decisions for his own funeral," Maggie said. "He told Father Cusick that he wanted a simple service and gave him a list of songs for the Mass. He'd arranged and paid for everything at the funeral home."

"How extraordinary," Doris said. "He must not have wanted you to have to deal with things after what you went through with Mark."

"A perfect example of George's thoughtfulness," Maggie said. "It really helped Jake to know that his grandfather had planned things and that we were carrying out his wishes."

The older woman's eyes filled with tears. "He was so very proud of Jake. This last year with you and the boy here in Delbrook made a great difference in George's life."

"I hope so," Maggie said, reaching in her pocket for a tissue, which she pressed into Doris's hand. "I wouldn't trade a moment of our time with him. For Jake's sake, as well as my own, I wish it hadn't come to such an abrupt ending."

She looked over at the children's room where Jake

and Kenny Rossiter had their heads together in a whispered conversation.

Oh damn! They're up to something, Maggie thought.

Under normal circumstances, she would have been quick to investigate, but after the last several days, she was expecting some rebellion or at least an emotional outburst to counter the somber atmosphere that had surrounded the boys.

The wake and the memorial Mass had been difficult for Jake, but now that the reality of his grandfather's death was beginning to sink in, he was accepting it better than she'd expected. Not that he hadn't loved George, but his grandfather's death was far less gut-wrenching than the major trauma of his father's death.

"I can see that Jake and the Rossiter boy are still thick as thieves."

"An apt comment, Doris. I was thinking much the same thing."

"The friendship has been good for both of them. Jake has brought Kenny out of his shell. When his mother left three years ago, Kenny was so withdrawn that it was worrisome."

"Does Kenny see his mother at all?" Maggie asked.

"No. No one knows where she went. She was here in Delbrook one day and then the next it was as if she'd been erased from the face of the earth. I never asked Hugh. I don't think anyone did."

"She was a local girl?"

"Yes. Her family lived just north of town. Julie Caldwell was a pretty young thing. Unfortunately she had such round heels I doubt if she could stand on the side of a hill without falling on her back. Everyone suspected she was carrying on behind Hugh's back. My guess is that she found someone who was better in bed."

"That must have been awful for Kenny."

"Hugh took Kenny to work with him. His landscaping business wasn't as successful then as it is now, so he had more time for the boy. Hugh said he hoped the physical chores around the nursery would keep Kenny busy and too tired to dwell on his loneliness. He'd been a solitary child, content to play by himself. Hugh provided the structure and the companionship when he needed it most."

Maggie scanned the room, spotting Hugh's curly head rising above the knot of men talking beside the bar set up in the café area. It was strange that she didn't really know more about him. He wasn't one to talk about his life. He was a physical man, comfortable doing things rather than discussing them. If she ever hoped to have any kind of continuing relationship, she'd have to get him to open up.

Suddenly Hugh looked up, catching her watching him. He didn't smile, but there was an intensity to his glance that warmed her. Then he turned back to Charley Blessington, who was speaking. By the gravity of the expressions, she suspected George's death was the subject of the conversation.

"Tully Jackson is still missing," Doris said.

The non sequitur threw Maggie for a moment. "I wondered if he'd turned up. Do you really think he would attack George?"

Doris shrugged. "Charley always thought he was a public nuisance. The man's been a thorn in his side for years. Said it didn't look good having someone like Tully hanging around town. Unfortunately he couldn't think of any legal way to get rid of him."

"How are you doing, Maggie?" Nell asked.

Maggie had been so absorbed in Doris's conversation that she hadn't seen Nell's approach, and her heart leaped at the voice so close to her ear.

"Don't sneak up on me like that," she said, patting her chest for emphasis. "You could give me a heart attack."

"You know, Nell," Doris said, "on anyone else that outfit might look a dash outré. On you, it has genuine flair."

"Being an artist of mature years has certain advantages," Nell said, patting her salmon curls. "I can wear what I damn well please, and people consider it eccentric rather than just plain peculiar."

"George would have appreciated your dressing up for the occasion," Maggie said. "Those shoes are definitely a work of art. How are your feet doing?"

"Not good." She made a face. "You know sneakers are more my speed. Unfortunately they didn't look right."

"Well, ladies, Charley's giving me the signal, so I better take my leave. Let me know, dear, if there's anything I can do."

Doris kissed Maggie on the cheek and walked over to join the men.

Nell leaned closer to whisper, "Did she have anything new to report?"

"No. Only that Charley and George had had what she called 'words' about a month ago and haven't been speaking. She didn't know what had caused the rift, but she said that luckily they had resolved it after dinner Saturday night, so that by the time the poker game started, they were back on friendly footing."

"Walter Kondrat was there, so I'll have to ask him if he knows what the fight was about," Nell said. "Typically male, however, he either won't have noticed or he'll tell me it was just a misunderstanding."

"Where is Walter?" Maggie asked. She glanced around the room, spotting the big man talking to Hamilton Rice on the far side of the dining room.

"I should have known he'd be with Ham," Nell said. "Rice doesn't look sixty-five. He was a good friend of my husband, you know. Once Ham moved down to Chicago, we didn't see that much of him. I always liked him. He's got a wicked sense of humor."

"Don't I know it," Maggie said. "I met him when I was first dating Mark, and he loved to tease me. We saw a lot of him when we lived in Chicago. Since Mark's death, only a couple times."

With his permanent tan and thatch of white hair, Ham was a good-looking man. He wasn't a great deal taller than Maggie was, but she thought of him as a big man with his broad shoulders, barrel chest and short but powerful legs. He moved with deliberation, walking with a rolling gait that got him to his destination without any appearance of haste.

His blue eyes twinkled out at the world from a nest of wrinkles. He had been George's oldest friend, and she was grateful that he had come to Delbrook to lend his support.

Nell's eyes narrowed as Grant Holbrook joined the

other two men. Her gaze was intense as she stared at Grant, who was bracketed by the two older men.

"I didn't get a chance to talk to that young man either yesterday or earlier in the evening," Nell said. "Walter just told me he's Mark's cousin. And he came all the way to Wisconsin for the funeral?"

"Yes." Maggie licked her dry lips. "He's related to George's wife."

"Edna?"

"Ham said he doesn't bear much of a family resemblance to Edna. She was not a handsome woman, I gather. Ham said Mark got his good looks from George's side of the family. I never knew Edna. She died when Mark was in his teens."

Maggie knew she was babbling, and she pressed her lips together to keep from blurting out any additional information.

"Yes," Nell said, her voice thoughtful. "One of those really nasty cancers. She was in a lot of pain for about a year. I used to stop by for a visit a couple times a week. To help her pass the time, I taught her to tat."

At Maggie's blank look, Nell rolled her eyes.

"It was a different age when I was growing up. Needlework, knitting, sewing were all considered necessary accomplishments for a young woman. Tatting, you ignorant child, is a form of lace making. You use a hand shuttle to weave delicate patterns that you can add as edging on a handkerchief or a tablecloth."

"I think I saw that demonstrated once on a PBS special."

Maggie tried to keep a straight face, but Nell caught the amusement in her voice and smacked her on the wrist. "You need to show a little more respect for your elders."

Maggie grinned an apology. "Mark never talked much about his mother. For that matter, neither did George."

"To be honest, Edna was only a presence in the household. She cooked, cleaned and sewed, making as little fuss as possible. I doubt if George ever paid her much mind. He was never unkind; he just never seemed to notice her. As far as he was concerned, her only real achievement was in giving birth to Mark."

"How sad," Maggie said.

"She was an unhappy and lonely woman. We really only got to know each other in that last year before she died. Not friends. Just two women talking."

Nell turned away from Maggie, her eyes resting on Grant. Maggie could feel the tension building up in the muscles across her back. She didn't know what was coming, but she didn't think she was going to like it.

"I don't know if you knew that Edna was from a little farming town in Minnesota." Nell's voice was soft but clear. "The summer she turned twenty, a tornado ripped through the town. It wiped out everything in its path."

"How awful," Maggie said.

"In those days there were no early warning signals, so the death toll was high." Nell stared at Grant, a calculating expression on her face. "The tornado killed everyone in Edna's family. When she came to Delbrook she was alone. She had no relatives. No family at all."

Maggie sucked in her breath at Nell's words.

"I know you're stunned," Nell said, bending close to

Maggie so she could whisper in her ear, "but the man is clearly an impostor."

"An impostor?"

"Don't be frightened, dear." Nell took hold of Maggie's elbow. "We'll work our way over to Charley Blessington. He'll know what to do about this. For all we know, Grant Holbrook could be the man responsible for George's death."

CHAPTER TEN

"GRANT HOLBROOK might not have killed George," Nell said, "but he is an impostor."

Maggie could not have spoken if her life depended on it. It was the very thing she had feared when Grant first concocted the charade. She could feel the rush of heat rising to paint her cheeks with guilty color under the intense scrutiny of the older woman.

"You're a party to this deception, Maggie?" Nell's grip tightened on her arm as she stared at Maggie in rising bewilderment.

"Yes. But. I-I . . ."

Before she could do more than stammer out a few words, Grant was beside her. He held out his hand as if he knew she was in need of support, and she grasped it with a sigh of relief at his rescue.

"George's wife Edna had no living relatives," she said, by way of explanation.

He faced Nell without flinching, one eyebrow lifted in amusement. "Then I assume you have already figured out that I am not one of Edna's shirttail relatives," he said.

"I see nothing funny about this subterfuge, Mr. Holbrook." She straightened her spine, lips pressed together in disapproval. "I don't want to create a scene, but I intend to speak to Chief Blessington about this situation."

"Don't get on your high horse, Nell." Hamilton Rice stepped into the space between Nell and Grant. "Not until you know more."

Ham's watery blue eyes crinkled in a tanned and leathery face. His voice wasn't deep but had a shivery warmth that made listeners believers. He opened his mouth as if he wanted to reassure her and was only waiting for her permission. Nell was unmoved by his charm.

"Don't con me, you old reprobate," she snapped. "Can any of you give me one good reason why I shouldn't denounce Mr. Holbrook?"

"I can," Grant said. He kept his voice low, words enunciated clearly. "I think George Collier was murdered and it was made to look like a robbery."

Nell's body jerked as if she'd taken a blow. Ham put his hand beneath her elbow and Maggie moved closer to steady her. Grant was all too aware of the people milling around the bookstore and knew that at any moment someone might realize that some drama was being played out in their midst. Despite that, he remained still, letting her focus her attention on him.

"I apologize for upsetting you," he said. "Both Maggie and Ham have had time to get used to this idea. I swear to you my impersonation is for a very good reason. I know it's a lot to ask, but do you suppose you could trust the three of us—all right, the two of them—until we have an opportunity to explain?"

"Please, Nell," Maggie said. "It's very important."

Grant wasn't sure what the older woman's decision would have been had Jake not chosen that particular moment to join the group. Nell's eyes softened as the young boy slipped his hand into his mother's and leaned his head against her arm.

"Kenny's going home, Mom."

Grant could see that the general exodus was beginning. Nell grimaced in indecision, but with one more glance at Jake, she sighed in obvious surrender.

"While your mom says goodbye to your grandfather's friends, Jake, why don't you and I keep Mr. Holbrook company?"

Grant could only smile as the older woman took hold of his arm and Jake's hand and led them, rather like recalcitrant children, to a circle of chairs in the teen section beneath the staircase. With a worried look over her shoulder, Maggie followed Ham Rice over to the people at the door.

Maggie's feet hurt from standing so long on the hardwood floors. Her mind was on rote as she bid people goodbye and thanked them for coming. As things slowed down, she looked around for Kim Shearman, who had been in charge of the buffet table. The heavy-set woman was carrying a cardboard box into the laundry room.

"Kim?" Maggie called, following the woman inside.

"Everything's all cleaned up, Maggie. Did everything go all right?"

"Wonderfully well. I just came back to thank you for helping out here tonight. George always said you did a fine job when you served them on poker nights."

A wide smile stretched Kim's mouth even as her eyes filled with tears. She set the box down on the top of the dryer, brushing at her eyes with a corner of her apron.

"They've been meeting at the club for the last twenty years. Ever since I was married. Your father-in-law was such a nice man," she said. "I still can't believe Tully Jackson stabbed him."

"The police don't know that for sure, Kim."

"Everyone was talking about it at the country club. It's real creepy that Tully ran off. He could be hiding anywhere around here. I'm that scared about going out to the parking lot at night. My husband drove me over here tonight and he's waitin' outside till I'm done."

"That's a good idea. No point in taking any chances until they find out what happened."

"Delbrook was always safe as a church picnic," Kim said. "It's like bizarre."

"I know what you mean," Maggie said. "Violent attacks happen in big cities, not in towns like this."

" 'Sides, Saturday night the card game was real quiet. Not like some weeks. Sometimes they'd fight all during the game and one of the players would just get so disgusted they'd throw stuff. You know, cards or chips. Nothing big."

"George said it could be a pretty noisy group."

"He should know. A couple a years ago, he was the worst of the lot." Kim snorted. "It was after your husband died. If you pardon my saying, George was drinkin' quite a bit in them days."

"That's what I heard. He didn't have much to drink on Saturday, did he?"

"No. He had a manhattan before dinner, but he didn't even finish it. Walter Kondrat was doin' the honors, if you know what I mean." Kim shook her head in disgust. "Between you and me, Mrs. Collier, Walter was really carrying a load."

Walter was a big man with a bushy mustache. He'd always reminded Maggie of a walrus, and she couldn't picture him staggering around drunk. Her amusement must have been apparent, because Kim lowered her voice, partially covering her mouth with the corner of her apron so her words wouldn't carry out to the bookstore.

"It ain't a pretty sight," she said. "Walter gets real feisty. Him and George had a nasty go-round after dinner."

"A fight?"

"Just words. Walter was real hot like. It happened right outside the ladies' room. That's how I heard it. Walter said it wasn't any of George's business."

"What wasn't?"

"I don't know. I missed that part," Kim said. "All I know is it was somethin' that George thought Walter should quit doing. He said it wasn't fair to anyone. Walter told George he better keep his mouth shut or he'd be asking for trouble. George said it was too late, she already knew."

"She?" Maggie asked, totally mystified.

Kim shrugged her shoulders. "I didn't hear anyone's name. Walter was getting madder and madder, and I got a little worried. I was just sure he was going to have a stroke and keel over. So I went back and flushed the toilet again just to let 'em know I was in the john. By the time I come out they was gone. I was that relieved."

"How strange. Walter never mentioned anything to me. Were they still fighting during the poker game?"

Kim shook her head. "When I got back to the dining room, George was pumpin' coffee into Walter, and by the time the cards were dealt, the booze had worn off a bit. It was a real quiet game. I was glad when George won the last pot."

"It was a grand way to end the day." Maggie patted Kim on the shoulder. "I'm sure you're tired and want to finish and go home. I appreciate your sharing your thoughts tonight. You've been very kind."

Kim picked up the box full of food trays and carried it over to the back door where she already had a stack of things.

"Let me help you," Maggie said.

She opened the back door and waved to Kim's husband, who was leaning on the side of his truck talking to Frank Woodman, the manager of the country club, who'd arranged everything for the buffet supper. The men hurried over and piled the bags and boxes into the pickup, and Kim and her husband drove away.

"You look tired, Maggie," Frank said. "Everything all right?"

"I'm pretty beat, but I'm glad I found you. I wanted to say thanks for making this such a lovely evening."

"It's the least I can do. You know how sorry I am about George." He took her hand and, after a moment of hesitation, leaned over and kissed her cheek. "You warm enough?"

Maggie nodded. It was a beautiful September night. Indian summer-like with a clear, almost cloudless sky.

"Who would have thought we'd have to be afraid in Delbrook?" Frank said.

"A sign of the times. Every time I turn on the news I get more frightened for Jake's safety. Gang attacks. Home invasions. School shootings." Even the words frightened her. Shivering, she took a deep breath of the fresh air. "It's hard to even think of violence on a night like this."

"Too true. " Frank smoothed a hand over the top of his graying hair. "I just wish I knew what happened. I've gone over and over everything with Charley, and I'm just utterly mystified."

Maggie didn't know Frank well. She'd seen him around town and when she'd gone to the country club. Tall, somewhat gaunt with even features, but nothing that set him apart. George had described him as competent and efficient. The kind of man who could be counted on to do his work with little complaint and retire after years of service without leaving much of a legacy behind.

"Did you play poker Saturday night?" she asked.

"Just for a little while. Brent Prentice was stuck at home, waiting for a long-distance call. Connie asked if I'd sit in until he arrived." Frank stared up at the sky, his voice contemplative. "By the time Brent got there at nine I was looking for any excuse to get out of the game."

"Losing your shirt?"

"No. Everyone seemed out of sorts. Walter was sulking for some reason, and Hugh Rossiter and Charley

Blessington got into an argument over Camp Delbrook."

"The camp?" Maggie asked.

"I don't know if you're aware that there's going to be a massive rehab of the camp this year. Right after the fall cleanup. They're going to modernize a lot of the cottages and the main buildings. The mews is one of the buildings up for rehabbing. Hugh was furious that he hadn't been consulted, because the birds get upset pretty easily and there was barely enough time to move them to temporary quarters."

"Why wasn't Hugh told earlier?" Maggie asked.

"Well, according to Hugh, Charley Blessington is on the board of directors and deliberately kept him in the dark so that one of Charley's cronies would get the contract, which included new landscaping. Saturday night, Hugh made a couple of comments about political influence, and Charley got on his high horse." Frank chuckled. "Hugh has lived in Delbrook all his life, and of course the chief's friend moved here from Illinois last year. You know how the folks around here feel about that."

"I was lucky when I moved from Chicago. Since my mother had lived here and George was a resident, I wasn't considered a carpetbagger."

"Illinois residents get blamed for a lot of the tourist troubles. The locals think they come to Wisconsin and use up the natural resources and screw up the environment. In truth, the nonresidents put millions of dollars into the economy that helps us maintain our parks and tourist attractions."

"You should run for mayor," Maggie said.

He reddened slightly. "Connie Prentice is talking to the Lakeshore party about drafting me for the next election. She's trying to convince me to accept."

"I think you'd be an excellent mayor. You certainly do a fine job running the country club, so how much different could it be to run the town?"

Maybe Frank wasn't flashy, but he would certainly be an asset to the town council. The people who worked at the club appeared contented with his leadership, and he dealt with the guests graciously without being dogmatic or obsequious.

"If Connie's in favor of it, you know Brent will back you," Maggie said.

"He owes me big time for the night of the poker game. He missed dinner, but I had the kitchen hold a plate for him. You know how fussy he is about his schedule. Once he'd eaten he was in better spirits, but by that time he'd ticked off Connie and she'd left in a huff."

"These poker players must be a cantankerous lot. Although I heard it was a quiet game until George won the final jackpot."

"The group gets a little ornery sometimes, but they manage to work it out." Frank chuckled. "I'm glad George won, but even that was strange. He rarely bluffs, so when he just kept betting, everyone dropped out. In my opinion, George wasn't bluffing, he was distracted and forgot he was holding only two pair."

"Why was George distracted?"

"I'm not sure. He'd been upbeat, showing off those photos of Jake's birthday party. He passed them around the table, and we all had a good laugh. There was a lot of reminiscing about kids and parties during dinner and even in the early part of the poker game. I was sitting across from George when I noticed how still he was."

Maggie leaned against the door frame as she listened to Frank.

"His face was pale and his mouth was pulled tight as if he were in pain. I thought he was having a heart attack. Suddenly he pulls the pile of pictures out and stares at the top one as if something has struck him. He looks up and catches my eye. Shaking his head, he stuffs the photos into his jacket and picks up the newly dealt poker hand."

"Those were the birthday pictures?"

"Yes," Frank said. "He plays several more hands, and he appears to have shaken off what was troubling him. I was still concerned, so I kept an eye on him, although this time I didn't let him catch me at it. About ten minutes later, George pulls the photos out of his pocket again, stares at the top one and then slowly flips through the rest. He stops once more about halfway through, then shuffles them together and puts them back in his pocket."

Maggie's nerves hummed with excitement. What had George seen in the pictures? Was it possible that Grant's premise was correct and that George had seen Tyler in one of the pictures?

"Did George say anything?"

"He said he needed to make a phone call. The group was ready for a break at that point, so there was a lot of milling around. When the game started again, he seemed in better spirits but was quieter than usual," Frank said. "I wondered if the earlier reminiscing had gotten him thinking about Mark. I couldn't help but notice, when I was looking at the photos, how much Jake resembles his father. My thought was that George was feeling Mark's loss and that was why he was so distracted during the card game."

"It's possible, I suppose," Maggie said. "I wish I'd seen the pictures."

"Don't you have them?"

"No. All of George's things were sent to the police lab. Charley gave me a list of what they had, but the photographs weren't on it. I've asked around, but nobody seems to know what happened to them. I don't suppose George left them at the club."

"Not that I'm aware of. I'll check with the dining room staff, but if anyone found them, they'd turn them in to me." Frank patted her arm. "They've probably just been misplaced. They'll probably turn up once things settle down."

Maggie wasn't convinced of that. If what Grant had suggested was true, Maggie suspected the photographs had already been destroyed.

"Would you like something to drink, Mrs. Gleason?" Grant asked. "I think Ham has the front door covered, and Maggie's got the back."

He caught a flash of amusement in Nell's eyes and felt some encouragement. She hadn't denounced him when she first discovered the deception, but he didn't fool himself that the main crisis had been averted. She was a smooth old gal. It had only been postponed.

"Could I have a Coke, Aunt Nell?" Jake asked. "Kenny and I only had one before dinner."

"You can think of this as a test," Grant said.

Nell sniffed. "One Coke for Jake. Make mine brandy. A double."

Grant poured the drinks, handed them out and sat down again. Although the older woman's attention was focused on Jake, he knew she was aware of his every move, assessing him as he talked to the boy.

"Your mother says you like to fish. Did you do any fishing when you lived in Chicago?"

"A couple times my dad took me. We didn't catch anything. I kept getting my hook stuck." He took several long sips of his Coke, then carefully set the glass on one of the tables from the café area. "Mom packed us a big lunch, and we sat on these huge rocks and watched the boats go in and out of the harbor."

"I know where you were. That's one of my favorite spots for boat watching. Which do you like better? Sailboats or motorboats?"

"Motorboats." He blew through his lips, a sputtering engine sound. "The sailboats are way too slow. The best part was when a monster sailboat almost smashed on the rocks. That would have been cool. But it didn't."

"Now I see why reality TV shows are so popular with the young male set," Nell said. "The more carnage, the better the ratings."

"Think it's the testosterone?" Grant asked.

Despite herself, Nell chuckled. "That and shit for brains," she said under her breath.

At the unexpected comment, Grant inhaled part of his drink. He coughed several times to catch his breath, but when Maggie and Ham arrived, his eyes were tearing and he was still sucking in air.

"Really, Nell, you don't have to kill the man," Ham

said with a quick glance at the amusement on the older woman's face.

"I'm OK," Grant managed to gasp out. "Everyone gone?"

"Yes," Ham said. "I hope you don't mind, Nell, but I told Walter I'd take you home later since I haven't had a chance to talk to you."

"How about a nightcap?" Maggie said. "It's getting late and Jake is itching to get out of his dress-up clothes."

"Mom made me wear my new school shoes," he said, raising his legs straight out so they could inspect his shoes.

"Very good looking," Ham said in admiration. "That's a dynamite shine."

"Grampa helped me pick them out." Jake's lip quivered.

"Time for bed, honey," Maggie said, walking over to the counter where she'd left her purse. It wasn't on the shelf. She looked around in growing bewilderment.

"Problem, kiddo?" Ham said.

"I can't find my purse," she said.

"Are you sure you left it here?"

"Yes," she answered shortly.

"What's it look like?" Grant said, joining them along with Nell and Jake.

"It's navy blue with three gold X's."

The group fanned out, searching the bookstore.

"I found it," Jake yelled from the bathroom.

Maggie hurried over to find him picking up the items that were spread out on the floor beside the washbasin.

"You probably left it on the sink and someone knocked it off," Nell said.

"Nice work, Jake," Maggie said. She took the purse and kissed him on top of the head. "Now say your goodnights and I'll tuck you in."

Upstairs, she helped Jake get into his pajamas and then sent him in to wash. Picking up her purse from the nightstand, she carried it out to the kitchen. She hadn't wanted to make an issue of it, but she knew with a certainty that she had left her purse on the shelf under the counter not in the bathroom.

Opening the clasp, she checked to see if her wallet was inside. It was there and so was the fifty dollars she had placed in the bill compartment. Lipstick, comb, handkerchief and other odds and ends.

At the funeral home she had placed the sympathy cards in her purse as she left. She pulled them out and noticed that each of the envelopes had been opened. The list of George's effects that had been given to her at the hospital had been taken out of the zippered pocket where she'd placed it.

Someone had taken her purse into the bathroom to search it.

Her hands shook as she put everything back inside. It gave her a sick feeling knowing that someone had touched her things. Who had taken her purse, and more importantly, what were they looking for?

"What you're asking me to believe," Nell Gleason said, "is that George's death was actually a premeditated murder committed by someone who was at the country club on Saturday night?"

"That's exactly what we're trying to explain to you," Ham said.

The voices drifted up the curved staircase from the bookstore as Maggie stood in the doorway to the second-floor apartment. Sliding her hand along the smooth oak banister, she walked partway down, then sat on the steps. Resting her forehead against one of the stair posts, she looked between the spindles at the group seated at the round mahogany table in the main room of the bookstore.

Grant leaned back in the captain's chair across from Nell, with Ham between them facing an empty chair.

Grant raised his head, the only one aware of her presence. His eyes were steady on hers, but she could read nothing in the dark brown gaze.

"If you believe that the killer was not a passing stranger, but someone in Delbrook, why haven't you gone to the police?" Nell's voice was shrill with indignation. "Why in God's name are you keeping this secret?"

"For the simple reason, Nell, that we don't know who committed the murder." Grant turned his full attention on the older woman, but Maggie realized much of what he said was for her benefit. "For all we know, someone on the police force may be the person who attacked George."

"You don't mean someone," Nell said. "You mean Charley Blessington."

Her words were met by silence. Nell's mouth pulled into a tight line of alarm as she swung her gaze between the two men. Maggie must have made some sound, because her friend turned her head and saw her sitting on the stairs.

"Dear God, Maggie, is this what you believe too?"

"I don't know what I believe." She rose to her feet and continued down the stairs to join the group. "It's only just dawned on me that this whole situation is so far out of my understanding that I feel as if I've just fallen down the rabbit hole. And I'm very frightened."

Ham stood up and came around the table to meet her at the bottom of the steps. He opened his arms, and she stepped into his embrace, feeling an immediate easing of the fear and confusion that had surrounded her since George's death. She felt as if the cavalry had arrived.

"I've barely had a chance to say hello to you," Maggie said, kissing his tanned cheek. "I'm so glad you're here. This is a god-awful mess."

Ham gave her a reassuring hug, then released her. "Jake's asleep?" he asked, jerking his head toward the second floor.

"Yes. I sat with him for a while after he dozed off to make sure. I don't want him hearing any of this. He's got enough to manage just dealing with George's death."

"Agreed."

Maggie stepped closer and spoke for Ham's ears only. "Can we believe this man?"

He looked over her shoulder, his eyes assessing Grant, then returning to Maggie.

"Yes," he said. "Grant and I have mutual friends who vouch for him. He may be a bit uptight and anal, but he's got a reputation for being honest and ethical."

"That's high praise for a lawyer," she said. "He has his moments of charm, but I don't think he trusts me any more than I trust him."

"If you'd hit me in the head with a canoe paddle, I might be a bit standoffish, too," Ham said, a wide smile accompanying the raising of his eyebrows.

"That was before I even knew him," she said. "I've been tempted to hit him again every time he brings it up. He's a bully. He's got his own agenda, and he's trying to guilt me into following it."

Ham's eyes were serious as he stared across the room at Grant. "He's hurting, kiddo. Like you and Jake, he's sustained a hellava loss."

Maggie sighed. "I hate it that you're right, Ham. I'll try to be less hostile and hope he's worthy of the consideration."

"Since I got here yesterday, we've talked a fair amount, and I'm getting a feel for who he is. He's the kind of man who doesn't like to delegate. If he had his way, he would have come up and nosed around on his own. Instead, you and I know who he is and what he's looking for, and now Nell is questioning him. It shook him up that she uncovered his charade so easily. He believes you and I have motivation for covering for him, but he doesn't know about her."

She turned her body until she had a good view of Grant. He was listening to Nell, his expression fixed in what Maggie thought of as his lawyer look. His expression was attentive, his brown eyes absorbed in observing every movement, yet despite his stillness, she suspected his mind was buzzing with decisions to be made.

It was interesting to watch him without being the object of his scrutiny. Despite his scar, Grant was a handsome man.

After years of dealing with Mark's infidelities, Maggie was less susceptible than most to the automatic confidence engendered by a good-looking face. Mark had used his appearance to manipulate and persuade. With a calculated look, he tried, usually successfully, to burrow deep into her emotions to get what he wanted. Worst of all, he had been able to lie with an ease that left her shaken in her own ability to judge character.

"What was your gut reaction when you first heard his story?" Ham asked. "Did you believe him?"

"Not at first," she said. "Even now, I don't want to believe him, but the more I hear the more I'm beginning to think his premise is correct. He's very compelling. When I listen to him I'm convinced that the story is true. It's only when I get away from him that it seems too bizarre. What do you think?"

Ham looked thoughtful.

"I have absolutely no doubt that he believes what he's telling us. The question that comes to mind is why he's so convinced that Tyler could be in Delbrook. I think we need to examine the entire picture so we know exactly which pieces are missing."

Maggie followed him back to the table, sitting in the empty chair beside Nell. The older woman reached out and squeezed her hand.

"I don't know what to make of all this, dear," she said. "So much to take in."

While Maggie had been upstairs with Jake, Grant and Ham had told Nell about Tyler's disappearance and the call from George that had brought Grant to Delbrook. It was clear that Nell was upset by the awful revelations, but she appeared to be taking the whole thing in stride. Whether it was her age or her personality, Nell had a capacity to listen without making judgments, keeping her mind open to even the most outrageous of theories.

"There's something that has been bothering me, Grant," Ham said as he sat down. "After George called me asking about the missing child, I did a bit of checking into the case. I went online and downloaded a lot of the articles in the Cleveland papers about Tyler's disappearance. It was grim but fascinating reading. What I'm wondering is why you haven't mentioned the other kidnappings."

"Other kidnappings?" Maggie asked.

The jagged scar stood out as the muscles rippled along Grant's jaw. From the glare he shot Ham, it was obvious that he wanted to discuss only George's death and his nephew's kidnapping.

"Well, Mr. Holbrook," Nell said. "If you expect us to give you any further help, you need to come clean."

Grant's head was bowed, his face in shadow. It intrigued Maggie that he had an ability to sit motionless without the usual nervous twitches others had when they were in a quandary. As a lawyer he would have learned to take a quick assessment of his options and then choose the one most suited to the situation.

"You're right," he said. He raised his head, his lips pursed as if his decision to speak had left a bad taste in his mouth. "When Tyler was taken we assumed it was by some kind of sexual predator."

Maggie shivered at the words. She wondered if she'd ever again look at the world the same. Delbrook had been a safe haven, but in the last twenty-four hours an evil presence had invaded the town. Like a child, she wanted to cover her ears but forced herself to listen to Grant's words.

"My sister and brother-in-law thought it was some local molester," he continued, "and that if we found him, Tyler would be returned. As a lawyer I've seen too much to be that sanguine. I was aware that after four or five days the chances of a quick solution to any case are poor. It was only later in the investigation that we discovered what we were up against."

Grant paused.

"The kidnapping fit a very specific pattern. It had happened before. In another city. In another state. Two other children had been taken in circumstances similar to Tyler's."

"Were the children found?" Nell asked the question that Maggie was too afraid to ask.

Grant didn't speak for a moment, and when he did, it was apparent he was upset.

"The boy was located and returned to his parents. The girl was found, but it was too late. She was dead."

CHAPTER ELEVEN

"ONE OF THE CHILDREN DIED? Murdered?" Nell's question was a horrified whisper.

"The girl was dead, but there was no hard evidence to prove it was murder." Grant bit off the words.

In his own mind, he had always considered it murder. If the child hadn't been kidnapped, she wouldn't have died.

"Why the hell didn't you tell me about the other children when you first told me about Tyler?" Maggie asked.

Maggie's face was flushed with anger and her hands were clenched on the edge of the table.

"I wanted to keep it simple," he said.

"You thought if I was sympathetic to your story about your nephew, I wouldn't go to the police," Maggie said.

Grant shrugged at her accusation. He could feel the stillness of Hamilton and Nell but ignored them, focusing all his attention on Maggie.

"Tyler is my first priority. I will do whatever I can. Use any trick, any subterfuge to get the information I need to find him."

His temper threatened to overpower his common

sense. He inhaled slowly through his nose to get his breathing back under control.

"Consider my position, for God's sake! When I left Chicago, I didn't know if George had kidnapped Tyler. I'd briefly checked on both George and Hamilton, but I still didn't know if either of them were law-abiding citizens. It occurred to me that they might be working some kind of scam to get the reward. Hell, for all I knew, they could have been the kidnappers."

"Once you understood that George wasn't involved," she said, "you could have told me."

"I'm a lawyer. I don't trust anyone. Once it became clear that you knew nothing about George's phone call to Hamilton, I felt reasonably comfortable telling you about Tyler's disappearance."

"But not everything," she said, her mouth thinned into a bitter line.

"Be fair, Maggie." He spoke directly to her, his voice soft. "Would you have held something back?"

She refused to meet his eyes, her head bent and her gaze fixed on the surface of the table.

"Yes," came the grudging reply.

Silence filled the room, but this time the edge of tension had dissipated slightly.

"All right, children," Ham said, "if you're done spitting, maybe we could move on. If we're going to get anywhere, we need, as the Gen Xers say, to be on the same page. Why don't I tell you what I've been able to find out, and Grant can fill in the blanks?"

Grant was grateful to be out of the spotlight. He was too close to the story. For twenty months he'd lived with the guilt that Tyler's disappearance was his fault. The boy was never out of his thoughts. In the daytime he could bury his emotions in work, but when he slept, his nightmares were filled with every kind of psychological and physical abuse of the boy.

Ham pulled a small notebook out of his pocket and flipped through several pages.

"Four years ago, a child disappeared from a movie theater in Detroit. His name was Eddie Harland, and he was five years old," he said. "No witnesses to a struggle. No ransom note. The kid's folks didn't have a lot of dough. They both worked to support Eddie and his two younger brothers. It was assumed that the boy had been kidnapped by a child molester."

"Eddie was at a movie? By himself?" Maggie asked. "Didn't anyone see anything?"

"No," Grant interrupted. "He was with his mother and his brothers. It happened when the show ended. The lights in the theater were still low. His mother was carrying the youngest and holding the hand of the middle child. Eddie was holding his brother's hand. When they got outside the theater and his mother discovered Eddie was missing, she went back inside to see if she could find him. It couldn't have been more than five minutes before she panicked and called for security. Just five minutes, but Eddie was gone."

Maggie's hand flew up to cover her mouth, and then she looked across the table at Grant. He could feel her reaction as if it were a physical thing.

"It makes me almost sick to my stomach to hear this," she said. "Every mother has probably had one of those moments when she loses contact with her child. First you can't believe it, and then, when you do, you're so shocked that you're almost paralyzed. After that, the panic sets in."

"That's exactly what my sister said when Tyler was taken," Grant said. "Barbara was so careful, and yet in the blink of an eye he was gone. Even when she started to search, she thought he had wandered away. Or was hiding."

Originally, when he'd told Maggie the story of Tyler's kidnapping, fear and horror had been her basic reactions. Once he explained his theory about George's murder, he could feel her resistance and resentment.

When he and Hamilton had arrived yesterday at the funeral home for the wake, Grant had caught the hint of hostility that accompanied Maggie's greeting. His presence in Delbrook frightened her. Without his story of kidnapping and murder, she would have accepted the fact that George had been accidentally killed in a botched robbery.

Grant felt some sympathy for Maggie's preferring to cast a blind eye to the presence of evil in her life. From what little he knew of her, until the tragic death of her husband, she had probably led the relatively uncomplicated life of a suburban wife and mother in Chicago. She was unprepared for the world of deception and danger that she found herself in.

Despite their mutual antipathy, he had been drawn to her from the beginning. He needed to fight any involvement. She represented a distraction to the focus and detachment required if he hoped to get to the bottom of this latest twist in Tyler's disappearance.

Only Tyler matters. He repeated the phrase in his mind, then turned his thoughts back to the discussion.

"The police investigated Eddie's disappearance thoroughly," Ham said, "but couldn't find a trace of the boy or any viable suspects."

"You said they found the first child. That was Eddie?" Nell asked Grant.

"Yes. Exactly one year from the day he was kidnapped in Detroit, Eddie was discovered in a Cineplex in Toledo, Ohio. The show was over, and the cleanup crew found him sitting all alone in the empty theater."

"Was he hurt?" Maggie asked.

Grant wasn't sure how to answer the question.

"According to what I read in the newspaper archives," Ham interjected, "Eddie was in excellent health. He was clean, physically fit and looked to have been well cared for during the year he was missing."

"One of the details omitted from most reports," Grant said, "was that Eddie was dressed in brand-new clothes: shirt, pants, underwear, shoes and socks. The movie theater was in a mall, and the clothes had been purchased that day. The police found the labels in a trash container in the men's room closest to the lobby of the theater."

"Fingerprints?" Nell asked.

Grant shook his head.

"The child was five when he was taken and was kept for a year?" Maggie asked.

"Yes. Exactly a year," Grant said.

"At six," she continued, "he would have been able to tell the police what happened to him, and despite the fact he was taken from Detroit and returned in Toledo, he should have been able to give the police enough information to conceivably pinpoint where he had been held. Maybe even who had kidnapped him."

When neither Ham nor Grant made any comment, she raised her head, glancing from one to the other, her eyebrows drawn together in question.

"When Eddie was found he couldn't speak," Grant said.

"Couldn't?" Nell leaned forward, her eyes intent. "Couldn't or wouldn't?"

"According to the doctors it's a matter of semantics." Grant clipped his words to hold back the emotion that swamped him when he thought about what trauma might have caused the child to go mute. "Nothing was wrong with the boy. Everything necessary for speech was intact. They examined him extensively and could find no physical reason for his inability to speak. Psychologically was another case altogether."

"When they examined him, did they find any indications of abuse?" Maggie bit her lip, waiting for the answer.

Grant spoke directly to her. "No. No bruises, broken bones, scars or any sign that he had been sexually abused. Aside from the fact that the boy was speechless, Eddie Harland was in better shape than when he disappeared."

Ham shifted restlessly in his chair.

"Eddie was returned three years ago. He's nine now," he said. "I picked up much of the basic story in a fast search on the Internet, but the one thing I didn't find was what the boy had to say when he finally broke his silence."

"Nothing," Grant said.

There was pain in the single word, Maggie thought as she looked at the man who until two days ago she'd never met. Grant took several deep breaths, as if to cover the break in his control.

"The parents refused to let the police see the boy after he was returned," Grant said. "They were grateful that he'd been returned to them, as they put it, 'undamaged.' They refused to let the police interview him. Then or later. Even after the second child was taken and the connection was made between the two cases, the parents denied all requests. And after Tyler, they refused again."

"Did Eddie ever speak?" Maggie asked.

Grant shook his head. "He began to talk shortly after he was returned. I got that information through a contact with the school Eddie attended. The principal obviously couldn't give me access to the child. All she would say was that, as far as she knew, he had never spoken about the year that he was missing."

Maggie pushed back from the table, her mind full of compassion for the child and his parents. Chilled, she rubbed her hands over her arms.

"I know how I'd feel if Jake was kidnapped. I'd feel enormous guilt that I had failed to protect him. Then the only thing that would matter would be to help him return to a normal life. I wouldn't let anyone near him to stir up memories of pain or fear." As she noticed the others looking at her, she shrugged. "Sure, I know it's big-time denial. But I wouldn't care. Only Jake would matter."

"I understand what you're saying, Maggie," Nell said, "but there's bound to be some payback for the psychological damage. Maybe not now, but what will happen in the coming years? I think Eddie's parents are making a major mistake."

"I do too," Maggie said, "but in a case like this, what does anyone know? Just in dealing with Jake after his father's death, I felt out of my depth, knowing when to push and when to back off. God knows what kind of resources Eddie's parents have to help them cope."

She stood up, too restless to remain seated. Walking around the bookstore, she touched the backs of the books, needing the tactile sensation of familiar and non-threatening objects. Just talking about Jake had brought her fear for him close. She wanted to distance herself from the intensity of the emotions around the table. She reached out a hand to the poster that had been brought over from the funeral home and was now suspended on an easel beside the front door.

Jake had made the poster from pictures they had gathered the day after George died. Maggie and Nell had helped him make a collage. He had laboriously cut and pasted the photos onto the thick posterboard until he was satisfied that it gave a good representation of his grandfather's life and interests.

The center picture had been taken the year before Mark died. The perfect family, she thought, staring at the smiling foursome. George was in the middle, holding Jake, while Mark and Maggie stood on either side, separated by only a few feet and yet worlds apart.

Her lips quivered as she fought back tears. Two of the four are gone. Please, God, keep Jake safe.

"Tell us about the second child," Maggie said, without turning around.

"The next child was from Minneapolis," Ham said,

picking up the story. "Her name was Noreen Flood. She was four years old. She disappeared from the Minnesota Zoo almost three years ago."

"How soon after the boy was found?" Nell asked.

"A month later," Ham said. "Eddie was returned in October, and Noreen was taken in November." He closed the notebook and continued. "One year from the day she was kidnapped, Noreen's body was discovered at the Milwaukee County Zoo in the moat around Monkey Island."

"Did she fall in? Did anyone see her?" Nell's questions ripped out in her impatience for answers.

"Her body was discovered by a security guard," Ham said. "It was late at night, and the zoo was closed. Despite extensive publicity, no one came forward to say they had seen or heard anything."

Maggie could hear Ham flip the pages of the notebook and waited for him to continue.

"According to the coroner's report, Noreen Flood died after midnight. The cause of death was listed as accidental drowning. There was evidence that she had climbed over the bar and across the grass which left stains on the knees of her blue jeans."

"No signs of abuse?" Nell asked.

Grant shook his head. "None. Like Eddie, the girl was extraordinarily healthy and unmarked by abuse either physical or sexual."

"Her clothes?" Ham asked. "New?"

"Yes. Once again they found the packaging, labels and tags in the men's room near the monkey exhibit."

"Men's room would indicate that whoever took the kids was male," Ham said.

"Most probably," Grant said. "Noreen's hair was cut

short like a boy. These days fathers are so involved with their children it's not unusual for a man to take a small girl into the men's room. It would be far less noticeable than if he tried to accompany her into the ladies' room."

Maggie touched one of the pictures on the poster, her finger sliding across the slick surface. George was pushing Jake on the swing in Wolfram Park. Behind them were the faces of other children, playing happily on the other playground equipment. How far away it seemed from the subject under discussion.

"Noreen died in November, and Tyler was taken in December," Grant said. "Once we knew about the other two cases, we began to hope that he would be returned at the end of the year. The anniversary day came and went with no sign of Tyler. In the opinion of the police, the fact that he was not returned suggested that he might be dead."

"Did you believe that?" Ham asked.

"I couldn't accept it. Neither my sister, Barbara, nor her husband believe it either. We don't talk about it now, but until we have hard evidence, we keep the hope alive."

Maggie remained beside the poster but angled her body until she could see all three of the people around the table. Grant's head was bent, his body sunk against the back of his chair. His hands gripped the wooden arms, and even at a distance she could see the white skin across his knuckles.

Except for an occasional slip, Grant kept his emotions under control, but she could hear the underlying pain in his tone of voice. His attempt to cover his agony caught at her heart. How often had he paced the floor at night? Awakened in a sweat? Visualized the circumstances in which his nephew existed?

Grant coughed, releasing his hold on the arms of the chair.

"You can imagine how I felt when I first got Hamilton's phone call. If there was even the slightest chance that George knew where Tyler was, I had to find out."

"What I still don't understand is how you know it's the same person who is taking the children?" Maggie asked.

"According to the police reports," Grant said, "there are enough similarities between the three cases that they believe it's the work of one man."

"That might be true of the first two cases, but not in Tyler's disappearance." Ham's voice was sharp as he confronted Grant. "In your nephew's case, a child is missing. Thousands of children are missing every year. Since you have such total confidence that it's the work of one man, you've got to be holding out a significant piece of evidence. What connects Tyler to the other two?"

For several seconds, Grant didn't move, then he sighed and released a slow stream of air. With a shudder, he pushed himself upright, propping his elbows on the table, his fingers tented beneath his chin. He gave Hamilton and Nell a quick glance and raised his head to look across the room at Maggie. Even though his eyes were in shadow, she could read the decision in his face. He had decided to tell them whatever it was that he'd been holding back.

"After Eddie Harland was taken, the police searched the movie theater. Aside from the usual trash, they found only one thing out of the ordinary. An eagle feather."

"An eagle feather? Now that's something I didn't hear about," Ham said. "And the girl? Noreen?"

"Noreen's parents were divorced. She was at the Minnesota Zoo with her father. It was the day after Thanksgiving, so the place was crowded. Noreen and her father were in the main Asian Tropics building. In the nocturnal tunnel the Asian animals are in lighted habitats behind glass windows set into the wall. The viewing room is illuminated along the floor."

Maggie had taken Jake to the Brookfield Zoo and the Lincoln Park Zoo in Chicago, so she was familiar with comparable layouts and could picture the scenario.

"Noreen and her father were about halfway into the exhibit when someone screamed. A white mouse was loose and scuttling along the floor, sending the people scrambling to get out of the way. In the general stampede, Noreen was separated from her father. Security was called, but she was nowhere to be found."

"Judas!" Ham smacked the arm of his chair with a tight fist. "This sick bastard has big brass ones to take such a chance."

"According to the police, the higher the risk, the more the kidnapper gets off on it if he succeeds." Grant's mouth was a grim line. "The police searched the exhibit and found a few things of possible interest, but then they hit the jackpot."

"Let me guess," Ham said. "An eagle feather?"

"On the nose. It might have gone unnoticed except for a very sharp-eyed detective who had a friend working the task force in Detroit. She had told him about Eddie's kidnapping and shared more than she should have. Although she knew they were keeping certain information out of the newspapers, she told him about the eagle feather."

Maggie felt the rise of tension in the room and knew exactly what Grant was going to tell them. He looked across at her and gave a single nod, his mouth curved into a smile that had little to do with humor.

"And yes, you've guessed correctly," he said. "When Tyler was taken from the department store, on the floor beneath the clothing rack he'd been hiding in, the police found an eagle feather."

Even though she'd been expecting Grant's words, Maggie felt goose bumps rise across her skin. Nell sagged back in her chair, and Ham let out a slow stream of air as if he'd been holding his breath.

"I think we could use a break," Grant said.

Nell reached for the pitcher of water in the center of the table and refilled the glasses, raising her own and drinking thirstily. Ham took the opportunity to locate the bathroom. Grant pushed his chair back, the legs scraping on the hardwood floor. He stood up, rolling his shoulders to loosen the tension in his back and neck, then picked up one of the water glasses and brought it over to Maggie.

"I like the pictures," he said, nodding his head toward the poster.

"Jake put it together. I think it gave him an outlet for his grief to be able to focus on the good times."

"I didn't get a chance to look at it during the wake." Grant leaned closer, his eyes scanning the pictures. "Your father-in-law had a lot of interests. Family. Fishing with Hamilton. The poker group. What's this?"

The photograph was one of George holding a hawk

on his gloved hand. Maggie smiled at the wary expression on her father-in-law's face.

"That was taken last fall when he went with Hugh Rossiter on a hunt sponsored by the falconry club. He told me later that he refused to make eye contact with the bird because he was convinced it would take it as a signal to attack him and peck his eyes out."

"A falconry club?" Grant asked. "Here in Delbrook?"

"Yes. George wasn't a member, but some of his friends were. There's a picture of the group somewhere on here." Maggie scanned the poster, finding the photo close to the bottom. "For a small town it's a good-sized club. Six members. Charley Blessington and Connie are pretty active in the club, and Hugh Rossiter is the master falconer."

"Half of the poker group," Grant said.

Maggie started in surprise and took a closer look at the photo.

"Where do they meet?" he asked.

"Over at Hugh's place on the south side of the lake. At least that's where they keep some of the birds. Hugh converted one of the buildings into a mews and a clinic."

"With a veterinarian?"

"No. Most vets don't work on wild birds. Falconers for the most part take care of their own birds. It's a pretty intense sport."

"Is Walter Kondrat a member?" Grant asked.

Maggie glanced quickly at Nell, but the older woman was holding a low-voiced conversation with Ham on the far side of the room.

"No. Walter's only interests, outside of work, are

poker and Nell. Not always in that order. Nobody knows how Nell feels."

"Who are the other three in the picture?"

"Lorraine Pickard is the woman on the left. Last year she moved to an Indian reservation in Minnesota to work on an agricultural project. I know it sounds loony, but it was something about birth control for chickens. Next to her is Mike Offenlach. He owns a body shop over on Cumberland." She tapped the face of the last man in the picture. "You might have met Brian Harper at the wake last night. He's into computers and kids. He's got six children already, and he said once that he's hoping to field an entire baseball team."

Grant studied the picture as she identified each person, then scanned the rest of the photos on the posterboard.

"Your father-in-law seems to have led a very full life. I'm sorry I never met him. His friends had a lot of nice things to say about him at the wake and earlier tonight at the dinner."

"He's definitely left a void in our lives." Maggie raised her eyes to the staircase. "Jake and I will miss him."

"That's what Hamilton says. I gather he and George had a lot of great times together."

"They were good friends. By the way, I invited Ham to stay at George's place with you."

"To keep an eye on me?"

She ignored the question. "You two seem to have hit it off."

"You don't sound as if you approve." Grant stared across the room, where Hamilton was still talking to Nell. "Hamilton arrived at George's after lunch yesterday, and we had a lot of time to talk before the wake. If you're interested, I'm sure he'd let you see a copy of my references."

"Personal or professional?"

It startled her that she felt so comfortable in his presence that she could joke.

"Do I actually see a possibility that you're beginning to have a little faith in me?" he asked.

"Don't get your hopes up, Holbrook. I'm not the trusting type."

"Funnily enough, I think you are."

"Break time is over, you two," Ham said, pulling out Nell's chair for her. "Nell and I have been talking, and there are a couple questions we'd like to ask."

Grant touched Maggie's elbow, and she walked over to join the group. She set her glass back on the tray and took a can of pop, opening the top and swallowing, hoping the caffeine would give her a boost of energy. She shook off the feeling of lethargy that threatened to envelop her and waited for Ham to begin.

"I understand why you're convinced that the kidnappings are the work of the same person or persons," Ham said. "But what I don't see is why you're so convinced that George's death is the result of his recognizing Tyler in the pictures from Jake's birthday party. There must have been hundreds of calls from people convinced they'd seen Tyler. Why are you so positive that George did see Tyler?"

Grant must have been expecting the question, Maggie thought. He looked relieved that someone had asked it.

"When Tyler disappeared I spent as much time with

my sister and her husband in Cleveland as I could. I went with them to the police station and I sat in on all the meetings. Once the actual investigation was in full swing I was at loose ends. I'd been asked to let the professionals take over."

The muscles in his jaw rippled. That request had clearly rankled him. As Ham had said earlier, Grant was not the sort of man to step back, leaving the decisions to others.

"Although I knew I was not at liberty to talk about the eagle feather, I asked if anyone had considered contacting law enforcement officials in the Midwest who might have come across some reference to eagle feathers. No one was particularly receptive to the idea."

"I thought the police or FBI had some sort of data bank that would have that information," Nell said.

"They have various data files, but the way it works is that the feather would only be noted if it was connected to the commission of a crime. If there was no crime, it wouldn't be in the data. My thought was that someone might have come across feathers in another context."

"So the police suggested that you do the research?" Maggie asked. "It would give you something to do and keep you out of their hair."

Grant looked across at her and smiled as if she were a particularly bright pupil. Maggie was surprised at the pleasure his approval gave her.

"You guessed correctly," he said. "Frankly, it didn't matter to me why they gave the project to me. I needed to be doing something."

"I'd feel the same way," Ham said.

"From the moment Tyler was taken I used all the resources at my disposal to get information. I'd never defended anyone charged with any kind of sexual deviancy. I found it personally repugnant. So I needed to start from ground zero."

Grant reached out and opened a can of beer, tipping his head to drink thirstily before he continued.

"I talked to experts. Read books and articles on sexual predators. Interviewed psychiatrists. Monsters like this usually have a long history of antisocial behaviors. My hope was that the eagle feathers might be the beginning of a trail I could follow."

He shrugged.

"I went online looking for organizations for retired police officers and other law enforcement professionals. My prime focus was the Midwest since that was where the three kidnappings had taken place. I kept my postings simple. I asked if anyone had run across a reference to eagle feathers in the commission of a crime or even the suspicion of a crime. Then I waited."

"Pretty good idea," Ham said. "Did you get any hits?"

"Unfortunately, more than I'd hoped for. It started out slowly, but eventually the response was overwhelming. Hundreds of e-mails. Each one had to be read and evaluated. A majority could be ruled out immediately. Kooks and crazies. People wanting to sell me eagle feathers. People telling me the dire consequences of selling and/or buying eagle feathers. Lonely people who just wanted to make a contact. It was about two months into the project that I finally got a break.

"I got an e-mail from a retired cop who said that for several years he'd had complaints from people about finding eagle feathers. No crime was committed, so it never made it into the books, but he remembered it because it was so unusual."

"What do you mean?" Nell asked. "How did they find the feathers?"

"According to this guy, people found feathers in their purses, in their houses and inside their clothing."

Maggie shivered. "I don't like that."

"Neither did the people who found them," Grant said. "The only feather this cop had actually seen was turned in to him at a carnival here in Wisconsin. A young woman found the feather inside her blouse when she went to change into her bathing suit. The only reason the cop knew about it was that he was in charge of giving out the prizes for the games that were played all through the day. The woman presented the feather, thinking it entitled her to one of the prizes."

"When was this?" Maggie asked.

"Twenty years ago."

"Twenty years ago? What possible bearing could that have on this case, Grant?" Maggie said, letting the irritation show in her voice.

"I know it's a long time ago, but hear me out," Grant said.

Ham cocked his head on the side, eyeing Grant through narrowed eyes. "You said the feather turned up at a carnival in Wisconsin?"

He nodded. "The carnival has been held for the past twenty-five years starting the Friday after Labor Day. It used to be sponsored by the Four-H Club in conjunction with the Chamber of Commerce. Lots of crafts and baking contests and even an auction of farm animals."

"You mean it's still being held?" Nell asked.

"Yes. An outside company runs the event, but it's still in the same venue. It used to be called the Falcon Festival, but the name's been changed," Grant said. "It's called the Renaissance Faire."

CHAPTER
TWELVE

"THE FESTIVAL where the feather was found," Grant said, "is called the Renaissance Faire."

"No shit, Sherlock!" Ham slapped the table with the palm of his hand. "So the Renaissance Faire is your connection between Tyler and the feather and George and the birthday pictures."

"Exactly," Grant said. "I'm cognizant of the fact that they could be unrelated events. In real life, however, bizarre coincidences do happen. Think about it. Twenty years ago the kidnapper could have been fairly young. Maybe not old enough for a driver's license or with no opportunity to travel anywhere. So it's plausible that when he acted out, he'd have done it in his home territory."

"So the first eagle feather was found in Delbrook," Ham repeated.

"The first feather we *know* about," came Nell's dampening comment.

"It's a weak case," Grant conceded, "but it's the only one I have."

He glanced across at Maggie. Her expression was

somber, and except for a startled look when he mentioned the Renaissance Faire, she'd remained motionless. Her eyes were focused on a spot somewhere over his left shoulder, and even when he shifted around to draw her attention, she didn't respond. Her detachment worried him, but Ham spoke before Grant could draw her into the conversation.

"You said a cop e-mailed you about the eagle feather. Did you talk to him?"

"Yes. At length."

"I was still living in Delbrook," Ham said, "twenty years ago. If the cop worked here then, I probably knew him. Who was it?"

"Artie Babiak," Grant said. "He said he had a place on the south side of the lake."

"I do know him. And so does Nell," Ham said. He looked at her, and she nodded her head. "He's been off the job about fifteen years. Pretty active around Delbrook. He ran the annual golf tournament at the country club. His wife, Arline, was the ladies' golf champ for about three years running. His kids are all in New York State, so when he retired he moved up around Lake George."

"That's the guy," Grant said. "Artie's got a great memory for detail. He says after that first feather got turned in, he heard rumors of others. Nothing concrete. No crime. Nothing on the books. Those were the days when people didn't sue for every real or imagined injury. Artie said they never identified the 'Eagle.' He always thought the guy would do something to get himself in real trouble, but it didn't happen on his watch."

"Too bad about that," Ham said.

"So basically you've got two threads that connect Delbrook to Tyler," Nell said. "The eagle feather that turned up twenty years ago at the festival at Camp Delbrook and your assumption that George saw a picture of Tyler at the same festival which is now called the Renaissance Faire. It's pretty thin, Mr. Holbrook."

"Agreed." Grant released a heavy sigh. "It would never get to the grand jury. I should state here that my hypothesis has met with little enthusiasm from the police. Before I came up here to Delbrook, I called Joe Moore, the detective in charge of the investigation in Cleveland. When I first came across the information on the eagle feathers, I contacted him. He didn't laugh, but it was obvious that he didn't think much of my conclusions. At least not enough to warrant a deeper investigation."

"I would have thought the police would jump at any lead," Nell said.

"You have to understand that they've had hundreds of leads. Elvis has been sighted fewer times than Tyler. Calls from people accusing relatives and friends, either for the reward or just out of spite. The usual village-idiot calls. My eagle feather theory ranks up there with the latter bunch."

"A child is missing. Every lead should be followed." Nell pursed her lips.

"I agree. Unfortunately I'm not running the investigation," Grant said. "So I called Joe Moore and told him that George might have seen a picture of Tyler. He wasn't impressed. He suggested I contact George directly to see if I could get a positive ID."

"If only we had the photographs," Ham said, "at

least we'd have some hard evidence to take to the police."

"Then I could prove that whoever has Tyler lives somewhere in the vicinity," Grant said, "and that whoever killed George was at the country club that night. Someone he knew."

"That's not possible," Maggie snapped. "It can't be true."

"Why not?" Grant countered. "Because you don't want it to be true?"

Maggie jerked back in her chair. Tears rose to her eyes as she struggled for words to refute his charge. She opened her mouth to speak, but closed it again because she knew that what he said was true. She didn't want to believe it.

She didn't want to accept the fact that someone in Delbrook had kidnapped a child and had deliberately murdered George. She had known ever since talking to Frank Woodman that Grant's theory was probably correct. If she told him what she knew, he would dig into every corner of Delbrook to find answers. Grant's investigation would put them all at risk.

The threat of exposure could drive the killer to desperate measures. He would attack again, and this time Jake could be in jeopardy. All she could think of was that she might be risking Jake's life.

"Easy does it, son," Ham said. "Maggie doesn't live in your kind of world. She's only just now trying to get a handle on something that's been gnawing your ass for two years. In fact, we all are."

Grant's face turned a fiery red, all except for the scar on his jaw, which stood out like a white-hot brand.

"I don't mean to be rude, but I'm running out of time. I need to find out what George knew about Tyler and how the photographs connect up. No matter what it takes, I'm going to find out what I need to know. If that offends you, I'm sorry."

Maggie shook her head, and the tears that hung on her lids overflowed, falling unnoticed on her cheeks.

"It doesn't offend me. It terrifies me. You're right. I don't want it to be true. I'm coward enough to want it to go away. I want to turn the clock back and pretend you never came to Delbrook. George is dead, and every instinct in my body tells me that Jake is in danger."

Ever since George's death, she'd felt she had to control her emotions for Jake's sake. Now she'd lost the battle. She cupped her hands over her mouth to muffle the sobs that ripped through her body.

Feeling Nell's arms encircle her, Maggie clung to her friend, letting her tears wash away some of the fear and loss she'd bottled up. Reeling from one new revelation to the next, she was exhausted, and every detail added to the nightmare quality that surrounded her.

Slowly the sobs lessened until only an occasional shudder shook her body. A handkerchief was tucked into her hand, and she took a deep breath and raised her head from Nell's shoulder. Too embarrassed to meet anyone's eyes, she kept her head bent and blew her nose. Her cheeks itched from the salt residue of her tears, and she rubbed the handkerchief over her face.

"You missed a spot," Ham said.

Letting out a watery sniff, she raised her head to glare at him. "No wonder you never married. Nobody would have you."

Ham chuckled. "In actual fact, the woman of my dreams was already married, but I take your point."

Maggie hated the fact she'd lost control in front of a stranger, but she finally found enough courage to look across at Grant. For once, his hard, brown eyes were filled with warmth and compassion, and his expression held nothing back, letting her see that he understood her fears.

"I'm fine," she said in answer to his unspoken question. "Apparently I needed to let off a bit of steam."

He nodded once, swallowing back whatever words he might have spoken.

"I'd say you were entitled to a breakdown, dear," Nell said. "Now that you've released all that pent-up emotion, I expect you'll feel a lot better. We're all here to support you. You don't have to carry such a heavy load by yourself." Suddenly she yawned. "Lordy, Lordy, I'm fading. Is there any coffee left?"

"Yes. Kim made a fresh pot before she left. Get some, and I'll run up and check on Jake," Maggie said.

She was grateful to be able to escape in order to regain her composure. She had left the door at the top of the staircase ajar, and now she pushed it open, walking along the hall to Jake's room. She eased open the bedroom door, and a wedge of light from the hall streamed across the floor.

The bedroom was stuffy, but she'd noticed a chill in the air as they came home, so she didn't want to open his windows. Being short of sleep, his resistance would be down, and she didn't want him to catch a cold. She tiptoed across to the bed.

Looking down at the sleeping boy, she flashed on

the picture of the missing child. Dear God, how does a mother survive? she thought. Just the suggestion that something could happen to Jake made it difficult for her to breathe. She leaned over and brushed her lips against the soft skin at Jake's temple. Heat rose from his body, bringing the earthy smell of an active boy to her nostrils.

It was an odor she associated with summer and children. A lump formed in her throat, and she swallowed painfully as she thought of the three mothers who had lost their children to some psychopath. She couldn't conceive of the pain. Jake was her whole life.

She stood at the top of the stairs to the bookstore, holding the railing, wondering what she should do. She knew that when she returned to the meeting downstairs, she had to be prepared to participate fully. No half measures would do.

Grant intended to investigate George's murder in order to find Tyler. She had two choices. She could either join the clandestine investigation or she could go to Charley Blessington and tell him everything she knew.

Could her involvement hurt Jake?

If the investigation heated up and the killer panicked, Jake could be at risk. Knowing that was a possibility, she would need to prepare for such an eventuality in order to safeguard her son. If the murderer wasn't caught, Jake and others could be in real danger. So, as far as she could see, her help in the investigation would ultimately bring safety to him.

She needed to consider his mental health as well as his physical. Jake partially blamed her for Mark's death, and she suspected he had transferred that blame to include some responsibility for George's death.

It was partially her fault that her relationship with Mark had deteriorated. Perhaps she had failed Jake by refusing to fight harder to keep the marriage alive. She wouldn't fail him again.

In her heart she knew something wasn't right with George's death, and she needed to find out what was wrong. She owed that to George as well as to Jake.

It appeared that the decision was easier to make than she had first suspected. She would do whatever she could to help find the person who had killed her father-in-law.

Walking back down the stairs to the bookstore, she felt more centered. Since George's death she had done what was required for basic survival. Like an old-fashioned pulp fiction heroine, she had let events dictate her actions rather than making her own decisions.

It was time to take control of her life.

The reviving aroma of freshly brewed coffee added to her sense of determination as she returned to the bookstore. Nell had set out a plate of crackers and cheese, and Maggie was surprised to find she was hungry. Ham was pouring coffee, and Grant was holding a basket of grapes.

"Just wait until Beth comes to work tomorrow," Maggie said. "She'll wonder who's been raiding the refrigerator."

"Who's Beth?" Grant asked, eyeing the grapes with dismay. "Are these hers?"

"No. They're mine. I buy them for Beth Witecki, who runs the bookstore. She's a thin wisp of a girl with a passion for grapes. She used to work for one of the bookstore chains in Milwaukee, but when she got married she moved to Delbrook. I was out of my depth when I first bought the store. Beth took pity on me and came to work here."

"You spoil her rotten," Nell said.

"Please. I'll do anything to keep her from quitting. I was really naive when I got into this business. I thought all you needed to run a bookstore was a love of books. I was an editor. I knew when to dot *i*'s and cross *t*'s, but I hadn't a clue how to read a balance sheet or an order form. The reality is that bookselling is a killer of a business. To be a successful bookstore owner you have to know all aspects of running a business and then layer on a wealth of knowledge about the publishing world."

"And this woman can do that?" Grant asked.

"Beth gets high creating graphs and designing budgets. She handles accounting, orders stock, takes care of returns and baby-sits the occasional author who wanders into town for a book signing. All in all, she's responsible for the day-to-day functioning of the store."

Grant chuckled. "If Beth quits, you'll sue me for cause. First thing in the morning I'll buy some grapes and bring them over. She will have no grounds for resigning."

Maggie picked off several of the grapes, popped one in her mouth and sighed at the rush of sweet juice. Pulling out a chair, she sat down at the table, nodding her thanks to Nell for the coffee.

"Before we continue I need to tell you what I learned tonight from Frank Woodman, the manager of the country club," Maggie said. "I think it goes a long way to proving your theory about the pictures, Holbrook."

She grimaced under the intensity of his look. She could almost read his accusation at her delay in bringing up the subject.

"Don't bother to ask," she said. "You know how resistant I've been to your theory. I didn't want to believe any of it. Tonight I needed to listen to everything before I could actually accept it all."

She told them what Frank had told her about George's reaction to the pictures, his preoccupation and his abrupt leaving to make the phone call, which she assumed was to Ham. It all fit together to make a complete picture of the evening.

"Someone could have overheard the conversation," Ham suggested. "George said he was calling from the pay phone in the hall. He was pretty cagey, but if someone was listening, they might have gotten the gist of the call, which was that George had seen the pictures of Tyler."

"That would explain why the killer struck when he did," Grant said. "He couldn't afford to let George leave the country club with the pictures. In fact, he couldn't let George leave at all."

Silence followed Grant's words. Maggie swallowed to get the dryness out of her throat.

"There's something else you need to know," she said. "My purse was searched tonight. I did not take it into the bathroom where Jake found it."

"Are you sure, kiddo?" Ham asked.

"Positive. I didn't have any proof that someone tried to steal my purse outside the hospital, but I do here. It wasn't a robbery. My money and credit cards weren't taken, but all of the sympathy card envelopes had been opened and the list of George's effects that were sent to the police lab was taken out of the zippered compartment where I'd put it."

Grant could feel his heart jerk at the revelation, and he could see that Nell and Hamilton were shocked.

"Shouldn't you tell the police?" Nell asked. "There's bound to be fingerprints."

"My guess is that it would be pointless," Maggie said. "Jake put all of the things back into the purse when he found it and then I handled everything when I looked through it."

Nell shivered, and Maggie reached over and squeezed her hand to reassure her.

"First the hospital, then George's house and now my purse," Maggie continued. "Someone is very definitely searching for something. We assume he has the photographs, and if that's the case, what is he looking for?"

Grant had been wondering that ever since he'd found the break-in at George's place. "Whatever it is," he said, "must not have been found yet. Maybe the conclusion is that there's nothing to be found."

"I certainly hope so," Nell said, "but until we're sure of that, keep your doors locked, Maggie."

"Luckily, George made sure the apartment was well supplied with dead bolts," Maggie said. "It would take a swat team to get inside."

She set her hand on the table, index finger extended, the tip of her nail tapping the table as if she were preparing to speak. She exhaled sharply and looked at each of the faces around the table.

"Much as I've denied this since you mentioned it,

Grant, George had to have been killed by someone who lives in Delbrook. Someone who knew him and was at the country club the night he died."

"What brought this on?" he asked.

"The missing pictures were shot primarily at the Renaissance Faire. If it was Tyler, he wasn't at the Faire alone," Maggie said. "Someone had to bring him there and take him away. This is a local fair. It doesn't pull in people from great distances."

"That's true," Ham said.

"I took the boys to see the falconry exhibit. Connie Prentice had both her birds there and demonstrated various aspects of the sport. She released one of the falcons and brought it back with a swing lure. It was a real crowd pleaser."

"I assume Brent wasn't too far away," Nell said.

"No. He was there, and so was Hugh Rossiter. Probably the rest of the falconry club, too. George told me Charley Blessington was there most of the day, but I didn't see him."

"I was there for a short time but went home before the rain," Nell said. "I met Walter for lunch, and he was still there when I left."

"That's pretty much the whole poker group with the exception of Frank Woodman," Ham said.

"I don't think we can count him out. He could have been there even though no one saw him," Maggie said. "So basically what I'm saying is that it could be anyone in town. We'll have to be careful who we talk to."

"I agree," Grant said. "Safety has to take precedence. This investigation has to be low-key. The killer is going to be feeling pressure from the police. We don't want to increase that level so that he panics and tries to cut and run."

"You think that's a possibility?" Ham asked.

"I don't know, but it's something I don't want to risk for Tyler's sake," Grant said. He faced Maggie squarely. "I'm not diminishing the importance of your father-in-law's death, but if my nephew is still alive, my first priority is to locate him. Hamilton and I have marked out some areas that we can concentrate on."

"I understand that," Maggie said. "George would want us to focus on Tyler. What can Nell and I do to help?"

"For the moment just go along with the fiction that I'm your mother-in-law's relative come to offer support. Naturally, it would be better if no one knew about George's call to Hamilton," Grant said, nodding toward the older man.

"So you're saying we should just sit tight?" Maggie persisted.

"Exactly. Don't talk to Charley Blessington," Grant continued. "I can't stress enough that we don't know who can be trusted. We have to assume that anyone who was at the country club the night George was killed is a possible suspect. That includes Charley."

Maggie could feel the blood pounding in her ears as it dawned on her that Grant had no intention of letting her get involved in his investigation. One look at Nell told her that she had come to the same conclusion. The older woman rolled her fingertips on the top of the table in a steady tattoo, a visible sign of her agitation.

"I don't want to rain on your parade, Mr. Holbrook, but there's something going on here that leaves me feeling that Maggie and I are out of the loop. You and Ham have the look of Peck's bad boys." She grimaced, sniffing the air. "I raised three children, and I could always tell when one of them had smuggled a frog into the house and was planning to release it during the night."

Maggie caught the look of guilt that passed between the two men. The compatible interaction hadn't been particularly noticeable before, but now that she thought about it, they had told the story of the crimes as if they were working together as a team. How had they managed to bridge the thirty-year difference in their ages and become allies?

"It's nothing you have to worry about, Nell," Ham said.

"Oh please," she said. "The next thing you'll do is pat us on our heads and tell us this is man's work."

He closed his mouth in a firm line and shot a quick glance at Grant.

"Since Hamilton's been up here, we've talked about the case and come to some conclusions." Grant had the grace to look slightly self-conscious. "We think it would be safest if you and Maggie distanced yourselves from any involvement in the investigation."

"And you expect us to go along with that decision?" Nell asked.

Maggie knew the older woman well enough to recognize the disdainful tone, but Grant was oblivious. Ham opened his mouth as if to offer a warning, but one look at Nell and he pressed his lips together.

"I was hoping you would," Grant said.

"Then you're an idiot," Nell said. "I'm not sure what sort of women you're used to dealing with, Mr. Holbrook, but you're off the mark here. If you expect either Maggie or myself to keep our mouths shut, we want a full partnership in whatever scheme you two have in mind."

"It's not that simple . . ." Grant started.

Ham covered his eyes and sank lower in his chair.

"And the horse you rode in on," Nell barked. "You have forgotten something very important here. George was Maggie's father-in-law and my friend. If we are to believe your story, then it was a premeditated murder, and we have a duty to join in any effort to discover the perpetrator."

"You can't shut us out, Holbrook," Maggie said. Her tone had a finality to it. "We're not discussing a business decision, nor are we dealing with a local voting issue. We're talking murder and kidnapping. You don't have any choice but to include us."

"Judas Priest!" Grant said. He flopped against the back of his chair and glared at Ham. "You should have warned me."

"You wouldn't have believed me."

"Well, Mr. Holbrook? What's it to be?" Nell asked.

Grant threw up his hands in surrender. In any other context the situation would have been comical. He could see in the somber expressions on each face an awareness of the risks involved.

"All right, ladies, you're in," he said.

Grant had found a yellow legal pad on a shelf in the kitchen and now he pulled it toward him and wrote the date and the time in bold letters across the top of the first page. When he looked up, he could see that this simple action had put an official stamp on the meeting.

"Two things I want to make very clear," he said. "First, my intention is not to set up an investigation that will lead to vigilante justice. What we're looking for is evidence leading to George's murderer or Tyler's presence that we can take to the police. Agreed?"

His glance moved around the table as each of the others nodded in agreement.

"The second thing to keep in mind is that if at any time I feel things are getting out of control, I'll pull the plug on the investigation and we'll take what info we have to the police."

"Absolutely," Ham said.

"I can live with that," Nell said.

Maggie's eyes were wide, and Grant could detect a hint of fear in the blue depths, but she met his gaze without flinching and nodded her head. He smoothed a hand across the yellow pad of paper.

"I've never run an investigation into murder," he said, "but I don't think it's much different than building a court case. I'd like to suggest we dig into the background of people involved and pool as much information as we can access in hopes that we'll see a pattern or find some evidence. That being the case, our first consideration must be Tully Jackson. Do any of you believe that he killed George?"

"He makes an easy choice," Ham said. "But from what I know and have observed, I don't think he did it. I've talked to him when I've been up here fishing with George. He'd have no reason to rob anyone. As far as I can see, his needs and wants are very small."

"I don't think Tully's stupid," Nell added, "but he's not a candidate for *Jeopardy*. If the person who killed

George is the mastermind behind the kidnapping, then Tully is definitely out."

"I agree," Maggie said. "I'm really worried about him. This is a man who's fragile. My guess is that he's gone into hiding because he's frightened. He might have seen whoever killed George, and that information would put him in dreadful danger."

"Do any of you have any idea how we can contact him?" Grant asked.

"No." Maggie shook her head. "It's possible that he might contact someone if he needs help."

"We have to pray that Tully doesn't pick the wrong person," Grant said. "It could be his death warrant."

CHAPTER
THIRTEEN

"IT'S NOT THAT EASY to get eagle feathers, you know."

Nell's comment came out of the blue, breaking through the tension that filled the room after the discussion about Tully. Her eyes were focused on the black bow she'd pulled out of her hair. She untied the ribbon and straightened it out, sliding it back and forth through her fingers.

"When I was first starting out as an artist," she said, "I decided that the way to fame and riches was to come up with some gimmick that would generate publicity. The theory was that once the art world became aware of my creativity and artistic genius, I'd become a media darling, travel throughout the United States and become filthy rich."

"Let me guess," Ham said. His blue eyes glinted with amusement. "You were twelve at the time?"

Nell pursed her lips and shook her head. "I was a very sheltered child. A late bloomer. Not a loose cannon, like some I could mention." She drew herself up, her ample bosom more prominent than usual. "I was sixteen. The age of optimum wisdom."

"Ah, I remember those days." Ham nodded. "Dare I ask if your gimmick had anything to do with painting naked while wearing a headdress of eagle feathers?"

Grant tried to hide his grin, but Nell's gaze swung to him, and she snorted in disgust.

"Men have no imagination beyond the sexual plane," she announced.

"Bless the little darlings," Maggie said.

"My gimmick, you old roué," she said to Ham, "was to paint with eagle feathers."

"A sixteen-year-old has few really creative ideas," Ham said. "I suppose that might have been considered avant-garde in those days."

"Don't make it sound like it was before fire, Ham," Nell drawled. "You were probably out of school and in the working world at the time."

Ham clapped a hand over his heart as if mortally wounded. The banter between the older couple added a much-needed lightness to the atmosphere.

"As you might have guessed, the project wasn't a wholehearted triumph." Her tone was rueful. "I couldn't paint worth a damn with the feathers. I actually might have had more chance of success had I painted naked. Several years ago, I decided to resurrect the project, and much to my dismay, I discovered that there were enormous penalties for owning or using eagle feathers."

"You're kidding," Ham said. "You mean fines?"

"Yes. They can be as high as ten thousand dollars for having a feather in your possession."

"Did you know about this?" he asked Grant.

"I didn't until I started researching the eagle feathers. The laws were set up on the theory that if you protect the feathers, you protect the birds. I think the only people allowed to own and work with eagle feathers are Native Americans, who can use them in art and in cultural rituals."

"It's curious that when the feathers turned up after the kidnapping, they were eagle feathers," Nell continued. "It might be worthwhile to call Artie back to see whether they were all eagle feathers and just which feathers they were. Wing, body or tail feathers."

"Let me call him," Ham said to Grant. "He knows me and will be more likely to talk to me."

Grant jotted down several notes. He'd call Herb Stebbins, a friend of his with the U.S. Fish and Wildlife Service, to get a refresher course on the regulations surrounding eagle feathers.

Nell bit into a cracker, sending a shower of crumbs down onto the top of her dress. She automatically brushed them away as she reached for another cracker.

"Shouldn't we be setting up a list of suspects?" she asked.

"Yes, and I think unless we find evidence to the contrary, we must consider the poker players to be our prime suspects." Grant could see by their expressions that they didn't like that thought. "I understand your reluctance to address this situation, but it's more likely that George was killed by someone he knew than by a complete stranger."

"It's tough for us," Ham said. "We know these people. They're friends of ours."

"I understand that," Grant said. "These people were with George during the evening and would have known if he had discovered any information about Tyler. Just because the people at the club are your friends doesn't make them above suspicion."

"I hate it that you're right, Holbrook," Maggie said, heaving a sigh. "Frank told me something else when I talked with him earlier. When Connie and Brent stopped by George's house to give me their condolences on Monday, Connie said George was still at the club when they left."

"So that gives them both an alibi," Nell said.

"That's what I thought," Maggie said. "However, when I talked to Frank Woodman tonight, he said that Connie was at the club for dinner but Brent didn't arrive until after dinner was over."

"That means two cars," Ham said. "I suppose they followed each other home."

Maggie shook her head. "According to Frank, Connie was angry with Brent and went home early."

"Why would she lie about it?" Nell asked.

"A very good question," Grant said, making a note. "Anyone want to do a bit of background research on Connie and Brent?"

"I can do that," Nell said. "I'm having lunch with Doris Blessington this week. I'll do a little pumping. Doris always knows where the bodies are buried."

Grant spoke quickly, before anyone registered the unfortunate wording. "I'd like to go over to Camp Delbrook and look around. I need to see where the Renaissance Faire was held. I understand the camp is closed."

"It's not like you're dealing with Camp David," Nell said. "There's no way to keep anyone out. The camp takes up about two hundred acres on the west end of the lake. Most of the cabins and outbuildings are located on a hill leading down to the south shore."

"There's a security guard just inside the main entrance to monitor who goes in and out, and there's another one down by the boat landing," Maggie added. "The place is closed, but there's always a lot of people around. The community college uses several of the buildings for administrative offices, so you can stop there if you have any questions."

"Between the woods and the lake, anyone could get into the camp without being seen?" Grant asked. The others nodded.

"In addition to that," Ham said, "Hugh Rossiter's landscape company is located next to the camp. His father started the business, and when he died Hugh took it over. He owns a piece of adjoining property, which he uses for direct access so he doesn't have to go in and out through the main entrance. His company takes care of the grounds maintenance for the camp, and he lives and has offices in a house on the shore."

"If you want to get a look at the camp, you can come with me tomorrow," Maggie said. "I told Hugh I'd pick up Kenny after school and drop him off at the landscape office."

"That would be great," Grant said. "It'll give me a quick overview so I'll have some idea what to check out at a later visit."

"You thinking your nephew might be held at Camp Delbrook?" Ham asked. He leaned forward, his eyes flashing. "It would be risky, but there'd be plenty of places to hide one small boy."

Grant nodded. "That's my thought. Maggie was

telling me a little about the falconry club, and I'd especially like to get a look at the mews."

"When we're over at the camp tomorrow, if Hugh doesn't offer to take you to see the birds, I'll ask him."

"What exactly are we looking for?" Nell asked.

"Whoever has taken the children has to have a place to keep them," Grant said. "I can't believe they're passed off as family members. It'd be much too dangerous. Someone could recognize them or just question their presence. So I think we have to consider an alternate place. Someplace a child could be confined."

Even though the sound was barely audible, Grant heard Maggie's cry of distress. Color had drained out of her already pale face.

"You must think I'm incredibly stupid," she said. "I've heard all the same things that Ham and Nell have, but it's as if I'm working out some intellectual puzzle. Then all of a sudden you'll say something and it hits me on an emotional level."

"Remember, Maggie," Grant said. "I've been living with this for twenty months."

"I know that, but just now all I could picture was a child caged up in some sort of cell. Eddie and the little girl, Noreen, were imprisoned for a year. And now Tyler. Dear God! Those poor babies." She was close to tears. "It's monstrous. Who could do such a thing?"

Grant reached out a hand and placed it on top of hers. Her fingers were entwined as if in prayer, and he could feel a slight tremor beneath the surface of her skin. He kept his touch impersonal, a reminder of a comforting presence.

"Don't be so hard on yourself, kiddo," Ham said.

"Nell and I have seen a lot more of life than you have. Besides, we haven't taken quite the series of shocks you have in the past two days. You must be a bit punchy at this point."

"I'm not sure that's a really good excuse." She gave him a watery smile. "I have to admit that I've avoided thinking about the ugly and sordid crimes in the news. I know they exist, but I've made a conscious effort to filter out the details."

"Most of us do," Grant said. He gave her hands a pat of reassurance and then withdrew his own. "Only when something happens that hits close to home do we really look into the face of evil. Circumstances force us to examine it."

Maggie took a deep breath, sitting up straighter in her chair. "If we're thinking of places where Tyler could be held," she said, "we need to consider the Falcon Lake Country Club. The clubhouse is old and rambling. Frank Woodman told me once that some of the rooms upstairs are kept permanently closed off to keep the heating and air conditioning costs lower."

"And don't forget the maintenance sheds and equipment buildings that are possible places to keep a child." Ham tapped his fingers in a nervous beat on the top of the table. "Dave Gerbitz is a pilot and a photographer. He takes shots of farms and other properties in the area. Sort of a strange cuss. He flies with a golden lab named Boo who sits up in the copilot's seat as if he's ready to take over the controls. I'll ask Dave if he's got some photos of the golf course so we'll know how many buildings there are and can check them off after we've judged them empty."

"Good idea," Grant said. He made a note to ask Hamilton to see if he could get other photos, especially of Camp Delbrook.

"How about Walter Kondrat?"

"Walter lives in McGuire's Irish Estates about a block away from George's house," Nell said. "He did a major renovation a year ago and knocked down the internal walls on the first floor so it's a totally open plan. Upstairs there are two bedrooms and a bath. No third floor or attic space and no basement. No place inside the house to hide a child."

"Does he own any other property?"

"Not that I'm aware of," Nell said. "His father had a house in town, but it was sold when he died ten years ago. Walter's wife died young. Do you remember when, Ham?"

"Maybe thirty years ago. No kids. I don't think Walter wanted any. He was always tied up with his insurance business. Going to make a million."

"And so he did, and now he's got no one to leave it to," Nell said, mouth pursed in disapproval. "His sister will have the last laugh yet."

"He has a sister here in Delbrook?" Grant asked.

"No. She moved to Colorado about twenty years ago. I went to school with Crystal. She married her high school sweetheart. B. D. Wintrick. Word was that the initials stood for big and dumb." Nell laughed. "But Lordy, Lordy, he was beautiful. At any rate, Walter didn't approve. He said B. D. had no business sense, and when they ran into financial trouble, Walter refused to lend them any money."

"Are they still in Colorado?" Grant asked.

"Last I heard. Crystal said that Walter would end up rich and alone. Looks like that's what's going to happen, except when he dies, his sister will get all the money. If Walter'd been the victim instead of George, Crystal would be the prime suspect."

"I always thought you'd eventually marry Walter," Maggie said.

"That's what everyone thinks," Nell said.

"Well?" Ham asked, his eyes sparking with curiosity.

"I'll be sure to let you know if I have any announcements," she said dismissively. "Let's move on, shall we?"

From the sound of it, Grant didn't think that Walter would pan out as a suspect in this case, but he'd have to wait and see if anything turned up. He looked down at the pad of paper. That left the Blessingtons. He'd make Charley his project, he thought, circling the name.

"We should probably have a list of the other people who were at the club but not in the poker game," Maggie suggested. "I can get that from Frank Woodman. I talked to him tonight to see if anyone had found the photographs from Jake's party. I can tell him I need the names so I can ask around about the pictures."

"I can't urge you strongly enough to be very careful," Grant said. "Someone in Delbrook is living a double life and will do whatever it takes to protect any disclosure. If we're right in our assumptions, George was killed out of fear of exposure."

"I agree," Ham said. "I know you want to help, Maggie, but if it looks like you're digging around for information, you could put yourself at risk."

Maggie's mouth was drawn into a grim line. "I understand the danger," she said. "Doing nothing won't keep me or Jake safe. Finding George's murderer will."

"I don't want to frighten you any more than you already are," Grant said, "but the killer will be watching you. He has no idea whether George told you about the photographs. Since you've mentioned nothing so far, he might be reasonably assured that you don't know anything, but he'll be on the lookout for any unusual activity on your part."

"I'll be careful," Maggie said.

"That goes for all of us," Grant said. "If the murderer gets the idea that our investigation is getting close, he'll strike out. He's murdered at least once. He won't hesitate to kill again."

The Warrior stomped along the path through the woods above the lake. The moon was so bright he could see his way clearly, and he could smell the rain in the air. The imminence of a storm always made him restless.

It had rained when he took his first trophy.

He'd taken the child to prove he had reached the highest level of counting coup. Completing the act, he was overwhelmed with exhilaration. He had the power of life and death over the boy.

As an excuse to keep First Child in his possession, he decided to train him as a warrior. The training period, although experimental, had gone well, and the Warrior decided if the boy could accomplish one coup, he would be released.

Since he had taken First Child from a multiscreen theater, the Warrior selected a similar setting for the test. It would be easy enough to blend into the crowd as children and adults mingled in the lobby. The risk factors were minimal.

As soon as they entered the theater, the Warrior knew he had miscalculated. A new animated film had opened the day before, and the Saturday afternoon crowd was enormous. He decided to abort the test just as a harried mother pushed forward followed by a stream of children wearing party hats.

First Child was swept away in the crowd.

The Warrior could see the panic on the boy's face just before he was lost to sight. It was pointless to search. His only hope was that once free of the throng, the boy would return to the lobby. Locating a vantage point where he could see all entrances, he waited. When the police car pulled up in front of the theater, he knew the boy had been taken from him.

The Warrior climbed the trail to his favorite spot overlooking Lake Falcon. He came through the trees on the top of a flat rock bluff, and in the moonlight the view opened up around him.

The Aerie. He had come to this particular spot for years. It was his sanctuary, a refuge where the sights and sounds worked into his soul, chasing out the fears and doubts that possessed him. He sat down on the natural rock ledge and stared down at the shadowed panorama of sky, trees and water.

A month after the debacle at the theater, he had taken a child at the zoo near Minneapolis.

Wearing a baseball cap, jeans and a Minnesota Vikings jacket, there had been no indication that the four-year-old wasn't a boy. When he discovered the mix-up, his first thought was to jettison the girl. She stared at him with wide eyes, blank of all expression. Her stoicism convinced him that she had the soul of a warrior.

A year later he discovered he had misread the signs.

Since he had found her at a zoo, he had set her test at the Milwaukee County Zoo.

The moment they entered the zoo, Girl had been drawn to Monkey Island as if it were a magnet. She stood at the metal guardrail, looking across the grassy expanse at the monkeys beyond the moat. Wanting to work with her strengths, he had chosen Monkey Island as the rendezvous point.

Aware of the human element that had resulted in the loss of First Child, he had found a place for them to hide until the zoo was closed.

The November night was cold. It was close to midnight when the trial began. When he gave the first in a series of three bird calls, Girl appeared, walking steadily toward the enclosure for the Kodiak bears. She leaned over and stuck a feather in the ground in front of the iron fence. She stood for a moment staring at the sidewalk as if she couldn't remember what to do next.

The Warrior held his breath. She looked around, her eyes catching the moonlight for an instant, then she started off down the path that led to the seals and polar bears. Pleased with her success, he let her get ahead of him.

She was not waiting for him at the rendezvous point. He wandered around the paths, searching for her, keeping to the shadows and listening for the sound of the security personnel. It wasn't until morning that he learned about the child who'd ducked under the guardrail at Monkey Island and drowned when she fell into the moat. In life, Girl had been drawn to the monkeys, and her curiosity to get closer to them had caused her death.

Above him, an owl cried out, and the Warrior felt his body tense.

Time was running out. The risk of discovery was always present during fall cleanup at Camp Delbrook, but in one month the place would be swarming with workers as each of the buildings was inspected to determine the amount of renovation needed to bring them up to code. He'd only just heard of the violations, so at least he had time to plan what to do about One Who Cries.

He should have released the boy at his year anniversary. His attachment to the child had put him at risk. When he had disposed of George, he thought the situation was under control. Now there was Maggie. She wasn't content to let her father-in-law rest in peace. He'd covered his tracks, but there were still some loose ends to tie up. Once that was done, he'd have to deal with her.

Maggie, along with One Who Cries, would have to be eliminated.

The man was angry. When he left, he banged the door.

Tyler peered out from beneath the shelf bed. He had heard banging outside the room and climbed under the shelf, pulling the blanket with him to hide behind. If the man brought the second dish, he didn't want to be seen.

Huddling under the blanket, his teeth chattered and his bottom was cold. He stuck one hand out and touched the mud floor. It was damp.

The man had yelled at him when he couldn't get the

feather into his pocket. It was a big feather, not the little fluffy ones he was used to. He tried it three times. He could see the red on the man's cheek. When he missed the last time, he thought the man would get the bird.

Instead, he used the knife.

Tyler pulled his knees up to his chest. He bowed his head until his forehead touched the blanket. Tears tickled the inside of his nose, but they didn't come out of his eyes. His throat hurt, and he tried to swallow, but it was hard.

Was Mouse Ears dead?

The man had held his knife over the top of the mouse cage. He stabbed it through the wires. One. Two. Three times. He squeezed his eyes shut. He could hear the knife go right through the cage and hit the table.

The man laughed.

When Tyler opened his eyes, he saw the blood on the back of the mouse. The man held it up by the tail. He took it with him when he left.

Tyler tapped his finger on the bottom of the shelf bed. He listened. No mouse sounds. He tapped again. When he heard nothing, he pulled the blanket over his head and closed his eyes to sleep.

CHAPTER
FOURTEEN

"WAITIN' ON JAKE?"

Maggie jumped at the sound of Charley Blessington's voice beside the open window of her car.

"Dear Lord, Charley, you just about gave me a heart attack."

"Sorry about that," he said. "I was passing when I saw your car and thought I'd stop and chat a spell."

Charley was so big that she felt at a decided disadvantage inside the car. She got out and leaned against the door, head back to look up at the chief of police. The afternoon sun was behind him, so his face was in shadow and Maggie had to squint.

"I'm picking up Jake and Kenny Rossiter," she said with a quick glance at the empty stairs leading up to St. Bernard's School. Just a few more minutes and the whole area would be swarming with screaming and shoving children. "Since Mark's cousin has never been up to Delbrook, we're going to take him for a drive around the area."

Still apprehensive about Grant's impersonation, she blurted out the information. She bit her lip to keep from further disclosures.

"Grant Holbrook," Charley said, his voice questioning. "He seems a nice enough fella for a lawyer. Surprised I never heard George talk about him."

"I don't think they ever saw much of each other. Ham knew him because they both live in Chicago."

"Chicago's a pretty big place," Charley drawled. "You didn't know Grant when you lived there?"

"No. Mark may have," Maggie said, grateful to come up with at least one answer that Charley couldn't verify. "Ham called Grant to tell him that George had died. It was very kind of him to come all the way up here."

"I understand he's going to stay around and give you a hand with George's affairs. Can't believe that Hugh Rossiter will cotton to having competition for the title of most eligible bachelor in Delbrook."

Talking to Charley about Grant was difficult for Maggie. She hoped he would take the heat rising to her face for a blush rather than an indication she was lying.

"By the way, Charley, do you know what happened to the photographs of Jake's party that George was passing around the night he died?" she asked, anxious to change the subject.

"Don't you have them?"

"No. They weren't listed among George's effects," she said.

"Well, that's funny." Charley tugged at his earlobe. "You're right though. I made the list out myself, and I don't recall seeing the photographs. We were looking at them during dinner, so if they weren't among George's things, they may be in his car."

"His car!" Maggie caught her breath. "Oh, my God, Charley, I totally forgot about it."

"You've had plenty to think about," Charley said. "We had it towed over to the motor pool, and the lab tech went over it. No sign that anyone had been in the car besides George. Why don't I have one of the uniforms drive it over later?"

"I'd really appreciate that, if you can spare someone."

"I'll have Wayne Brody run it over."

"You better have him bring the car to the bookstore. Parking is tight with both Ham and Grant over at George's place. Tell Wayne to call and let me know when he's coming so I can drive him back to the station house."

"Let him walk back," Charley said. "He's on my 'S' list. Called in sick last week, and I found out he was up at the Fernley Casino. Got an addiction to the one-armed bandits."

Maggie laughed. "I know Wayne and always thought his weakness was bridge."

"Since his divorce he's picked up a lot of new vices."

The dismissal bell rang, and almost in the same instant the doors of St. Bernard's sprang open and children exploded from every exit.

"Anything new on the investigation?" she asked.

"Nothing very promising." Charley raked his fingers through his hair. "We've interviewed everyone who was at the country club that night, and as you might figure, no one saw anything."

"Dennis Nyland was the only one who saw Tully Jackson?"

"Yep. Wish he'd seen the actual attack. I'd like to be able to take a strong case to the grand jury."

Maggie waved as she spotted Jake coming out the

door of the school. He raced down the concrete stairs, leaping the last three steps and landing in a heap on the sidewalk. His bulging backpack cushioned his fall, and he scrambled to his feet.

"Hi, Mom. Kenny'll be right out." He threw his arms around Maggie's waist, and she leaned over to give him a kiss. "Hi, Chief Blessington."

"Looks like you got a ton a homework in that backpack," Charley said. "What all you got in there?"

"Just books and stuff." Jake flushed under the police chief's scrutiny. "We're learning about Egypt. The pyramids and those funny-looking statues without noses."

"Sphinxes?" Charley asked.

"That's it," Jake said.

"I can see you're learning a lot of important things. You musta had a good day at school?"

"All except for lunch. It was puny," Jake complained. "And I'm starving. Can we stop on the way to Kenny's for some fast food, Mom?"

"No. Mr. Rossiter said he'd have something for you when we got there," Maggie said, looking around for Jake's shadow. "Where is Kenny?"

"He'll be right out. He had to finish a paper."

"Why don't you change out of your school shoes and keep an eye out for him while I finish talking to the chief?"

Jake opened the back door of the car and climbed inside. He rolled down the window, watching for his friend as he pulled off his shoes. Charley leaned a hip against the fender of the car.

"You still haven't found Tully Jackson?" Maggie asked.

"Not a sign. I swear to God, that man has lit out of town. I've had every officer on the police force looking for him. We've combed all his usual haunts and haven't picked up so much as a scent of him."

"Does he have a permanent place here in Del-brook?" Maggie asked.

"Beats the hell out of me."

Charley's voice was harsh with frustration. His eyes were focused on a spot behind Maggie, and she finally realized he was staring at Jake. He lowered his voice.

"Sometime when I'm not around, you might ask Jake and Kenny if they know where Tully lives. I have the distinct feeling that they know more than they're telling. They always spent a lot of time hanging around the boat ramp, and they may be the only ones who know how to get in contact with Tully."

"I'll ask," she said, "but I'm sure if Jake knew, he would have told you when you asked him before."

Maggie really wasn't so sure of that. Jake counted the eccentric loner as his friend and wasn't particularly fond of the chief of police. If Jake thought Charley was un-fairly pursuing Tully, he'd balk at telling him anything.

"Tully's been a thorn in my side for ages. I've tried to get rid of him for years, and now my failure to do that has cost George his life."

"You don't know for certain that Tully killed George," she said, all too aware of Jake's listening ears.

"It's just the sort of thing people who are living on the fringe of society are capable of. They're so alienated from the rest of us that when something happens to set them off, they just go berserk."

Charley pushed away from the car and paced a few

feet away as if he was too wound up to remain still. His face was flushed, and his hands were squeezed into fists.

"I feel so damn bad about George, Maggie," he said, facing her. "Doris has been pushing me to run for mayor in the next election, but I haven't been all that keen on it. But I tell you true. If I can nail Tully and wind this case up, I believe I will do just that."

"Mom says it's going to rain tonight," Jake said.

The rest of his words were inaudible as he leaned over to whisper in Kenny's ear. There was something furtive about the gesture that gave Maggie the uneasy feeling the boys were hatching something. She wished she'd talked to them before she picked up Grant. It was too late now. Camp Delbrook was just ahead.

"Try to stay out of trouble while we're at the camp," she said over her shoulder to the boys in the backseat.

"We will, Mom," Jake said much too quickly. "Do you think Mr. Rossiter will take him to see the birds?"

Maggie eyed Jake in the rearview mirror, but his head was bent, so she couldn't see his face. Unwilling to lie to him, she had let Grant introduce himself as Edna's nephew from Chicago. For some reason, Jake refused to address Grant directly. She had suggested "Mr. Holbrook," "Cousin Grant" or simply "Grant," but Jake didn't seem comfortable with any of the names.

"That depends on his schedule and the birds," Maggie said.

"I don't think I've ever seen a hawk up close," Grant said. "Are there a lot of birds, Jake?"

After a short silence, Jake replied, his tone grudging. "No. Just four."

"In one big cage?" Grant asked.

"No, separate. It's hard to explain."

Maggie cleared her throat, and Jake saw her watching him in the mirror. He ducked his head, but not before she'd seen his awareness of his rudeness.

"Mr. Rossiter has two birds that he keeps in the mews," he said. "The other two birds belong to Mrs. Prentice."

"That's Connie," Maggie said to help Grant keep the names straight.

She turned in between the square stone pillars at the entrance to Camp Delbrook and pulled up alongside the gatehouse. She rolled down the window as Joyce Albrecht looked up from the book she was reading. As near as Maggie could tell, the uniformed guard read only World War II novels, preferring the ones with garish swastikas on the cover. Joyce set the book down and walked outside the security office, smiling as she recognized Maggie.

"I heard about your father-in-law and I was sorry," she said. "George was an upright man. I'll miss seeing him around here."

"We all will, Joyce. Thanks for your kind thoughts." Maggie indicated Grant in the passenger seat. "This is Grant Holbrook."

"Ah, Edna's nephew. The lawyer from Chicago." Joyce leaned over, hands on her thighs so she could look in the window. "Glad to meet you. I heard you were living at George's house with Ham Rice. Will you be staying long?"

"I'm not sure," Grant said. "I'm giving Maggie a hand settling George's affairs."

"Hi, boys," Joyce said, her gaze shifting to the backseat. "If you're running around in the camp, stay away from the dining hall. A ton of volunteers are arriving today to help with the fall cleanup this week."

"Kenny's dad already warned him," Jake, the spokesman, said.

"They're creating a temporary dormitory out of half the dining hall, and they don't need any distractions from you two," she said, standing upright, her eyes frosty as she stared at the boys. With a nod, she stepped away from the car and waved them through.

"Word is out," Maggie said with a sideways glance at Grant. "It's a small town. Everyone knows everyone's business."

"So I gather." Grant grinned. "Do you suppose for the rest of my life people will refer to me as Edna's nephew?"

"For as long as you're here," Maggie said. She pointed to the empty flat land along the top of the ridge. "This is where the Renaissance Faire is held. Nothing much to see now. The village houses are just stage sets, and they're folded up and stored until next year. Just over the hill beyond this flat area are the stables. Bleacher seats are put up around the exercise ring to create the jousting arena."

"It's sad when they take everything down." Jake stared morosely out the window. "It was cool when all the banners were up and you could walk around the village and see the jugglers and magicians. Now it's just trees and dirt and the old buildings."

"Make-believe can be much more exciting than real life," Grant said, clearly in sympathy with the boy.

"Maybe so, but this view is hard to beat," Maggie

said, bringing the car to a halt as they rounded a bend and came to the top of the steep hill leading down to the lake.

The dirt and gravel road wound past, dark red- and green-sided buildings nestled among the foliage on the hillside. The green shingle roofs blended into the landscape, and even the white trim on doorways, porches and windows didn't look out of place. At the base of the hill, flickering through the leaves like an aquamarine, was Falcon Lake.

Maggie drove slowly, pointing out the administration building, the dining hall, the outdoor theater and some of the cottages, feeling self-conscious between Grant's intense scrutiny and her awareness of the boys in the backseat, listening to every word.

"In case you're housebound," she said, "this is a great place to get some exercise. If you stop by the administration office tomorrow, you can get a map of Camp Delbrook. Along with indicating the roads and hiking trails, it shows a layout of the whole campground."

Grant nodded absently as if his mind were already making an inventory of the structures and the terrain beyond the windshield. Maggie knew she'd never view the camp the same again. She stared at each building, wondering what secrets were held behind the walls.

Driving through the camp on the way to Hugh's, Maggie could feel a rising tension. Suggesting that Grant come with her today had been easy enough to propose, but now that they were here, she felt a vague sense of betrayal.

How could she even consider that Hugh could be involved in George's death or the kidnapping of a child?

She knew Hugh. He was a friend. Could she be such a bad judge of character that she wouldn't recognize a truly evil person?

Her mind buzzed with questions as she thought back over all the conversations she'd had with Hugh, searching for clues to his moral center. It was frightening that she couldn't say with any certainty that Hugh was innocent.

If she couldn't exonerate Hugh, how on earth would she be able to evaluate the rest of the people on the list of suspects?

At the bottom of the winding road, she drove along the lakefront, passing the swimming beach and the boat docks until she reached an L-shaped turn that meandered back up to the entrance to the camp. Beyond the turn was a parking lot that led into Hugh Rossiter's landscaping business.

She pulled into a parking space in front of the two-story house with the white porch that faced out onto the lake. Jake and Kenny bolted out of the car, bounding up the porch stairs to disappear inside as the screen door slammed behind them.

"Not a bad view," Grant said, getting out of the car to stare at the lake. "I've never been up to Falcon Lake before, and I can't imagine why. Not only is it beautiful, but it's incredibly peaceful."

Maggie laughed. "You ought to see it before Labor Day. The people who live along the shore put up with the chaos just for days like this after the summer crowd goes home."

The screen door squeaked, and Maggie turned to see Hugh Rossiter framed in the doorway.

"Is it OK for Jake to have something to eat? Kenny said they were starving," he said.

"School was boring, and their lunches were too skimpy," Maggie said. "I heard a litany of woes on the way over here."

"I turned them loose in the kitchen." Hugh came down the stairs, holding out his hand to Grant. "Good to see you again, Grant. I didn't realize you were staying on."

"Just giving Maggie a hand," Grant said. "This is quite a place you've got. I can't believe how extensive the camp is. When it's in full swing the place must be pretty busy. Doesn't that get in the way of your business?"

"When the camp's in session, we come and go through the other side of the parking lot. This entrance is gated. That discourages most of the intruders." Hugh smiled, his teeth flashing in his tanned face. "Occasionally we find some idiot wandering through the nursery or the greenhouses, but they're usually lost. They're grateful to be led back to the camp."

"Do you live here?" Grant asked.

"I used to have a place in town, but eventually I was spending all my time here anyway, so I couldn't see any sense in driving back and forth."

"It probably gives you more time with your son, too," Grant said. "How much land have you got?"

"Just twenty acres. Most of it's uphill, but the college rents us some tillable fields as a part of an agriculture internship they run. It's a win-win situation. They train future farmers and agrochemists, and we grow plants and trees for the nursery business. Would you like a tour?"

"If you've got the time," Grant said.

Maggie couldn't believe how talkative Hugh was.

Usually he answered her questions with a series of grunts or nods of the head. It must be a guy thing, she thought with some resentment. As if Hugh sensed her annoyance, he turned to her.

"Want to come too?" he asked, putting an arm around her shoulders and leading her up the stairs.

"No. I'll keep an eye on the boys," she said, flushing when she saw Grant's sharpened interest at Hugh's familiarity. "I have a feeling they're up to something."

"Crap! Don't tell me we're in for another suspension from school."

"Last time," Maggie explained to Grant, "they smuggled a snake into school and let it loose during lunch hour. The boys explained to Mrs. Micheff, the principal, that it was just a baby and wasn't even poisonous, but she didn't see a lot of humor in the prank."

Grant laughed. "Remind me to give you both my card. I have the distinct feeling these boys will need a good defense lawyer in their later years."

Inside, the room on the left, originally the dining room, held a large counter across the open archway, behind which three women were working. Computers, phones, fax machines and copiers were part of the equipment that covered the desks. On the right, the living room had been turned into Hugh's office and was enclosed by a set of oak French doors that opened off the foyer. Along with a desk and credenza, there was a round conference table covered with landscape drawings and plant catalogs.

Hugh led the way down the hall toward the back of the house and pushed open the door to the kitchen to the accompanying sound of breaking glass. Kenny and

Jake were staring down at the jar of mayonnaise that had shattered on the tile floor.

"Sorry for the mess, Dad," Kenny said in his whispery voice. "We were making sandwiches."

"So I see." Hugh's voice boomed around the walls. "Well, don't just stand there. Get this mess cleaned up."

"Yes, sir," Jake said, pulling Kenny by the sleeve of his shirt toward the sink. "You get the paper towels, Kenny. I'll get the wastebasket."

"Why don't you show Grant around, and I'll give the boys a hand?" Maggie suggested.

Hugh reached up to the pegboard beside the refrigerator and took down a ring of keys attached to a round plastic disk. Inside the disk there was a picture of a hawk, wings spread wide in flight.

With one more sharp glance at the two boys, Hugh led the way back outside.

Grant was surprised at Hugh's strong reaction to the mishap. Spills and kids generally went hand in hand. A single father should be used to it. More worrisome for Grant was the flash of fear he'd seen cross Kenny's face as the boy stared up at his father.

"I'll take you over to the mews," Hugh said.

"That'd be great. Jake was telling me a little about the hawks," Grant said. "I never realized there were falconry clubs around. How'd you get interested in it?"

Obviously Grant had hit the right subject. Hugh's tight-lipped frown was replaced by a lighter expression.

"My dad had a friend, Patrick O'Shea, who had learned falconry in Ireland. I used to spend a lot of time at his place. O'Shea saw I was willing to give the time to the sport, so he took me on as his apprentice. It's a highly regulated sport."

"Does it take a long time to get proficient?" Grant asked.

"Two-year apprenticeship with an experienced falconer. You can't get a hawk before you take an exam and have the required housing for the bird."

"Why so tough?"

"For the bird's protection. Falconry is a major commitment. Anything less is detrimental to the bird's health and well-being." Hugh paused. "Don't get me started. I'm pretty obsessive about the subject. I'll take you up to the mews, and you can see for yourself. That's better than a lecture any day."

Hugh led the way around the side of the house to a mulched trail that led off the service road toward two red-sided structures in a clearing. The first building was a large equipment storage and repair shed. The double doors stood open, and Grant could see a submerged pit for oil changes on the left. Around the sides and along the back there were enough used parts for garden, hardware and automotive equipment to rival any repair superstore.

"We use a lot of machines," Hugh said. "Give them hard use. I had this equipment garage built about ten years ago and hired a full-time mechanic. April through October, when we're busiest, we usually take on one or two additional guys."

Grant liked the fact that the equipment garage had been built to match the older structure on the other side of the clearing. Dating back at least seventy years, the red-sided building was oval with a steeply slanted, green shingled roof that rose to a netted center opening.

"This is the mews," Hugh said, pulling out the ring of keys on the plastic disk.

He unlocked the dead bolt on the door and led Grant into the building, closing and locking the door behind them. Walking through the tunnel, they entered the inner circle of the mews.

The center yard, a hard-packed dirt surface, was open to the sky, and the late afternoon sun illuminated a row of three-sided roofed structures. Plastic netting was fastened securely to close off the fourth side on the front of each cage. Some sort of blind was pulled down on the outside of the netting in three of the cages, but Grant had an unobstructed view into the fourth. He had been expecting to feel sorry for the birds in confinement and was pleasantly surprised at how spacious their living quarters were. Each cage was twelve foot square with a ceiling height of nine feet.

"In England this is called a weathering. The birds require a place to shelter from the elements that's safe from predators and easy to keep clean. With this arrangement I can power hose inside the cage and spray the place with disinfectant. I like to keep things pretty simple. The floor is uncrushed pea gravel. It's rounded stone so if a bird picks up a piece to aid in digestion, it won't do her any damage when she regurgitates it."

"One bird to a cage?"

"Yes. We've got plenty of room here."

As he approached the cage, Hugh let out three short whistles followed by soft squeaking sounds as he drew air in through his closed lips.

"This is Morgana. She's a female goshawk. A shortwing. I've had her for three years. Keep your voice low and your movements to a minimum," Hugh cautioned. "She's a solitary bird and fairly shy, especially around strangers."

"A female?"

"The females are bigger and stronger than the males, so they can strike down larger prey."

Grant eyed the bird that was standing on the shelf, high on the back wall of the chamber. He had to admit she was impressive. She stood about fifteen inches tall. Her chest was gray with thin horizontal stripes in black, black wings and a black-and-gray-striped tail. A slash of white feathers, like eyebrows, gave her a haughty look and added to the piercing quality of her red eyes.

"What does she hunt?" Grant asked, keeping his voice low.

"A wide variety of prey. She'll fly at squirrels, rabbits and even pheasants."

"How long does it take to train a bird?"

"Ten to twelve weeks initially," Hugh said. "The process is called manning. Basically the hawk has to lose its natural fear of man. I chose a bird that will imprint. During the training period, I'm the one who provides food, shelter and entertainment. She depends on me for everything."

"A parent and child relationship," Grant said.

He stared hard at the beautiful bird in the cage, all too aware that part of his objective was to find out if somewhere else in the building there wasn't another caged animal. Not a bird this time, but a child.

"I saw a documentary once that showed a falcon hunt," he said. "Even on film it's exciting, so I can imagine the thrill when it's real. Don't you have to worry the first time you release the bird that she won't come back?"

"Not if you've trained her right." Hugh's gaze was intense as he watched the hawk and scanned the inside of the cage. "Before she's entered, she's been flown on a creance, which is a braided field leash, and she's become familiar with a swing lure."

He turned his head and grinned, and this time the smile was genuine.

"I know much of this is gibberish to you," Hugh said, "but it's hard for me to break it down into really simple terms. That's why I don't do many of the show-and-tell programs at the schools. Connie is good at those, but I'm not patient enough. I always get some smart-mouthed kid who asks a stupid question to see if he can get a laugh from his peers."

"I'll keep that in mind," Grant said.

Hugh let out a sharp bark of laughter, cutting it off immediately when the hawk spread her wings and hopped along the shelf. Grant was curious to learn more about the exotic sport. He could see why someone could get hooked on it.

"Do you bring the hawks inside during the winter?" he asked.

"No. Because of the way the building's constructed, we don't have to worry about the wind, only falling temperatures. If you look, up above the perch there's a heat bulb that I can turn on when the weather is really nasty. The shade on the outside of the netting rolls down to keep the drafts out and hold in the heat."

"How many birds do you have here?" Grant asked, looking along the line of cages.

"Connie keeps two birds here." Hugh pointed to the cages at the end of the line. "They're both gyrfalcons. She prefers them because they're the largest and fastest of all the falcons. They're also willful, refusing to do anything they don't see any point in doing. Sort of like Connie herself."

"I've only just met her," Grant said, "but she has the same elegant poise as your hawk and gives the impression she's only waiting for a moment of freedom so she can spread her wings and soar."

"Not a bad assessment, Grant," Hugh said. "I'm sorry you can't see her hawks now, but they're in the last stage of the molt. That's why the blinds are drawn. If a hawk gets upset, the new feathers could grow in with fret marks, sort of a fault bar which weakens the feather."

Hugh pointed to the closed cage beside Morgana's.

"My second bird is a peregrine falcon. She's a long-wing in her fifth season, almost at her full potential. She's got a case of bumblefoot from a trauma to her ankle. I'm treating her with an antibiotic and trying to keep her quiet for a couple days. As the master falconer I can have three birds, but with my business I don't have the time for another one."

"From what I've seen, it's an enormous time commitment," Grant said. "Where do you get the birds?"

"Connie bought her two from a breeder. Paid big tickets for them." Hugh snorted in disapproval. "Thirteen thousand for Rowena and a whopping fifteen thou for Isolde."

"Judas! Not only a time-consuming sport," Grant said, "but a costly one as well. Just this building is a major investment."

"I've only had this arrangement for the last ten years. When I decided to build the equipment barn, Connie suggested I renovate this building into a mews. Brent designed the plans and worked with the construction people to get it right. Connie and I split the expenses, and we've hired someone to do most of the cleaning and some of the day-to-day checking on the birds."

"Who watches the birds when you're on vacation?" Grant asked.

"Most falconers don't vacation without their birds."

Grant thought Hugh might be kidding, but he could hear no hint of amusement in his voice. He had noticed that when Hugh smiled, it rarely touched his eyes. Probably his business sense had taught him to be gracious and charming, but in actual fact, he appeared to have little sense of humor.

Aware of Grant's surprise, Hugh continued.

"That's not totally true. Connie's going to Europe next month for four weeks, so I'll be taking care of her birds. It coincides with some renovation work being done on the mews, so I'll probably move all of them to a temporary site so they aren't upset by the noise and confusion."

"Do you breed the birds?" Grant asked as he followed Hugh around the complex.

"No. I leave that to the experts. The bald eagle is a great example of a successful breeding program. It brought them back from the brink of extinction. In 1963 there were only four hundred seventeen pairs in the lower forty-eight states. Now there are more than five thousand pairs."

"So many things to learn," Grant said.

Hugh shrugged. "Sorry. I tend to run on."

"To be perfectly honest, I'd like to hear more. Does anyone in your club hunt with an eagle?"

"No. Because of their size and weight, the logistics are complicated," Hugh said. "You need a much larger cage to accommodate the wingspan, and all your equipment needs to be heavy-duty. Even the glove. An eagle could crush your hand in an ordinary falconer's glove. They're aggressive, and combined with the fact they're so fiercely territorial, a falconer has to be aware of the presence of danger whenever he works with them."

"Sounds more like drudgery than fun."

"If you want fun, you ought to see the peregrine in flight. You can see why she merits such high esteem from falconers. She's built for speed chases and steep plunging dives, called stoops."

For the first time, Grant could see that Hugh was answering on an emotional level rather than an intellectual plane. He had wondered how the man could devote so much time and energy to the sport, but as he talked about the falcon, his face lit up and his words were almost poetic.

"Silhouetted against the sky she appears to be filled with joy as she circles and waits on the prey," Hugh continued. "At times it's like she's playing. She'll harass other birds by stooping at them without striking, tapping them with a closed foot. Just one touch and the falcon soars back up into the sky. Ultimate power. The choice of life over death."

CHAPTER FIFTEEN

"CAN I GO UP in the treehouse, Mom?" Jake asked as they pulled into the parking lot behind George's house.

Maggie couldn't help the sinking feeling that she got in the pit of her stomach. She never would have believed a time would come that she'd be nervous about leaving Jake alone outside George's house, but each day her fear for his safety grew stronger and made it more difficult for her to let him out of her sight.

"Mom? Can I?"

"Sorry, Jake. I was daydreaming," Maggie said. "Yes. You can play out here for a bit, but not long. It's five o'-clock, and I'm already starving."

"You can stay here for dinner," Grant said. "Ham and I are going to order chicken."

"I like chicken," Jake said, getting out of the car and pulling on his backpack.

"Not tonight," Maggie said. "It's a school night, and you've got homework."

She waited below while Jake climbed the ladder. He looked unbalanced with the bulky backpack, but he moved steadily up the rungs and opened the trapdoor in the bottom of the treehouse. She held her breath as he teetered on the top step, pulled off the backpack and shoved it through the opening, then disappeared inside.

"What a great place for a kid to play," Grant said as he followed Maggie to the back door of the house. "I went up there yesterday and I was impressed. I tried not to think of insurance claims and viewed it from the perspective of a child, and I had to admit, it's a winner."

"It took me a while before I was comfortable with him playing up there. George and my husband convinced me that a boy needed independence and that I had to let him go. It's not easy being a mom," Maggie said with a final glance at the treehouse.

"You must have heard me opening the refrigerator," Ham said as they entered the kitchen. "I was getting a beer. How about you?"

"Draw two," Maggie said.

"Make it three," Grant added.

Ham pulled the cold bottles out of the refrigerator, opened them and handed them around. Maggie sat down at the kitchen table.

"How'd it go over at the camp?" Ham asked. "Did you get in to see the birds?"

"Yes," Grant said. "It's quite a setup. Hugh showed me all around the mews. As far as I can tell, we saw every part of the place, including storerooms and the clinic. I tried to consider the outer dimensions of the building, and there were no spaces unaccounted for. No secret rooms. No locked doors."

"Don't sound so discouraged," Ham said. "It's early

days yet. You didn't really think you'd hit the jackpot first time out."

Grant shrugged. "I'm the optimistic type. Then Hugh took me through the greenhouses and chemical sheds. No hesitation that I could pick up about looking through any of the buildings. He was very hospitable for a man who's got a business to attend to. By the time we'd covered the lot, Maggie and the boys were waiting by the car. I never did ask what you and the boys did."

"It took a while for Kenny and Jake to finish cleaning up the mess from the broken mayonnaise jar. They suggested we take a march up into the woods. The boys took their backpacks and enough supplies to last us if we got lost. We went up past the mews and then crossed over into the campground. They dragged me through the outdoor theater and a couple other buildings. They were all empty."

She took a sip of the cold beer, sighing at the bite in the back of her throat as she swallowed. She understood how Grant felt. Each time she and the boys had approached a building, she was disappointed when she found it vacant.

"By the way," Ham said. "I got hold of Dave Gerbitz. He's making copies of some aerial pictures of the golf course and the camp, and I added Connie and Brent's place on the south side of the lake."

"It's a pretty substantial piece of property," Maggie explained to Grant. "It was her grandfather's estate, and Connie inherited it when her father died."

"Any chance of finding out what killed her father?" Grant asked. "I gather there's some mystery there."

Ham tilted his head back and scratched under his

chin. "Connie and Brent have been married seventeen years. Her father died about a year after the wedding. I was already in Chicago when I heard about the fire, but I don't remember any of the details. I'll ask Nell. If she doesn't know, she'll know whom to ask."

"Nell may have an idea of the layout of Connie and Brent's place. We'll need to check it out," Grant said. "Once you get the pictures of the camp and the country club, we'll mark off each of the buildings as we inspect them. That way we'll have less chance of missing one."

"Look, Grant, we're never going to find Tyler working this way," Maggie said, verbalizing her frustration at the enormity of the project. "At least when you're looking for a needle, there's only one haystack."

"Don't get discouraged, kiddo," Ham said. "Crimes are never solved without one hellava lot of footwork."

"When I was walking with the boys over at the camp today, I realized that if whoever is holding Tyler gets wind of the fact we're searching for him, all he has to do is move him to one of the places we've already ruled out."

"You're right, but we have to make a try at finding him," Ham said, looking to Grant for support.

"I've had similar misgivings, although my real fear is that the kidnapper will decide that Tyler is a risk." The scar rippled as Grant clenched his jaw. "The clock is ticking. The longer we investigate, the more chance there is that the kidnapper will become aware of our activities."

"Today is Wednesday," Ham said. "George died on Saturday. How long do we have?"

"By Sunday my continued presence in Delbrook will be hard to justify," Grant said.

Damn, Maggie thought. He was an annoyance she could do without, but she had to admit she'd hate to see him go back to Chicago. Despite his uptight attitude, he had a solid reliability that she appreciated since her entire world seemed to be shifting and changing.

"What can we do to improve the odds?" she asked.

"Using the facts we have, we've got to narrow down the list of suspects," Grant said. "The only real hope we have of finding Tyler is to figure out who killed George. Once we know that, we'll be able to pinpoint where to search."

"So we investigate the people, not the places?" Maggie asked.

"We do both." Grant grinned. "Even if I'm a hard-assed lawyer, I was raised on Perry Mason and those last-minute miracle endings. Who knows? We could find Tyler."

"Why not?" Ham said. "I drove over to Milwaukee today to look up an old girlfriend of mine. Paula Craig is on the police force there. Paula used to be with animal control but now works homicide. She told me if I came back tomorrow, she'd get me a look at the police reports on the little girl found at the zoo."

"Great work, Ham," Grant said, saluting him with his beer bottle. "I've been talking to Michelle Hoppe, the principal at Eddie Harland's school. She tried to convince Eddie's parents to talk to me after Tyler disappeared. She was devastated when they refused. She's always been convinced that the boy will eventually self-destruct if he doesn't talk about his experiences."

"Poor little bugger," Ham said. "I've investigated a lot of child abuse cases. Bottling up traumas only increases the pressure, and these kids eventually explode."

"Mrs. Hoppe called me about a month ago," Grant said. "She wanted to know if Tyler had been found. Apparently she's established a solid relationship with Mrs. Harland and has been talking to her about getting psychiatric help for Eddie. Eddie's nine, and according to Mrs. Hoppe, he's depressed. Failing in school and generally withdrawing."

"It's so hard being a parent," Maggie said. "All you want is what's best for your child, but there are no hard and fast rules to guide you. I'm sure Eddie's parents thought they were doing the right thing by letting him bury the experience. First they have to deal with their guilt over the kidnapping, and now a double whammy if he's coming apart."

"That's exactly the situation. Mrs. Harland won't let anyone talk *to* Eddie, but she may be willing to talk *about* him."

"That would at least be something," Ham said.

Grant looked across the table at Maggie. The muscles across her shoulders began to tighten with the intensity of his gaze.

"I talked to the principal earlier today, and she thought Mrs. Harland might talk to you," Grant said.

"Me?" Her stomach fluttered at his words, and her hand tightened around the beer bottle. "I'm not qualified. I don't know enough about the case."

"It doesn't matter," Grant said. His gaze held hers, refusing to let her back away. "You're a mother of a boy Eddie's age. You'll be able to understand her fears more easily than I can. In my opinion, she'll speak to you more freely than she will to me."

Maggie's gaze traveled back and forth between the two men, seeing the appeal in their eyes. The whole idea terrified her. The responsibility was too much.

"Not a chance. You're the lawyer. You've had training on how to interrogate a witness. I'd screw it up," she said, verbalizing her fear.

"We'll be no worse off than we are at this point. Besides, you owe me one," he said, wincing as he touched the cut on the side of his head.

"Really, Holbrook, you can't throw that in my face at every turn. The damn thing's nearly healed, so give it a rest."

A boyish grin stretched his mouth, and his eyes flashed.

"I'm not too proud to beg," he said. "If the principal can get Mrs. Harland to talk, will you do it?"

It was strange, Maggie thought. Although she had agreed to help Grant with the investigation, she had never really believed that she would have anything of importance to contribute. As much as the prospect frightened her, here was at least a chance for her to do something concrete.

"Yes," she said. "I'll talk to her."

As she looked at the two men, it seemed to her as if she'd passed some test. That thought didn't offer a great deal of comfort when she compared it to the possibility that she might fail to learn anything of consequence. She'd just have to wait and see.

"I'm supposed to call Mrs. Hoppe back tonight,"

Grant said. "If it's possible, I'd like to set it up for tomorrow."

"So soon? Where does Eddie live?" she asked.

"Detroit. We can fly up in the morning and be back before Jake gets out of school," Grant said.

"I can't just take off for Detroit at a moment's notice," Maggie said.

"Why not?" Ham asked.

"Because," she said. Seeing Ham's grin, she wanted to smack him. "Does it have to be tomorrow?"

"Mrs. Harland is very ambivalent. We have to act quickly, before she gets cold feet and backs out," Grant said. "I know it's asking a lot of you, but could you go tomorrow?"

Maggie threw up her hands in defeat. "Yes, I can go. Let me know if the interview is on and what time the flights are so I can make some arrangements for Jake."

"I'll call you as soon as I know," Grant said.

"I'd like to make a suggestion," Ham said. "I think you should say you're going into Milwaukee for a day of shopping."

"What?" Maggie said.

"For you to fly off to Detroit for a day trip is out of the ordinary for you," Ham said. "It will raise more questions than you want to answer. Someone in Delbrook is watching for any strange behavior and might put two and two together and come up with Eddie Harland."

"I hadn't thought it through," Grant said, "but I think you're right."

"Do you know how many lies I've told since I met you?" Maggie set her beer bottle down on the table with a thump and glared at Grant. "I'll have to lie to Jake. I hate lying. I'm not good at it."

"Actually, kiddo," Ham said with a smirk, "you're getting better at it every day."

"Oh stuff it," she snapped.

"I'll take care of everything," Grant said.

He pulled open one of the kitchen drawers and reached in for the yellow lined pad he'd used the day before. He seemed perfectly at home in his surroundings, she noted with annoyance.

"Shouldn't you be going back to Chicago? What about your job?" she asked.

"Technically, I'm on vacation," he said. "I managed to shuffle a few cases around and got a continuance on an upcoming trial, which gives me a bit of breathing space."

"Does your firm know why you're in Delbrook?" Ham asked.

"Only one of the partners. I talked to him Sunday morning before I drove up here."

Maggie couldn't resist asking the question that had been nagging at her ever since she'd heard Grant's story. "Did you tell your sister that you might have a lead to Tyler?"

"No." Grant bit off the single word.

"If it were my child," Maggie said, "I'd want to know, no matter how slim the possibility was that it would amount to anything."

Grant didn't answer immediately. The muscles along his jawline rippled, and she could see the scar clearly.

"When Tyler disappeared, Barbara had just discovered she was pregnant. With the trauma of the kidnapping, she had a miscarriage."

"Oh, God. I'm so sorry," Maggie said.

"She's pregnant again. Seven months along," Grant said. "I can't risk doing anything that might upset her. It would kill her if she lost this baby, too."

Grant propped his feet up on the railing of the redwood deck, watching the play of lightning over the lake. Since his arrival at George's house four days ago, he'd made a point of sitting outside as much as he could. The early evenings had been perfect deck weather. No bugs, mid-seventies with a breeze off the lake. When he returned to Chicago, he'd miss this pleasant interlude.

It had been so long since he'd permitted himself any moments of quiet solitude. His every waking breath was taken up with surviving another day with the twin demons of guilt and regret riding herd on any attempts at self-analysis.

Neither Barbara nor Ken had ever blamed him for Tyler's kidnapping by as much as a glance or a sharp word. Perhaps if they had, he would have been able to deal with his own sense of responsibility. If he'd stayed in Cleveland one more day, Barbara wouldn't have taken Tyler shopping.

So much had changed since Tyler's disappearance.

He'd put his law practice on hold while he lived in Cleveland, helping his sister and her husband during the first weeks after the kidnapping.

Before the kidnapping, Grant had been a celebrated criminal defense attorney, representing any client who had the money to pay for his high-priced services. The guilt or innocence of a client had no bearing on his performance or dedication. Like most lawyers, he had a good idea of culpability after building the case and listening to the presentation by the prosecution.

If the price was right, it didn't matter what kind of a scumbag he returned to the streets. He had an occasional twinge of guilt when the crime was particularly brutal and he won the case, but he'd soothed his conscience with the adage that he was only an instrument of justice.

During the investigation into Tyler's disappearance, he'd learned more than he wanted to know about the perverts who preyed on children. He'd listened to the horror stories of repeat offenders in child molestation and pedophilia cases and no longer had the stomach to defend some of the clients who wanted his services.

When his engagement to Veronica ended, he'd left the law firm where her father was a partner and moved to a small firm, taking only clients whom he unconditionally believed were innocent. Most who wanted his services didn't fall into that category, so he had plenty of time to devote to his investigation of Tyler's disappearance.

And that had brought him to the redwood deck overlooking Falcon Lake. His mind was drifting, lulled by the beauty of the reds and purples of the sunset, when he heard footsteps coming along the side of the house. He was surprised that Ham had returned so quickly with the fried chicken.

"How close is that chicken place?" he asked. He turned to see Connie Prentice standing at the bottom of the steps to the redwood deck. "Oh, sorry. I thought you were Ham."

"I hope that's not some sort of pork reference or I'll be insulted," she said.

"Here, let me help you," he said. He crossed the deck to stand above her, holding out his hand to take the bag she was holding. "Bearing gifts?"

"Actually, it's dinner. I thought I'd better bring it over before the rain hits. I can't believe Hamilton is much of a cook, and I didn't know if you were. It's a chicken casserole, but I gather a chicken is already on the way."

"It is, but this will be a welcome addition to our bachelor stocked refrigerator." He took the bag and waited while she climbed the stairs. "I think we have twelve beers, two bags of chips and assorted dips. And of course, since it's Wisconsin, we have a couple sticks of spicy venison jerky and a bag of cheese curds."

"I hate curds," she said. "They squeak when you bite into them. I'd take one of those beers, if you're offering."

"Coming up. Make yourself at home."

Grant opened the screen door and took the bag to the kitchen. He unpacked it, putting everything in the refrigerator except for the brownies, which he set on the counter for later consumption. He opened two bottles of beer, found a beer glass in the cupboard and headed back to the deck. Connie was in the living room, looking at the pictures over George's desk.

Several of the drawers were partially open, as if she'd been searching for something.

"Shall we go back outside?" he said, holding the

screen door open for her. "Ham should be back momen-
tarily, and I'm sure we'll have enough chicken if you'd
like to share."

"Thanks, no. The beer will be fine. Brent and I ate
earlier."

He poured part of the beer into the glass and
handed it to her. She took it and walked across to stare
out over the trees at the lake, then turned around and
hitched a hip up onto the railing. She saluted him with
the glass, and he raised his beer bottle in response.

"To George. Damn, but I miss him." She sipped her
beer, one eyebrow raised in amusement as his eyes
roamed over her.

He had to admit, yellow enhanced her bronzed skin
and blond hair, adding depth to her green eyes. She was
a beautiful woman and she knew it. Definitely high
maintenance with her diamond earrings, diamond and
emerald rings and the wide gold bracelet on her wrist.
He'd known enough women like Connie in Veronica's
circle to recognize that her appearance was the tool
she'd use for manipulation and barter.

Maggie's face flashed into his mind, and he was surprised at the feeling of warmth that invaded his body as
he contrasted the two women. He preferred Maggie's
softness to the brittle quality of Connie's overt sensual-
ity.

"Do you always wear yellow?" he asked as he noted
the expensive lemony silk shorts and matching blouse.

"How clever of you," she said. "You've only seen me
a few times and yet you figured it out. It took Brent almost six months. Of course, he's my husband, so he
doesn't have to notice."

"Lawyers are paid to be observant."

"You look like you're enjoying your visit to Delbrook," Connie said, looking at him over the rim of her glass.

"I feel downright decadent in blue jeans. I spend the better part of my life in button-down shirts and suits. My casual wear is a blazer. I'm enjoying the change."

"My mother always thought that a woman who was not wearing a dress, nylons, a slip and a girdle had gone 'native.' I can't imagine what she would think of this outfit."

She held her arms out wide to give him the whole effect.

"I'm sure she'd be jealous of the tan," he said. "I don't mean to be offensive, but may I ask you a question?"

Her eyes held his for a moment, speculation in their depth. "Go ahead. I can always refuse to answer."

"What were you looking for in George's desk?"

Aside from an archly raised eyebrow, his straightforward question didn't appear to ruffle her. She didn't answer immediately, and he sensed that she was deciding whether to give him the truth or make something up. She took a long swallow, finished the beer, and set the glass on the top of the railing.

"Thanks to my mother's obsession with golf and the fact there was a swimming pool there, I grew up at the country club. Mark Collier, Maggie's husband, was just a couple years younger than I was. We spent a lot of time together when George was playing cards."

Grant wondered where Connie's discourse was heading. She seemed content to talk, and he pulled up a chair, propped up his feet and watched the play of emotions across her face.

"Mark was your first love?"

"Lover, yes. Love, no." She gave him a quick smile, teeth a flash of white in the tanned face. "The story in Delbrook is that Mark Collier was the model son, loving husband and all-around great father. The truth is, he was a real bastard. The original roving eye. I doubt if he had it in him to be faithful. The only person he loved was Mark Collier."

"Did Maggie know about the other women?"

"Yes."

The revelation surprised Grant. He mentally apologized to Maggie for assuming she had led a storybook life up until Mark's death. He should have known most fairy tales have a villain.

"So that's why you're hanging around Delbrook," she said.

Grant wanted to deny his interest in Maggie but knew she would see through his bluff. Besides, it was safer if people speculated that he was staying in town because of his attraction to her.

"I'll admit she intrigues me," he said.

"Just like Mark. At first I couldn't understand why he married Maggie. It's the eyes." Connie's mouth pulled into a twist of bitterness. "Blue eyes full of truth and goodness and honesty. Beneath that soft, sweet exterior, there's a banked fire that's a real challenge."

"She strikes me as a person with a strong moral compass. Why didn't she divorce her husband?"

"She would have stuck out the marriage for Jake's sake, but eventually Mark wanted out. When he asked her for a divorce, she agreed. I may be the only one to know that except Maggie."

"Mark told you?"

"Yes. We used to call each other a lot. I'm sure I knew more about his love life than Maggie. He liked to tell me about his other women. He told me once he loved the chase, not the conquest," Connie said, twisting the wide bracelet on her wrist. "Once he bedded them it was over. Most of the women let him go without too much of a fuss. Until he met Joy Edwards."

"Ah, I like the name," Grant said. "She gave him more joy than he'd expected?"

"You might say a whole bundle of joy." She laughed, the sound a sharp bark that held little amusement. "Joy Edwards was young, practical and determined to marry Mark when she discovered she was pregnant. She wanted the child to have a name."

"Just an old-fashioned girl."

"The last time I talked to Mark was the day of his accident. He and Joy were coming up to Wisconsin the next morning to tell George about his decision to divorce Maggie and remarry. Joy had insisted that he get George's approval. She was the traditional sort; she wanted to be part of a family, not an interloper."

"Was Mark pleased with the prospect of a new child?" Grant asked.

"No. He didn't like change. He didn't want to give up his established lifestyle. He did his best to hide his infidelities. He wanted everyone's approval, especially Jake's and his father's. He was worried that they would be angry when he told them about the divorce." She sighed, staring across at Grant for a moment before she continued. "The irony is that he and Joy and the baby were killed before he could tell anyone except Maggie and me."

"He went to the grave with his secrets intact," Grant said. "Hard on Maggie. Hard to live with that knowledge."

The chirp of crickets was the only sound to break the silence on the deck. Connie was relaxed, her legs crossed at the ankles as she leaned against the railing. Grant waited, wondering how they'd come so far afield from his original question.

"You're a good listener. Just like George," she said as if she had read his mind. "As I told you, I spent a lot of time at the country club. When it rained, I used to watch the card games. George was always kind to me. He never shooed me away from the table. That's how I learned to play poker."

"At George's knee?"

"Exactly. It wasn't until I was married that I was permitted into the weekly games. Things were fine until Mark died. Then George took up drinking as a serious endeavor. That and poker were his only interests. Sometimes he was so drunk that I'd drag him outside and walk him around the golf course until he was sober enough to play. All the time we walked, he would talk. Ranting mostly about the unfairness of life."

She must have seen the questioning expression on his face, because she grinned suddenly.

"You're probably wondering if there's a point to all this. I've been enjoying myself. I don't have that many people I can confide in. Do you suppose this conversation is covered under the lawyer-client privilege?"

"I think we could stretch it for that," he said. He returned her smile, liking her much more than he thought he would when she first arrived.

"All right, I'll get to it. During one of our walks, I told George that I thought Frank Woodman would make a good mayor and that I was encouraging him to run. I was worried that Charley Blessington would make a try for it. George said not to worry, that he had the one piece of evidence that would stop Charley in his tracks."

Grant dropped his feet to the deck and leaned forward in his chair. "And that was?"

Connie shook her head. "I don't know. He said he'd stumbled across something in Charley's background that would take him out of the running. When I asked what it was, he snapped his mouth shut and refused to tell me. All he'd say was that if Charley announced he was running, George would show him the report and that would be the end of that."

"So George had some kind of report," Grant said.

"Yes. That's what I was looking for in the desk. It was stupid, because I can't imagine he'd have left it right out in plain sight if it was something explosive. George said Charley would do anything to keep the information from getting out."

CHAPTER SIXTEEN

MAGGIE WAS HALFWAY DOWN the staircase to the bookstore, carrying a laundry basket of dirty clothes, when a crash of thunder exploded over the house. Below her, lightning flashes illuminated the steps. Knowing the fragility of the electrical connections in the old house, she remained where she was.

The lights flickered and went out.

"Oh damn!" she muttered as she inched her way across the step until her hip touched the banister.

"Mom?" Jake yelled.

"Give it a minute," she called back.

She held her breath and waited. The lights blinked once, then popped back on. Overhead, the thunder grumbled as the storm closed in.

She retraced her steps, set the laundry basket down at the top of the stairs and headed along the hallway to the kitchen. The phone rang, and Jake tore out of his room, skidding past her.

"I'll get it," he yelled as he raced for the phone in the kitchen.

By the time Maggie arrived, Jake was talking into the phone.

"Just do it, Kenny," he said.

He turned his back to Maggie and spoke under his breath so that she didn't catch any more of the conversation. She opened the junk drawer, pulled out a flashlight and pressed the switch. A minuscule circle of light beamed out, slowly faded and died. No amount of tapping or pressing could rejuvenate it. Tossing it back in the drawer, she opened the cabinet over the stove and took out three votive candles in glass holders. Behind her, Jake hung up the phone.

"Can I have a candle in my room?" he asked, flinching at the boom of thunder outside.

The lights flickered, but this time they didn't go out.

"I'm not too keen on that," she said. "I'm going to light a couple candles before I go back down to finish the laundry, so if the lights go out you won't be in the dark."

She lit one and placed it on the counter. Carrying the other two, she went into the living room and lit another one and set it on the coffee table in front of the loveseat.

"What if the lights go out during the night?"

"I'll put one in my room and leave the door open so you can see the light. OK?"

"I guess so," Jake said.

"It's eight o'clock, so if you've finished your homework you can watch a half hour of television in here."

"I'm all done. I was just reading some stuff," he said, flopping down on the loveseat and reaching for the remote control.

"Keep the volume down," she said as the sound of the television followed her into the hall.

Maggie took the last candle and set it in the laundry

basket just as the telephone rang. Rats! She'd never get finished at this rate. Once more Jake raced out to the kitchen and she stood at the top of the stairs waiting.

"It's for you, Mom. It's Aunt Nell."

Maggie went into her bedroom and picked up the portable phone. "I've got it, Jake."

"I'm sorry to be such a disappointment," Nell said after Jake hung up. "Obviously he was expecting someone more exciting. He's not at the age when the girls call all the time, is he?"

"No. Thank goodness. I'm not sure what's up. He's been jumping for the phone every time it rings," Maggie said. "I think Kenny's involved as well, so I'm expecting a call from school in the next day or so telling me that they've both been suspended again."

"Can you see why I was so thrilled to have girl children? They're wonderful to shop with and talk to, and hopefully they might even take care of me in my old age." Nell chuckled. "Although Jean Frances says the moment I look a bit shaky, it's bam, right into the rest home."

"First you've got to find a place that will take all your art supplies. How's the painting going?"

"Slow. I was planning on working late tonight, but with the light show outside it's hard to concentrate."

Maggie shivered as rain pelted the bedroom window. Wind whipped against the trees, and in the streetlights along the boardwalk she could see it roughening the surface of the lake. The temperature had dropped earlier in the evening, so it looked to be a cold, nasty night ahead.

"It's the same here. I'm doing laundry." Maggie jumped at the sound of the door buzzer. "Damn it, now someone's at the door."

"I'll get it," Jake yelled.

"Go ahead and see who it is," Nell said. "I didn't have anything of importance. I just wanted to make sure you were all right. Talk to you tomorrow."

Maggie hung up and walked along the hall as she heard the rumble of voices coming up the back stairs. To her surprise she found a very wet Brent Prentice standing in the middle of the kitchen, breathing heavily from the stair climbing.

"Sorry for not calling first, Maggie," he said, looking awkward as he stood holding a ceramic bowl covered in aluminum foil in one hand and a bag in the other. "I'm getting your floor all wet."

"Don't worry about the floor," she said, reaching out to take the foil-wrapped dish.

"I can take the bag," Jake said, earning a smile of approval from Maggie.

Even after his hands were free, Brent seemed unsure of what to do about the water that dripped off the edge of his raincoat, so he just remained where he was.

"Connie was taking something over to Ham and that cousin of Edna's and wanted me to bring this casserole over, but I suspect you've already had dinner. I had some errands to run and didn't realize it was getting so late."

"What's in the casserole?" Jake asked, prying up a corner of the aluminum foil.

"Jake," Maggie said, swatting his hands away from the dish.

"It's a chicken-and–water chestnut thing." Brent chuckled at Jake's less than enthusiastic expression. "Don't worry. There are chocolate brownies in the bag along with some rice and a salad."

"Thanks, Mr. Prentice. Brownies are my favorite," Jake said. He set the bag on the counter and disappeared into the living room.

"It'll be a real treat not to have to think about cooking a meal. Please tell Connie how much I appreciate her thoughtfulness," Maggie said.

She suspected that the gesture had been prompted by Brent. The old-fashioned tradition of providing food after a death seemed more in keeping with his character than Connie's.

"I'll tell her," he said. With the tips of his fingers, he smoothed the damp white hair at his temples.

"What a boob I am to let you stand around when you're soaked," Maggie said. "Would you like a drink before you head back out into the storm?"

Brent shook his head. "No. Thanks for the offer, but it's getting late."

"Well the least I can do is lend you an umbrella."

She flipped on the light in the stairwell and reached for the umbrella she kept with her raincoat on one of the clothes hooks on the wall. The hook was empty.

"Jake? Have you seen my umbrella?" When there was no immediate answer, she called again. "Jake? The umbrella?"

"Isn't on the stairs?" came the drowsy answer from the living room.

"No. It's not." Maggie frowned, trying to remember when she'd last seen it. She was too tired for guessing games. If she could remember where she'd left her raincoat, she'd probably find her umbrella.

"Please don't fuss," Brent said. "I'm parked right out in back and I'm heading home. Just thought I'd stop by and make sure you were both all right. What with the storm and all."

"A couple of those thunderclaps were right overhead," Maggie said, walking back to the counter to put the casserole in the refrigerator. She smiled when she opened the bag and found a new flashlight. "You must be psychic, Brent. The lights went out a little while ago, and my flashlight died in my hand."

"I had to stop at Mackie's Hardware Store to get one for myself, and knowing how precarious the electricity is in these old houses, I thought you might need an extra."

"You're very thoughtful," she said.

For some reason Brent's kindness brought tears to her eyes. When he realized she was upset, he looked positively stricken.

"Please don't worry," she said. "I was thinking of George. He used to fuss at me about things like flashlights, squeaky hinges and oil for my car. Sometimes I'd get so impatient with him, but it's silly things like that that remind me of him."

"I know just what you mean. I remember when Connie's father died, I didn't realize how much I'd miss the little everyday things."

Now that he was talking, Brent seemed more at ease. He crossed to the sink and unrolled several sheets of paper towels. When Maggie tried to take them, he waved her away.

"Did you know Edmund Falcone, Connie's father?" he asked as he knelt down to wipe the floor.

"No. He was gone before my mother moved back to Delbrook."

Resting his forearm on his knee, he looked up at

her, a thoughtful expression on his face. "He wasn't a big man in size, but he had the kind of power that made you think he was taller. He bustled when he walked. It's an old word, but it describes how he moved. He gave the impression that there were not enough minutes in the day to get things done unless he hurried through each task."

"I've known people like that," Maggie said, leaning against the counter. "They usually end up having a heart attack or a stroke."

"That's what happened to Edmund." Brent gave the floor a final sweep of the towels and rose to his feet. "He had a stroke the night Connie and I were married."

"How dreadful," Maggie said, reaching out to take the paper towels and throw them in the wastebasket.

"He must have had the attack right after the wedding guests left. He had a housekeeper in those days. Cait Darlington. She had fantastic managing skills but was a bit too sharp-tongued for my taste. Mrs. Darlington found Edmund the morning after the wedding. Connie and I were on our honeymoon when we got the call that her father had been taken to the hospital."

"How serious was the stroke?"

"The worst. Although his mind still functioned, he was almost totally paralyzed and had lost his capacity for speech."

Maggie shuddered. How would it feel to be imprisoned inside your own body? As Brent had said, worse than death. "How long did he survive?"

"He died just short of our first anniversary."

"Dear God. A year."

"It wasn't quite as bad as you'd imagine. Connie was

devastated. She couldn't bear to look at the man she had adored in such a weakened condition. We agreed that she would go to work and I would stay home to care for him. Don't look so astonished," he said. "Men can be excellent caregivers."

"My look wasn't meant to be disparaging," she said. "I've never known much about you, and it was a side of you I hadn't seen before. I've always thought you were very kind, so I'm not surprised that you would opt to take on Edmund's care."

Brent's shoulders rounded and a blush rose to his cheeks.

"I'd hate for you to think I selflessly sacrificed my life for my father-in-law. I'm practical by nature, and it seemed the most logical solution. Edmund would have hated being dependent on nurses."

"Yes, I can imagine if he was the bustling sort, he would prefer to keep his infirmities a private matter."

Brent nodded. "I had the help of nurses and therapists, but I was the one who was responsible for his day-to-day care. Knowing his mind was still intact, I read to him as much as I could. Newspapers, magazines, books. Anything I thought might be of interest."

"That must have been a godsend for him."

"I hope so." A shadow crossed his face. "One never knows."

"It must have been hard on both you and Connie, especially since you were newlyweds."

"Not really," Brent said. "I was comfortable with Edmund. I'd lived in the house on and off over the years since I was sixteen. One of my teachers brought it to Edmund's attention that, although I was a bright child, my mother couldn't afford to send me to a private school, let alone college. Connie's father sponsored me all the way through school and, after my mother died, gave me a room in the house where I spent vacations and holidays."

"How good for all of you," Maggie said. "It must have been good for Connie and her mother to have someone else in the house if it was so big."

"Actually, Edmund's wife left when Connie was ten. My addition to the household took the pressure off Connie to be the son that Edmund never had."

Brent laughed, but the sound was harsh rather than lighthearted. He paced across the floor to look out the window at the rain, his face thoughtful as he turned back to Maggie.

"It was a case of poor little rich girl," he said. "Connie was totally different then. Looking at her now you'd never guess that she was quite a tomboy in those days. She never wore anything feminine. Her hair was cut short, and she had a swearing vocabulary that would rival any longshoreman's speech."

Maggie couldn't picture the elegant Connie as Brent described her. "She's definitely changed for the better."

"I think so," he said, his voice soft and admiring. "She had always been desperate for her father's approval, and when her mother left she tried even harder to please her father. If he wanted a son, she would be one."

"Was Edmund blind to the fact?" Maggie asked.

"I don't know. Maybe that's why he chose to mentor me. He transferred his expectations to me, and eventually Connie learned to enjoy her role as a female."

Brent's comments made Maggie feel some guilt over not liking Connie more. She'd automatically stereotyped her as a spoiled only child but should have known there was more to the story.

"I understand there was a fire in the house. Is that how Edmund died?"

"Yes and no. When Edmund discovered the house was on fire, he had another stroke. This one was fatal. I carried him outside, and Connie and I stood beside his body and watched the house burn to the ground."

"Dear God, how tragic," Maggie said, hearing the remembered horror in his voice.

"I designed the new house," he said. "It's lovely, even though it can't compare in size to the original. Old Delbrook Falcone, Connie's grandfather, had hopes of housing a dynasty on the shores of Falcon Lake. It was a huge rambling affair. Next time you're at the library, ask to see the pictures of the place. It was called Falcon's Nest."

Falcon's Nest. An aerie. The name sent a shiver through Maggie's body. Feathers, birds, eagles, falcons. The continual references frightened her, as if the words held some special warning. Like a bird of prey, fear hovered over her, threatening to swoop down at any moment and carry away everything she held dear.

Mouse Ears and Shorty were still alive.

The mice were shivering in a corner of the cage. There was blood on the shavings at the other end. Tyler pushed his finger in between the wires to touch his friend's fur. He could feel the warm body beneath the scratchy coat.

Tyler sorry. Tyler help.

The man would be angry. He might bring the bird and let it bite Tyler. He jerked his hand back away from the cage. Mouse Ears scrabbled in a circle as if he were searching for his friend.

Tyler reached out and pulled the cage toward the edge of the table. Picking it up, he set it on the floor. He sat down cross-legged in front of it. His fingers touched the latch. The hinges squeaked as he opened the little door.

Tyler made clicking sounds with his tongue. Come Mouse Ears.

Shorty ran toward him, but his friend crawled under the cedar shavings. The end of his nose twitching, Shorty stuck his head out the cage door. Before Tyler could grab him, he jumped onto the mud floor and raced toward the back of the room until he was lost in the shadows.

Tyler snapped his fingers.

The shavings rustled and Mouse Ears raised his head. Tyler snapped them again. The mouse crawled across the cage to the door. Tyler reached out and grabbed the mouse in his hand. He sucked in air at the feel of the wriggling body. Standing up, he carried his trophy across to the shelf bed. He held on to the tail as he set the mouse in the nest of blankets.

With the tip of one finger, he stroked the top of Mouse Ears' head. The mouse went still, no longer pulling at his tail. Tyler sang the ABC song and then with a sigh released his friend.

Mouse Ears remained motionless. Tyler touched the rounded back. The mouse turned and jabbed his pointed nose against his fingers.

Tyler cupped both his hands. Inching along in a circle, Mouse Ears brushed his palms, nuzzling against them. He could feel the tickle all the way up his arms.

Beyond the door, he heard a sound. His heart hammered in his chest as his hands closed protectively around the mouse. With a shudder he opened his fingers.

Run Mouse Ears.

Tyler snapped his fingers. The mouse raised his head, then with a bouncing run, he jumped off the bed and disappeared in the darkness beneath the shelf.

Maggie finished folding the last of Jake's shirts and set it on top of the pile of clean clothes. Rain was still falling outside, and she was grateful that she'd been able to spend the evening at home. After Brent left, she'd come downstairs to do the laundry. While she waited, she'd tried to read, but her mind had been filled with all the things that he'd told her.

It struck her that one could socialize with people and yet know very little about their lives. Most people had secrets, either things they preferred to keep private or things no one ever asked them about.

She was pleased that Brent had volunteered the information about Edmund Falcone. She'd sensed a kindness in him, and his care of Connie's father added another layer to his personality that she might never have suspected.

It made her all the more curious about Brent's relationship with Connie.

Maggie'd only seen the couple in social situations, but even then she'd been aware of a tension between the two. Although Connie was the demonstrative type, Maggie had never seen her give Brent the kind of loving touch that most couples exchanged. Never a caress in passing or even the sort of visual cue that was tantamount to an embrace.

Nell had told her that Connie had had an affair with Hugh Rossiter several years ago. It was after Hugh's wife left. The gossip ran rampant, and neither one had been particularly discreet. If Brent knew about it, he apparently had forgiven Connie. In conversation, his voice was either conciliatory or self-deprecating. It was Connie's tone that held the sharp edge.

No matter what Brent said about his closeness to Edmund, it was strange that Connie hadn't been the one to take care of her father. Brent said that she adored her father, and yet she preferred to put his welfare in her husband's hands. Although it didn't reflect well on Connie, Maggie tried not to condemn her. Many people couldn't handle acting as a nurse for a loved one.

She wondered why they'd never had children. It was hardly a question she could ask. Perhaps they couldn't have them. In any case it was a shame. Brent would have made a loving father, and perhaps a child would have softened the brittle edge that Connie showed to the world.

Life had been simpler before George's death. Now she wondered if anything was ever what it seemed to be. Was Grant? So much depended on whether she could trust him.

He had called earlier, and she had to admit she'd enjoyed the conversation. Even through the phone he'd been able to sense her uneasiness. He talked for a while

as the storm crashed overhead, and she'd been so involved the majority of the thunder and lightning had
passed unnoticed.

It was only then that he told Maggie that Eddie
Harland's mother had agreed to speak to her. He gave
her the flight information and told her he'd pick her up
at nine in the morning for the drive to the airport. Despite her apprehension, she said she'd be ready.

Please, God, let it go well, she thought.

Maggie placed her hands at the small of her back
and stretched backward to ease her stiffness. One
glance at the clock and she sighed. Ten o'clock. "Never
enough time," she muttered. Balancing the laundry basket on her hip, she switched off the light in the laundry
room and walked through the kitchen into the darkened
bookstore.

The upstairs hall light streamed through the open
door. The phone rang as she started up the staircase,
and she cursed the fact that she'd forgotten to bring the
portable. She quickened her steps, but before she could
get to the top, Jake's door opened and he ran across the
hall to her bedroom and the ringing phone. She could
hear him talking as she closed and locked the door to the
bookstore. When she entered the bedroom, he was
whispering into the phone, one hand curled around his
mouth so she couldn't hear his words.

"Who is it, Jake?" she said, her voice sharp with
worry.

"It's for you," he said.

She set the laundry basket on the bed and held out
her hand for the receiver. After a momentary hesitation,
he placed the portable phone in her hand.

"I didn't think you'd get upstairs in time to answer the phone," he said.

"I appreciate your concern," she said. "Now get back to bed."

"Night, Mom."

He hurried past her and into his own room, closing the door with a solid click of the latch. Maggie raised the receiver.

"Hello?" she said.

For a moment all Maggie could hear was the sound of rain. It took her a moment to realize that whoever was on the other end was calling from a phone that was outside. Either a cell phone or a pay phone. She pressed the receiver to her ear as she heard the rasping voice on the line.

"Missus Jake?"

Her fingers tightened on the telephone at the unfamiliar greeting. "Who's calling? Who is this?"

"It's Tully, missus."

"Tully! Are you all right?"

"Yes, missus. I had to get away because I was afraid of what would happen."

"That's what I thought, Tully. But you need to come back. It's not good for you to be hiding and frightened. No one means you any harm."

Even as Maggie said the words she wondered if they were true. Someone might want to keep Tully from talking.

"I can't come back yet. Blessington has been looking for a reason to put me in jail. I'd die in jail. I've got some thinking to do. Need to find out who's against me. Soon's I know, I'll come talk to you."

She could hear the withdrawal in his voice. She didn't know what to do for the best. The sound of the rain decided her.

"Do you want to come here, Tully? You need a place to stay and you'd be safe here. Jake and I would be glad to have the company."

"He's a good boy. And you too, missus. It's risky to come there. People will be watching. No time to be reckless."

Frustrated at her inability to convince Tully that he might be in danger, she felt like crying. "Do you need anything?"

"I wanted to tell you I didn't hurt George," he said, ignoring her question.

"Jake told me you wouldn't, and I believed him. Do you know who did?"

"I didn't see. I don't know why he was killed." His voice sounded baffled, as if he were trying to work out some puzzle. "Maybe I can find out."

"Please, Tully, it's dangerous to be out there on your own. You have friends here in Delbrook who can help you. Will you come and talk to me?"

"Not yet, missus. Don't worry about Tully. I'm good at hiding. Just wanted to tell you I wouldn't never hurt George any more than I would hurt you or Jake."

Tully's voice faded away. For a moment Maggie heard the sound of rain, then a click and the line went dead.

CHAPTER
SEVENTEEN

DENNIS NYLAND STROKED his fingers along the row of silver rings lining the edge of his ear. The soft tinkling sound was soothing. He'd gotten in the habit of doing it whenever he talked to his mother. It made it easier to ignore the whine in her voice as she cataloged his sins of commission and omission.

He was twenty-five. Too old to live at home. If he didn't get out soon he'd be trapped forever.

Dead as old Collier.

Dennis shivered as he remembered touching the dead man. Even though George Collier's body had still been warm, he had felt as if the heat were being sucked out of his fingers wherever he touched the man's flesh.

Getting up from his desk, he walked across to the far side of the garage to the beat-up refrigerator and opened the door. It was stuffy in the garage, and he breathed in the cool air before leaning over to take out a beer. He shut the refrigerator with the heel of his shoe and opened the entry door beside it.

He stood in the open doorway, looking out at the dark night. The sky was clear, but the air was heavy after the fury of the rain that passed through earlier. He enjoyed working in the garage during a thunderstorm. He'd turn up the volume on his CD player and blast the music. It was what he imagined it would be like inside the eye of a tornado.

It was midnight, and the neighborhood was quiet. Everyone was in bed. Wednesday night. A workday tomorrow. He stuck his head out until he could see around the corner of the garage to the back of the house. Just one light in the kitchen so he'd be able to see his way when he came inside.

Ma'd gone upstairs. He could see the faint blue light from the TV in her bedroom window. Every night when he came upstairs, she'd be sound asleep, the TV blaring in the silent house. Some nights he wanted to smash the screen.

He had to get out of Delbrook.

Leaving the door open, he made a circuit of the garage, making sure that everything was ready in case his visitor wanted the tattoo immediately. He checked to see that the autoclave was plugged in. Everyone was paranoid about catching AIDS. New clients always checked to see that the sterilizer was functional.

Back at his desk, he flipped through the pages of flash, pleased with the new designs he'd created for his display book of tattoos. He was driving to Madison on Saturday to see about a full-time job and had been working for the past week setting up sample books of photographs so he could show the owner the kind of tattoos he'd done.

A month earlier he'd gone over to Madison to a body modification convention and met Tony DeVita, the owner of Tony's Tattoo Parlor. They'd hit it off immediately. The parlor was two blocks from the University of Wisconsin, and when he had stopped by to check it out, the place had been loaded with students.

Tony had an opening, and Dennis wanted the job. Although several tattoo artists worked there, no one could do custom work. Dennis could draw anything freehand anywhere on the client's body. He was convinced that once Tony saw the kind of work he could do, the job was his.

Nobody'd hassle him in Madison. The cops weren't as provincial as Charley Blessington.

Blessington had been on his case for years. Giving him the hard eye whenever he saw him at the country club. Just like Sunday when the cops had picked him up at his girlfriend's place. You'd have thought he was the one who offed Collier.

Thank God he'd told the chief that Collier was already dead when he found him. It made him panicky to think that someone else might have been there and overheard Collier.

"Tattoo."

That's what Collier had said. Just the one word. Dennis had been in his shirtsleeves, and in the bright moonlight the dying man must have seen the tattoos on his arms. If Blessington heard about that, he'd take it as a deathbed accusation and slap the cuffs on him, despite the fact he'd already told the chief that he'd seen Tully Jackson running away.

Dennis heard a car pull up outside the garage. He touched the drawing on his desk for good luck. He hoped he'd gotten it right. He'd only gotten a quick look at the original tattoo.

He grinned, remembering his surprise to find someone coming out of the shower tonight at the country club
when he thought the locker room was empty. He'd started
to clean earlier than usual, but it was no big whoop.

And then to be accused of staring like some kind of
pervert!

Shit! All he cared about was the tattoo. He'd just
gotten a quick look before the towel covered it.

He couldn't resist asking who'd done the drawing. It
wasn't anyone local. Dennis knew the few artists in the
area.

Despite the glare and his own feeling of discomfort,
Dennis refused to retreat with his tail between his legs.
He pulled out one of the new business cards he'd printed
up. The colors were vivid and the design was original.
With a flourish, he flipped it on the bench between the
lockers. He mentioned he did custom work and offered a
discount on a tattoo before he left the room.

Dennis stroked his hand across the stencil paper on
his desk. He was pleased with the colors he'd chosen.
The original must have been an old tattoo, because the
colors weren't as vibrant as the ones he'd placed.

An eye-catching gold for the arrow and a bright
cherry red for the bleeding heart.

"Why do I have to go to Aunt Nell's after school?"

Jake stood at the bottom of the back stairs of the
bookstore, his body rigid, elbows out and his fists
jammed against his waist. Maggie wondered why she
hadn't told him about her trip at breakfast to avoid this
last-minute confrontation. Probably because she knew
he'd put up a fuss, she thought.

"Let's not get into an argument," she said. "I've already arranged for Nell to pick you up after school."

"Why can't I go to Kenny's?"

"Because I said so." She hated falling back on the motherly defense, but she had to admit it came in handy in cases like this. "We're not going to discuss this further. I'll try to get back in time to pick you up, but in any case, we'll go out for dinner when I get home."

"I won't be hungry."

If it hadn't been so frustrating, Maggie would have smiled at the hangdog expression that accompanied his words. He'd been sullen and uncooperative since she'd told him that she was going to Milwaukee for the day. She couldn't imagine how he'd react if he knew she was going to Detroit.

"I'd like to think that by the time I get back you'll be in a better frame of mind."

"I won't be," he said. "I still don't see why you have to go to Milwaukee with him."

Jake's oblique reference to Grant gave Maggie a clue as to the reason for his antagonism. It wasn't the trip he was angry about; it was the fact she was going with Grant. What on earth did he have against Grant? Oh rats! Why did a crisis always occur when she had no time to deal with it?

"Look, Jake," she said, "I know you're unhappy about this, but give me a break. I have to go to Milwaukee today, and since Grant is going there too, it only makes good sense that we go together. When I get back, you and I need to sit down and have a little chat."

"I don't want to talk about him. Why doesn't he go

back to Chicago? Every time we go someplace, he has to come too. I don't like him."

He'd apparently bottled up his resentment against Grant, and the words spilled out in a whiny litany of complaints. Seeing Hugh Rossiter's car coming down the street, Maggie sighed. At least she knew the source of Jake's latest round of hostility, and when she returned she'd have to deal with it.

"Enough," she said, her voice sharper than she'd intended. "We'll talk about this tonight. Give me a hug and don't give your teacher any grief today."

Hugh pulled up beside her, and she opened the back door of the car. She gave Jake a squeeze, but he hung limp in her arms, not responding in any way except for a mumbled goodbye. Hugh looked at her quizzically, and she rolled her eyes.

"Thanks for picking up Jake," she said, leaning in the open passenger window. "I've got to go over to the police station and make a report about George's car."

Hugh turned off the motor and stepped out, walking with her over to George's dark green Malibu. "I see they broke the side window to get in. They take anything?"

"Not that I can tell. Whoever it was looked through the glove compartment, under the seats and in the trunk. I doubt if there was anything to take. The police already went over the car, so they have an inventory of what was there. When I called to report it, they told me to come in and take a look at the list. They didn't seem too concerned about fingerprints."

"Only idiots leave prints nowadays," Hugh said. "Did it happen last night or this morning?"

"It must have been after the storm came through, because the inside of the car is dry."

He walked around the car, peering at the maps and papers littering the inside. "You didn't hear anything?"

"No. It was still raining when I went to bed. Nell called me to tell me about it. She needed a sugar fix this morning and went out to get chocolate éclairs." Maggie shuddered at the thought. "She walked over to Corky's Bakery and didn't see the window until she was coming back."

"You better call George's insurance company," Hugh said.

"Damn. I didn't think about that."

He put his arm around her shoulders as they walked back to the car. She could feel the strength of his body as he pulled her close against his side. Normally she tried to be self-reliant, but she was just tired enough that she appreciated the protective feeling that radiated from him.

"I'll call a friend of mine and have him repair the window," he said. "He can do it here without your bringing the car into the shop."

"That would be great. Are you sure you've got time to call him?"

"For you, I've got time," he said, getting back into the car. "I'd like to do more. How about dinner when you get back from your shopping spree in Milwaukee?"

Maggie blushed at the thought of the number of lies she'd told since George's death. The worst of it was that she was finding it easier to do and she felt less guilty when she did it.

"I think I'll pass on that, Hugh. Some other time."

"I'll give you a call tonight. I didn't get a chance to talk to you yesterday."

"Thanks for showing Grant the birds," she said. "He was really impressed."

"He certainly asked a lot of questions. For a while I thought he was planning to give up the law and open his own falconry club."

"He's the curious type. I suppose that's what comes from being a lawyer. Always building a case," she said. "You driving in to Milwaukee?"

"No. Grant has some business there, so I thought I'd tag along."

Hugh's brows bunched over his eyes, and he gave her a comprehensive glance. "How long is he staying over at George's?"

"I don't know," she said, awkward with the question.

"Delbrook's an interesting change of pace for him. Eventually he'll get his fill and return to his life in Chicago."

Uncomfortable under the intensity of his gaze, Maggie stepped away from the window. "I better let you go or you'll be late. Have a good day, boys."

She waved as the car started up. Kenny was the only one who returned the wave. So, along with Jake being angry about her spending the day with Grant, Hugh was ticked. She didn't see that he had any reason to be. She hadn't given him any reason to believe that he had the inside track to any relationship with her.

At least she didn't think she had.

Did Hugh? He'd acted unusually territorial when she brought Grant over to look at Camp Delbrook and the birds, touching her in a more intimate manner than he usually did. Did the mere fact that another male was around bring out that sort of competition?

"Oh, damn!" she said aloud.

Thank goodness she had plenty to do to keep her from thinking about the irrationality of men. She drove over to the police station and completed the paperwork on the car break-in, then returned to the bookstore to help Beth shelve the new stock and pack up returns until it was time to get ready for her trip to Detroit. She couldn't decide what to wear, and when she found herself considering a frilly sundress she hadn't worn in five years, she was so annoyed at herself she grabbed an old denim skirt and plain white blouse.

Why was she acting so weird? She didn't usually obsess over her appearance. The thought that it was Grant who was making her crazy irritated her, and she was crabby when he picked her up for the drive to the airport.

"I'd offer a penny for your thoughts," he said as she climbed in and buckled her seat belt, "but by the look on your face, I'm not sure I want to know."

"Jake hates you," she said, blurting out the first thing that came to her mind.

"Ah," he said. "I wouldn't worry about it. He'll get over it."

She turned at the cheerful comment and caught the almost puckish grin on his face.

"What's so funny?"

"It's a guy thing. He's protecting his territory."

"You're kidding!"

"Look at it from Jake's viewpoint. He's been the main man in your life since his father died. With his grandfather gone, he's once again the man in charge. He's not going to welcome anyone into your life, let alone a stranger."

"He's never reacted this way to Hugh," she said, deciding not to tell him about Hugh's display of jealousy.

"I wondered if you were dating him."

"We've gone out a few times. A movie. A dinner. If it's any of your business."

"I see."

Grant's voice was noncommittal, and Maggie kept her eyes focused beyond the windshield, unwilling to look for any reaction to her comments.

"So why isn't Jake hostile about Hugh?"

"Probably because he doesn't see Hugh as a threat."

"What's that supposed to mean?" she said, turning to glare at him.

"For starters, Hugh is the father of his best friend. Jake's used to seeing you two together. He probably doesn't see Hugh as someone who might want to have an intimate relationship with you. Besides, I suspect Jake senses you're not head over heels in love with Hugh."

Maggie took a breath, prepared to defend her position, then thought better of it. Just because Grant was easy to talk to didn't mean that she needed to blab out her life story.

"So I can expect Jake to react this way to every man that comes into my life?"

"Not every man," Grant said. "Just certain ones."

At the husky note in his voice, Maggie was disgusted at the blush that she could feel flooding her cheeks. She refused to rise to the bait, staring out the window as if she were fascinated by the scenery. What on earth was the matter with her? It wasn't as though she was interested in Grant Holbrook. He had come to Wisconsin by chance, and he would be leaving to return to his life in Chicago.

She had given up her life in the city to raise Jake in the small-town atmosphere of Delbrook. She had been happy here, and when Grant left, she would be contented with the life she'd chosen for herself and Jake. Maybe she'd discover she could love Hugh. Anything was possible. In the meantime she needed to remember that her relationship with Grant was one born out of necessity not shared interests or mutual attraction.

As they drove she told him about George's car being broken into. He didn't look surprised. It was almost as if he'd expected it.

"Nothing was taken?" he asked.

"Not as far as I could tell. At the police station I looked over the list that they made when they checked the car. Everything seemed to be intact. I guess I was hoping I'd find something missing that would explain the break-in."

"Whatever it is that someone is looking for," Grant said, "must not be very obvious."

"Why?"

"The thief must have known that the police had already been over the car. If there was anything incriminating, they would have found it."

"What could it be?"

"I haven't a clue, but the search has come full circle. Whoever it is searched George's house, your purse, the hospital bag and now his car. Maybe they'll conclude there's nothing to find, but in the meantime you'll have to be very cautious. Your apartment and the bookstore might be the next on the list."

Maggie closed her eyes and breathed deeply. She'd worried about that right after George was killed, but in the last few days she'd thought the danger had passed. She'd have to remind Jake to be careful about locking the doors.

So much had happened since Sunday morning. Just five days. It seemed like a lifetime.

"Oh, I forgot to tell you," she said. "Tully called last night."

Grant's hands jerked on the steering wheel, and the passenger-side wheels skidded in the gravel along the shoulder until he got the car under control again.

"You might give me some warning that you're planning to drop a bomb like that when I'm driving eighty," he said.

"You shouldn't be speeding," she said.

He glared at her, then returned his eyes to the road. "Are you purposely trying to annoy me?"

Although it was a rhetorical question, she gave it some thought.

"I think I might be. It's a bad habit I have when I'm nervous. My husband never figured that out," she said, surprised that Grant had caught it. "I've been worried about Jake and I'm taking it out on you. All last night he was as nervy as a cat with his tail in a light socket. Every time the phone rang, he ran to get it as if he were waiting to get the news he'd won the lottery."

"That's interesting. He didn't say anything about it?"

"No." She sighed. "And I didn't ask. He's growing

up, and I'm trying to respect his privacy. Being a single parent really bites sometimes."

She stared out the window, aware that part of her ill humor and apprehension was just a holdover from her own lack of confidence in her mothering skills.

"At any rate, Tully called," she said. "He wouldn't tell me where he was, and I couldn't convince him to come talk to me."

"What did he say?"

"He wanted to tell me that he hadn't killed George."

After a moment of silence, Grant asked, "Did you believe him?"

"Yes." Maggie gave the one-word answer without hesitation. "I'm frightened for him. He said he was going to think about who might have killed George. That could be dangerous."

"You're right about that. No clue as to where he might be?"

"No. He was calling from a pay phone or at least someplace outside."

"Any chance that Jake was waiting for Tully's call?"

"Whoof." Maggie hadn't thought about that. She'd just assumed that he and Kenny were up to something outrageous. "If he was, he only had time to say a few words to Tully before I got upstairs."

"It was just a thought. You might ask Jake if he's had any contact with Tully since George died."

"Yesterday I ran into Charley, and he asked me to talk to Jake too. Do you think he really knows anything?"

"He might. It's worth asking him," Grant said.

Maggie was silent the rest of the way to the airport. The flight to Detroit left on schedule, and before she knew it, they were in a rented car on their way to her appointment with Eddie Harland's mother.

"Where are we meeting Mrs. Harland?" she asked.

"At Gifford Elementary. It's on the north side of Detroit. Small private school with a good reputation for working with kids on an individual basis. Eddie and his family live right in the neighborhood, and the community has been helping out financially since he was returned."

"I don't need to tell you that I'm really apprehensive about this," Maggie said. "Are you sure you shouldn't be the one talking to Eddie's mother?"

"To be honest, I wanted to be the one to interview her, but Mrs. Hoppe, the principal, said no. The mother's name is Katrina, she's from Russia, and her husband is from Germany. They've been in the United States for ten years, but according to Mrs. Hoppe, she's still afraid of any kind of authority figures. Men especially."

"How did Mrs. Hoppe convince her to talk to me?"

"Katrina Harland is beginning to realize that Eddie needs psychological help. Except for some counseling through the school, her husband won't consider it. Mrs. Hoppe told Katrina that if she spoke to you about Eddie, it might help locate Tyler, and if that happened, I'd arrange to get the help Eddie needs."

"And you would?"

"Without question," Grant said.

"What should I ask?"

"Try to get any information you can about what Eddie told his parents after he started talking again. Things like what the kidnapper looked like, whether the place he was held was urban or rural, if there were other people involved. Visual clues would be crucial. Anything specific could help us to pinpoint Tyler's location."

"I feel totally inadequate," Maggie said.

"Have a little faith. Take your time and feel your way through it. Go with your heart. You're a mother. Ask whatever you feel is appropriate. If she gets upset, back off a little and maybe just listen."

Maggie clasped her hands in her lap and tried not to think of all the things that could go wrong.

It didn't take long for them to reach Gifford Elementary, a neat brick building in a residential area. The school yard and the parking lot were surrounded by a wrought-iron fence that looked more decorative than functional. Grant pulled up in front of the school and handed her a paper with a phone number where he could be reached when she was finished. With a two-fingered salute, he drove away. Maggie swallowed hard as she headed up the stairs.

A hall monitor met her just inside the door and pointed out the principal's office. Heels clicking on the highly polished linoleum floor, she walked along the silent hall.

"Thank you for coming such a distance for this meeting. The flight must have been right on time," Mrs. Hoppe said. The tall, slender woman rose from her desk and came around to shake hands. "I've been looking forward to meeting you since talking to Mr. Holbrook. He told me about your father-in-law. May I offer my condolences?"

"Thank you," Maggie said. "It's still hard to believe that it happened only five days ago. In many respects it seems like it was much longer than that."

"I've always found it interesting that in stressful situations time is either compressed or elongated." She took Maggie's arm and led her back out into the hall. "I'm sure you're anxious to meet Mrs. Harland, so I won't keep you waiting. Katrina arrived just a few moments ago, and I've put her down the hall in a conference room. One of the teachers is keeping her company because she's a bit skittish. Her husband doesn't know that she's here and would disapprove strongly if he did."

"I appreciate the warning. I'll try not to upset her any more than I have to."

Mrs. Hoppe's mouth tightened. "Don't let her tears deter you. She cries easily because she's afraid. Afraid of her husband. Afraid for her son."

With that caution, the principal opened a door leading into a small lounge. The deeply cushioned couch and chairs were upholstered in a bright chintz pattern that looked warm and inviting. Mrs. Hoppe introduced Maggie to Eddie's mother, and then she and the other teacher left the room. Mrs. Harland's eyes flickered owlishly as the door clicked shut.

"Is that coffee?" Maggie asked, pointing to the tray on the table against the wall.

"Yes. It's very strong."

A trace of an accent gave Mrs. Harland's voice a soft, buttery sound. Without makeup and with her limp brown hair pulled back behind her neck, the woman looked to be in her late thirties, but her skin texture indicated she could be ten years younger. She was wearing a formless black skirt, a faded print blouse and sensible shoes.

Katrina clasped her hands together just beneath her breasts and stood uncertainly in front of the couch while Maggie poured herself a cup of coffee and brought it over to the table.

"I can't tell you how much I appreciate your seeing me today," Maggie said. "It must have been a very difficult decision."

"I don't know if this is a good thing. My husband, Lothar, would not approve," Mrs. Harland said. "If only I could be sure it would help Eddie."

She looked as if she might make a bolt for the door, and Maggie tensed, wondering how to get the woman to relax. She should never have let Grant talk her into this. She tried to think of something to say, but the exhaustion of the last week made it difficult for her to concentrate.

"Would you mind if we sat down?" Maggie said. "I think I need a little of that coffee."

The request startled Mrs. Harland, and she peered closely at Maggie.

"You are very pale. You are not well?" she asked.

"I'm just tired. My father-in-law died this week, and my legs are still aching from standing so much during the wake."

Mrs. Harland crossed herself and reached out to pat Maggie's arm. "It was sudden?"

"Yes." Maggie could see no point in explaining the situation.

"How sad for you and your husband. Was he close to his father?"

"My husband died two years ago. It's just myself and my son, Jake."

"Oh, my dear, please do sit down. The coffee is very good, and it's strong enough to revive you."

Although Maggie would have never thought to use her own circumstances to gain the other woman's confidence, she realized the revelations had given them a sense of bonding. In the ancient tradition of women sharing and mourning their losses together, they drank coffee and talked about their children. Katrina was pleased to know that Jake was so close in age to Eddie.

"The principal mentioned that Eddie was having problems in school?" Maggie asked to ease into the subject that had brought her to Detroit. "I remember that Jake had a hard time after his father's death. His teacher called me on several occasions to talk to me about it."

Katrina's shoulders sagged, and she nodded.

"When Eddie first came here to school four years ago, he was normal. Like the other children. Each year he has had a little more difficulty. Now he is failing all his classes. He is not making trouble in the classes. He seems to have lost interest in school. And he doesn't play with the other boys."

"When he's home, does Eddie play with his brothers?"

"No. He doesn't go outside and play ball with the boys, and he didn't go to the pool this summer. He stays in his room. When I ask him what's wrong, he tells me nothing."

Katrina's voice was thick with tears of frustration.

"Does he listen to music or play computer games?"

"Music, yes. Loud and hard on the ears. All the time, the music. And he ties knots."

"Ties knots?" Maggie asked.

"Yes. Every day. He ties knots in everything. Everywhere I look there are knots."

Maggie felt out of her depth. She didn't know anything about obsessive behavior. She wondered if the psychiatrist at the school knew about this.

"What kind of knots?" she asked.

Katrina jerked to her feet, and for a moment Maggie thought she was distraught and was ending the interview. Instead she went across to one of the chairs and picked up a bulky black fabric handbag. She brought it back to the couch and sat down. Opening the top, she reached inside and withdrew a metal key ring. A short black string, the thickness of a shoelace, was tied to the ring with a fancy knot, and beneath it was a second knot.

"I brought this to show you," Katrina said, handing the ring to Maggie. "I used to keep my house keys on this ring, until one day Eddie tied this on it. I couldn't bear to untie it, and yet I didn't want my keys touching it. It would be bad luck, I think."

Maggie held the ring and the knotted cord in the palm of her hand. The knot was unusual, but she didn't know enough to be able to recognize it.

"May I keep this?" she asked.

"Yes. I don't want it back. I have knots everywhere to remind me. This was the first one, and it still troubles me."

Maggie didn't want to jam it into her purse for fear she'd change the position of the knot. She folded the key ring inside several tissues and placed it carefully in the zippered compartment of her purse for added safety.

Once the knot was out of sight, Katrina appeared less agitated, as if she'd made the commitment to talk about Eddie. Maggie didn't push, but eventually she asked about the kidnapping, the investigation and the awful year that followed Eddie's disappearance. The joy in his return was tempered by the realization that as time passed, the boy appeared to be failing physically, mentally and socially.

"You said that according to the doctors, Eddie was not injured in any way while he was gone."

There was a slight hesitation before Katrina answered. "No. He was very healthy." She shuddered. "My husband was frantic when Eddie came back. He was so afraid that he had been hurt in a sexual way. He kept asking, and the doctors all told him that Eddie was 'untouched.' I'm not sure that Lothar believed them."

"I think my husband would have worried about the same thing," Maggie said. "Mothers are different. Our first priority is to have our children returned home and safe again."

Tears overflowed Katrina's eyes. "You understand what I feel."

Maggie waited as the woman blew her nose and wiped her eyes.

"I know that Eddie didn't speak when he first returned home," she said. "That must have been awful for you."

"It was. It confirmed for Lothar that something dreadful had happened to Eddie. I don't think my husband wanted to know what it was that had gone on in that year. Maybe if he knew, he would not be able to love Eddie again." Katrina hunched her shoulders, pulling her body in on itself. "For me, not knowing is worse. I've pictured every unspeakable horror. If I knew, I could accept it."

"Did you ever ask Eddie?"

"Once," she said, her voice just above a whisper. "Lothar heard me. He flew into a rage, screaming at me to let the boy forget. I could see that Eddie was terrified by his father's fury, so I did not cry out when Lothar hit me. I smiled at Eddie and told him I was sorry."

Maggie could have wept listening to Katrina. What a terrible situation. All three of them torn apart by the aftermath of the kidnapping. No wonder Eddie was self-destructing.

She felt as if she ought to have been able to learn more in the interview. She knew that Grant was hoping for actual information about Eddie's year of captivity. Any clue that might give the police a lead as to the whereabouts of Tyler. She had learned nothing of value.

A question came to her mind, and she wondered if she was reading more into Katrina's answers than was there. Maybe she was grasping for straws. Deciding not to second-guess herself, Maggie asked, "You said Eddie wasn't hurt, but there was something different about him when he returned, wasn't there?"

Katrina caught her breath and looked so frightened that Maggie was afraid the woman might faint. She remained motionless, knowing that her stab in the dark had hit a nerve.

"It was the tattoo," Katrina whispered.

Her voice was so low that Maggie wasn't sure she'd heard correctly. "Tattoo?"

Katrina reached out and took Maggie's hand and

placed it on her own chest. Beneath her fingertips Maggie felt the woman's frantic heartbeat.

"A tattoo. On his skin. Right here."

Maggie blew out her breath at the shock of Katrina's revelation. "It wasn't there before?"

Katrina shook her head. "Lothar told the police it was. He didn't understand what the tattoo meant. He thought it marked the boy. Like the evil eye. Lothar was ashamed."

"Oh, Katrina, how hard this has been for you."

Maggie put her arms around the woman and hugged her. For so long Katrina must have bottled up her fears and anger, because she burst into tears, sobbing uncontrollably for several minutes. Maggie held her, ignoring the tears that slid down her own cheeks as she thought about Jake and how she would feel if anything happened to him.

Please, God, keep him safe, she prayed.

When the shaking of the other woman's body eased, Maggie gave her a reassuring hug. Katrina pushed away, her eyes swollen and her cheeks red with embarrassment. Maggie rose and poured more coffee. The caffeine helped.

"What does the tattoo look like?" she asked.

"A heart. Drawn on his skin," Katrina said. Her voice shook with revulsion. "And there is an arrow, too."

"Could you draw it for me?"

Maggie searched her purse for a piece of paper, eventually settling for a deposit slip that she tore out of the back of her checkbook. She handed that and a pen to Katrina. The woman set it on the table. With angry strokes, she drew the picture of a heart with a short, stubby arrow running through it from right to left. Beneath it, she drew several dots.

"This is how I see it on his body," she said. "It is in color. The arrow is gold. The heart is red. And also the circles are red. Red tears of blood. Like the heart is crying."

"No words?"

Katrina looked confused.

"Sometimes there are dates or names or several words along with the picture," Maggie explained.

"No." Katrina shook her head. "No words. Just the arrow and the heart that bleeds."

CHAPTER EIGHTEEN

"WHY CAN'T I PLAY up in the treehouse until you get back?" Jake said, taking off his backpack and setting it on the ground beside the tree.

"Oh, Jake, give it a rest," she said. He'd been whining since she'd picked him up at Nell's and told him she was bringing him over to George's house. "While I'm gone you can give Grant a hand making dinner."

"You're just dumping me here?" Jake's voice grew shrill. "Aren't you going to eat with us?"

"Yes, but first I have to go see Chief Blessington."

She had just gotten back from the airport and was on her way to pick up Jake at school when Charley called asking her to come to the police station. Grant had offered to make dinner, so she phoned to say she and Jake would be late. He suggested she leave Jake with him while she talked to Charley.

"Why can't I come with you?"

Maggie threw up her hands in exasperation and walked down the path to the back porch.

"Because Chief Blessington wants to see just me," she said, speaking over her shoulder.

"You told me this morning we were going out to dinner as a treat," Jake said. He stomped along the path behind her.

"This is out," she said. "And any time I'm not cooking is a treat."

"Who's cooking? Is he?"

"His name is Grant," she snapped, realizing with a start that she was now calling him that instead of "Holbrook." Somewhere during the trip to Detroit, they had become friends. "I'd appreciate it if you'd start using his name."

Jake's eyes widened, and she turned to see Grant standing in the open doorway.

" 'Master Chef' to those who have tasted his exotic cuisine," Grant said.

Maggie flushed, aware he had overhead their conversation. "Are you sure about this?" she said with a nod of her head toward the sulking boy.

"Positive," Grant said. "We'll rattle along here while you're gone."

"I won't be long." She thrust a salad bowl into his hands. "Connie sent this over yesterday. I froze the casserole, but this will spoil if we don't use it."

"It must have been her day for good works. She brought some for us bachelors, too. Run along. We'll have dinner ready when you get back."

Maggie didn't know if she was doing the right thing, leaving the two of them alone together, but with a shrug of resignation, she leaned over and kissed Jake on the forehead before he could duck away. Refusing to look back, she hurried down the path and headed for town.

She had assumed the chief wanted to see her about George's car, but when she spotted several mobile news vans parked in front of the station and a crowd of reporters milling around outside, she could feel a zing of excitement at the possibility there'd been some break in the case. Her stomach lurched at the sight of the activity, and she was grateful that Charley had told her to park in the back and she wouldn't have to run the gauntlet of reporters. She parked close to the building and hurried up the back steps and was buzzed inside.

The police station had been recently renovated. Outside it retained its small-town charm, but inside it had the look of a modern organization with the latest in technology and manpower. A quiet efficiency pervaded the atmosphere, which she found somewhat intimidating.

"Come on in, Maggie." Charley Blessington came to his feet as Maggie was shown into his office. "Why don't you sit right here? Would you like some coffee or some soda?"

"No thanks. I'm fine." She sat down in the battered leather-and-steel chair in front of his desk, crossed her legs and smoothed the skirt over her knee. "I saw the news people out front. Has something happened?"

"I just had a press conference to bring them up to speed on the status of the case." Charley returned to the chair behind his desk. "The dispatcher told me about George's car. Nothing was taken?"

"No. And I don't even know if the insurance will pay for the repair of the window," she muttered. "You know I almost left the car unlocked yesterday when Wayne drove it over. Just picture trying to explain to Marty Karac that I'd left it unlocked if the car had been stolen instead of burglarized."

Charley let out a bark of laughter. "Marty's my insurance agent, too. Years ago I was transporting a horse to my dad's farm when I stopped to have lunch. While I was eating, someone stole the horse, and I had to tell Marty I hadn't locked the trailer. He groused about how much it was going to cost the insurance company, and I got mad and told him the damn premiums were high enough to cover a singing eunuch and a dancing horse."

His humor eased a little of the tension that had been building since she saw the reporters out in front of the station. She sat back in her chair, trying to relax.

"By the way, Maggie," he said, "did you manage to ask Jake if he knew where Tully might be holed up?"

"Yes, I did," she said. "He said Tully used to have a lean-to in the woods behind the Pat Jackson War Memorial over at Camp Delbrook. Tully told Jake that he was related to the Jackson family and felt most at home near the memorial. Jake says it's kind of hidden and Tully doesn't like for anyone to know where it is."

Charley made a couple of notes, his big hand dwarfing the pen. "I'll send one of the uniforms over there to snoop around. Has Jake been in touch with Tully since we talked last?"

"I saw you Wednesday. Was that only yesterday?" Maggie said, nervous under his steady gaze. "As far as I know, Jake hasn't seen or talked to Tully."

She didn't know whether to be appalled at the fact she hadn't told Charley that she had talked to Tully or to be shocked that she felt no guilt for omitting that information. She had decided in her own mind that Tully was innocent, and she couldn't bring herself to do anything that might lead to his arrest.

Almost as if he sensed that something wasn't right,

Charley looked up from his notes and stared at her, his eyes hard and challenging.

"I have the feeling, Maggie, that you're holding something back. I don't know why that would be, since you surely want to get to the bottom of this case as much as I do," he said. "But if you are, it's a dangerous game you're playing."

Maggie clasped her hands in her lap. She had so much information that might or might not have to do with George's murder, but she didn't know where the danger lay. Without knowing if Charley was to be trusted, what could she tell him? After some thought she made a decision.

"I know this sounds stupid, Charley, but I think George's death has something to do with the pictures from Jake's party."

Charley drew his head back so that his chins doubled as he looked down his nose at her. "You mentioned those pictures before. What do they have to do with anything?"

"I don't know, Charley. Maybe I'm grasping at straws, but at least hear me out."

She opened her hands, brushed them together, then placed them flat on her lap. She leaned forward in her chair, trying to organize her thoughts so that he would understand what she had worked out.

"I talked to George before he went to the poker game. He was perfectly normal, teasing Jake and talking easily about Mark. As far as I could tell there was nothing on his mind other than a slight guilt that he wouldn't be taking Jake to the movies. He said he'd pick up the pictures from Jake's party and bring them to our place for dinner the next day. Are you with me so far?"

Charley was tilted back in his chair, looking relaxed, but she could see by the intensity of his gaze that he was taking in every word. "I'm following you," he said.

"George gets to the club, and during dinner he passes the photos around the table. Now, according to Frank, who was sitting across from him, George suddenly focused on one of the pictures. He seemed troubled and he gave the pictures another look. Frank didn't know which photo had caught his attention. The game ends, and George goes out for a cigar and is attacked. His wallet and his watch are stolen. Something else is taken. The photographs."

Charley's chair tilted upright, and his feet hit the floor with a hard smack.

"What do you mean the pictures were taken?"

"Frank said that George put the photos in the pocket of his sport coat. They were not there when his body was found."

"Why would anyone take the pictures?"

"I don't know," Maggie said. "I can't believe if it was an actual robbery that anyone would take them. George never carried a lot of money, and the watch was worthless. It seems to me the real purpose of the robbery was to take the photographs."

"That's just plain crazy," Charley said. "George coulda left them in the club or in the car or just lost them."

"No," she said, shaking her head. "I'm not being stubborn, but I've checked everywhere and talked to as many people as I could. The pictures are gone. My question is why?"

"Damn it, Maggie, what kind of question is that?" He glared across the desk at her. "How would I know why or where the pictures are? I looked at them, and they were just a lot of silly shots of the kids at the Renaissance Faire. Nothing exceptional or newsworthy."

"Then why did the person who killed George take them?" She could see by Charley's expression that she had done little to convince him. "I guess my problem is that I can't believe Tully killed George. Somebody could have put the watch in his car, and Dennis Nyland could have been mistaken about seeing him on the green."

Charley ran the thick fingers of one hand through his hair, the strands standing up like blond spikes. His eyes were hooded as he stared across the desk.

"You haven't heard about Nyland?" he asked.

"Heard what?" Maggie could feel her heartbeat speed up.

"Dennis had a graphic arts business that he ran out of his garage. His mother called a little while ago. She said Dennis generally works late at night and she didn't see him when she left for work this morning. She's a bookkeeper for Rouse Accounting over on Fairview. When she came home today, she discovered his bed hadn't been slept in. She went out to the garage and he was there. Dead."

"How awful." Maggie had a panicky feeling in the pit of her stomach as she thought about Dennis's death. "How did he die?"

"He was stabbed. Just like George." Charley's mouth pulled tight in a grim line. "A direct hit to the heart."

Maggie sat in the car outside the police station. She gripped the steering wheel to keep her hands from shaking. Poor Dennis. What had he known that made him a risk to the murderer? Had he seen something or heard something as he bent over George's body that jeopardized the security of the killer?

She started the car and drove slowly back to the Estates, where Jake was waiting. She would have to be careful that he got no hint of this latest murder until she'd had a chance to talk about it with Grant. As she pulled into the parking area behind George's house, she felt a bit like Scarlett O'Hara. She'd think about all of this tomorrow.

"What took you so long, Mom?" Jake had heard her drive up and stood on the back porch, hopping from one foot to another. "We're starving."

"Sorry, guys," she said as she came down the walk. "I must have talked to Chief Blessington longer than I thought."

"Just wait until you see what I—what we made," Jake said. "It's way cool."

"I can't wait," she said, hugging him.

Jake raced into the house, and Maggie looked at Grant with newfound respect as he stood back to let her into the house.

"What happened to the crabby son I left with you?" she whispered as she passed him.

"You have such little faith in me, Maggie. He's a great kid. Once we had a chance to talk he decided I wasn't so bad. Besides, I showed him how to make something he really likes. I'm not allowed to tell you. He wants it to be a surprise."

"Sounds like bribery to me," she said. "I hope it's chocolate chip cookies. He considers that one of the food groups. And so do I."

"Can I get you a drink?" Grant narrowed his eyes as he pulled out a chair at the kitchen table for her. "You look done in."

"It's been a long day," she said with a flickering glance at Jake. "Something cold, wet and nonalcoholic would be a godsend."

"I can make lemonade, Mom," Jake offered.

"Do you think Grampa has any?" she asked.

"Sure, and I know right where it is."

He pulled a chair over to the counter and climbed up to reach the cabinet door.

"I found it," Jake said, holding out a packet of pre-mixed pink lemonade. "It's the same kind we use."

"Do you know how to mix it?" Grant asked, setting a plastic pitcher beside the sink.

"Cinch-o," he crowed.

"What can I do?" Maggie asked.

"Nothing," Grant said. "We thought you'd be home pretty soon, so we have dinner already in the oven. You just relax."

Maggie was amazed at how well the two worked together. Grant showed no hint of annoyance when Jake spilled the lemonade as he poured it into glasses, tossing the boy a towel without missing a beat. Grant put ice in the glasses but let Jake bring the drink to his mother.

"Boy, that's just what I needed," she said after taking several swallows. "So what are we having for dinner? I didn't smell anything when I came in, but I'm starting to get a very nice aroma from the oven."

"Grant showed me how to make it. Guess what it is?"

Maggie was pleased that Jake was actually referring

to Grant by name. She considered that a fair indication of how far they'd progressed during the short time they'd been together.

"Tuna noodle casserole?" she asked.

"Oh gross, Mom. You know I hate that."

She sniffed. "Smells Italian. How about spaghetti?"

"You're getting warmer."

"Meatballs?"

"You'll never guess," Jake said, too impatient to wait. "Grant showed me how to make pizza."

"No way," she said.

"Way," he said. "You should have seen the kitchen when we were done. There was flour all over everything."

"I can imagine. How soon do we eat?"

"Soon?" Jake said, turning to Grant.

"Couple more minutes. Just enough time to set the table and serve the salad."

Without any argument, Jake helped find silverware and dishes. They worked with a minimum of conversation, but the silence was an easy one. They'd come a long way in a short time, Grant thought.

Earlier, while they worked on the pizza, Jake had talked a lot about his life in Chicago, and it had become apparent that although the boy hadn't seen that much of his father, Mark had done a good job of parenting. According to what Connie had told him, Mark might have been a disaster as a husband, but he had been a strong and stable influence in Jake's life.

The bell on the oven dinged, and Jake leaped to his feet. He crouched in front of the oven door, peering in through the lighted window.

"Just wait'll you see it, Mom. It's got pepperoni and onions and olives and tomatoes. You're going to love it."

He opened the oven door and watched with wide eyes as Grant pulled out the first of two baking sheets and carried it across for Maggie's inspection.

"Did you really make this, Jake? It smells terrific and it looks very professional."

"It's a bit lumpy on that end." Jake, his face flushed with pride, was quick to point out a slight flaw.

"I think it will eat just fine," she said.

"A very impressive first effort, Jake," Grant said. He grinned at the boy, who responded with a wide smile of his own.

"I'm beginning to drool," Maggie said. "Let's eat."

"Apparently George didn't make a lot of pizza," Grant said as he set the baking sheet on the counter. "We couldn't find either pizza pans or a pizza cutter. Your son has great imagination and decided that scissors would work just fine."

He cut the pizza and set it down in the center of the table. Jake was practically vibrating with impatience, and Grant was impressed that he waited for his mother to take the first bite, his face apprehensive as he waited for her verdict.

"Mmmm," she said. "This is really good, Jake. And I'm not just saying it because you made it. It's excellent."

"Dig in, Chef Jake," Grant said.

Grant kept the conversation general during dinner. He could see that it was an effort for Maggie to keep up the cheerful banter. Something must have happened at the police station to upset her. To keep Jake occupied, he asked about his classes and told him an anecdote about his own school days.

"I can't eat another bite," Maggie said, pushing her plate toward the center of the table.

"An exceptional dinner, Jake." Grant got up and poured a cup of coffee. "Normally I'd let you off from doing dishes, but your mom looks tired. Let me get her settled on the deck with this coffee, then I'll come back and we'll get this place cleaned up."

"You're spoiling me," Maggie said, rising to her feet. "And I love every minute of it."

Carrying the coffee, Grant followed Maggie out to the deck. She walked over to the edge, placed her hands flat on the top of the railing and stood quietly, staring into the night.

"What happened at the police station?" Grant said, setting the mug of coffee on the picnic table. "I assumed Charley wanted to see you about George's car, but it's clear that you've been upset all evening. Do you want to talk about it?"

She turned, and he moved closer so that she could speak quietly.

"You're right. It wasn't the car." She took a deep breath and, lowering her voice to a whisper, said, "Dennis Nyland, the man who found George's body, has been murdered."

"What?!" Grant shot a glance over his shoulder to make sure Jake wasn't within earshot. "Murdered?"

"Yes, he was stabbed," Maggie said. "Just like George."

"God Almighty! What did Charley say?"

"Only that Dennis's mother found his body this afternoon when she got home from work. According to Charley, Dennis was working last night in his garage, where sometime after midnight, someone attacked and killed him. Why would anyone kill Dennis?"

Grant didn't immediately answer her question. He knew what he had to tell her would upset her further, but she had to know, and the sooner he told her, the sooner she'd be able to come to terms with the implications.

"What is it?" Maggie asked.

She seemed to sense he had something unpleasant to tell her. She placed the palms of her hands on his chest, and he could feel the slight tremor of her body.

"Dennis was into graphics," Grant said, "but he also had a hobby. He was a tattoo artist."

"Oh dear Lord! Eddie's tattoo?"

Maggie raised her head, and he could see a frightened bewilderment reflected in the darkness of her blue eyes.

"I don't know," Grant said. "But if Dennis knew about the bleeding heart tattoo, the knowledge killed him."

"Yes, I heard about Dennis," Maggie said, cradling the phone against her shoulder. "It's really frightening, Hugh."

"I thought you might be upset," he said. "I've been out most of the day and just picked up my messages. Connie left me a voice mail about Nyland's murder."

"Charley called me in to the station when I got back this afternoon. He didn't tell me much other than that Dennis was stabbed. Do they know any more?"

"Not much according to Connie. Might be another

robbery. Nyland's mother says someone took his tattoo design pictures."

"What?" Her knees gave out, and she dropped down onto the foot of Jake's bed.

"She says he kept books of all the tattoos he drew. The books are missing. Strange, huh?"

Knowing about Eddie Harland's tattoo made this new information even more damning than before. Her mouth was dry, and she was afraid to comment. Hugh would hear in her voice that she was holding something back.

"Are you still there?" he asked when she didn't respond.

"I'm here. It's just the whole thing is so scary."

"You should consider it a warning."

"A warning?" Maggie said. "What do you mean?"

"First George was killed and now Nyland. That guy must have known more than he told the police. He might have seen who did it."

"He told Charley he just saw Tully."

"Maybe yes, maybe no." Hugh pronounced each syllable slowly and precisely. "He must have known something, or why would he be murdered?"

To Maggie it was unimaginable that they were discussing murder as if it were a normal topic of conversation.

"What are you suggesting?" she asked.

"I think Nyland tried to make some money and got caught in his own trap. Meddling in murder is a dangerous business. It got Nyland killed.

Hugh's voice was angry, almost threatening. She shivered.

"Don't tell me any more. It's frightening me."

"Do you want me to come over?"

"No." She cleared her throat to cover the sharpness of her reply. "I appreciate the offer, but it's late, and I want to get Jake into bed. I still haven't decided whether to tell him about Dennis tonight or wait until tomorrow."

"News like that can wait until morning," Hugh said.

"You're right," she said, speaking quietly so that her voice wouldn't carry down the hall to where Jake was just finishing his shower. "There's no school tomorrow because of teacher conferences. I'll have more time in the morning, and I won't have to worry that it'll give him nightmares."

Just talking about it made her feel less apprehensive. Standing up, she pulled back Jake's bedspread and stared at the sheet-covered bed, wondering where the blanket had disappeared to. It had been warm the last several nights, but usually Jake just kicked off the covers. She looked under the bed but couldn't find it.

"What time is your teacher conference?" he asked.

"I drew the evening shift. Eight o'clock."

Too tired to look for the blanket, she turned on the table lamp, switched off the ceiling light and walked across the hall to her own bedroom, sitting down in the chair beside the window.

"Then I won't see you there. I'm going after lunch, then I'm taking Kenny up to Door County to see my mother. I'm coming back Saturday morning, and she'll bring him back Sunday late. Oh, before I forget, could you check to see if Jake has Kenny's windbreaker? We've got Jake's. Kenny says they got mixed up yesterday when you brought him home."

"Does he need it before you go to your mother's?"

"No. He's got a spare."

"It's probably in Jake's backpack. If I find it, I'll drop it off sometime tomorrow," Maggie said.

"That's great. If I'm not there, it'll be in the mud-room closet."

"I'm done, Mom," Jake yelled from the open door of the bathroom. "Can I have some cookies?"

"Just a minute, Jake. I'm on the phone," she said. "Sorry, Hugh. Jake's just getting out of the shower."

"Kenny's still in the tub. He spends more time in the bathroom than the bedroom. He's content for hours with that flotilla of boats he's got. Not much room left for water, let alone soap."

It was out of character for Hugh to chitchat. Get to the point, she thought, holding back a sigh.

"Jake's just as bad," she said. "I would have thought they'd give that up now that they're getting so grown up."

"Kenny's starting to lengthen out. All of sudden he's eating more. I suppose a sign his body's changing. He and Jake polished off a loaf of bread and a package of ham the other day when you were here."

"It's funny you should mention that. Jake's been taking apples and oranges to school and still complains that he's hungry. Times are changing, Hugh," she said. "By the way, thanks for getting the window of the car fixed. I called the insurance company, and it's covered. Let me know how much I owe you."

"We'll call it a deposit on dinner," he said. "I'd like to get together. Just the two of us."

Maggie grimaced at the tone of his voice. She wondered why he was suddenly pressing her. It couldn't just

be the fact that he was jealous of Grant. It seemed as if
there was a new urgency in his voice.

"Since George died there's been no time," she said,
knowing it was a weak excuse.

"Time enough for shopping in Milwaukee."

She might have been more sympathetic if Hugh had
sounded like he felt neglected. Instead his tone was
angry, as if she were purposely avoiding him. Oh rats! I
don't have time for this.

The awareness of how supportive Hugh had been
over the past year and how many secrets she was keeping from him combined to make her feel guilty. Perhaps
he sensed that she was shutting him out. Although un-
founded, he clearly saw Grant as a threat to their developing relationship.

"It would be good to get together, Hugh," she said,
leaning her head against the back of the chair, too tired
to argue. "Since Sunday it's been hectic, but now things
are loosening up. Today's Thursday, and you get back
from Door County on Saturday. Would Sunday about six
o'clock work for you?"

"Absolutely. Kenny won't be back until nine. How
about Hills' Haufbrau Haus?"

"Sounds great," she said. "Now I better get Jake off
to bed. Thanks for calling, Hugh. I'll see you on Sunday."

Maggie could hear the relief in his voice as he said
goodnight. She'd have to give some serious thought to
their relationship before Sunday. It would be unfair to
string him along if there was no interest on her part.

"Now can I have some cookies, Mom?"

Jake was waiting in the kitchen, his hair standing up

in damp spikes and his cheeks pink from his vigorous towel drying. He was wearing pajama shorts, and the fresh scent of soap rose from his skin to fill her senses. She leaned over and kissed the top of his head.

"Since you don't smell like an old tennis shoe anymore, you can have a treat," she said.

She put some chocolate chip cookies on a plate and poured him a glass of milk. He carried them to the kitchen table and sat down, pulling his bare feet up onto the seat of the chair. He picked up a cookie and then set it back down on the plate and looked over at Maggie.

"Mom, I'm sorry I was mean about Grant this morning. I think he's a good guy."

"I'm glad you like him. I do too," she said, "but I have a confession to make. I didn't like him when I first met him."

"You didn't?"

"Next time you're with him, ask him to tell you about the canoe paddle."

"The canoe paddle?" Jake asked.

"Yes. I know you want to know now, but I'm not going to spoil the fun. I think you'll really get a laugh out of hearing the story from Grant."

"OK."

He raised the cookie again, stopping just short of his mouth, then returned it to the plate. Apprehension was clear in his expression.

"Mom, I had a talk with Grant and told him some stuff, and he's going to tell you about it. Promise you won't get mad?"

She felt a momentary stab of jealousy that Jake had talked to Grant about something that was clearly troubling him. Part of the problem with being a single parent was that she tried to be all things to Jake. Mother, father, friend, playmate, teacher. The list was interminable. Any time he turned to someone else, she felt a twinge as if she were inadequate to fill her roles.

"You know how I hate when you want me to promise I won't get mad. Best I can do is promise to listen and try to understand." She worried when his expression didn't lighten. "I hope it's not too bad. You didn't rob a bank, did you?"

He shook his head. "Grant will tell you."

As if Grant's involvement relieved him of all responsibility, he went back to eating his cookies with a look of contentment.

"After you're in bed," she said, "I'm going down to the bookstore. Grant's coming over shortly. I'll leave the door open, so if you wake up all you have to do is call."

"Uncle Ham and Aunt Nell are coming too?" Jake said, wiping the milk mustache off his lip with the back of his hand. His eyes crinkled at her start of surprise. "I heard you guys talking."

"Don't you know it's not polite to eavesdrop?" She rubbed her knuckles on the top of his head.

"If I didn't, I'd never know anything." He looked up at her, eyes wide and serious. "You know, Mom. I'm not a baby anymore."

Maggie sighed. "I know, Jake. Sometimes I forget that. Moms have a tough time when their boys grow up."

For an instant she could hear Katrina Harland saying much the same thing. It was hard to believe that she'd been in Detroit earlier in the day. No wonder she was tired. Thinking about Eddie's mother triggered another memory, and she let out a small gasp.

"What's the matter, Mom?" Jake asked.

"I just thought of something I forgot to show Grant," she said.

She picked up her purse from the kitchen counter where she'd dropped it when they came home. She carried it across to the table and set it on the edge.

"Do you know anything about knots, Jake?"

"Some. Kenny showed me how to do some fancy ones. He's a wizard at them."

She opened the zipper compartment of her purse and withdrew the tissue-wrapped package she'd put inside for safekeeping.

"Somebody gave me this today, and I forgot all about it."

She unwrapped the tissue, setting the key ring with the knotted cord in the center of the table. Jake crammed the last cookie in his mouth.

"I don't recognize the knot," she said. "Do you?"

"Sure," he said, chewing and swallowing before he continued. "Kenny showed me how to tie one just like that. It's called a falconer's knot."

CHAPTER NINETEEN

"A FALCONER'S KNOT?" Ham said, staring down at the key ring with the knotted cord attached. "Jake's sure?"

"Yes. He tied some knots for us, and they were identical to this one," Grant said. "Kenny Rossiter showed Jake how to tie the knot, and he thought it was really cool because you only use one hand to do it."

"You tie the knot with one hand?" Nell asked.

"Yes. Picture this. The hawk is sitting on your gloved left hand, and you need to secure his leash. You only have your right hand." Grant demonstrated, using a piece of string. "Jake showed me the basics, but it takes me a couple tries before I get it looking right. You should see him. He can do it at lightning speed."

"What's the second knot for?" Ham said, touching the original knotted cord.

"It's sort of a safety knot so you don't release the first one unintentionally," Grant said. "The knot's designed to be untied quickly. You just take out this free end and pull sharply."

Maggie could feel the tension rising as Grant tried

to bring Ham and Nell up to speed on what they'd learned about the knot. She sat back, letting Grant do the talking.

Trying to appear normal during the dinner with Jake and Grant had taken a toll on her energy. They had just finished when Ham called to tell Grant that he and Nell had just come back from dinner and heard about Dennis Hyland's death. After a low-voiced conversation, Grant asked if they could all meet later at the bookstore.

Maggie had been grateful that she could get Jake safely tucked into bed while Grant told the other two about her meeting with Katrina Harland. She'd brought a pot of coffee and a bottle of brandy when she came downstairs.

Ham leaned across the table, speaking directly to Maggie. "Grant called me after you had your meeting with Katrina Harland. He knew I was going to Milwaukee. Noreen Flood, the second child kidnapped, died at the zoo there. My friend Paula Craig was going to let me look at the files."

"Did you learn anything?" Maggie asked.

"Grant told me to check if there were any identifying marks on Noreen's body," Ham said. "There was. She had a tattoo."

"Oh God!" Maggie cried, thoughts of Eddie Harland and Dennis Nyland fresh in her mind.

He took out a Xerox sheet, unfolded it and passed it across to Maggie. Her hands shook as she smoothed the paper. It was a copy of a close-up photograph of the dead child's chest. Above the left nipple was a red heart with a golden arrow through it. Beneath the heart were several droplets of blood.

"It's just like the drawing Eddie's mother made," Maggie said.

She swallowed hard as she stared down at the tattoo. Grant handed Ham the drawing of the bleeding heart that Katrina Harland had given Maggie.

"Hearing about it was bad enough," Maggie said. "Seeing the actual picture is even worse."

Her eyes filled with tears, and she covered her shaking lips with her hand. Grant placed a comforting hand on her arm. She could feel the warmth of his touch, but it didn't diminish the chill of fear that invaded her body.

"I asked Paula if they had ever come across any other tattoos. She's tracked several similar in Wisconsin and Minnesota," Ham said. "Over the last ten years four bodies have turned up with tattoos that were similar to the one on Noreen's chest. Paula said there could be more in other states, but she's only been able to find these four."

"Four? God in Heaven!" Maggie said. "Were they children?"

"No, thank God," Nell said. "That was my first question too. They were young men. Two of them were runaways in their late teens. The other two were in their twenties. Homeless and heavily into drugs."

"Two in Wisconsin. Trego and Green Bay. Two in Minnesota. Minneapolis and Grand Rapids," Ham said. "They'd been stabbed. A single wound from a thin-bladed knife. The tattoos were done after death. They were similar but not as refined or as professional looking as the one that Noreen had. Paula thought the killer might be a tattoo artist in training."

Even though Ham spoke in an impersonal tone,

Maggie could not hold back the sense of horror that surrounded her. It was like Pandora's box. Once the investigation was opened, there was no holding back the ripples that spread out to include even more shocking details. Suddenly a new thought jolted her.

"Do you think Dennis Nyland was killed because he did the tattoos on Eddie and Noreen?" she asked.

"I don't think so," Grant said. "The kidnapper is intelligent. He's made few mistakes. It would be too dangerous to have someone local do the tattooing. Besides, he isn't aware that we know anything about the tattoos. I think it's more likely that Dennis was killed because he found George's body."

"I agree," Ham said. "He must have known something that represented a threat to the killer. It's possible he could have recognized him."

"Not Tully," Maggie said.

"No," Grant said. "Dennis had already told Blessington about Tully. Maybe he saw someone else, too, and for some reason didn't mention it. Dennis might have approached that person later. If so, the killer would have no choice but to eliminate him."

"If only we could talk to Tully," Maggie said. "Dennis Nyland's death proves that Tully is in danger."

"The killer is getting rattled," Ham added. "Nyland's death suggests he's cleaning up loose ends."

"We've been looking for something to narrow down the suspect list, and it's my opinion that the falconer's knot tips the scales toward the falconry club," Grant said.

"I'd have to agree," Maggie said. "At least we should put them at the top of the list of suspects. Ham?"

"I can see where you're heading, but I still think we can't leave anyone who was at the poker game off the list."

"OK. Let's combine the two and see what we end up with." Referring back to several pages of the yellow pad, Grant wrote down two lists of names. After he'd completed it, he stared down at what he'd written, then passed it to Maggie. "We have eight names."

"I can help you eliminate one of the names," Maggie said after scanning the list and handing it to Nell. "Mike Offenlach is in the falconry club, but he and his wife were in Illinois visiting her mother last weekend. I talked to Mike at the memorial service, and the night George was killed he was at an antique auction."

Nell drew a line through Mike's name.

"While I'm at it, I can take out another member of the falconry club. When I was at the bakery this morning, Donna Harper was telling the owner that her husband was rushed to the hospital Wednesday evening with an appendicitis attack. So that lets Brian Harper out.

"We're making some progress," Nell continued. "I've got one more name I think we should take off the list. Walter Kondrat."

"Is that a sentimental choice?" Ham asked, his mouth drawn tight in disapproval. "He was at the dinner and the poker game. He might not be into falconry, but hanging around with that bunch, enough of it could have rubbed off so that he'd be familiar with a falconer's knot."

Nell glared across the table at Ham.

"I'm not making a sentimental decision, you

dunce," she said. "Walter is not the brightest bulb in the chandelier when it comes to anything outside of the insurance business. He doesn't have enough intelligence to pull off a murder, let alone a kidnapping."

"It doesn't take intelligence to stab someone. Unrestrained anger would do it," Ham said. "It's entirely possible that George was killed not only because he had seen the pictures but for another reason altogether. We know that Walter had an explosive fight with George that night over money. More people are killed over money than over fear of exposure."

"Walter didn't kill George," Nell said. "I know what they were arguing about. George called me that night from the club and told me."

"What?" Ham yelped.

If Nell had dropped a bomb in the center of the bookstore, she couldn't have gotten a more shocked reaction. Maggie stared at the older woman, who tried to appear unconcerned at the consternation she'd created. She smoothed one hand across her salmon-colored hair, then reached out to the bottle of brandy, pouring a substantial dollop into her coffee.

"Why didn't you tell us?" Maggie said.

"Because it had nothing to do with the investigation. All George and I talked about was his argument with Walter, and I didn't think it had any bearing on his death."

"Judas Priest!" Ham said. "You're a very exasperating woman. Don't you know that in a murder case everything has relevance? Each detail fills the holes in the puzzle and eventually helps the investigators find a solution."

He threw himself back in his chair, spreading his arms and raising his palms to the sky in resignation. He looked at Grant, who had been silently watching the by-play but now leaned forward to speak.

"I'm sure you had cogent reasons for not telling us about George's call," Grant said, "but it would be constructive to hear what you talked about."

Nell took another sip of her coffee and set the mug back on the table. She picked at a spot of paint on her denim blouse and then looked up and began to speak.

"My husband, Hal, and Walter were partners in the insurance company. After his wife died, Walter spent a lot of time at our house, and the three of us became good friends. When Hal died, people assumed that after a suitable mourning period Walter and I would marry. Even my children pushed for it. They only saw that he would be a solution to their worries about my being alone."

Nell stared down at the table, running one hand along the edge, her face thoughtful.

"About ten years ago, Walter asked me to marry him. I wasn't in love with him, but I was going through a lonely period and I strongly considered it. One night I ran into George at an election rally and we got talking, and I asked him if he thought Walter was ready to marry. George misunderstood and said Walter had told him he had no plans to marry Jeanne Vadnais but was content with their long-term affair."

"The randy old bastard," Ham muttered.

"Naturally it was a bit of a blow to my pride, since I'd had no idea. Jeanne and I were friends. She was sort of a psycho bitch in her younger days but eventually mellowed into a very nice woman. Always wears great shoes."

"Oh for God's sake, Nell. What do her shoes have to do with anything?" Ham asked.

"It was just an observation. No need to foam at the mouth," she said. "George realized that I didn't know about Walter's affair, and I made him promise he wouldn't tell him that I knew. I gather that for ten years George kept his word. Until Saturday night."

"So George was fighting with Walter about his on-going affair?" Grant asked.

"Yes. When he called me he was very upset for breaking his silence. It seems that Walter was drinking and made some disparaging remark about my refusing to marry him. George lost his temper and said I'd never marry a man who I knew was having an affair with an-other woman. Then the you-know-what hit the fan."

"All the more reason to keep Walter on the list," Ham said, his eyes flinty.

"According to Doris Blessington, Walter spent the night at Jeanne's house after the poker game," Nell said. "Jeanne lives next door to the Blessingtons. Doris said she thought it was Charley coming home, and when she looked out the window, she saw Walter driving into the garage. It was about twelve-thirty, and if George was killed right after the game, Walter wouldn't have been able to get to Jeanne's by that time."

"The time of death isn't all that accurate," Ham said.

"Give it up, Ham," Nell said. "Walter is not a man of action. He'd have sued George, not killed him. I appre-ciate your championing my cause, but just because you don't like Walter, you can't nail him for murder."

Maggie caught the smile that passed from Nell to Ham, and her eyes opened wide. Why hadn't she noticed that the two of them had established some kind of relationship in the last few days? She shot a glance at Grant, who had obviously come to the same conclusion.

"Since we're trying to narrow down the list," Grant said, "I think I'd agree with Nell. Walter looks like a poor suspect. But something you said makes me wonder about Charley Blessington. You said Doris thought it might be Charley coming home. Where was Charley?"

"He's in the falconry club and he was at the dinner," Maggie said. "I know he's the police chief, but it worries me that he keeps asking about Tully. It's like he has a personal reason to get hold of him. Do we have any evidence against Charley?"

"Yes," Ham said. "I would have mentioned it, but I only confirmed it today."

Maggie wondered if this was the information that Connie had been looking for. Grant had told her about his conversation with Connie and had asked Ham to look through George's papers to see if he could find any report that would sabotage Blessington's chances to be elected mayor.

"You have to go back twelve years ago," Ham said, "when Amelia Fowler was the mayor. She'd been a movie actress and had been elected not for any governing qualifications but rather because it was rumored she'd slept with some big-name stars. Turned out to be a good, tough mayor. She was running for reelection and she'd just fired the chief of police for sexual harassment of his female personnel."

"It was the best scandal in Delbrook history," Nell

said. "The chief's wife caught him spanking a bare-assed beat cop—if you'll pardon the expression—in his office and screeched so loudly there was no way of covering it up. It was such a hot topic of conversation that the chief, his wife and the rosy-bottomed cop all left town."

"So Amelia was desperate for someone who could restore dignity and discipline to the office of chief of police," Ham said. "One of the names mentioned for the job was Charley Blessington, and the newspaper did a story on him. It turned out that Charley was a genuine hero. He'd saved the life of a young girl during a bank robbery down in Florida. The robber panicked when the alarm went off and started shooting. Charley shielded a little girl with his body and took the bullet that might have killed her."

"Way to go, Charley," Grant said.

"When Charley was questioned he tried to downplay his role, but they had a picture from the newspaper showing him strapped to a gurney with his bandaged arm around the little girl trying to comfort her. I've seen the picture, and it's a real heart tugger."

"How come I never heard that story?" Maggie asked.

"It happened twenty-three years ago," Ham said. "Charley was twenty-one or two."

"During the election campaign, the newspaper gave the story plenty of space," Nell said.

"Amelia thought Charley was the perfect candidate. He'd been an assistant chief of police in a mid-sized town in Ohio, had an excellent reputation and was an all-American hero to boot. So Amelia appointed him chief." Ham paused, poured some brandy into his coffee and took a sip. "Charley's done a good job as chief. There's no question of that. The only problem is that the story that got him the job wasn't true."

"The picture was a hoax?" Maggie asked.

"No, the picture was real. The report I found among the papers in George's desk was a letter from Brandon Terrell, who's the photo editor of the *Park Ridge Advocate* newspaper. When he was starting out as a photographer in Florida, he took the picture that appeared on the front page of the paper after the shooting. I don't know how George got onto this whole thing, but the letter Terrell sent confirmed that the name beneath the photo had been misidentified. It was not Charles Blessington but Charles Lester who had saved the child's life."

"Poor Doris," Nell said. "She really loves Charley. Gossip's always been her thing, but this would be tough to deal with. He'd either end up as a laughingstock or get labeled as an opportunistic liar. In her eyes, I don't know which would be worse."

"How did the mix-up happen?" Maggie asked.

"Charley had been at the bank, but he wasn't the one on the stretcher who saved the girl. Brandon Terrell, the man who wrote the letter to George, shot a bunch of pictures at the scene of the shooting, including one of Charley being interviewed as one of the witnesses. The man on the stretcher was also named Charles, and Terrell identified him as Blessington instead of Lester."

"If Charley runs for mayor, the lie is bound to surface," Nell added. "Connie knows there's something in Charley's background that could hurt him politically. She has the money and the resources to do a thorough check."

"These days I don't know if something like that would be enough to cause a scandal. Look at what goes on in Washington," Grant said. "Charley could always say that once the story was in the paper, there wasn't anything he could do about it. The more he denied it, the more people would believe it."

"That might be true, except when I went back to the newspaper archives, I came up with at least five instances where Charley talked about the story as if it were true," Ham said.

"Would Charley kill to keep this information from getting out?" Maggie asked.

"I don't know him well enough to say," Grant said. "One thing to consider is that, if he was the one who searched George's house, he would have found that letter and destroyed it."

"Maybe that's what he was looking for and just didn't see it," Ham said. "Charley was at the poker game, he saw the photographs and he's a falconer, so he'd know the knot." Ham didn't want to take anyone off the list. "He could have had two reasons for killing George."

"All right. Blessington is still a suspect," Grant said. He took the list back from Ham and put a check mark in front of Charley's name. "Next is Hugh Rossiter."

Maggie was aware they were waiting for her to speak. She felt awkward, since they all knew that she'd dated Hugh.

"I hate this, you know," she said. "I've never had to look at everyone I know and wonder if they have the capacity to do evil things. Shouldn't it be apparent?"

"My mother always said, when you touch pitch, it

sticks to your fingers," Nell said. "I wish there were a lit-
mus test for killers."

"The thing is," Maggie continued, "I'm so paranoid,
I'm afraid to leave Jake with anyone. I realized this
morning when Hugh drove Jake to school that there was
a part of me that wondered if I could trust him with my
son. How can I suspect a man who's been so good to
both of us?"

"It's natural," Grant said. "It would be naive, knowing what you know, not to question everyone in Delbrook. Jake's safety is most important. The thing to
remember is that, unless George's killer is unmasked,
you will never be able to trust anyone again and you will
never feel that Jake is really safe."

Maggie stared down at her hands, letting his words
sink in. She didn't know if he'd said what he'd said to reassure her, but it hadn't worked. Examining her friends
made her sick to her stomach. It took all of her resolve to
think about Hugh in an objective way.

"Facts against Hugh? He's the master falconer, so of
all people, he would know the falconer's knot. He was at
the Renaissance Faire, at the dinner and poker game and
saw the photographs. On the pro side, he's a caring father,
a hard worker and appears reasonably normal," she said.
"You know what's sad? When I started to think about
Hugh, I realized how little I really knew about him. I
know dumb things like what kind of movies he likes and
that he prefers Italian food over Mexican, but I don't
know anything about his past or even his present life."

"If you had wanted to know, you would have asked,"
Grant said.

"I guess what I'm saying," she continued, ignoring

his comment, "is that I don't know anything negative about Hugh, unless it's that at times he's a bit tough on Kenny."

Grant shifted in his chair, suspecting that Maggie would feel a general sense of betrayal with what he was about to say. He wanted to tell her that it was not personal, just a part of the investigation process, but he didn't think she'd believe him.

"While you were meeting with Katrina Harland, I went to see Hugh Rossiter's sister-in-law, who lives in Detroit."

Maggie's eyes widened, and the glow that had been reflected in the blue depths faded. Grant swallowed to get the dryness out of his throat before he continued.

"According to the rumor mill here in town, Julie Rossiter left Hugh three years ago for another man. No one seems to know who this man was, but he wasn't local. It seemed to me unusual that she wouldn't still be in contact with her son, but apparently that's the case. More than once I heard the phrase 'she disappeared off the face of the earth,' and I decided to find out where she was."

"Why the hell didn't you tell me this before?" Maggie asked.

"I didn't think you'd like it," Grant admitted. "I called Amy Caldwell, Julie's sister, and asked if I could talk to her about Julie. She agreed because she was curious to know why I was looking for her."

"I knew Amy," Nell said. "Married a lazy good-for-nothing who used to spend his days watching game shows and the Home Shopping Network. She must have taken back her maiden name after her divorce."

"She did. She's got two kids, five and six, and has a good job with a computer repair company in Detroit. She doesn't know where Julie is. According to her, Julie has never contacted her since the day she left three years ago."

"Did she know why her sister left?" Ham asked.

"According to Amy, Julie ran off because Hugh beat her."

"What a rotten thing to say," Maggie said.

"I'm telling you Amy's story, not mine," Grant said.

"I can't believe it," Maggie said. "No one has ever hinted at anything like that."

"If it was true, probably no one was aware of it," Nell said. "Women keep it a secret because of misplaced shame. They give a million excuses why they have a bruise or a cut. Sometimes members of a family suspect what's going on but are afraid to say anything or purposely ignore it."

Grant could see Maggie withdraw at Nell's comments. He suspected she was equating it to her own life and the fact she had kept Mark's infidelities a secret. Everyone had something they would rather not talk about.

"Amy said that she'd seen evidence of Hugh's abuse," Grant said, "and when she confronted Julie, she admitted that he'd beaten her. She said he was sorry and had sworn it would never happen again. The abuse must have continued. Amy said that Hugh was very jealous, and she thinks the reason that Julie has never contacted anyone is that she's afraid of Hugh finding out where she is."

Grant glanced at Maggie, who was staring down at the tabletop, her mouth drawn into a tight line.

"I don't know if Amy's story is true," he said. "All I can tell you is what I heard. It will take further investigation to prove any of this."

"Even if it's true, that doesn't make Hugh a murderer or a kidnapper," Maggie said.

"That's right," he said. "Everything we're learning about the people on the list is just information. We haven't come up with anything that makes us point to one person and say that's the killer. Our only hope is that by a process of elimination we can come up with one person who had the opportunity and the motive to commit murder."

Grant placed a check mark in front of Hugh's name. He could feel Maggie's resistance to the idea as if it were a physical thing. Knowing that each day he was drawn more strongly to her, he wondered if any relationship would survive the soul-searching that was required in this investigation.

"Frank Woodman?" Ham asked, eager to change the subject.

"I don't know of anything that would put him on the list except for the fact he was at the club," Nell said. "The strongest reason to assume he's innocent is that I don't think he would have mentioned anything about George looking at the photographs if he had killed him in order to keep them a secret."

"That's a good point," Grant said. He started to cross off Frank's name but instead put a question mark in front of it. "We'll keep him on the list until we do a bit more checking into his background. We know he was at the country club when George's body was discovered, so he had the opportunity. Dennis Nyland was killed around midnight. If Frank is normally at the country club at that time, someone may have seen him and be able to give him an alibi."

"The killer appears to have picked times and places to attack George and Dennis where he is unlikely to be seen," Grant said. "He either arranged for George to meet him on the fairway or he waited outside until he could approach him through the trees. He went to Nyland's place after midnight, and once again no one saw him."

"I keep meaning to bring this up," Nell said. "I object to the use of 'he' for the killer. Nothing suggests that the killer is male. It wouldn't take only a man's strength to stab someone. I don't think you can rule Connie out."

"I agree," Maggie said. "She's a falconer, and she was at the dinner and the poker game."

"My use of the male pronoun was strictly for ease of speaking. Connie's name is on the list. I'm not sure I consciously discounted her," Grant said.

Maggie wasn't so sure about that. She could see in both the men's faces that they could not picture Connie Prentice as either a murderer or a kidnapper.

"All right, let's talk about Brent and Connie," Maggie said. "Do we have any evidence against either of them?"

"They were both at the Renaissance Faire, and neither one has an alibi for the time George was killed," Nell said.

"Maybe they didn't leave together, but as a couple it would be hard to be gone long without the other person knowing about it," Ham said. "Doris knew that Charley wasn't home."

"Charley could always tell Doris he was on police business, and that would be enough of an explanation," Grant said. "But what excuse could Brent and Connie make to each other?"

"None would be necessary," Nell said. "Connie and Brent live in separate wings of the house. They don't live as a married couple and haven't for many years. I doubt if either one would be aware of the other's comings and goings."

"That might explain why Brent has that air of sadness about him when he looks at Connie," Maggie said. "He told me once he'd fallen in love with Connie the first time he saw her and there's never been anyone since."

Grant shrugged. "Things change. Connie sounds caustic and bitter around him. Like something's happened that she doesn't understand."

"Does everyone lead a secret life?" Maggie asked. "God, this is awful."

"Doris did drop a piece of information that might have some bearing," Nell said. "Connie and Brent wanted children. Connie was pregnant when Falcon's Nest caught fire. She went into labor, and the child lived only a few hours after it was born. It was a boy."

"You're suggesting that they might kidnap children in order to replace the child they lost?" Grant asked.

"I'm not suggesting a thing," Nell said. "I'm reporting what Doris told me."

"Brent missed the dinner, so he wasn't there when the photographs were passed around," Ham said. "Does anyone know if he saw them?"

"No. I think we need to make an assumption here. If

he didn't see the actual pictures, he would have heard them discussed and known they were taken at the Renaissance Faire," Grant said. "He also could have overheard George's phone call. Even though he's not in the falconry club, Connie is, so he would be familiar with the falconer's knot."

"Are we making any progress?" Maggie asked.

"We've got a list of prime suspects." Grant held up a finger as he ticked them off. "Hugh Rossiter, Charley Blessington, Brent Prentice and Connie Prentice."

"I can't believe any of them could commit a murder," Maggie said. "We have nothing but bits and pieces. Nothing that points to a killer."

"That's how police work is done, kiddo," Ham said. "You compile as much info as you can, and then eventually a pattern begins to emerge. It's hard work. Killing's fast. Catching a killer takes time."

"We don't have a lot of time." Maggie splayed out her fingers and pressed them on the table in front of her. "First George is killed and now Dennis. I have this sick feeling that Tully will be next. He may have a key piece of information, and therefore he's in terrible danger."

"Isn't there any way to contact him?" Nell asked. "Doesn't anyone know where he is?"

"Yes, someone knows where he is," Grant said. "Someone's been hiding him for the last couple of days."

"No shit, Sherlock," Ham said. "Who?"

"The one person Tully trusts," Grant said. "Jake."

CHAPTER
TWENTY

"JAKE IS HIDING TULLY?" Maggie sagged in her chair, expelling a slow stream of air. "That's why he's been acting so strange. I suppose Kenny was involved, too."

"Yes. Reluctantly, I gather," Grant said.

"God in heaven! How am I ever going to explain this to Hugh?" Maggie muttered.

"Very enterprising boys," Ham said.

"Aren't they cute, the little darlings?" Nell said, salmon curls quivering as she shook her head.

"You'll have to give Jake points for confessing before I got out the thumbscrews," Grant said. "I've been trying to piece together where Tully could be, and I decided if he was still in Delbrook, someone was helping him. Once I got suspicious of Jake, everything fell into place."

"I can't believe Tully put Jake in danger by contacting him," Ham said.

"He didn't," Grant said. "Jake made the contact. He was afraid Charley Blessington was going to arrest Tully."

"No wonder Jake wanted me to promise I wouldn't get mad when you told me something tonight," Maggie said. "I forgot about it when I came downstairs because I didn't know it had anything to do with the investigation. You better give me chapter and verse so I know how much trouble he's in."

"Tully lives in a lean-to in the woods over in Camp Delbrook. When Jake goes over to Kenny's, he usually brings some Snickers bars, along with anything else he thinks Tully would like. He leaves everything in a hollowed-out tree in the woods beyond the mews that the boys refer to as the mailbox."

"I think the military could use these kids," Ham said.

"The first couple days after George died, Tully stuck to the woods. Jake was worried that he wouldn't be able to buy groceries, so he got Kenny to make a drop at the mailbox. Kenny supplied sandwiches, and Jake added fruit and a couple bottles of juice. Do you remember when Kenny broke the mayonnaise jar?" Grant asked. "I wondered why he looked so frightened. It seems they'd just made a bunch of sandwiches for Tully, and he was sure we'd discover them."

Maggie groaned. "Hugh and I were just discussing how the boys' appetites have increased. And of course that's why they took their backpacks on the hike. They were taking the food to Tully. I can't believe I didn't pick up on any of this."

"Well, dear," Nell said, "you've had a few things on your mind. The trouble with children is that they're born provocateurs. Their minds cope much better with conspiracies than adults' do."

"Everything was going all right until yesterday," Grant said, "when the volunteer cleanup began over at Camp Delbrook. With the additional people around, the chances that someone would spot Tully increased. Besides, rain was predicted."

"This just gets worse and worse," Maggie said. "All right, Grant, how the hell did you figure it out?"

"The tip-off was Tully's call. You said Jake had been jumping to answer the phone, so I wondered if he was waiting to hear from him. That was it. On Wednesday, the boys left a note along with the food for Tully and told him where to go to get out of the rain."

"I'm too old to play guessing games," Nell said.

"Tonight when Maggie left Jake with me at George's house, I noticed that he'd left his backpack beside the ladder to the treehouse. I realized the treehouse was the perfect place for Tully to hide." Grant shrugged. "I asked Jake straight out, and he confessed the whole thing."

Maggie remembered yesterday when they'd returned to George's house. She had a mental picture of Jake climbing up to the treehouse with the bulging backpack. It was so clear now, but then it had meant nothing.

"What did Jake have in the backpack yesterday?" she asked.

"A blanket, your raincoat and an umbrella." He grinned at Maggie's start of surprise. "Missed those, did you? Don't worry, they're still up there. Jake and I checked it out tonight before you got back from the police station. From what I could tell, Tully had been there during the storm."

"Where is he now?" Ham asked.

"I don't know," Grant said. "Jake wrote Tully a note, asking him to come and talk to me. He left it in the tree-house along with the sandwiches that Kenny passed him at school today. After you and Jake left tonight, I took up some leftover pizza and a thermos of coffee, but there was no sign of Tully. All we can do is wait and see if he comes back and if he's willing to talk."

"He's got to," Maggie said. "There's a killer running loose here in Delbrook. I can't let Jake continue to shield Tully. It's too dangerous."

"I agree," Grant said. "George might have been killed on the spur of the moment out of fear of discovery, but Dennis Nyland's death is different. He was deliber-ately murdered. For some reason Nyland was a danger that had to be eliminated. The murderer won't think twice about killing the boys if they get in his way."

The sleep of the innocent, Maggie thought as she stared down at Jake. He lay on his back, his arms spread wide, his little boy's chest achingly vulnerable in its nakedness. Since Mark's death, she had stood many nights beside Jake's bed, aware of the fragility of life and terrified of losing Jake.

She leaned over to kiss his cheek, inhaling the soapy smell that clung to his hair after his shower. Please, God, keep him safe.

Picking up the dirty sneakers beside the bed, she took them out to the kitchen, where she sprayed them with disinfectant. They were only a few weeks old, yet they looked and smelled as if Jake had been wearing them for years. He hated socks. He said his feet couldn't breathe. In the winter it wasn't too bad, but when it was hot, the sweat combined with the materials in the sneakers to create an odor that brought tears to the eyes.

She set the shoes on the floor by the stairs and picked up his backpack. She unzipped the bag, finding Kenny's windbreaker jammed on top. She shook it out and hung it over the back of a kitchen chair.

The backpack needed airing, too. She made a mental note to wash it on the weekend. She pulled out several schoolbooks and set them on the counter along with a plastic pencil case, two dog-eared Batman comic books, old brown paper sandwich bags and a collection of rocks, bottle caps and intriguing metal parts.

When the bag was empty, she inverted it over the sink and shook it. Crumbs, scraps of paper and miscellaneous grit showered down on the metal surface of the sink. She gave the backpack one final shake, and out floated a feather.

The feather was pure white with a little clouding near the shaft. She recognized it immediately. It was the tail feather of a bald eagle.

Her fingers tightened on the backpack, and her heart pounded in her ears. The feather was perfect, with no gaps or crimping along the edges. The flawless condition of the feather indicated it had not been scrunched in the bottom of Jake's backpack for days on end.

Hands shaking, she picked up the receiver of the phone and dialed George's telephone number. Grant answered.

"I just found an eagle feather in Jake's backpack," she said, swallowing to loosen the dryness in her throat.

"I'll be right there," he said.

Maggie blinked several times as she heard the dial tone droning in her ear. She hadn't expected such an immediate reaction, but she felt instant relief at Grant's response. Hanging up the phone, she unbolted the door to the stairwell and walked down the stairs. She unlocked the outer door and opened it, standing in the darkness, looking out into the night.

The air was cool, the crisp chill hinting at the winter ahead. Her face was warm, and she rested her head against the frame of the door, sighing as a puff of wind fluttered across her skin. She tried to shut her mind off, floating above her emotions until she heard the sound of an approaching car. Footsteps crossed the wooden floor of the porch.

Grant closed the door as he entered, enclosing them in the darkened stairwell. He put his arms around her, and she clung to him, transferring her fear to him as naturally as if she had known him for a long time instead of only a week. They stood together, pressed into a single unit, and she drew the strength she needed from his presence. He seemed to sense when she had recovered her equilibrium. His arms dropped, and he released her.

"Show me," he said.

She led the way back up to the kitchen. She pointed to the feather that still lay in the bottom of the sink. He seemed as reluctant as she to touch it, leaning over to look at it more closely.

"It's definitely an eagle feather," he said. "It was in Jake's backpack?"

"Yes. But not long."

"Agreed." He paced across to the living room archway. "Do you think Jake could have found it?"

"It doesn't look as if it's been outside in the elements," Maggie said. "I didn't want to wake him up, but I'll ask him in the morning. Usually when he finds a feather of any kind, he sticks it in a buttonhole or tucks it behind his ear. This one was down in the bottom of the backpack."

Grant frowned, walking back to stand in front of the sink.

"Jake left his backpack outside beneath the treehouse when you dropped him off, and we didn't bring it inside until just before you came back from the police station. Anyone could have put the feather inside."

"Why?" Maggie clasped her hands to keep them from shaking. "Why would someone do that?"

"A joke? A warning?" Grant shrugged. "I wish I knew."

"Jake's in danger. I know he is," Maggie said, unable to keep the quiver out of her voice.

"It could be intended as a warning to all of us, but we can't ignore the fact that the feather was left in Jake's backpack. I think for the next several days we should keep him in sight."

"We've unleashed a monster," Maggie said.

"Wrong. The monster was always there. Just think of the situation if we didn't know he existed."

"Could it be Tully?"

"I don't think so. Ham and I checked the treehouse after we left here. Nothing has been touched. Tully hasn't been there. Ham's keeping watch for him while I'm over here." Grant picked up the feather. "What do you want me to do with this?"

"Get it out of my sight." Maggie shuddered.

Grant slipped the feather into the inside pocket of his jacket.

"What have you got planned for tomorrow?" he asked.

"Nothing much. I was hoping Kenny could come over, but Hugh's taking him up to Door County to stay with his grandmother. Jake can help Beth and me downstairs in the bookstore for most of the day. Then after dinner, I've got a conference with Jake's teacher, and I'll take him with me."

"Why don't I pick Jake up in the afternoon, and he can knock around with Ham and me? We'll fast food it for dinner and go to a movie while you're at the conference."

"That would be great, but are you sure you're up to all of that?"

"I had a good time with Jake yesterday. Besides, I suspect you could use a bit of time when you don't have to worry about him," Grant said.

"It would be bliss," she admitted. "Jake could use some time away from me, too."

"Would you like me to stay here tonight?" Grant asked.

His sudden question came as a surprise. She didn't know if he was asking in order to soothe her anxiety or for more personal reasons. She didn't know which she would prefer.

"When do you go home?" she asked, answering his question with one of her own.

"I'm not sure. If it looks like I'm not getting anywhere, I'll have to leave."

"That's a safe lawyerly response," she said. She

opened the door at the top of the stairs. "I appreciate your coming over. Just having someone to talk to has calmed my initial panic. Thanks for the offer to stay, but I'm turning you down. It's a small town, Holbrook. By morning everyone would know."

"Can't handle being thought of as a fallen woman?" he asked.

She started down the stairs, aware of his presence behind her. At the bottom, she opened the door to the side porch and turned to face him.

"It was your reputation I was worrying about," she said.

As he passed her, he leaned forward and kissed her on the mouth. "Next time I'll walk over and no one will know I'm here."

"There won't be a next time," she said, grinning despite a heaviness in her heart. "Carpetbaggers aren't welcome in Wisconsin."

"You won't have to suspend Jake again," Maggie said half-jokingly as she faced Rachel Velasco across the teacher's desk. "We had a nice talk today, and he said to tell you he wouldn't talk so much during class."

"Generally he's not disruptive," Rachel said, "but this week I've had to reprimand him several times."

"Kenny Rossiter?" she guessed.

"Yes. The two of them are trouble with a capital T. Thank heavens, they're mischievous not naughty."

"I think you'll have a quieter week from both of the boys. They had a scheme in progress, but it's been curtailed."

Maggie's morning talk with Jake had been difficult.

To alleviate some of her own fear, she would have loved to scream and rant at his actions, but if she had any hope that he would confide in her again, she needed to keep things in perspective. After she extracted a promise from him that he would not have anything to do with Tully without letting either her or Grant know, she felt considerably calmer.

She had not slept well. Finding the feather in Jake's backpack had brought home with explosive force the danger that surrounded them. She had left her door open when she went to bed, getting up several times in the night to check on Jake and to pace the halls, testing doors and listening to the creaks and groans of the old house.

In the morning, when she asked Jake, he knew nothing about the feather, confirming that someone had placed it in the backpack deliberately.

Most of the day she had kept him busy helping shelve books and doing general cleanup chores in the bookstore. Jake could hardly contain his delight when Grant arrived with an offer of fishing and a movie. After she'd agreed to meet them on George's deck for drinks and a summary of their day, Grant and Jake sauntered out of the bookstore, looking very pleased with themselves.

Freed of her immediate worry over Jake, she'd had a peaceful day, and after a dinner of salad and fruit, she drove to St. Bernard's and her conference with Jake's teacher. As she looked through Jake's papers and drawings, she could feel the tension easing across her back. She handed the folder back to the teacher with a smile.

"These look good," Maggie said.

"Yes. The purpose of today's conference is to look at the first couple weeks of work and identify any problem areas. Jake's doing fine academically," Rachel said, consulting her notes. "His spelling's a bit weak, so it would help if you could work with him on it. Math is good. Reading excellent. Your owning a bookstore gives him validation and a strong motivation to do well."

"How do you think he's doing emotionally?" Maggie smoothed the cotton wrap skirt across her knees. "He tries to hide his feelings from me so he won't add to my own grief."

"I've talked to Alice O'Neill, the school psychiatrist, and we both agree that he's handling his grandfather's death appropriately. Dr. O'Neill and I were worried that the violent nature of the crime might be too strong a reminder of his father's death and precipitate a regression in his attitude."

"Poor kid's really under a microscope," Maggie said. "Both here at school and with me at home."

"It's only natural that you'd be concerned. From the school perspective, he seems to be moving through the mourning process properly."

"That was what I thought too. We had an excellent therapist after my husband died, so it's not as if Jake hasn't had to work through this before."

"He's a very mature child," Rachel said.

"Necessity, I'm afraid."

"After your father-in-law died, the teachers planned several sessions of the school day so that the children could discuss violence and their feelings about death," Rachel said. "Dr. O'Neill has helped us prepare lesson plans for just this sort of situation. Unfortunately violence has become a national problem, and we need to deal with it in the schools as well as the home."

"Sometimes when I'm watching the news I wonder if anyone can really be safe," Maggie said. "How do you prepare for random violence?"

"You can't. Here at school we're learning to deal with the aftermath of violence. What we need are programs that will identify and prevent problems that can escalate into some sort of incident."

"Amen to that," Maggie said.

After the conference was over, Maggie stood on the steps of the school, looking at the lake. Only a few boats skimmed across the surface, heading for home as the evening began to close in. It was eight-thirty, and Grant and Jake wouldn't be out of the movie until nine. With the temperature in the seventies and a light breeze, she was looking forward to a peaceful interlude on George's deck until they returned.

She walked down the stairs, stopping at the bottom, trying to recall where she'd left her car. Lately her brain had been on automatic pilot. She took several steps to the right, then remembered she was parked closer to the shopping area and abruptly turned around. She didn't see Connie Prentice until she collided with her.

"Oh, sorry!" Maggie cried.

Connie staggered, dropping her purse and the paper bag she was carrying. Maggie made a lunge for the bag. The corner ripped and spilled the contents onto the sidewalk.

"Really, Maggie," Connie snapped. "Can't you look where you're going?"

"I'm so sorry. I wasn't paying attention," Maggie said. "Here, let me help you."

"Oh, don't fuss. Nothing's breakable. It's just plates and napkins for the Ladies Golf Luncheon at the country club," Connie said.

Maggie stuffed everything back in the bag, then with the torn edges held together with one hand, she clasped the bundle in her arms and stood up.

"My car's over there," Connie said, pointing to the light blue BMW convertible beside an expired parking meter.

Connie scooped her purse off the sidewalk and reached inside for her keys. She unlocked the car and opened the passenger-side door.

"Just put it on the seat."

Maggie set the bag down. The tear promptly opened again, and the contents tumbled onto the floor of the car. Connie sighed in exasperation.

"Leave it," she said. "I'll take care of it when I get home."

"This is my day to be inept," Maggie said, closing the car door. "Next time I'll watch where I'm going. Actually, though, I'm glad I bumped into you. Thanks for sending over the dinner the other night. Even Jake's getting tired of fast food."

Connie waved her hand in dismissal. "Don't thank me. It was Brent's idea. He's Wisconsin's answer to Ms. Manners."

Maggie laughed. "Even so. I appreciate the thought and the deed."

"It forced me to cook a meal. We seem to be eating out more these days. Brent's gone so much I may end up living the life of a recluse, raising cats and talking to myself. Thank God the food is good at the country club.

Poker nights lure me out of the house a couple times a week."

"Speaking of poker, do you remember the pictures George was passing around at the country club?"

"Yes. And between you and me, Maggie, I don't think Jake will ever earn a living as a photographer."

Maggie was so used to the bite in Connie's voice that until she saw the smile she didn't realize the woman was joking.

"I agree," Maggie said. "By any chance, did you see what happened to the photos?"

"Don't you have them?"

"No. No one seems to know where they are. I know Brent came late. Do you suppose George might have given him the pictures?"

"Why all the interest in these photos?" Connie asked.

"They were from Jake's party. It would be nice to have them."

Connie passed her car keys back and forth between her hands, eyeing Maggie with sharpened interest.

"I don't know if Brent even saw the pictures. He missed dinner."

"Maybe George showed him the pictures when they took a break," Maggie said.

"Trust me, Maggie. The boys don't go to the bathroom in pairs like us girls do." Connie snorted in amusement. "I think you're beating a dead horse. The only time Brent left the table was when I got ticked at his snide remarks and quit. He came chasing after me to apologize."

"Did you leave the club right away or did you hang around?"

Connie's fingers stopped twisting the wide gold bracelet on her wrist. "And this would be your business how?"

"I was curious about something that you said when you stopped by George's house," Maggie said, all too aware of the other woman's annoyance. "You said George was still at the club when you and Brent left. I assumed you'd driven together, but now I realize that you left at separate times."

"Yes. I left early," Connie said. "I was furious with Brent and I went home early. What does it matter anyway?"

"I don't know if it does," Maggie said. "I just wanted to know what had happened the night that George died."

"What did you think? That I had come back for a secret tryst with him and then, in a fit of passion or rage, killed him?" Connie laughed. "By your expression I'd say that was exactly what you thought."

"That's not what I was thinking," Maggie said, suspecting that she was blushing in her embarrassment.

"Oh, don't mind me. I've got a headache."

"Want to walk in the park for a bit?" Maggie asked. "The fresh air might help."

Connie looked surprised by the invitation but nodded her head. "I'd like that."

They crossed the street to Wolfram Park, angling down to the lakeshore and the lighted boardwalk. Maggie raised her face, sighing as the breeze cooled her cheeks. Connie stood beside her, eyes closed, drawing in deep breaths of the moist air.

"I should have thought of this earlier," she said. "Brent's in Milwaukee. I'm going to meet him there for the weekend. With this headache, I was dreading the drive, but I'm already beginning to feel better. Thanks for the suggestion."

"Lake air always rejuvenates me," Maggie said.

"If you had lived here in Delbrook after you married Mark, do you think we would have been friends?"

The question came out of the blue. Looking at Connie, Maggie could see a genuine curiosity in her expression. She thought about it for a moment before she answered.

"With Mark as our connection we might have been. I could have used a friend," Maggie said.

"Yes, I know."

Maggie had always assumed that no one knew about her situation with Mark. Connie's knowledge came as a surprise.

"Mark told you?"

"Yes. We were always close. Perhaps I should have married him, and things might have turned out differently for all of us."

Maggie wasn't offended by the comment. Mark had told her they had been lovers when they were younger and that after it was over they had gone back to being friends.

"Were you in love with Mark?"

"Good heavens, no." Connie sounded shocked by the question. "I understood him. And he understood me."

"Didn't either of you consider it?"

"Mark might have, but for me it was out of the question. Very early in life, my father explained that I would be making an advantageous marriage and he would choose my life's partner. A bit archaic, but I didn't question it. Mark was two years younger and not what my father would have considered the kind of man to father a dynasty."

Maggie walked along the boardwalk, wondering if she'd misjudged Connie. Listening to Brent Wednesday night, she had automatically taken his side. She had always felt he was unfairly the target of Connie's sharp words. But looking at Connie's pale face and nervous gestures, Maggie saw a vulnerability she'd never noticed before.

"And your father chose Brent?" she asked.

"Brent was born here in Delbrook. You probably know that my father sponsored him," Connie said. "My father was the controlling sort who loved playing Lord Bountiful to the starving masses. He never spent money unless he got a good return. He thought Brent was the answer to his prayers. Father groomed him to take over as the head of the Falcone dynasty."

According to Brent, Connie had tried to be the son her father never had, suppressing her own femininity to please Edmund. It was difficult to picture her as anything but a beautifully poised young woman. Had she been grateful or resentful when her father turned his attention to Brent?

"How old were you when you married?" Maggie asked.

"Twenty. Brent was fourteen years older. Father

thought he would be a steadying influence on me," Connie said, an acid tone creeping into her voice. "Brent idolized Edmund. He saw himself as a mirror image of my father. He was convinced that our children would be exceptional. He, like my father, wanted a large family. Unfortunately, when I miscarried, we discovered there would be no other children."

"I'm sorry," Maggie said. "Sometimes life conspires to take away our choices."

"Don't mind me," Connie said. "I don't usually bare my soul. I used to talk to George a lot. It's been a crappy week, and I miss having him around."

Under the park lights, she didn't look well. Her makeup didn't hide the dark circles under her eyes, and the blush stood out starkly against the pallor of her cheeks. She looked as if she were living on her nerves. Her manicured fingers flashed in constant movement, touching her earrings, her bracelet and then reaching down to pick at a loose thread on her yellow pleated skirt.

"Is everything all right?" Maggie asked.

Connie looked startled. "Well of course it is," she said. "What makes you think it wouldn't be?"

She flipped her hair back away from her face and brushed her hands across the material of her skirt. The safety chain of her gold bracelet caught on a loose thread. The movement of her arm was so quick that the clasp snapped open and the bracelet dropped to the boardwalk and rolled into the grass.

"Damn it all," Connie muttered.

"I see it," Maggie said, leaning over to pick up the bracelet. "The chain's broken, but the clasp looks OK."

Connie rubbed her wrist as Maggie handed her the wide gold band.

"Are you hurt?" she asked.

"It's just a scratch," Connie said.

Seeing a trace of blood, Maggie reached in the pocket of her skirt for a tissue.

"Here. Don't get blood on your clothes."

Maggie reached out to dab the cut when she spotted the drawing on Connie's wrist.

"You have a tattoo," she blurted out before she could help herself.

"Don't sound so horrified," Connie said. She snatched the Kleenex and wiped the blood away, then covered the mark with the gold bracelet. "I got it a long time ago. Brent hates it. He doesn't like being around the birds, and I don't think he likes my obsession with them. That's why I always wear a bracelet to cover it."

"I wasn't being critical," Maggie said. "It was seeing the tattoo that made me think about Dennis Nyland. I assume you heard about him."

"Yes," Connie said. "It's frightening."

"Did you know that Dennis was a tattoo artist?"

"Yes. We talked about it a couple of times when I saw him at the country club," Connie said. "It's sad. He was very talented. He created some beautiful designs. And, if you're wondering, Dennis didn't draw my tattoo."

Maggie was stunned at the coincidence of Connie, Dennis Nyland and the two children all having tattoos. Were they all connected?

"When did you get it?" she asked.

"It was right after Brent and I were married. I'd just

gotten involved in falconry. Growing up, I always felt like an outsider. Poor little rich girl angst. I knew my father had wanted a boy, so my gender made me feel inadequate. In falconry, there was little bias. I could do the same things the men could do. I had found my niche and I excelled in it. Training the birds came naturally to me, and my gyrfalcons were first-rate hunters."

"I saw your program at the Renaissance Faire, and I was impressed," Maggie said.

"Thanks. As you can see I love the sport. It's a wonderful obsession. The tattoo was to celebrate my hawk's first kill. It's on the inside of my left wrist. A falconer carries the hawk on his left hand. That's the gloved hand. Every time I put on my glove I see the tattoo. For me it's a constant reminder of my success."

"Is it a picture of a hawk?"

"No. That was more of a commitment than I wanted to make. I'm not really into pain. I didn't have a lot of designs to choose from."

Connie unsnapped the bracelet and held out her arm. The sight of the tattoo raised goose bumps on Maggie's arms. It was a line drawing, the black ink sharp against the light skin tone of Connie's wrist.

"I wanted the tattoo to have some connection to falconry," Connie said. "This seemed the right choice. Instead of a hawk, I chose an eagle feather."

CHAPTER
TWENTY-ONE

"HOW COME UNCLE HAM didn't want to go to see *Tarzan*?" Jake asked as he bounded along the pavement to keep up with Grant.

"He's not into animated films, I guess."

"Oh."

After a few more steps the boy stopped, and when Grant looked down, his face was scrunched up in thought.

"What's up?"

"Did you like the movie?" Jake asked.

"Actually, I did. I have a fondness for dancing animals." Grant ruffled Jake's hair. "You worked that out just fine. You may have a career ahead as a lawyer."

"Mom says that lawyers—"

Grant held up his hand. "I can just imagine what your mother has to say about lawyers. I don't think she likes me very much."

"Yes, she does," Jake said, starting to walk again. "If she didn't like you, she just wouldn't talk to you."

"Not a bad system. I may have to try that."

They walked along the sidewalk toward Grant's car in companionable silence.

"I was impressed last night when you told me about helping Tully," Grant said. "I know you were feeling bad about keeping the secret from your mom."

"Uh-huh. It wasn't *ezactly* a lie, but I knew she wouldn't like it."

"Well I've been feeling bad about something I told you. And in my case it was a lie."

Jake tilted his head, looking up at Grant out of the corner of his eyes. "Is it about bein' Dad's cousin?"

Grant came to a halt, staring down at Jake as a grin crept across the boy's face.

"You knew?"

"Dad told me he didn't have any cousins."

"Oh. How come you didn't say anything?"

"I was scared at first that you were a bad guy."

Grant put his hand on Jake's shoulder, squeezing it for reassurance. "I'm very sorry I frightened you. Even for a second."

"That's OK. I told Kenny about it when his dad took you to see the hawks. He said to wait and see."

"And?"

"The pizza we made was good."

Grant bent his knees until his face was on the same level with Jake's. He held the boy's shoulders between his hands and looked him straight in the eye.

"You're a fine boy, Jake. I promise I will never lie to you again. Friends?"

"Friends," Jake said. They walked a short distance in silence, then he asked, "Do you have lots of money?"

Grant was surprised by the sudden question. "Do you need a loan?"

"Uh-uh. I just thought it would be really cool if you

could buy Grampa's house. Then Kenny and I could still play in the treehouse."

"I see. Do you think your mom would like that?"

Jake thought for a minute, then shrugged his shoulders. "Maybe. You better ask her though."

"Speaking of your mother, we better get moving. She's going to think we've gotten lost."

"Can I have something to drink when we get to Grampa's?" Jake asked. "I'm really thirsty."

"Next time don't put so much salt on the popcorn. Did you finish the whole box?" Grant asked.

"Yep. I'm stuffed." He pulled his knit shirt down tight to show off his rounded belly. "Dinner was good too. I don't think I ever ate three whole tacos before. Wait'll I tell Kenny."

"Speaking of Kenny, your mom is going to talk to Mr. Rossiter about Tully."

"That's what she told me. I hope he won't be too mad. It was my fault. I made Kenny help out."

Grant heard the anxiety in his voice. "Mr. Rossiter has a temper, huh?"

Jake's gaze flashed up to meet his. "Sometimes he's pretty mean to Kenny. Even when it's not Kenny's fault."

"I used to feel bad when I was your age because I'd get my sister to do something really dumb and then she'd get in trouble."

"That happens all the time." There was guilt in the rounded shoulders as Jake said, "Taking the snake to school was my idea."

"I had a feeling it was." Grant laughed. "Remember this, Jake. People choose what they want to do. You might come up with the plan, but each person has to decide if they want to go along with it. Do you understand what I'm saying?"

"Maybe. I still have to watch out for Kenny though."

Grant opened the door of the car. "Hop in. We've got one more stop before we head home."

"Did Tully come to the treehouse last night?" Jake asked as he buckled his seat belt.

"No. Ham and I took turns watching for him, but he didn't show up."

"You don't think something's happened to him, do you? Mom told me about Dennis Nyland." His voice shook slightly.

"My guess is that Tully heard about Dennis too and he's laying low. I put fresh coffee and some fried chicken up in the treehouse in case he comes back tonight."

"Thanks, Grant. Tully might be getting tired of the sandwiches." Jake stretched his neck to see out the window. "Where are we going?"

"Kruckmeyer's Pharmacy. I stopped by earlier to see the owner, but she doesn't come to work until after nine. I wanted to talk to her."

"Mrs. Kruckmeyer talks to everyone. Except kids. She can be real grouchy when they're in the store."

"I'll keep that in mind," Grant said as he parked the car and led the way into the store.

"Can I get some gum?" Jake asked.

"As long as it's sugar free," Grant said.

"That's just what Mom always says."

Jake rolled his eyes and wandered down the candy aisle as Grant walked over to the heavyset older woman behind the checkout counter.

"Mrs. Kruckmeyer? My name's Grant Holbrook."

"Ah," she said. "Edna's nephew. The lawyer from Chicago."

"Guilty as charged," he said, grinning at the familiar designation.

"Just call me Ann." She held out her hand and gave his a hearty shake. "What can I do you for?"

"I wondered if I could ask you some questions."

"Shoot."

"It's about the disposable camera Maggie brought in the other day for developing."

"The one from Jake's birthday party?" At his nod, she drew herself up, frowning across at him. "I'm real sorry the photos are lost, but we don't keep copies. We develop everyone's pictures in town. Can you imagine if we tried to keep copies of every roll of film?"

"You'd need a bigger store." Grant smiled at her, and her expression lightened. "Actually, what I wanted to ask you about was George. I understand he picked up the pictures on Saturday."

"Yes, he did. I waited on him myself. Imagine how I felt when I heard about his death. It's just a shame that something like that could happen in our town. A lot of riffraff hangs out around the lake. They get to thinking we're easy pickings."

"Crime always goes up in lake communities during the summer," he said.

"You got that right. I'm always bending Charley Blessington's ear that he ought to do more to curb that element." She waved a hand at the theft detectors in front of the doors. "I had to install those damn things because I was losing my underdrawers to shoplifters. Little pissants no bigger than Jake here."

Arriving at the counter just then, Jake jerked his hand up and dropped a package of gum on the counter as if she were accusing him.

"That'll be eighty cents," she said, passing it across the antitheft strip.

Grant handed her the money. "So George picked up the photographs?" he asked, hoping to get her back on track.

"Yeah. And four cigars." Ann rested one ample hip on the stool behind the counter. "You know, Mr. Holbrook, this is a small town and everyone knows everyone else's business. George's doctor told him to give up cigars about six months ago. I knew he shouldn't be buying them, but hell, I ain't his mother."

"I can understand that," he said.

"I sold him some nicotine patches a couple months back, so I asked him if he'd given up on the patches. He said they didn't help." She tipped her head forward and looked down her nose at Jake. "I hope you won't ever take up that filthy habit."

"No, ma'am," Jake said, his eyes wide. "My mom told me she'd be really cross with me if I did."

"Good boy. You mind your mother and you'll grow up just fine." She shifted her gaze back up to Grant. "So I told George he ought to give the patches another try. I'd been a pretty heavy smoker, and it took me three times before it took, I told him. Three times is the charm, I said."

"Did he buy them?"

"Naw. He paid for the cigars and the pictures. He tucked one of the cigars in his inside jacket pocket and winked. He said he'd just take one to smoke after the poker game."

"What happened to the others?" Grant asked.

"I put them in a bag. There wasn't anyone else in line, so he opened up the package of pictures and took them out to show me." Once more she looked down at Jake. "Your granddad was real proud of you, Jake. He got quite a laugh over the picture of Kenny Rossiter tossing his cookies. When you get a bit older you better take a photography class. You wasted a lot of film. Some of those pictures woulda looked better if you hadn't cut the heads off."

"Mom says I have to remember to hold the camera still."

"That'd be good for starters," she said. "So then George sticks the pictures in the folder and puts them into the pocket of his jacket. After promising to buy a box of the patches next week, he puts the negatives in with the cigars and leaves."

It took a moment for Ann's words to sink in, and when they did, Grant thought he'd taken a shot to the stomach.

"What did you say about the negatives?" he asked.

"George put them in the bag with the cigars."

"Judas. Why didn't I think of that?"

"Think of what?" She looked totally confused.

"Nothing," Grant said. "What did he do with the bag?"

"How would I know?" she said.

"Thanks so much for your help," Grant said, anxious to be away from the woman in order to have time to think. "I've got to be getting Jake home, but I appreciate all you've told me."

He pushed Jake out the automatic doors, unlocked the car and got inside while his mind was busy reviewing everything the woman had told him.

The negatives. The killer had taken the photographs from George, but he didn't get the negatives. That's got to be what he's been searching for. If only the negatives were still in the bag with the cigars.

"All I have to do is find the bag of cigars," he muttered aloud, smacking his hand on the top of the steering wheel.

"I know where it is."

Grant jerked around to stare at Jake.

"You know where the bag with your grandfather's cigars is?"

"Sure. It's up in the treehouse."

The matter-of-fact response left Grant speechless. He shook his head to clear it and tried to keep the strain from showing in his voice when he asked, "What's it doing up there?"

"Grampa didn't want Mom to find the cigars. He always hid them up there." Jake sounded surprised at Grant's question. Apparently his grandfather's deception was well accepted.

"Is the bag still there?"

"I guess. I just put it in the coffee can like Grampa showed me. That's so the cigars don't get soggy."

"How about we go see if we can find them?" Grant said as he flipped on the headlights and put the car into gear.

His fingers cramped on the steering wheel as he

drove through the dark streets on the way to the Estates. He had to make a conscious effort not to speed when his first inclination was to press the gas pedal to the floor. Jake sat quietly beside him, unaware of the explosion he had set off with his comments.

Adults tended to ignore the presence of children, speaking freely, forgetting the small ears that sucked in everything for later processing. Kids knew far more than adults realized. Once Grant had determined the existence of the negatives, he'd have to consider what other information Jake might have.

He pulled into the parking spot beside Ham's car. Jake scampered out the door and climbed the ladder and disappeared inside the treehouse. In a flash he was back, his face framed by the open trapdoor.

"I got it," he said. "I'll drop it to you."

Grant caught the coffee can and waited for Jake to return to the ground. He held out the can and nudged the boy.

"Let's take it inside," he said.

"I heard the car," Ham said, handing Grant an open bottle of beer as they entered the kitchen. "Coke, Jake?"

"Super," Jake said, setting the metal can on the kitchen table.

Ham reached into the refrigerator for a bottle of pop, opened it and handed it to the boy. "What's that?"

"The jackpot, I hope," Grant said, waiting as Jake took a long swallow of the soda. "OK. Let's see what you've got."

Jake pried off the plastic lid of the coffee can and pulled out the white bag with the red letters of Kruckmeyer's Pharmacy. He opened the top and turned the bag on its side. The contents slid out onto the oak surface of the table. Three cigars and a transparent plastic envelope containing narrow strips of film.

Grant opened the envelope and slid out one of the strips, holding it up toward the ceiling light. He was barely able to control his elation as he stared at the film.

"What have you got?" Ham asked.

"The film from Jake's party pictures," Grant said. "The negatives from the Renaissance Faire."

The security guard at Camp Delbrook was gone for the day when Maggie drove in through the entrance. Lights flickered through the trees in the dining hall, and she could see people moving around beyond the windows. Music and laughter floated across to her as she passed. Apparently the volunteers weren't too exhausted from the fall cleanup.

She parked the car in front of Hugh's place, anxiously checking the clock on the dashboard. Nine o'-clock. Grant and Jake should be getting out of the movie now. If she hurried, she'd arrive at George's about the same time as they did. She felt a sense of urgency to talk to Grant. Time was running out.

With Kenny's jacket slung over the strap of her purse, she got out of the car and climbed the stairs to the front porch. She lifted up a corner of the mat, picked up the key Hugh had left for her and unlocked the front door.

A lamp was on in Hugh's office, spilling light across the foyer. Her footsteps sounded loud in the empty house, and she hurried along the hall to the kitchen. She pushed the door open and felt along the right-hand wall for the light switch. She pressed it, and the overhead light flashed on, the illumination so bright that Maggie couldn't hold back a gasp of surprise.

Her heart pounded as if she'd been running, and she could feel an uneasiness creep through her as she scanned the room. Don't be so jumpy, she muttered to herself as she crossed the tile floor to the open door of the mudroom.

She pressed the light switch, prepared this time as the lights popped on to reveal a washer and dryer on one side and a long closet on the other side. Jake's jacket was on a hanger inside the louvered doors of the closet. She exchanged the jackets and closed the doors, turning off the lights as she returned to the kitchen.

She took the key to the front door out of her skirt pocket. Hugh had told her to hang it on the pegboard beside the refrigerator, since the front door would lock automatically when she closed it. She hooked the key on one of the empty pegs. As she released it, her fingers brushed against the round plastic disk attached to the ring of keys for the mews. The disk swung back and forth, and the hawk inside looked as if it were in flight.

Birds. Feathers. Tattoos.

Maggie had to admit that the sight of Connie's feather tattoo had shocked her. Despite her attempt to downplay her reaction, Connie had seen it and become defensive. Minutes later she announced that she needed to leave or she'd be late meeting Brent in Milwaukee. Maggie was left staring after the blue BMW and wondering what conclusions she could draw from their conversation.

Now, as she stared at the ring of keys hanging on the

pegboard, she thought about everything she knew about Connie.

Connie had been at the Renaissance Faire. She'd been at the poker game and had seen the photographs. She was a falconer with knowledge of the falconer's knot and access to feathers.

Everyone had assumed that George had been killed by a man, but as Nell had pointed out, there was no reason that a woman couldn't have done it. Connie was used to talking to George, so it would be perfectly natural for her to walk along with him as he smoked his cigar after the poker game. Without raising his suspicions, she could have gotten close enough to him to stab him.

"It can't be Connie."

Maggie winced at the sound of the spoken words. She crossed her arms over her chest. Pacing over to the sink and back she moaned softly as if she were in pain. It can't be any of them. She didn't want it to be any of them. Charley, Brent, Connie and Hugh. Especially Hugh. She knew these people. She loved them.

They were all George's friends. They had mourned his death. She could see that they missed him. None of them could have killed him.

Charley was the chief of police. No secret in his past would be worth murder. And Hugh. Even if it turned out he had beaten his wife, it didn't mean that he would commit murder. Just the thought of it felt like a betrayal of her friendship. He had been nothing but kind to her and Jake. What reason would either of these men have to kill George?

The same reason as anyone else. George had recognized Tyler's picture.

Full circle and no closer to the truth.

She looked at the key board and thought again about Connie.

A kidnapper? What had Connie said about her marriage to Brent? Maggie closed her eyes and tried to bring back the exact words. She said after the miscarriage, she couldn't have any more children.

Maggie swallowed hard, her throat suddenly dry. She had read about women who were so desperate to have children they went to hospitals and stole babies out of the nurseries. Surely if Connie was that emotionally disturbed, someone would have noticed.

Maggie stared up at the hawk swinging from the ring of keys. Connie kept her birds in the mews. Hugh had taken Grant through the building, and he had found nothing suspicious. Could Grant have missed something?

She'd never have a better chance to find out. Hugh was in Door County, and Connie and Brent were in Milwaukee. She didn't know where Charley was, but if she was going to search the mews, this was the perfect opportunity.

It was the flashlight lying on the counter beneath the pegboard that decided her. Knowing that if she thought about it she would chicken out, Maggie grabbed the flashlight, the ring of keys and at the last moment remembered to take the key to the front door.

Outside she walked quickly, her footsteps muffled on the mulched path that led up toward the mews. She came to the clearing, and the equipment garage loomed ahead of her. Bushes crowded close against the sides of the building, leaving much of the area in deep shadow. She walked around to the side, looking for a good place to leave her purse and the windbreaker. Tucking the front-door key into the pocket of Jake's jacket, she folded it and shoved it under the edge of a small shrub and anchored it with her purse.

Flashlight in one hand and the ring of keys in the other, she continued along the path to the mews. Shielding the beam of the flashlight with her body, she found the key and unlocked the door.

Standing inside the tunnel, she waited for the pounding of her heart to slow enough for her to breathe without gasping. The air was still, musty smelling. Taking a last fortifying breath, she pushed away from the door and walked out into the open yard.

Not wanting to startle the birds, she flashed the light into each of the cages, keeping the beam low. The slight rustling of the hawks was the only sound to break the stillness of the night. She made a full circuit of the cages, then started on the infirmary and the storage areas. By the time she was finished she was sweating.

The search had been a waste of time.

Frustrated by her failure to discover anything and anxious to get away, she hurried out through the tunnel, locked the door and started back along the path.

Had Grant seen the inside of the equipment garage the day he'd gone to the mews with Hugh?

She stared down at the keys in her hand, wondering if one of them would open the door into the building. She should be getting back, but she hated to lose the opportunity to search.

"If the key fits, I'll check it."

The whispered words sounded loud in the silence of the night. Forcing her feet to move, she approached the door and switched on the flashlight, shining the beam of light on the lock. The second key slid in easily. She turned it and heard a click.

Her hands shook as she pulled the key out. The plastic disk hit the doorknob, and the ring of keys flew out of her hand. They hit the ground with a soft thud. She was afraid to take the time to search for them. She'd look for them on her way out.

Taking a deep shuddering breath, she pulled the door open and stepped inside. The door closed silently behind her on well-oiled hinges. She kept the beam of light close to the floor as she walked farther into the building. She played the light slowly, sliding it over and around the boxes piled along the walls and jutting out into the room, searching for a storage closet or a door to another room. Anything that might be worth investigating.

The darkness beyond the beam of light closed in around her, increasing her fear. Every muscle was tense as she strained to see the slightest movement or hear any sound to indicate her presence had been discovered.

Hurry! Get out!

Her nerves screamed at the passage of time, but she knew she'd never get another chance to search the garage. Steadying her hand on the flashlight, she worked her way around the perimeter of the room. The light flickered across the stacks of equipment and shelves of parts, up and down, probing every shadowed crevice.

Nothing.

She clenched her teeth in disappointment, breathing loudly through her nose as she completed the sweep of the room. The garage was empty. Nothing even slightly suspicious.

The floor was a vast array of concrete, littered with parts, hand tools and electrical equipment. Toward the far side of the room was a long pit where the mechanics could work on the underside of the vehicles without having to rely on a pneumatic lift. She walked over to the edge, shining the flashlight down into the opening.

She didn't hear anything, only felt the presence of someone behind her. Before she could move, fingers dug into the hair at the back of her head and dragged her away from the pit.

She let out a small cry as her head was yanked backward. Instinctively she raised her hands, lashing out with the flashlight. It connected with a hard body, but the impact jerked it out of her hand. There was the sound of breaking glass, then darkness.

"Why couldn't you leave it alone?"

Words shrilled in her ear, accompanied by wrenching shakes of her head. She struggled to tear the hand away from her hair, scratching at the flesh in a frenzy of pain. In the darkness she fought blindly, twisting her body to face her attacker.

A fist crashed into her face, glancing off her cheekbone. She cried out and raised her arms for protection. Another blow caught her on her forearm, and as she pulled away, she was rocked by a punch to the side of her head, next to her ear.

Her knees buckled. The hand in her hair was the only thing holding her up. The darkness closed in around her, and her head fell forward as her attacker released her. She collapsed, her hands breaking her fall, so that when her head hit the concrete, there was an instant of pain before she lost consciousness.

CHAPTER TWENTY-TWO

"KRUCKMEYER'S DOESN'T HAVE anyone there who can develop the film," Grant said, hanging up the phone. "What's open at this hour on a Friday night?"

"Nothing," Ham said. "Besides, we need the pictures now. Not in three days. Let me call Alexis Beckwith. She's a retired photographer who lives here in the Estates."

Ham grabbed the phone book and flipped through the pages until he found the number he wanted. Grant looked at his watch, then stepped outside where Jake was sitting on the top step of the porch.

"Where's Mom?" Jake asked without taking his eyes from the parking space behind the house.

For the last fifteen minutes, Grant had been wondering the same thing. Maggie knew the show was over at nine, and he was surprised that she hadn't called or left a message to say she'd be late. He'd already called both the bookstore and the second-floor apartment, but there'd been no answer either place.

"I don't know, Jake. I thought she'd be waiting for us on the deck. She said she had errands to run and the conference with your teacher. Maybe she stopped to get something to eat."

The kitchen door opened, and Ham came out holding the plastic envelope of negatives.

"We're in luck. Alexis has a darkroom. She told me to bring the negatives and she'll print them right now."

"Dynamite. Jake and I will stay here and wait for Maggie," Grant said.

He'd already voiced his concerns to Ham. They'd agreed to give Maggie another half hour in case she had car trouble or was just running late. Grant didn't like it. He knew Maggie wouldn't be away from Jake this long unless she'd run into an emergency.

"Want something to drink, Jake?"

"Nuh-uh," he said.

His elbows rested on his knees and his chin was cupped in the palms of his hands as he watched Ham disappear down the street. Grant leaned against the kitchen door. The silence lengthened and the small night sounds returned, slowing his pulse even though his anxiety level remained high at Maggie's continued absence. Ten minutes later, Jake leaped to his feet.

"Hey, Tully," he said, racing down the path toward the treehouse.

Grant picked out the dark shadow standing close to the trunk of the tree. He remained on the porch, afraid that any movement on his part might spook the man into bolting. He had to trust that Tully had come in answer to Jake's note and let the boy make the initial contact. His muscles cramped as he tried to appear at ease, listening to the soft murmur of voices beneath the treehouse.

Tully paced away from the tree, stepping into a thin

patch of light. Grant's first impression wasn't encouraging. Although at a distance he couldn't distinguish Tully's features, he could see the long hair and scraggly beard topped by what appeared to be a white top hat. He wore shapeless khaki pants and a short-sleeved undershirt, the front of which had been torn in a jagged cut from neck to the middle of his chest. The plastic raincoat he had on over his clothes completed the bizarre look of the man.

Grant heard the pleading note in Jake's voice and inhaled sharply as Tully turned to face the porch. He released his breath in a slow stream of relief as Jake came down the path holding the hand of the enigmatic Tully.

"This is my friend," Jake said.

Grant smiled, wondering which one of them the boy meant. In the light from the kitchen he could see a reflection of his own amusement in the other man's eyes.

"Grant Holbrook," he said, holding out his hand.

Removing his hat, Tully brushed his free hand against the side of his pants and gave Grant a surprisingly firm handshake.

"Tully Jackson." His voice was raspy, as if he weren't used to speaking. "Jake says you need Tully's help."

"We'd appreciate whatever you can tell us," Grant said, intrigued by the third-person reference. "It'll be safer to talk inside."

He led the way into the kitchen, but Tully hesitated at the threshold.

"Don't be a baby. It'll be OK," Jake said, pushing the man inside.

Tully looked around, settled the top hat back on his head and chose the chair farthest from the door. The plastic raincoat crackling with each movement, he sat down facing Grant. Jake walked over to stand beside him. The boy didn't crowd him, just stood close enough so that Tully could feel his presence.

"Did you kill George Collier?" Grant asked without preamble.

"No."

"Did you see who did kill him?"

"No."

Jake cleared his throat, and Tully looked over at the boy. His closed expression softened. His eyes, shadowed by the brim of his hat in the overhead light, crinkled at the corners.

"Tell what you saw," Jake prompted.

"Tully saw someone kneeling beside George. He was too far away to tell who it was. Better?" Tully asked.

"Some," the boy said.

"How did you happen to be on the golf course?" Grant asked, leaning against the sink counter.

"Tully was dozing in the chair at the boat ramp when something woke him. He started packing stuff away when he heard someone yelling. Outta control kind of yelling."

Tully looked at Grant to see if he understood. Getting a nod, he continued.

"It came from the golf course. He climbed the fence. Tully don't like to get involved in other people's business. Too easy to end up in the crosshairs."

"Then what happened?" Grant asked.

"Tully came out about halfway between the clubhouse and where he heard the shouting. There's a raised part where the golfers stand to hit the ball. It's all dark like with trees and bushes behind." Tully's tongue shot out and licked his lips in a circular motion, the skin glistening in the nest of hair. "Tully looked up there and saw someone. Light cloth reflecting in the dark night. Tully didn't like what he saw, so he let out a shout. Whoever was there got up, all crouched over, and scuttled like a crab into the bushes at the back. Running to beat all."

"Away from you?"

"Toward the fence by the boat ramp. Tully loped along to the tee and found George." Tully turned to Jake in apology. "Your grandfather didn't have any truck with Tully, but Tully wouldn't hurt him."

"That's OK," Jake said. "I knew it wasn't your fault."

"Tully couldn't help him," he said. "Tully turned him over and saw the blood and the wound and knew it was too late. Then someone called out, and Tully knew he couldn't stay. Next would be the police, and Blessington would be there to say Tully did it. It was better for Tully to go to the other side of the lake."

"Why didn't you take your car?" Grant asked.

"When Blessington left the country club, he drove through the parking lot of the boat ramp. He always does that. He slowed his car when he drove past Tully dozing in the chair. If someone saw Tully leaving after George died, Blessington would be down on him like a ton a bricks. Better to leave the car there. Safer to walk."

"Do you have any idea who killed George?"

"No. Tully's been listening and watching, but he can't get a clear idea. No reason that Tully can see for anyone to hurt George."

Depression clamped around Grant. He'd hoped for more. Some clue that might point to the killer. Nothing.

He tried not to show his disappointment, but as he looked at Tully, he realized the man knew exactly what he was feeling.

"Tully's sorry."

The kitchen door opened. Tully shot to his feet as Ham Rice came into the room. Jake stepped in front of Tully, his arms out, palms facing the startled man.

"He's Grampa's friend."

Ham stood still, head up as he faced Tully, blinking owlishly in the sharp illumination of the overhead light. Slowly a smile spread across his face.

"Hi ya, Tully. It's Ham Rice."

Tully flopped down in his chair, exhaling like a deflating balloon. A sheepish grin lightened the impression of a cornered animal. He raised a shaking hand to touch the corner of his head in a jaunty salute.

Grant spotted the folder in Ham's hand.

"Did you get them?" he asked.

"Have a look," Ham said as he started to spread the newly printed photographs on the kitchen table.

"My party pictures," Jake cried. "Way cool."

Grant, Jake and Tully gathered around, leaning over to inspect each picture. Ham began the second row. He snapped down the third picture, and Grant sucked in his breath, staring at the boy in the background. His hand shook as he picked up the photo, holding it by the corner. His eyes swept back and forth across the half-turned face of the boy.

Tyler.

The lump in his throat threatened to choke him. He closed his eyes, counted to three and opened them again. He stared at the boy, seeing the cowlick of blond hair shooting up at the front of his head. No amount of gel could keep that spray of hair in place. Despite the fact that it was twenty months since he had seen him, there was no doubt in Grant's mind that he was looking at his nephew.

"There's another one," Ham said. His voice was tinged with emotion, and he coughed to cover it.

Grant searched the rows of pictures, finding the second one. In the center of the picture was a knight in full armor, astride a horse, his gauntleted hand holding a long striped pole. At the side, closer to the camera, Tyler stood with his back to the fence that circled the jousting arena.

"That's him," Grant said, touching the edge of the print.

"I know him," Jake said.

"You know him?" Grant asked in disbelief.

"I mean I saw him at the fair. It's the deaf kid."

"What do you mean?"

"We were all jumping around except for this kid who was sitting at the end of the bench," Jake said. "We were making faces and trying to get him to move, because Kenny wanted to sit there. The kid just sat like a statue and didn't look at us. Not even when Kenny threw up."

"So why did you think he was deaf?" Grant asked.

"Right after Mom hauled Kenny away to clean him up, the trumpets blew for the start of the jousting. The boy stood up, and he was shaping out words with his hands just like the deaf kid we have at St. Bernard's. I felt real bad that we'd been laughing at him."

"Then what?"

Jake shrugged. "I don't know. The horses came out and the fighting started. He wasn't there when it was over."

"Was he sitting with anyone?" Ham asked.

"Nope. He was sitting by hisself."

"There's your proof," Ham said, his voice quiet but firm. "Two weeks ago Tyler was at the Renaissance Faire."

"Who's Tyler?" Jake asked.

"The boy you call the deaf kid is my nephew, Tyler McKenzie," Grant said. "He's been missing for a long time. I came to Delbrook to find him."

"Oh wow," Jake said. "He lives here?"

"Someplace around here. I don't know where. That's what we're trying to figure out."

Tully picked up the picture of Tyler. He held it close to his eyes, his body hunched over in concentration. "Tully saw him with the birds."

"You saw this boy?" Grant asked.

Tully recoiled at the intensity of Grant's question. With the tip of his index finger, he tapped on the chest of the boy in the picture. "Tully saw him in the birdhouse."

"The birdhouse over by Camp Delbrook?"

Tully set the photo back on the table and nodded, his head bobbing up and down several times. "Tully goes at night to see the birds."

"How do you get inside?" Grant asked. "The place is all locked up."

"Tully goes over the roof to the open spot and climbs down. He doesn't hurt the birds or scare them. Tully whistles, and they know he's there."

"When did you see the boy?" Grant said, pointing to the picture.

"Tully's seen him lots of times. Sometimes in the woods. Sometimes in the bird place. Always at night."

"Is he alone?"

"No. He's with the trainer."

"The trainer?" Grant asked. This time he kept his tone quiet so he wouldn't spook the man. "Do you know who it is?"

"No. When they're with the birds, Tully's too far away. When they're in the woods, Tully has to hide. You can see someone's face real clear against the trees and bushes. The trainer wears blackface, but his eyes glow like beacons in the night."

Ham gathered up the photos, leaving the two of Tyler on the table. "What do they do in the woods?" he asked.

"He makes the boy run and jump. Sometimes he marches him just like the army. Other times he takes him up to the high place."

"What's the high place?" Grant asked.

Before Tully could answer, Jake chimed in.

"I think it's the rock cliff Grampa took me to a couple times. In the woods by Camp Delbrook. It's way up on the top, and you can sit on the rocks and see all the way to Chicago. At least that's what I used to think when I was a little kid."

"Before the peregrines died out," Tully said, "they had a nesting spot on the ledge. The falcon would scratch around with her claws to form a bare hollow and then lay her eggs. It's called an aerie."

"An aerie is a nest. Falcon's Nest," Ham said. "That was the name of Edmund Falcone's house. Connie and Brent's old house. The one that burned."

For Grant, the pieces of the puzzle were beginning

to fall into place. He couldn't see the whole picture, but he knew they were getting closer. If only they had enough time.

Time! He glanced at his watch. Eleven. How could he have forgotten about Maggie? Where was she? She had to be in trouble to be this late.

"Jake, do you know what your mom was going to do today besides go to the conference at school?"

Jake's eyes widened as he was reminded of his mother's absence. "Where is she? Why isn't she here?"

"I don't know," Grant said. "That's what we have to figure out. What was she going to do today?"

"Work downstairs in the bookstore. Then she was going to clean the house and go grocery shopping." Eyes squinched tight, he rocked back and forth, thinking.

"Was she going anywhere? Did she have any appointments?" Grant asked, hoping to coax some memory out of the boy.

"She was going to the library. I had a book overdue. And Kenny's jacket."

"What about Kenny's jacket?" Grant asked.

"We got 'em mixed up. She had to take Kenny's to the Rossiters' and pick up mine."

"Why don't we call over there and see if she's still there?" Grant said, grasping at any explanation for Maggie's lateness.

Jake shook his head. "Kenny's not home. Him and his dad went to see Kenny's grandmother."

"Damn, I forgot," Grant said. "I think we better give Charley Blessington a call."

"Are you sure?" Ham asked.

"I don't think we can wait," Grant said. He nodded at Tully. "Something you said makes me think Charley's no longer a suspect. You said that he drove through the parking lot of the boat ramp after he left the poker game. Just like he always did. If that's the case, he couldn't have been walking along the fairway with George."

"Damn straight," Ham said.

"It's time to lay all the cards on the table," Grant said. "Can you call Charley and tell him everything, Ham?"

"Me?" Ham asked. "Where are you going to be?"

"I'm going over to Camp Delbrook to look for Maggie."

Maggie woke to pain. Her entire body hurt, and there was something wrong with her eyesight. She blinked to bring things into focus. Her head was tipped forward. Her hair hung loosely in front of her eyes, blocking her vision.

Memory of the attack in the equipment garage flooded back.

She cringed as she remembered the fists beating her and the final blow that had dropped her to the concrete floor. Even as she lay helpless, her attacker continued to scream and rant, and she curled into a ball, trying to protect her body as he kicked her.

Her cheek throbbed where she had taken the first blow. When she looked down, she could see that the left side of her face was swollen. She licked her lips and tasted blood. Her bottom lip was split, dried blood caked at the corner of her mouth. Her entire body felt bruised, but aside from an intense pain that might indicate a broken rib, she didn't think any of her injuries were serious.

Breathing shallowly through her partially open mouth, she strained to hear any sound that would indicate she wasn't alone. She counted to twenty. Even though she heard nothing, she kept her movements to a minimum as she lifted her head. A sharp stab of pain lanced through her at the motion. The veil of hair parted, giving her a frightening view of her situation.

She was seated in a chair inside a narrow rectangular room. A string of lights hung around the perimeter, sending fingers of illumination across the white acoustic ceiling tiles. A door was set in the short wall on her left, and across from her was a shelflike cot piled with blankets. A small chest of drawers, another wooden chair and an old Formica kitchen table were the only other pieces of furniture in the room. On the floor beside the table was an animal cage, door open and apparently empty.

In the dim light, she stared around the room trying to figure out where she was. The floor was hard-packed earth. She breathed in the chill air. It smelled musty and had a metallic taste. She tried to move, only to discover that her wrists were tied with black nylon cord to the arms of the old wooden desk chair. Although she couldn't see them, she could feel the ropes binding her feet to the legs of the chair. She strained at the rope, twisting and turning to free her hands. The cord cut into her skin, but it didn't loosen.

She sagged against the back of the chair, clenching her teeth against the panic that threatened to overwhelm her. To have any hope of survival, she had to stay in control.

Who had attacked her? She had been so busy defending herself, she had only an impression of a black-clad figure before the flashlight broke and she passed out.

"Why couldn't you leave it alone?"

Maggie remembered the words screeching in her ear. Voice high-pitched and shrill. Oh God! Connie! She ground her teeth together to keep from screaming aloud.

Connie must have seen her suspicion, and instead of driving off to Milwaukee, she had followed her to Hugh's place. When she snuck into the mews and the garage, Maggie would have confirmed the fact that she was searching for answers.

How long had she been unconscious?

Her watch was broken. The crystal was smashed and one of the hands was missing. She wondered when Grant would begin to worry. If only she'd left a message, telling him where she'd gone. Jake would be frantic.

Jake. Oh God, help me.

If she thought about Jake, she would go insane. She needed to stay focused in order to find some way to escape. She might be alone now, but she knew with a certainty that Connie would return to kill her.

She strained at the nylon cord. She twisted on the seat and felt a slight give in the joints of the chair. She pressed her feet against the ground, shoving her body against the back of the chair. Her head hit the wall with a jarring blow, and for an instant she thought she would pass out again. She opened her mouth and pulled in a slow, steady breath, holding it for an instant, then blowing it out through her dry lips.

She rocked the chair from side to side, hoping to loosen the cord. When the ropes remained tight, she gave it up. She was afraid to continue, for fear the chair would tip over. She'd be worse than helpless if that happened.

Closing her eyes, she swallowed the lump in her throat.

A slight rustle on the far side of the room sent her heart racing. She clenched her teeth to keep from screaming as the blankets on the cot moved. She scanned the far side of the room until she spotted the figure wedged into the corner of the shelf, partially covered by the blankets.

She squinted, and as her eyes focused she saw the child.

It was a boy. Four or five years old. A cowlick of blond hair fanning out over his forehead. Wide, staring blue eyes.

"Tyler. Tyler McKenzie." Maggie breathed the name in a soft whisper.

No flicker of recognition in the eyes of the child.

"Tyler," she said, speaking louder this time. "Tyler? Are you Tyler?"

The boy's eyes remained fixed on her. Aside from a slow owlish blink, he showed no reaction to her presence.

"Can you hear me?"

She scratched her fingernails against the arms of the chair. The child jumped at the unexpected sound.

"So you can hear. Thank God."

After all the searching she had come face-to-face with the missing child. Part of her was filled with elation that he was alive, but the other part acknowledged the fact that the discovery had come too late.

"Tyler. My name is Maggie. Maggie Collier."

Maggie didn't know why she continued to speak, because he either would not or could not respond to her. She remembered the pain in Katrina Harland's voice as she spoke of her frustration with Eddie's inability to speak. It didn't matter. She needed to hear a voice, even if it was her own, to remind her she was not alone.

"Do you remember your uncle? Uncle Grant. He's come here to find you."

Maggie wondered if the boy was drugged. He didn't respond to her in any way. It was almost as if he were in a trance. Even though he hadn't acknowledged her presence, she knew he was aware of her. Hoping to break through his silence, she kept talking.

"Your uncle told me you have a dog, Tyler. His name is Barney. Barney Google."

Maggie began to hum the tune to the song.

"I have a son named Jake," she said, catching her breath in a hiccup as she struggled to keep her emotions at bay. "His grandfather used to sing him that song too. 'Barney Google with his goo goo googly eyes.' "

She repeated the refrain but couldn't remember any of the words to the verse. She sang it again, then hummed it. Still no reaction from Tyler. She thought about all the songs she'd sung to Jake over the years, and one by one she sang them, hoping for some sign of recognition from the child on the cot.

She announced the name of each song, and after

she sang it she repeated the title to the boy, finishing up with another rousing chorus of "Barney Google." She talked to him between times, telling him the little she knew about his mother and father and talking about Grant and the dog and anything else she could think of. Nothing penetrated the mask of detachment.

Eventually he relaxed, sliding down until he was lying stretched out on the cot. His eyes were open, and he stared at her blankly, as if she wasn't really there.

"That's all right, Tyler. You can go to sleep. I'll be right here."

Maggie hummed quietly. He stared at her for a while, then he closed his eyes, and she could hear the rhythm of his breathing change as he fell asleep. She continued to hum, resting her head against the wall behind her chair. She needed to conserve her energy if she hoped to make one last bid for freedom. Closing her eyes, she let her mind drift.

She came awake with a racing heart as she heard the lock click and the door of the room opened. She swallowed down the knot of fear as she faced the doorway. The dark figure stepped forward, and she let out a gasp of surprise.

"Oh, thank God, Brent!" she cried. "You've found us."

CHAPTER
TWENTY-THREE

"FOUND YOU?" Brent asked. "I didn't know you were lost."

Brent's conversational tone and expression of amusement sent a chill through Maggie. In a heartbeat she realized her mistake.

"Oh, God, Brent. Not you."

"Why not me? Were you expecting someone else?"

Maggie squeezed her eyes shut, wanting to block him from sight. All the bumps and bruises her body had sustained could not compare in pain to the knowledge of Brent's duplicity. He had been George's best friend, and she and Jake had been fond of him. How could they have missed the fact that, beneath the mask of civility, he was a monster?

"Connie said you were in Milwaukee. What are you doing here?" Maggie asked, blurting out her first thoughts.

"So that's why you look so surprised," Brent said. "No need to worry about Connie. When she gets to the Pfister Hotel, she'll find a note saying I'm delayed on business."

He glanced over to the shelf bed and smiled when he saw the two blue eyes staring at him from the mound of blankets.

"I gather you've met the boy," he said.

The focus of attention, Tyler scrambled into the corner, pulling the covers close around his neck. His face was expressionless, eyes wide and alert.

Brent's foot brushed the side of the wire cage. He stared down, his head extended forward on his neck. Bending over, he picked up the cage and turned toward the boy on the bed. Maggie could see the blanket shake as Tyler drew his body into a tighter unit.

Holding the cage at eye level, Brent peered inside. The door swung back and forth as if to emphasize that the cage was empty. Eyes focused on the child, Brent released his hold on the cage, and it fell to the floor. It bounced once, then came to rest against the wall beside the bed.

Brent turned his back to the boy and walked across the room until he stood directly in front of Maggie. He towered over her, and she had to tip her head back to stare up at him. She gripped the arms of the chair to keep herself from shaking.

She could only wonder at the transformation in the man. Externally he was the same. He was dressed more casually than usual in black slacks and a black turtleneck, but he looked as distinguished as ever. With the white wings of hair at his temples, he looked more like an elder statesman than a killer or a kidnapper.

The way he carried his body and the change in his voice tone were a reflection of the internal changes that had taken place. She had the distinct impression that he had become another person entirely. A new person she didn't know.

"I'm sorry about the bruise on your face," he said.

"Why did you attack me?"

"Ah, such an innocent."

He reached out to touch her face. Unable to bear his touch, she pulled her head back, knowing it was a mistake when she saw the flash of anger in his eyes.

He drew his hand back, then he slapped her.

The blow wasn't hard, but it was devastating, pointing up her helplessness. The total detachment on Brent's face as he watched her reaction was a sharp reminder that she was not dealing with a rational human being. The aftermath of murder and kidnapping had taken a toll on the man she had once known. Whoever he had become was evil, impervious to arguments or pleadings.

She had two options. She could cringe and whine in hopes that Brent would not hurt her any more before he killed her, or she could forget about her own pain and try to figure out a way to save herself and Tyler.

There was only one way. She would have to kill Brent.

A spurt of adrenaline shot through her. Frightened he would read the new resolution in her eyes, she dropped her head, hiding behind the curtain of hair that swung in front of her face. She'd play the whining coward he expected and look for her chance.

She'd only get one chance to defeat him. She'd have to make it count.

Slowly she raised her head. She didn't have to pretend to be cowed by Brent's presence. His closeness was stifling as he waited for her full attention. He continued speaking as if there had been no break in the conversation.

"I've been worrying about you, Maggie. You've been prying into things that don't concern you. If you'd left them alone, you wouldn't be in this predicament. So for the last few days I've been keeping a close eye on you. I still haven't figured out where you went with Grant Holbrook, but I suspect it wasn't Milwaukee."

Maggie pressed her lips together, trying to keep her expression from giving away any of her thoughts. Brent stood in front of her, rocking from foot to foot as he talked.

"Today I got worried when you ran into Connie. I saw her showing you the tattoo. I wondered if that would set you thinking. Did you come to the conclusion that Dennis Nyland drew it and that she had killed him?" He chuckled, and his mouth twisted into a smug smile. "I can see you did. Well, I'll tell you a secret. Dennis didn't do the tattoo. I did."

"You drew Connie's tattoo?" Maggie didn't have to fake astonishment at this piece of information.

"Everyone underestimates my talents," Brent said, voice tinged with anger. "I was eighteen when I got a tattoo. The whole process intrigued me. I've always been drawn to a mixture of pain and pleasure. Watching my own blood bubbling up around the pen aroused me. I wish I had time to initiate you into the art. I think you'd see what I mean."

He placed his open palm against her throat, pressing her chin upward with his thumb.

"I'm sorry I had to hurt you," he said. With his free hand he touched the bruise on her cheek. Even though he didn't press against the bone, she winced at the pain. "I followed you to Rossiter's. I had to park my car farther up in the woods so no one would spot it. When I got back you were gone. I waited for a while beside the car, but when you didn't come I got worried. Then I realized you'd gone up to look around the mews. I walked along the trail, and just as I came to the clearing, I saw you entering the garage."

He brushed the hair away from her face with a brisk sweeping motion of his fingers.

"Snooping again," he said. "When I found you standing beside the pit, I was so angry that I couldn't help but strike out at you."

His hand moved up and down on the column of her throat, his touch light and caressing at first, then slowly his fingers began to tighten. Maggie pressed against the back of her chair, trying to pull away from the hand that was choking her. She thrashed from side to side, gasping for air as Brent watched her, his eyes glowing with excitement.

Oh, God, don't let me die yet! Her strength ebbed, and she sagged in her chair, sinking into the darkness.

Suddenly he released her.

"Such a shame I can't keep you here for a while," he said. "I could teach you pleasures you've never known."

Brent's voice came from a distance as she fought to pull air into her lungs. Tears blinded her, and frightened sobs welled up inside her. It was one thing to know she was going to die, but it was quite another thing to fight the fear. For an instant she wanted to beg and plead for her freedom. His indifference to her pain reminded her that he was beyond compassion, beyond rational thought.

Brent reached into the pocket of his shirt and brought out a thin sheet of parchment paper. He unfolded it and held it up toward the light so that Maggie could see it. It was a drawing of the bleeding heart tattoo.

"Dennis Nyland was very talented. He drew this to show me, the night I visited him. It's beautiful, isn't it? He was kind enough to sign it before I killed him."

Maggie closed her eyes, wanting to block out the picture of the bleeding heart and the triumphant smile on Brent's face.

"I had planned to draw it on your body," he said.

Her eyes flew open as he placed his open hand on her chest, sliding it inside the neck of her blouse. His fingers pushed beneath her bra strap, pressing lightly over her racing heart.

Terrified of provoking him, she kept her eyes down, her body submissive. She screamed inside her head with the effort to remain still.

Brent sighed and withdrew his hand.

Maggie shook with the aftermath of fear. She tightened her muscles, trying to convert her terror into anger. She wanted to beg God for the chance to kill Brent, but she didn't know if He would grant such a request.

"No time for pleasure," he said, folding up the parchment paper and returning it to his pocket. "They'll begin searching for you soon. They'll never think to look at Camp Delbrook until tomorrow though."

"We're still at the campground?" Maggie's voice was raspy, and her throat was raw from the choking.

"You haven't figured it out yet?" Brent leaned over and pulled at the black cord around her wrists, checking to make sure it was still tight. "We're actually in a room underneath the equipment garage."

"Underneath?"

"Ingenious, isn't it?" Brent smiled. "I read about a man who kept a child in a room he'd built under his garage. No one found it even though they searched the place several times looking for the girl. So when Hugh began talking about a mews, I suggested that he build a storage and maintenance garage. Since Connie was going to pay for half of the mews project, I offered to draw up plans and oversee the construction of both buildings."

He checked the cords on her ankles, satisfied that she was secure in her chair. Then he walked across to the shelf bed.

"There are definite advantages to being the architect and construction supervisor. Hugh was busy and only saw the completed garage. He had no idea of the additions I'd made to the original blueprints. Two rooms marked for underground storage. Also a tunnel leading from the equipment garage to the mews and another one leading outside into the woods."

He pulled the covers back and motioned to the child. Without hesitation, Tyler swung his feet over the side of the shelf and stood up.

"This is my apprentice," Brent said, placing a hand on Tyler's shoulder. "He has been training to be a warrior. He's learned the discipline of silence and communicates through sign language. He is very proficient."

Tyler stood motionless, staring at Maggie. Despite

her singing and talk of his past life, there was nothing in his expression that acknowledged her presence or indicated he had made any connection with her. Brent released him, signing to him to sit on the edge of the cot.

It dawned on Maggie that Brent had no idea she knew who Tyler was. She would have to be careful that she gave none of her knowledge away, or the life of the boy could be in jeopardy.

"Where did you get the boy?" she asked.

"It doesn't matter," Brent said. "He belongs to me."

"Do you keep him here in this room?"

He caught the edge of horror in her question and glared at her.

"He is well cared for," he snapped. "There is a kitchen area and a play area in the other room. This one is for sleeping. He gets fresh air and good food and a system of education that suits us both. You can see how fit he is. I have been training him."

"Why are you training him? Why is he here?"

"This is not like in the movies where you keep me talking until the cavalry arrives," Brent said. "There will be no rescue for you, Maggie."

"I know that, but I'd still like to know why."

"It's simple," he said. "Connie couldn't have any more children."

"If you wanted children so badly, couldn't you have adopted some?"

Brent's face darkened, and he glared at Maggie. "I wanted Connie's children. That was why I married her. She was Edmund's daughter. Together we would carry Edmund's genes into a new generation. We would create the dynasty that he had envisioned."

"Did Edmund know that was your plan?" Maggie asked.

"I told him the night we were married." Brent paced back and forth in front of Maggie. His rising agitation frightened her. "I thought he would be thrilled when I explained it all to him, but he threatened to have the marriage annulled."

"On what grounds?"

"Edmund Falcone was my father. Connie is my half sister."

Brent's words left Maggie speechless. It was obvious he was pleased by her shock.

"Didn't guess, did you? Nobody knew but Edmund. And he had forgotten."

Brent's momentary smirk changed back to narrow-eyed fury.

"He didn't have the slightest remembrance of the fact he'd impregnated my mother. He'd given her some money, but that was long gone. My mother told me who my father was, but she refused to beg him for anything more. We lived in soul-crushing poverty, and I swore that eventually he'd accept me as his true son."

"Why didn't you tell him when he began sponsoring you?"

"I was angry that he could have forgotten my birth. I decided that I would present him with an accomplished fact once I was married to Connie. I expected him to be delighted. Instead he was appalled. He ranted and raved at what he called an unnatural act. As his fury increased, his body betrayed him and he had a stroke."

"I thought you were on your honeymoon when that happened."

"That's what everyone thought. He fell down on the floor of his bedroom. He was paralyzed and couldn't speak. I thought he would be dead by morning. I told Connie that he was tired and was going to bed. We left, and it wasn't until the next morning that the house-keeper found him. Unfortunately he was still alive."

Maggie couldn't even imagine what that long night must have been like for Edmund. And the year that fol-lowed. Dependent on Brent for everything.

"Edmund must have prayed for death," Maggie said.

"I think he did."

Brent chuckled, and the sound sent a shiver down Maggie's spine. He switched back and forth between anger and amusement, triggered by a single word or ac-tion. He was losing control, and his unpredictability would make him more dangerous to deal with.

Opening the top drawer of the dresser, Brent took out a pair of blue jeans and a dark blue knit shirt. Even in the dim light, Maggie could see that they had never been worn and was reminded of the new clothes worn by the two other children Brent had kidnapped.

"Put these on," Brent said, placing them on the cot.

Without a change in expression, Tyler removed the loose-fitting shirt and sweatpants he was wearing and put on the jeans and pulled the shirt over his head. When he picked up the new sneakers that Brent set on the floor, Maggie's mind was filled with images of Jake, and she had to bite her lip to hold back a cry of despair. She turned her head away, concentrating on Brent.

He stood facing her, holding a gun in his hand. When he saw he had her full attention, he tucked it into the belt at his waist.

"You will not be tied up when we leave here. You will walk ahead of the boy. If you try anything, I will shoot him. Do you understand me?"

Her mouth was too dry for her to speak, so she nodded.

"Good," he said.

Maggie swallowed, forcing herself to make one plea for Tyler. "Do what you have to do with me, Brent, but don't involve the boy. If you release him, I won't give you any trouble."

"You have no say in this," he said. "If you'd learned to mind your own business, you wouldn't be here. Just like George. Do you think I wanted to kill him?"

"George was your friend, Brent. He would have given his life for you. That's the kind of man he was. And you killed him."

"I had to kill him. He recognized the boy."

"George was your friend. You could have explained about the boy. He would have tried to help you. It was a cowardly thing to do. You killed George because you were afraid," Maggie said.

"Don't say that," Brent shouted.

As he charged across the room, Maggie glimpsed Tyler frozen in place, back pressed against the wall and eyes so wide they were ringed with white. She had no time to react before Brent was on her. He grabbed her by the hair and jerked her head backward until she was staring up into his enraged face. For Tyler's sake, she tried not to whimper.

"Don't be stupid, Brent," she said through gritted teeth. "You'll gain nothing by killing me. Don't you see that everything is falling apart? The police are already searching for the person who killed George and Dennis. If you kill me, the investigation will intensify. You know Charley. He'll keep hunting until he finds the murderer."

"You're the one who's stupid," Brent said.

He threw his hand up, releasing her hair, and her head snapped back, hitting the wall. When she cried out, his anger was replaced by satisfaction at her pain.

He paced back and forth between Maggie and Tyler. She could see Tyler watching him, his eyes following every movement. Obviously months of captivity had taught him to be wary of Brent's anger.

"Once you're gone," Brent continued, "the investigation will end for lack of interest and lack of evidence. I've been very clever to cover my tracks. There's no connection between me and either of the murders. No reason for me to kill George, and no reason that I would even know Dennis Nyland. No motive. No evidence. No case."

"I don't think Charley will give up."

"Of course he will. Just think about it, Maggie," he said. "Everything is working out perfectly."

She looked at Tyler standing motionless beside the cot.

"And the boy?" she asked.

"I think he will accompany you on your journey," Brent said. "Connie and I are going away on vacation. Time enough when I return to look for another child."

Brent's voice had taken on a singsong cadence, and his face had the intensity of a fanatic. Maggie bit her lip to keep from crying out as she realized Tyler's fate.

"Can't you let the boy go? Please?"

"He has not worked out as well as I hoped. I thought

about bringing you here to help me train the boy. I've been impressed with how well you've raised Jake. If you hadn't poked and pried, such a plan might have been possible. Look how you've spoiled everything."

Maggie closed her eyes so that he wouldn't see the fear in her eyes at the mention of Jake. The thought of her son, alone without her protection, terrified her. It was the one thing that could weaken her resolve. She wanted so badly to live.

"Enough talk," Brent said, words sharp in returning anger. "I have made my decision. It's time."

Brent stopped his pacing and stood directly in front of Maggie. He raised his shirt and turned sideways so she could see the knife bound to his side in the leather sheath.

"It's called a *misericorde*," he said. "In medieval times, it was worn every day. Close to the body so it was ready to use against an enemy. Or a friend."

As he spoke, he unfastened the straps, holding the sheath in his hand so that she could see the hilt of the knife. The braided silver wire on the handle gleamed in the dimly lit room. He slid the knife out of the sheath, turning it so that the light reflected off the thin blade.

He held the knife by the steel blade, between his thumb and index finger. Reverently he placed the *misericorde* across the palm of his left hand. Walking to Tyler, he held the knife out.

"As my apprentice," Brent said, "you will make the first cut."

Grant drove the last hundred feet without lights, easing into the parking spot next to Maggie's car. Knowing sound would carry on such a quiet night, he kept his voice low as he spoke to Tully.

"I'll check the house."

He got out of the car, touching the hood of Maggie's car. It was cold. He went up the stairs to the front door of Rossiter's house. The door was locked. He looked through the windows but could see nothing to indicate anyone was inside.

When Grant returned, Tully was waiting several yards along the trail that led up into the woods. He looked almost reassuring. Once he had volunteered his help, he had left behind his plastic raincoat and traded his top hat for Jake's baseball cap. At Grant's approach, he pointed down at a footprint, clearly visible in the soft mulch at the edge of the trail. The small size and shape indicated it was Maggie's.

"Up that way is the mews," Tully said.

There was enough moonlight to make it easy to walk on the path. Tully, used to the woods, moved soundlessly. Grant let him take the lead, his eyes moving from side to side as he searched for any other signs of Maggie's passage. They reached the clearing and the equipment garage, and Tully angled off toward the mews. Grant had only gone a few feet when he spotted something at the side of the garage and whistled softly.

Tully loped back, joining Grant. Grant's mouth went dry as he recognized the windbreaker on the ground beneath one of the bushes.

"It's Jake's," Tully said.

"Maggie's purse, too. Looks like she left them here."

He flashed the beam of light along the ground, searching for tracks, and caught a metallic flash in the grass beside the door. Leaning over he picked up the ring of keys attached to the plastic disk with the hawk inside. The keys were the ones that Hugh Rossiter had used when he gave him a tour of the mews. Maggie had either dropped or thrown the keys on the ground. Either way it wasn't a good sign.

Grant found the right key, and when the door of the equipment garage was unlocked, he pulled it open. He stepped over the threshold, Tully crowding in behind him. The door swung closed, leaving them in darkness.

Both flashlights clicked on at the same time, sending a V of light across the concrete floor. The garage appeared empty, but Grant was taking no chances. He flashed his light around the walls, then swung it back and forth across the floor as he moved deeper into the building. Something sparkled in the beam.

The flashlight lay at the edge of the pit, the glass face shattered. Grant knelt down to pick it up, moving the switch back and forth. The flashlight had been on when it broke. Grant could feel a tightening in his stomach as he pictured Maggie dropping the flashlight as she struggled with an attacker.

Shining his own flashlight around, he saw the drops of blood.

"Missus Jake is hurt," Tully said.

Heart pounding, Grant got to his feet and walked over to the edge of the pit. He gritted his teeth as he shined the light down into the pit, half expecting to see Maggie's body. His relief was enormous when he found it empty.

Tully scrambled down the ladder, flashing his light along the floor of the pit. At his low whistle, Grant joined

him, leaning over to stare at the blood spot in the circle
of light.

"Tully thinks he brought her down here."

Grant agreed. They worked their way along the
side, checking each of the shelf units attached to the
wall. Midway they found what they were looking for.
The metal shelf unit was more securely attached than
the others had been. Running the lights underneath
each shelf, they found a latch against the wall under the
third shelf.

Grant turned it, but it didn't give. There was a lock
beneath the latch, and he pulled the ring of keys out, trying each one. The door was locked, and they didn't have
a key.

"He's got Maggie and probably my nephew in
there," Grant said. "We've got to get help, Tully."

They climbed up the ladder and hurried across the
floor to the door. Grant cursed the fact he didn't have his
cell phone. Their best bet would be to break into
Rossiter's house and call from there. He doused the
flashlight and opened the door, waiting to let his eyes adjust to the night.

As he stepped outside, Tully grabbed his arm in a
grip of iron, pointing up toward the mews. Grant froze,
straining to hear above the beat of his heart. Silence,
then a muffled cry and the sound of a slap, a sharp crack
of hand against flesh. After a pause he could hear the
low murmur of voices, then the noise of people continuing up the trail faded into the distance.

"He's taking her to the high place," Tully said. "He'll
kill her there."

CHAPTER
TWENTY-FOUR

"I COULDN'T HELP IT," Maggie whispered. "I tripped."

She cried out as Brent hit her on the shoulder with the barrel of the gun to urge her to her feet. She'd have to be careful not to overplay her hand. Each time she stumbled or lagged behind he lost more of his control. If she pushed him too far, he might injure her so badly she would be incapable of making a bid for freedom.

She looked beyond Brent's menacing figure to Tyler, waiting patiently beside the trail. When she fell to her knees, Brent had pushed forward, shoving the boy to the side of the trail. She'd have to wait until Tyler was close enough for her to reach before she made her move. She couldn't escape without him, and she wasn't convinced he would come with her if she ran.

"Get up," Brent hissed.

He reached out with his free hand and pulled her to her feet. The motion ripped at the already bruised muscles in her shoulder, and she let out a low moan.

"Shut up."

He raised his hand to slap her again, and she threw up her arm in front of her face.

"Don't hit me," she said. "I'm doing the best I can."

"It's not good enough. If the boy can do it, so can you."

"He's been in training," she argued. "And he hasn't been beaten like I have."

"Get moving, damn you."

In the moonlight Maggie could see his clenched teeth and knew he was close to the breaking point. Knowing that he was rattled was enough, and she turned away and started walking again.

As the trail got steeper, she had more trouble catching her breath. She held her left arm against her side to try to steady her rib cage, but each step jarred her and she had to continually bite her lip to keep from crying out. The effort to keep moving was tiring her, and the shallow breaths of air didn't give her enough oxygen to restore her energy.

She tried not to think of anything except the placement of one foot in front of the other. She was grateful to be outside. She had been afraid she was going to die in the underground room.

When Brent had given the knife to Tyler, Maggie thought he was going to force the boy to stab her. Her heart raced as the boy approached. Tyler raised the knife, and she closed her eyes, praying silently. The sawing motion as he cut the ropes made her giddy with relief. As circulation flooded back into her arms, she grabbed the arms of the chair, fighting against the waves of painful sensation.

Brent slid the knife back into the sheath and

strapped it around Tyler's chest. How incredible to watch the interchange between the psychotic killer and the small boy. Brent spoke firmly but with great patience as he explained to the child the importance of the night mission.

"We will take her to the Aerie," Brent said.

Maggie had no clue where that was, but thought it might be another name for the mews. She focused on her breathing, knowing that the time for action would be soon. When Brent dragged her out of the chair, she walked haltingly, trying to overcome her pain and stiffness. She had little awareness of her surroundings as Brent took them through a tunnel that eventually led outside. She'd fallen to her knees, sucking in the fresh air, stalling to regain some strength.

Now as Maggie struggled along the trail, her energy dissipated with each step. Brent was right behind her. He shoved the gun against her back.

"Keep moving."

"How much farther?" she asked.

Suddenly the leather sole of her shoe slipped on the mulch, and she sprawled full-length on the trail. Her fall was unintentional, and the mistake was costly. Pain lanced through her rib cage, and she pulled her knees up to her chest to relieve the strain. Tyler came to stand beside her, moving off the trail as he waited for Brent.

"Get up," Brent snarled in her ear.

"Please," she whispered. "I think my ribs are broken. I can't catch my breath. Just let me rest a minute."

He bent over to stare at her. He must have seen the pain reflected in her face.

"I'll count to thirty," he said.

"Where are we going?" she asked between gasps for air.

"You'll know soon enough."

He was staring up the trail, paying little attention to her. For a moment, she debated attacking him. She knew she'd only have one chance, and she couldn't squander it unless she was sure of success.

"It's time," Brent said, nudging her with the muzzle of the gun.

He stepped back, putting some distance between them as she rose to her feet. He jerked his head in the direction of the trail, and they began the ascent again. The wind had picked up. The woods were noisy with the scrape of branches. She had the feeling they were approaching the top of the bluff, because the trail was growing steeper.

She was tiring, and her steps slowed. Tyler came up alongside her, and she wanted to reach out and take his hand. She had tried so hard not to think about Jake, but as time ran out, he was in her mind and heart, and she could barely hold back the agony that cut through her.

What would happen to him? How would he survive if he lost her too?

Oh, God, please help me.

Knowing she couldn't afford to break down, she tried to concentrate on her breathing. She adapted each breath to her steps. Right foot, breathe in. Left foot, breathe out. It helped her establish a rhythm.

She glanced sideways at Tyler. He climbed the steep trail without effort. His mouth was moving as he walked. Knowing Brent had forbidden him to speak, she strained to hear, and a thin whispery sound came to her ears.

Tyler was humming. She picked up the tune, and tears began to roll down her cheeks. Tyler was humming "Barney Google."

Knowing she had broken through the barrier to remind him of his past gave her a jolt of energy. They were walking nearly side by side. It was time.

Her eyes searched the trail ahead until she spotted a slim branch that crossed the path at shoulder height. She slowed her steps, letting Tyler pull ahead slightly. It was the steepest part of the path, and she had to reach out to the surrounding bushes for handholds to pull herself forward.

Ten more feet.

Five.

One foot in front of the other. She kept her breathing even, drawing in the oxygen to give herself additional energy.

Tyler was three feet ahead of her. He walked beneath the branch, and as Maggie approached, she raised her arms to grab hold of it.

Her fingers clutched the rough bark, and as soon as she sensed she had a solid grasp, she turned her body until she was facing downhill. Brent looked up. He started to raise the gun. Maggie gripped the tree branch as she pushed off the ground, and her body swung out over the trail. Pain ripped through her rib cage, but she held on to the branch.

Her feet slammed into Brent's chest.

The impact tore the breath from his body. His arms windmilled as he fought for balance. His hand smacked against the trunk of a slender tree, and the gun dropped into the underbrush. With a guttural shout, Brent toppled over and rolled backward down the trail. Maggie didn't wait. She released the branch and clawed her way up the trail.

As she passed Tyler, she grabbed his hand and scrambled up the trail. She could hear Brent thrashing around in the woods, and it gave added incentive to her race for freedom.

Tyler clung to her hand, neither helping her nor struggling for release. Her ribs burned, and she knew she couldn't climb much farther. She was afraid to leave the trail for fear of getting lost. Her only hope was to reach the top and then follow the path down the other side and pray she had enough of a head start on Brent.

Ahead, she could see the trail branching off to the left and sobbed in relief. Her ribs were in agony, pain tearing at her with each step. She had to make it to the top.

Five more steps.

Two more.

Oh God, she'd made it.

As her muscles collapsed, she let go of Tyler and slid to the ground. He stood beside her, his eyes questioning.

"Go down the path, Tyler." She gasped out the words. "Go for help."

The boy didn't move. He turned his head, looking back down the way they'd come. She could hear nothing above the sound of the wind in the trees, but she knew it was only a matter of time before Brent would be on them. She searched the woods on either side of the trail for anything she could use as a weapon.

"Go fi Grant, Tyler. He's down there," she said, nodding to the path where it turned downhill.

She spotted a dead tree branch and pulled until a piece broke off in her hand. It was futile against the gun, but at least it gave her a sense of control. Then she remembered the *misericorde*. She pulled Tyler toward her, until she was face-to-face with him.

"I need this," she said, unfastening the straps on the leather sheath around his chest. Just as it came free she heard the sounds of pursuit and struggled to her feet, jamming the sheath into the waistband of her skirt. "He's coming."

Tyler's eyes widened, and he took her hand again. He opened his mouth, but no sound came out. With his free hand, he pointed into the woods, his finger jabbing in silent agitation. A game trail cut through the underbrush, and she could see on her left the top of a rock ledge.

She didn't want to leave the path, but Tyler was insistent. Knowing it was useless to argue, she followed him. The path was narrow, and he released her hand. He led the way along the top of the bluff just below the rock ledge. She walked behind him, and when the wind died down, she could hear Tyler humming.

"Barney Google." The bouncy tune was incongruous with the tension of their flight.

Maggie used the stick and her forearm to push her way through the bushes. Tyler walked with ease and soon was well ahead of her. She stopped for a moment to listen, but the wind had picked up again and she couldn't hear anything over the whipping branches and her own breathing and the beat of her heart.

Ahead she could see moonlight as the underbrush thinned out. She quickened her pace, afraid of losing sight of Tyler. She came through the opening and froze when she saw him.

He was standing on the top of a flat rock bluff, the toes of his shoes touching the very edge. The moonlight illuminated the scene, picking out the details of trees and boulders and far below the shimmering surface of Falcon Lake.

Hearing her approach, Tyler turned to face her. He extended his arms, moving them up and down as if he were a bird landing on a rock ledge.

"Aerie," she said. "Falcon's nest."

The words were a whisper on the wind. With a sinking heart, she realized Tyler had brought her to the one place where Brent would find them.

Tyler stood on the edge of the precipice, and she was afraid if she spoke again she would frighten him. She beckoned to him, and without hesitation he came to her side. She looked around the flat top to see if there was some way to escape. The ground fell away on one side, and straight ahead was the rock ledge she had seen from the trail. It jutted out in a series of flat planes that rose about three feet over the place where they stood. She wished they had gone farther up the trail, since she would have felt safer on the ledge than in this cul-de-sac.

The only way off the top of the aerie was back along the game trail.

"Come," she said.

She used the stick to steady herself as she walked across the rock surface. Tyler kept pace with her, and when she arrived at the rock ledge, she searched along the edge until she found a narrow cleft in the rock.

"Sit here," she said, pointing at the crevasse with the stick.

He looked at the crack, then back at her. When he didn't move, she opened her mouth to repeat the command.

"I know where you are, Maggie," Brent shouted.

Although she couldn't see him, she knew Brent was coming up the game trail toward the opening.

"Go and sit down," she said. Her voice was firm, and with only a momentary hesitation, Tyler obeyed.

"Stay where you are, boy," Brent shouted. "I'm coming."

Maggie could see his outline as he trotted along the game trail. She dropped the stick and grabbed the sheath stuck in her waistband. One of the leather straps caught on her hand. She jerked her arm up, and the sheath along with the knife flew out of her hand, falling over the edge of the rock ledge.

Maggie let out a cry of despair as her only hope to save either Tyler or herself disappeared into the night. She bowed her head in defeat.

"Welcome to the Aerie, Maggie," Brent said.

He stood in the opening, the moonlight lighting his face as he stared across at her. A long gash ran on an angle from the end of his eyebrow to the middle of his cheek. Blood ran from the end of the wound in a crimson line to his jawbone. As he stepped out in the open, she could see he was limping.

"Where is the child?"

"I don't know."

Brent limped toward her.

"I would have been here sooner, except I had to look for this."

He raised his hand, and she could see the dark shape of the gun.

"Where is he, Maggie? What have you done with him? Stalling will make it worse for you. Where are you, boy?" Brent shouted. "Come to the Warrior."

Hearing the sounds of movement behind her, Maggie turned. Tyler stood up and moved into the open where Brent could see him. She should have known that months of captivity would supersede any commands that she might give him. Brent had trained him too well.

"Come to me, boy," Brent said.

Suddenly there was a rush of movement behind Brent, and Grant appeared in the opening to the game trail. Brent whirled, aiming the gun at the new threat.

"Don't shoot," Maggie shouted.

When she took a step forward, he swung the gun back in her direction.

"It won't do any good to kill us, Brent," Grant said, his voice calmly reasonable. "It's all over. The police are on the way."

"You're lying," Brent shrieked. "Why would they come? No one suspects me. There's no way they can connect me to George's murder."

"Charley Blessington knows everything. He knows about the boy found in the movie theater, and he knows about the girl who died at the zoo. And he knows about this child," Grant said, pointing at Tyler.

"That's not possible." Brent's voice had dropped to a

hoarse whisper, as if he couldn't believe what he was hearing. "No one knows about this boy."

"I know," Grant said. "He is Tyler McKenzie. He is my nephew."

Grant took a step forward, and Brent pointed the gun at Tyler.

"Stay away from the boy," he shouted. "Get back or I'll shoot him."

A scream of anger tore through the night, the sound ricocheting off the rock face. Brent staggered backward as a dark figure rose above him on the rock ledge. Tully tore off the baseball cap he was wearing and threw it like a Frisbee. It sailed through the air, landing with a soft plop inches away from Brent's feet.

With another shriek Tully leaped off the ledge, arms spread as if he were flying. Brent raised the gun and fired.

The shot was muffled as Tully crashed into Brent, knocking him to the ground. Bodies locked together, the two men rolled across the rock surface and disappeared over the edge of the cliff. There was a single thud, followed by a high-pitched scream that was cut off abruptly as something bounced and tumbled down the side of the hill.

Then silence.

Tyler, his face blank, eyes wide and staring, started toward the edge.

"Hold him," Grant said, shoving him into Maggie's arms.

The child struggled against her. He was in shock, and Maggie was afraid of what he would do now that his master was gone. She sank to the ground, dragging the child with her. Wrapping her arms around him, she pulled him against her chest. She held the shaking child in an iron grip, rocking back and forth and humming under her breath as she stared across at Grant.

He lay down on the rocks, inching his upper body out over the edge. He turned on the flashlight and played the beam down the side of the hill. Fifteen feet below there was a narrow ledge. The light was diffused, and at first he could only see the slashes of white where branches had been broken.

Then he saw Tully.

His body was wedged between the face of the hill and a small sapling that clung to the very edge of the ledge. He was lying on his back, one leg doubled under him, his face turned toward the rock face. Grant flashed the light around but couldn't see any sign of Brent.

"Tully!" Grant yelled.

"Oh, God, you found him," Maggie cried. "Is he alive?"

"I don't know. He's not moving."

Grant shone the light on Tully's face, but the beam was too weak for him to tell if the man's eyes were open or closed. He could see a bloodstain on the right side of his shirt. Even if the fall hadn't killed him, Brent's gunshot might have.

"Tully! Can you hear me? It's Grant!"

Down below, Grant heard a wail of sirens. Beams of light slashed through the leaves of the trees. Car doors opened and slammed shut, and the crackle of police radios cut into the night's silence.

"Damn it, Tully. Answer me."

"Tully hurt."

The words were only a whisper, but Grant heard them.

"Oh, thank God, Tully!" he shouted. "Don't move. Help is coming."

He flashed his light down toward the police cars, waving it back and forth as he shouted.

"Up here. We're up here."

For a moment he wasn't sure that anyone had heard him. Then a spotlight shot up through the trees, and he could hear voices shouting back at him.

"Just stay very still, Tully," Grant said, hanging over the edge so that Tully could hear him clearly. "We'll have you out of there in no time."

"Missus Jake?"

"She's safe, thanks to you. And the boy, too," he said. "I'm going to tell them about you, and when the police get up here, they'll have rope to bring you up. Just stay still."

Grant pushed away from the edge, rose to his feet and walked across to where Maggie sat holding Tyler.

"I think Tully will make it," he said.

"And Brent?"

"No sign of him. I think he's at the bottom."

Maggie nodded, and he knelt down beside her. Tyler's face was pressed into the curve of her neck, his body slack against her chest. Grant couldn't believe the child was safe. There would be years of therapy ahead, but it didn't matter as long as the boy was alive. He ignored the tears that slipped down his cheeks as he stroked the soft blond head of his nephew.

Tyler froze at his touch. Maggie continued to rock him, humming softly. Slowly Tyler turned his head until Grant could see his face. The boy's eyes were wide and unblinking. Moonlight lit the child's features, and Grant could see the mouth pulled tight in fear.

"Don't be afraid, Tyler. I've come to take you home." Grant swallowed the painful lump in his throat. "Do you remember me? I'm your uncle Grant."

Tyler stared unblinking, then turned his head back into the hollow beside Maggie's throat. He sighed, his breath a thin flutter of air in the stillness of the night.

"Uncle," he said.

Grant closed his eyes and offered thanks. He wiped at the dampness on his face, smiling across at Maggie. She was crying too, and he raised his hand to wipe away her tears.

She looked at him, her face white in the moonlight. He could see the bruises on her cheek and the cut and swollen lip. He had come close to losing her, and he hadn't known until it happened how much she'd become a part of him.

"It's over, Maggie. You and Jake have nothing more to fear."

"I can't take it all in." She looked down at the boy in her arms. "Will we ever know the whole story?"

"I don't know. Perhaps Eddie Harland will be able to help. Together he and Tyler could find a healthy bond in their ordeal."

"Will you take Tyler to your sister's in Cleveland?"

"Yes. Then I'll come back," Grant said. "Jake wants me to buy George's house."

"If you lived here in Delbrook, you wouldn't be a carpetbagger."

He squeezed her hand, and they sat quietly as the

rescue party approached. Lights and voices cut through the sound of the wind. Maggie let out a soft cry as one voice rose above the rest.

"Don't worry, Mom," Jake called. "We're coming to get you."

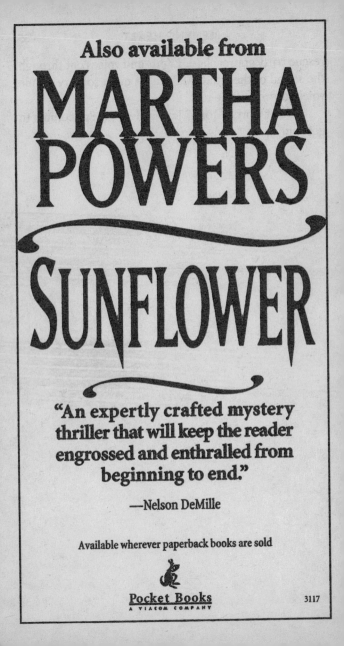

Also available from

MARTHA POWERS

SUNFLOWER

"An expertly crafted mystery
thriller that will keep the reader
engrossed and enthralled from
beginning to end."

—Nelson DeMille

Available wherever paperback books are sold

Pocket Books
A VIACOM COMPANY

3117